To Crown a Caesar

Book Two in the Ongoing
Praetorian Series

Edward Crichton

Acknowledgments

Once again, I'd like to thank the usual suspects: Alex, Amanda, Anita, George, Michelle, and Taras. Each of you offered one piece of advice or another on how to make this story better than what it was before, and I can't thank you enough for it. Let's just be a little quicker about it next time.

Books by Edward Crichton:

The Praetorian Series
The Last Roman (Book I)
To Crown a Caesar (Book II)
A Hunter and His Legion (Book III)

Starfarer
Rendezvous with Destiny

Table of Contents

Mission Entry #1
Jacob Hunter
Valentia, Transalpine Gaul - April, 42 A.D.

If you're reading this, and not in the military, you should know that those of us who are perform something called after action reports. If you are in the military, skip to the next paragraph and pick up there. After Action Reports, or AARs, are done after the completion of a military action or mission. Whether successful or not, these AARs serve as evidence of what occurred in the field and a way to identify missteps or mistakes.

By now, you've probably already become familiar with my previous journals, the ones that have chronicled the last few years of my life. Those were silly, informal affairs meant to keep my own mind from slipping into delirium as my friends and I fought our way towards the present. What is to follow from here will be a more precise accounting of our actions and decisions, but I'll try to keep it interesting in case it isn't some hardass military officer with a stick up his ass that finds these things. Believe me, things are about to get far more interesting than what you may or may not have already read to date.

Trust me.

So. Where to begin?

I guess the beginning would be as good a place as any.

If you're not already wondering, and you really should be by now, especially if my other journals haven't been recovered, there's a reason why the words in this notebook are written in blue pen, in English, and with poor syntax and grammar. Manuscripts dating back to the first century generally aren't, but I implore you to keep an open mind if I say something that contradicts what you think you already know.

So. Again. Where to begin?

My name is Jacob Hunter and here's my sit-rep.

That's "situation report" for you non-military type folk. A... summary update, if you will.

The world I once called home had been engulfed by a global war, the third of its kind. It began early in the 21st century, but by 2021, the world had been on the brink of destruction. I had spent most of my short adult life in the U.S. Navy fighting in that war, but for reasons I had been quickly regretting and it wasn't long after my own brush with death that my life – my war – found meaning once again.

Approached by a representative from the Vatican, I accepted a job that took me from the U.S. military and into the service of the Pope. I had become a Papal Praetorian, a modern day equivalent of the ancient bodyguards who protected Rome's emperors two thousand years prior. I, along with six other individuals, composed the second of such teams, tasked with the elimination of threats against the Pope.

Two Brits, a former Swiss Guardsman, a Frenchman, another American, and a female German made up the team, each as diverse as the next, but joined by a common cause. Our commander, Major Dillon McDougal, was killed in action on our very first mission, an accident that was mostly my fault. James Wang, small and deadly, was our team medic. Vincent (I never did learn the rest of his name) was a priest, at least that's what he started as before he admitted to being nothing but a fraud. His reasoning for the subterfuge had been sound, but I still never completely forgave him from keeping the truth from us.

He served as our defacto commander after McDougal's death.

Jeanne Bordeaux was our heavy gunner and demo man. John Santino had been a very close friend of mine before we had independently joined with the Pope. He was a fucking asshole, with an annoying talent for cracking horrible jokes at inopportune times, but even though his personality could grate on even the most stalwart, he was a good soldier, and I wouldn't trade him in for anyone. Except Helena van Strauss, of course. She's our sniper and something far more special to me.

With the team assembled and on our very first mission, after very nearly botching it completely, we were accidentally transported through time and space to ancient Rome during the reign of Caligula.

Let me give you a second to let that sink in.

Sunk?

I'm not going into the theoretical science behind it because it's so confusing, I don't even understand it anymore – and I thought most of it up! All we know is that upon our arrival in

Rome, we were met by real Praetorians and taken before the emperor. Caligula was nothing like he was supposed to be, at least, as he was supposed to be a few months from when we showed up. I'm something of a history buff, and know quite a bit about the time period we found ourselves in, but while it was initially useful in understanding what was about to happen, we quickly found that the more we got involved, the less a benefit our hindsight became.

As for Caligula, he immediately took a liking to us, and made the decision to use us for his own purposes. As ominous as that sounds, he wasn't crazy, and despite my reservations about interacting with the timeline, I felt we could have actually done some good for him.

Others were not so sure.

Caligula's uncle, Claudius, was also nothing like he was supposed to be. You won't know this, but Claudius was supposed to be an intelligent and soft spoken man disguised as a bumbling fool. I don't really know what you know about him, but that's what I knew, even if he was everything but: tall, good looking, athletic and devious to the core, he was no friend of his nephew or us.

Don't short change the cheesy "traitorous family member plot-line."

Learn your history.

Anyway, when Caligula became very ill, an event some considered a possible reason for why he originally went insane, Claudius took advantage. With the help of disloyal Praetorians, he attacked the House of Augustus. Luckily for Caligula, if not the timeline, we were there to nurse him back to health, changing history in the process. Then, with the help of a few loyal Praetorians, we escaped Rome and made our way north, hooking up with a legion in training that was camped for winter.

And then Agrippina showed up.

Sister of Caligula, mother of Nero, master conniver, slut, and traitor to Rome.

She brought with her a story about how her son had been kidnapped by Claudius and that it was imperative we rescue him. In order to secure my participation in the rescue mission, she tried to seduce me, which I, of course, refused, but I agreed to help *anyway. With the aid of Santino, we set off to rescue her son. Once in Rome, we were betrayed, captured and crucified (obviously we survived that one), but only I suspected Agrippina's involvement.*

I suppose now would be a good time to mention the time traveling blue ball. No, it's not a sexual problem, but in fact the object responsible for our temporal journey. A time machine. How does it work you ask? Good question. No idea. All I know is that past events can be altered, unlike some theories that state that whatever is done in the past by a so called "time traveler" was somehow already done by him in some kind of circular existential existence. Like for instance a guy that was sent back in time to father the child that would, in turn, send him back to knock up his mom to ensure that the robot rebellions would...

Never mind.

It's confusing.

To make matters worse, Claudius thought I was the key to working it, but I was little more than a hapless victim. He tried to extract information out of me, but his plan was foiled by Vincent and company when they infiltrated Rome under the cover of Galba's besieging army. Santino and I were pretty messed up, and it took us weeks to fully recover, but we had plenty of time to burn before the climactic battle scene at the end of the movie.

But I won't go into the details concerning that. They're still too painful to recall, but it ended in a return to the status quo. More or less. And only temporarily.

After the battle, things could not have seemed more perfect. While Wang, Bordeaux, and Vincent moved on to other endeavors away from Rome, Santino, Helena, and I stayed on as honorary bodyguards for Caligula. It was the cushiest job of my life. But it wouldn't last.

When the three of us attended a dinner party thrown by Agrippina, still innocent in the eyes of Roman high-society, Caligula used the opportunity to announce his decision to name Nero as his successor. The boy had been at the party, and even though he was only a few months old, I could already see the monster he would become.

Again, I have no idea what you know about history but try and keep up.

No more than two minutes after the announcement, Caligula was assassinated by poisonous mushrooms.

Except only I knew who did it.

In my timeline, which by now you may have determined is far different from your own (Again, I have no way to predict either way), Agrippina was married to Claudius and many thought she later murdered her uncle-husband with poisoned mushrooms. The look she gave me as Caligula convulsed on the floor all but confirmed it, and I knew our lives were in danger as well. Santino, Helena, and I fled Rome that night and haven't been back since.

That was three years, eight months and nineteen days ago.

At the time, I knew of only one man who could take on the job as emperor of Rome. Someone who could take it back from the clutches of someone like Agrippina and lead it back to prosperity. I knew he could do it because he had already done it in my history books.

Flavius Servius Vespasianus.

Vespasian.

So, armed with a vague outline of a plan and the idealistic fantasies of childlike optimism, the three of us set out to make sure the reign of Nero never arrived. It would be bad enough with Agrippina in charge, ruling in regency until her son was old enough to take over.

We'd gone north and waited, spending years helping those who couldn't help themselves, every act of kindness leading us to the here and now. Please see my other journals for further information – a series of wonderfully fun and whimsical short stories – but, to be honest, if you're reading this, you may already know more than I do about what happens than I do. Then again, you might not, but I'm glad if you do because the suspense is killing me. Hopefully, things turned out all right, but if they didn't, at least this log will be a record of what happened.

Okay. Got to go. Things are about to start getting interesting.

Oh, by the way.

Before I go.

If this shit ever gets turned into a movie, I want my name on it. Jacob Hunter. And for crying out loud... have some respect for the source material.

Part One

I
Goodwill

I put my pen on the table, leaned back and shook some life into my cramping hand. I hadn't written that much since college and the never-ending stream of essay tests that were the fate of any history major. Since then, the only time I'd ever needed to put pen to paper was to sign my name. All of my correspondence and after-action reports back home had been done electronically and I hadn't written in my previous journals in months.

Kneading away the soreness between thumb and fingers, I leaned back in my chair and took in the strange surroundings I had somehow found myself in this time – just one of a hundred random towns visited over what seemed like a lifetime.

My companions and I had been on the move ever since we fled Rome all those years ago. We'd been to Illyria, an old Greek province on the eastern side of the Adriatic Sea, east of the Rhine river in German country, then made our way to the Iberian peninsula in modern day Spain and Portugal, spent some time in North Africa, and had toured extensively around Gaul before we wound up here, a small city on the east bank of the Rhone River, in what I remember as southern France.

After all that time in the ancient world, I'd gotten quite used to its idiosyncrasies. While I still missed my home in 2021, I felt at ease in the rustic backcountries and Romanized provinces that made up Europe during what was left of the Julio-Claudian dynasty's reign of power, a time made even shorter by none other than me. The latest deaths in the family had been the emperor Gaius Julius Caesar Augustus Germanicus, better known as Caligula, and the should-have-been emperor, Claudius. Between the two of them, their reigns should have lasted until 54 A.D., but things were no longer as they should have been.

Claudius had been killed on the battlefield and Caligula had been poisoned; both events culminating in the naming of Caligula's nephew, Nero, as the heir apparent. He was currently too young to rule, so Agrippina the Younger, his mother, had become the first and only sole empress of Rome.

Agrippina.

The woman was best described as a double edged sword, rather than a two sided coin. Her beauty, poise, and allure were equally matched by her cunning, ambition, and avarice, both of which she used equally well to achieve her innermost desires.

I shuddered as my heart raced at the thought of her. It was a testament to her demeanor and beauty that, as someone who had every right to hate her, I could feel such attraction to her. There was more to it than her physical appearance, of course, but it certainly helped. Memories of how she could so easily command a room flooded into my mind, how every head would turn to gape and stare as she strutted about. The way her large breasts shifted beneath her slinky outfits and her mane of yellow hair tumbled around her shoulders, swaying alluringly with every step she took. It wasn't a rare occurrence for a man to trip over himself in her presence.

Something I could testify to personally.

It was her unbridled ambition that drove her to poison her own brother, as well as the sole reason for my presence here and why I no longer had a home to speak of. She had been the tool through which Claudius had arranged my capture and torture all those years ago, and after poisoning Caligula, she had wasted no time in labeling us as enemies of the Republic.

We were number one on her Most Wanted list, with bounties on our heads large enough to set someone up for life. My companions' bounties were smaller but labeled as wanted either alive *or* dead, whereas Agrippina wanted me alive and unharmed. Word had spread quickly around the empire, and Wanted posters had become a common sight throughout its vast expanse of territory. There was even one here, posted right above my head on the wall behind me, and I knew that as I propped my chair against the wall, my face on the poster was in full display just above my real one.

Fully aware of how exposed I was, I placed my hands behind my neck and drank in my surroundings.

It was dirty, dark, musky, and... homey. Unlike the bars or clubs back home, this one was devoid of anything meant to actually draw in patrons – dollar drafts, bright lights, DJs, scandalously dressed women gyrating to loud, obnoxious techno music, and the asshole frat boys who sought such women – and generally failed. This place wasn't somewhere people went to have a good time on the weekends, but somewhere people felt obligated to go because there was simply nowhere else. It was filled with regulars and the occasional drifter like me, and while music was strummed lazily from a corner, the only thing needed to entertain these people were gossip, stories, good jokes, and companionship.

As I sipped a cup of the local, dry vintage wine, I couldn't help but appreciate their simplicity. Life wasn't about obtaining the newest and fanciest gadget, wearing the trendiest clothing or planning the next vacation. It was about getting by with what you had and trying to enjoy what few moments of leisure was available at any given moment. Like residents of the Deep South in ante-bellum America, life was slow and lazy, which wasn't necessarily a bad thing, just different from the progressive hustle and bustle of the world back home.

I sighed at the thought. It was becoming harder to remember, but life back in 2021 was hardly worth remembering, and perhaps shouldn't be used in comparison. For years, the world had been consumed by a war that engulfed every nation on the planet, and even America had been unable to remain immune to the perils of total war. The Pacific Northwest and southern Border States were constantly in conflict, and while those in the Midwest, South, and East Coast remained without conflict, its residents were just as involved in the war effort as those living in contested areas. Factories meant to support the massive war machine had pockmarked the land east of the Mississippi, and its people had been pressed into service.

It had been a scene straight out of an old black and white World War II propagandist film about the home front and the importance of its industrial output – only in glorious high definition.

While children still went to school, the elderly retired, and most citizens continued to work their menial nine to five day jobs, life had been unraveling for years. If the war had continued, it would only have been a matter of time before the war effort became an all-encompassing endeavor with everyone forced to become involved.

I shook my head. With every passing day, my memories of home failed more and more to acknowledge how much of a cluster fuck it had become. Instead, they reverted back to older, happier memories, muddying my perspective. In many ways I had no desire or even a reason to go home. I even almost liked it here. But I couldn't live with myself if I one day learned we'd somehow messed with the future, irrevocably altering the lives of billions, all because of my own failings.

With that thought in mind, I remembered we couldn't go home yet, and why.

I shifted my attention back to the men and women around me. They seemed gloomy and certainly unfriendly towards strangers. Only the barmaids seemed to pay us any attention – barmaids who were also quite attractive. I suppose they had to be. It took more than just a steady pouring hand to squeeze as much money as possible from passing travelers like Santino, who sat at the end of the bar with an attractive, red headed barmaid in his lap. He laughed and joked with her innocently so I ignored them, analyzing the remaining patrons instead. I had already classified some as potential threats, an old habit born from years of service in the military and a few missions that had me play the part of spy more than operator. Cross-referencing nervous eye contact with body posture and clothing style had made it easy to identify those I had to worry about.

But my precaution was merely just that. I was confident no one would try anything out here. Despite Agrippina's best efforts to vilify us, our reputation was generally positive in the empire's back country. Crime in the Roman Empire was more than rampant, its issues plaguing the empire far more than they did in the modern world. Kidnappings, murders, thefts, battery, sexual crimes, and the like were no more prevalent than they were back home, but there was no one here to help the victims. There was no real police force or justice system to protect them, so with nothing else to do, we'd taken on the role of Sheriffs of the Roman Empire, available for hire to anyone with a grievance who could use a helping hand and met our minimum moral standards. After a few months, we had achieved the moniker, *Vani*, the plural form of the Latin word, *vanus*, which in this context meant, "shadow" or "stealth," in reference to how we did business.

Real sneaky like.

Which is what brought us to this dingy tavern today.

We were on a mission to help a grieving Roman widow who had lost her husband and two sons to roaming vagabonds who had raided her Gaulic villa. The family had been of equestrian class, upper echelon Roman business owners with more money than they knew what to do with. They had been vacationing in the lush Gaulic countryside when the attack had happened. Her only surviving family member was her seventeen year old daughter, who had been taken by the bandits. God only knows what they had in mind for her, but she'd been captured over a week ago, and the question of her survival was uncertain.

I glanced at my watch, one of the few bits of modern equipment still operational thanks to the rechargeable power of their solar cells. It also remained a useful tool because, while Romans had no such device, they could still tell time fairly accurately.

I noted that it was just before noon on this cloudy and cool spring day.

Time to start paying attention.

I finished my surveillance and looked at the last person of note in the building.

She was seated across from me, her back to the door and her head leaning over a bowl of stew that she was voraciously shoveling into her mouth. She wore tight fitting combat fatigues made out of a water resistant but breathable material lined with Kevlar, arranged with protective polyethylene gel pads. The pads were squishy when inert, but turned as rigid as titanium when impacted by any sizable force. They were comfortable and protective, the next generation of body armor back home.

Draped over her back was a grey colored cape of local design – typical wear for travelers. Its exterior was nondescript, but had been modified as reversible, with the side now pressed against her back outfitted with numerous strips of multi-colored frayed cloth. It was a make-shift ghilli suit, not as efficient as the full body suits she and I had, but one that was useful in a pinch if needed. It had been her idea, and one that had become quite useful over the years.

Her hair was tied back messily with sticks and more modern feminine hair products, but some of it dangled to either side of her face, obstructing her feeding motion and constantly finding its way into her stew. She had grown it so long that it fell to the small of her back now, just above her backside. Currently, it looked as though it hadn't been washed in weeks and dirt and grime covered her lovely face as well. The poor woman hadn't bathed in days, and the way she ate suggested she hadn't eaten in just as long either.

She looked horrible, but I knew what lay behind the filth.

Her delicate features, some combination of German and Turkish that had first come together back when Istanbul was still Constantinople, had produced a rare beauty. Light chestnut skin, black hair, but German features with full lips, high cheekbones, wide open eyes, and neat eyebrows made her a sight to see.

Helena noticed my inspection, and while still leaning over her bowl, looked up at me with those vibrant green eyes that almost seemed to glow.

"What?" She asked as broth streamed down the side of her mouth.

I laughed. She was a mess, not even pausing to swallow before she spoke, apparently still famished while she worked on her second serving. Even so, she was well within her rights to look as she did and gorge herself like she was. She'd been in the field for the past three days, and probably hadn't had much time to eat or refresh herself. It had been her turn to retrieve supplies from our hidden cache that remained hidden about a day's march away. She'd returned a few hours ago but hadn't been able to relax until just now, having posted herself a few miles away from the tavern, waiting for our targets to arrive. When she sighted them an hour ago, she indicated they were taking their time, but on their way. Thirty minutes later – now – she was sitting across from me, a fresh batch of God-knows-what awaiting her eager spoon

She'd brought with her another journal from the cache, a spot we had discovered after a delivery had found its way to us a few months after we'd fled Rome. It contained all the gear we'd brought with us from the future with a brief note. All it said was, *"G & M, Amici"*.

"G & M, Friends".

It was from our Praetorian friends Gaius and Marcus. Of all the people we could trust in our new lives, they were amongst the foremost, and it must have been a pain in the ass for them to arrange for the delivery of our supplies. Those containers were damn heavy.

As for our supplies, we didn't have much left. Spare ammunition, a few extra rifles, replacement parts, survival gear and clothing. We only had a few dozen MREs left, and had been force to relegate them to survival food a year ago. Besides our weapons, we were living pretty much like every other ancient person.

"What?" Helena repeated insistently as she stirred her dinner.

"Nothing," I told her, a smile still on my face. "I just can't get over how beautiful you look tonight."

She kicked me in the shin beneath the table and I felt a spark of pain shoot up my leg. Despite her beauty, she had a fiery and violent temper. I'd lost count of how many times she'd punched, poked, kicked, or prodded me over the years. Her temper stemmed from a repressive father and an entire life before joining the Pope's military trapped in a prearranged engagement. The relationship had been everything but loving or intimate, but before they could wed, her fiancé had died in a car accident, and she had been free of it just before I met her. We had quickly connected, sharing annoying fathers and sad love lives, and it hadn't taken long before I'd learned just how volatile she was, and I loved her for it.

"Sorry," I said, rubbing my shin. "It's just that I really want to take you home and have my way with you."

She pointed her spoon at me accusingly, an annoyed expression on her face. "You haven't said anything like that to me in months, so don't think I'm going to be impressed now."

I frowned. Relationships were hard, especially when forced to live the way we had. We weren't the crazily intimate couple we had been after the first few years. The love and affection was still there, just buried beneath years of survival, pain, and a sense of loss at our predicament. We had nothing permanent to latch onto, nothing for us to call our own. All we had was each other, and over time, even that sentiment grew flimsy. Lately, things had grown worse, but I figured it was just a phase.

Probably.

I ignored her flippancy and tried to push away the annoyance I felt at it.

"Since you seem to be done gluttonizing yourself," I asked, "I think it's time I asked whether you brought everything we need or not?"

She looked down at her bowl, perhaps noticing for the first time that she'd been scraping away at nothing but wood for the past twenty seconds. Wiping her mouth on a sleeve, she pushed it away. It was quickly swiped up by a passing barmaid who smiled at me. I gave her a wink along with a smile full of teeth, only to receive an ice cold stare from Helena in return.

"Yes," she replied sourly, holding up one of the three large bags she'd brought with her. "Everything on the list is here, plus a few things I added at the last moment. Plenty of ammo for each of us, some C4, NVGs, a few MREs, don't worry, no beef patties..."

"Thanks," I interrupted. For some reason the beef patties had never set well with me.

She ignored my interruption. "...Santino's UAV, our ghilli suits, a grappling hook with rope, tranquilizer darts, your wetsuit and Santino's, along with your breathing apparatuses, some soap and shampoo for me, three bedrolls, and... two tents." She described the last item with a bit of disdain, which caused me to wince. Normally, we shared a tent with no problem, and have a good time of it, but lately the cramped space had gotten awkward.

I broke eye contact with her for a moment, distractedly flaking away some decaying meat that had fused itself with the table. "Did you get in contact with our sleeper?"

"Yes," she said. "His answer was, 'I'll think about it.'"

I nodded. No surprise there.

All the vital details concluded, we found ourselves with little else to talk about. I spread my hands out along the edge of the table and gave her an awkward smile. Her expression was blank as she stared in my direction, clearly not interested in further conversation. I put my hands in my lap and tried to think of something to say, but just before the silence grew unbearable, a third figure sat down at the table.

I glanced over to see Santino plop himself down between us, apparently finished womanizing his waitress. I looked at his scarred and roguish face, the result of a grenade accident during basic that left him with a series of scars along his left cheek and brow, scars that women always found dashing. He sported a short, but scruffy beard these days, a practice he'd picked up during his days in Delta, and had grown out his hair to just before his shoulders, just as I had – only his was curly, whereas mine was more wavy. His most enduring physical quality, however, was his shit eating grin that spread from ear to ear, and never seemed to leave his face. Even in the heat of battle, the man's smile rarely faded.

He leaned his chair back and crossed his feet up on the table, interlocking his hands atop his stomach. He looked at me, then to Helena, back to me and then her again, before staring directly between us.

"Boy... you could cut the tension between you two with a spork." He shifted his look towards each of us in turn again, hoping for a laugh, before settling between us with a sigh. "I miss sporks."

Both Helena and I looked at him with mixed looks of pity and annoyance. I'd long ago determined Santino would always be Santino. He would never change. It was a personality quirk I had gotten a kick out of since I'd known him but one that had grown slowly on Helena.

I heard a commotion outside and looked over Helena's shoulder at the door. I saw agitated men outside the windows tying up their horses.

"Looks like it's time for you to go," Santino informed Helena.

She looked back at us, her eyes lingering on mine just slightly before nodding and getting to her feet. She stood, but before she could straighten completely, she suddenly doubled over, one hand reaching for the table to steady herself, the other to her abdomen, her face cringing in pain.

"Are you all right?" Santino asked, rising to help.

She held out the arm she had used to steady herself before answering. "I'm fine."

Grabbing one of our bags and pulling her long traveler cloak's hood over her head, she quickly transformed from the beautiful but disheveled woman I'd known for years, to yet another random female denizen of the town. She turned quickly and left.

Ever since Helena had been at death's door from a sword wound all those years ago, she'd been experiencing an odd, intermittent pain in her abdomen. It was probably nothing serious, just some side effect from the extensive procedure needed to save her life. Even so, I've seen her in some of our most tender moments cry out for no apparent reason, only to collapse in pain, her teeth grinding against themselves. In moments like those, I felt her pain as well. I had promised her I'd be there to protect her, but I hadn't been, and she'd paid for it in the end.

The only person I blamed was me.

"What's wrong with you two, anyway?" Santino asked as he sat back down, watching Helena open the door and leave.

"I really don't know," I replied, watching her go as well. "Things have been kinda shaky for a few months now, but I don't know where I went wrong. She's been acting weird."

"Women," Santino said mockingly. "What good are they, anyway?"

"Well, lots of things," I told him, not rising to the bait. "They're pretty to look at, fun to play with and are the vessels through which life is created."

"That all?" Santino asked, unimpressed. "Anything else?"

"Well," I thought about it, the last few months replaying in my mind. "Yeah... you're probably right."

"Like I said," Santino finished with a wink, helpful as ever.

When the tavern door finally opened again, I folded my arms across my chest and waited patiently as the men responsible for a family's murder and the kidnapping of their only daughter walked inside the room and approached our table. I put on my business face and shut down my emotions, allowing me the fortitude to do what I needed, no matter what that entailed.

I'd need to because we were going to change the timeline today, and even though I should, I couldn't care less. Not when a young girl's life was at stake.

The five men who walked in were tall, burly and had really bad blond hair – long and fizzed with gnarly curls – and only a few of them had all their teeth. They came bursting in as though they owned the joint, and didn't even pause as they marched straight for my table. They stopped short with looks of anger and intimidation on their faces, but some with a hint of fear as well.

"You!" The lead man said in heavily accented Latin. "*Vani.* We were told we could find you here!"

Santino looked lazily at the speaker, his feet atop the table. "We've been here for two days, champ. Way to keep up."

I smiled at my hand while I picked at some grime underneath my fingernails. I did my best to look uninterested. Santino took a long swig of the dry wine in his cup, his eyes still locked on the speaker.

The Gauls looked amongst themselves in confusion, unsure how to respond to such a statement. One of them, perhaps the dumbest of the group, had the bright idea of placing a hand on Santino's shoulder. Santino reacted instantly, snatching the man's hand in his own and twisting it violently while forcing his attacker to his knees. The wrist didn't break, but the pain was so bad that Santino simply kicked the man to the ground with a light tap of his foot. The entire exercise went down all the while Santino took another pull of his wine.

The downed victim clutched his hand while the leader, who merely smiled, took a seat in the chair Helena had just vacated. He calmly folded his hands together and looked directly at me, ignoring Santino, who was once again preoccupied with the cute barmaid he had been flirting with earlier.

"If you are *Vani*," he began, "what are you doing here with the likes of us?" He spread his left arm out to encompass the entirety of the bar, numerous heads turning to look in our directions.

The ones who did were the ones I'd earlier identified as potential problems.

I ignored him and held out my tumbler for Santino's wench to refill as she sat perched on his lap. She laughed as he tickled her and I brought the cup to my lips, noticing the seated man's patience wan and his hand move threateningly towards his lap. His body language suggested he was about to stand up, but I held up a hand to dissuade any aggression. Santino continued his games.

"There is no need for violence, gentlemen," I informed them. "My name is Buzz, and this is my friend, Woody." I gestured at Santino who smiled at the men stupidly. Their confusion was more evident than ever. I leaned in and lowered my voice just a bit. "I'll just be honest with you. Life isn't as exciting as it used to be and we're not getting paid nearly what we want, so we're seeking... alternative employment opportunities."

"I find that difficult to believe," the man in charge said as he sat back in his chair. His face seemed deep in thought, something I hadn't been so sure he was capable of. But he must have run out of synapses quickly, as his face relaxed and he glanced between Santino and me. "Are there more of you?"

I shrugged. Between Santino, Helena and I, we'd never given anyone a real opportunity to tell how many of us there really were. Besides the quick regrouping here, the only time the three of us were together was when we were off on our own in the wilderness. Our missions were mostly conducted in pairs, consisting of the few combinations the three of us allotted. Because of our precaution, some people thought there were at least five of us, and I had heard the random rumor of as many as ten.

The man looked around skeptically, perhaps fearing how others would view him in the future were he to trust us, but we'd run into guys like him everywhere we went: leaders of small bandit groups with more balls than brains, and a lust for gold and riches that overwhelmed more rational thoughts.

He had been as good as convinced long ago.

"I've heard many rumors," the man explained, "about your abilities and skills. Some even say you are gods."

Roman gods, Greek gods, Gaulic gods, it didn't matter. Everyone we ran into always jumped to that conclusion first, and we never gave them any reason to doubt it.

"We can demonstrate our worth if you require," I told him. "But if you're satisfied, I want fifty percent of all our earnings."

My negotiating partner crossed his arms and looked up at his companions. Not a one said a thing but some glanced amongst themselves awkwardly. They'd all heard the stories as well and knew we'd be powerful allies... or deadly enemies.

"Thirty percent," the man haggled.

"Fifty," I said.

"Forty?" He asked, knowing full well where I was going.

"Fifty," I repeated a final time.

The man looked beaten, but still pleased. "We must see what you can do first. Where?"

"Outside. Now."

Taking my cue, Santino whispered in the barmaid's ear, and she got off his lap to complete his request, pausing only slightly to giggle after Santino pinched her butt.

The Gaul didn't look impressed.

"Why not here? Now?" The man asked.

He was cleverer than I thought.

"This tavern pleases me, as do its staff," I said, throwing another wink at another waitress, a gesture I made sure he observed. "I would not like to inadvertently harm it or those within."

"Why should gods worry about such things?"

"It's not me that I'm worried about," I said as I rose to my feet. "It's you."

***

Once outside, I immediately felt the chill of the April air against my skin.

I hated this time of year.

The weather was unpredictable and its spontaneity was too difficult for my body to keep up with. I regularly felt either too warm or too cold. It was an annoying sensation for me but I didn't let it show on my face, for a god wouldn't find discomfort in such things.

In the brief seconds it took for everyone to emerge from the tavern, I allowed myself the pleasure of taking in the view. Lush and beautiful, the alpine wonderland around us was breathtaking. The tavern sat on a small crest, a cliff that jutted from a small mountain, the first stop before continuing further up into larger and higher mountain ranges. It offered a perfect view of the city below and was an ideal place to rest before continuing the arduous upward hike. Down the road, off in the distance, I could see the small town of Valentia at the foot of our mountain, little else of note except the wide open vistas that encompassed the city. Opposite the tavern was another steep hillside filled with trees that continued up into the mountains.

That's where Helena would be.

I paused on a spot a few meters from the horses and indicated the Gauls should stop where they were, just a few feet away, between me and Helena.

"What now?" The leader asked.

"Patience," I said.

Before the words escaped my mouth, Santino's barmaid came running from inside, a large coconut in her hands. Where they'd found the coconut, I hadn't a clue, my only guess revolving around migrating swallows. Whatever its origins, the young barmaid handed it to Santino and stepped up on her toes to kiss his cheek, but he turned his head at the last second and kissed her full on the lips. The small woman giggled again and her hands flew to her mouth. She scampered in place for another second before rushing back inside, Santino grinning after her.

I gave him a dubious look as I snatched the coconut from his grip, which he returned smugly. Still looking at him, I shook my head and offered the fruit to one of the Gauls.

It wasn't the leader, so when he looked at it in confusion, his question came out in Gaulic.

"What does he do with it?" The leader demanded.

"Tell him to hold it out in front of him, as far from his body as possible."

When the man did so, I held out my hand so that my palm faced the hillside.

"When I snap my fingers, I will make this piece of fruit explode."

Some of the men laughed, while two traded money in preparation for a bet. The leader gestured with his hand, an eerily similar gesture to the one Caligula had offered us four years ago when he was given his own demonstration. It was a gesture of uninterested skepticism, one that always made me smile.

I counted down on my hand, starting with all five fingers extended, but when only my middle finger remained, clearly directed towards the leader, I snapped them together. Not a millisecond later, the fruit exploded gloriously in a sticky mess. There had been no sound from Helena's suppressor equipped DSR1, so from the god fearing perspective of ancient Gauls, I had indeed caused it to explode.

The leader laughed as he wiped coconut milk from his face and came to slap my shoulder. "A fine show!" He yelled. "You will be good, I think. My name is Madriviox. Come. I will take you home."

***

I gathered our bags from inside the tavern while Santino said goodbye to his fair, young lass. She was sad to see him go, but he promised he would return. She perked up at the news and gave him another kiss. He squeezed her butt in return and I rolled my eyes at how she loved every minute of it. I tapped my foot as I waited for him at the door, but at least he didn't make me wait long. We were soon on our horses and falling into line with Madriviox.

The horses had actually been Agrippina's. Ones Santino and I had rode when we had accompanied her to Rome before she'd betrayed us all those years ago. They were black Spanish stallions, some of the best I'd ever seen. We'd stolen them, along with Helena's pure white mare, from Agrippina's stable the day we fled Rome. I'd named mine Felix, the Latin word for lucky. I figured it was appropriate.

Just another reason why Agrippina had it out for us.

We rode in the middle of our new employer's formation, with wary and distrustful eyes all around us. I would have been worried had Helena not been pacing us at a distance where she could cover us with her long rifle should she need to. We'd only been travelling for a few miles when Madriviox randomly peeled off the main road. From then on, we took a disorienting route as we wove our way through the forest. It wasn't long before I found myself completely lost, with no idea where we were or what direction we were going. The sun was behind clouds, all the trees looked the same and there were zero distinguishing features along the way to guide me.

However, one of my watch's more advanced features was a basic GPS function that mapped out a journey as it rode on a wearer's wrist. At automated increments, it updated a waypoint and calculated the distance between it and the previous waypoint. It would also indicate the direction needed to retrace my steps.

The watch even transmitted the waypoints to Helena through Santino's UAV, an invisible guardian angel, flying above us as it broadcasted an internet connection capable of reaching Helena miles away.

I spent the long hours of our trip trying to focus and think, but quickly found myself bored senseless. Endless trees didn't offer much inspiration and I fell asleep in my saddle on a number of occasions. After what seemed like half the day, we finally found ourselves standing before a thicket of bushes. As we approached, Madriviox called out and the bushes separated, allowing us entrance into a cave.

I laughed, never actually believing that secret lairs used by bandits, highwaymen and the like actually existed. I'd always thought they were something Hollywood and the video game industry had made popular with little thought toward historical accuracy, but the hideout before me was in fact something straight out of Robin Hood.

As we entered, I immediately sensed that the cave system was indeed more like the ones in the movies than I first thought. We had to abandon our horses at the entrance, moving the rest of the way on foot. The winding corridors reminded me of the caves we'd traversed back in 2021. I didn't like those then, and I didn't like these now. The narrow hallways and honeycomb of passages left too many unknowns lurking around hidden corners and the feeling of claustrophobia only grew worse as we continued.

I glanced at Santino as we walked with two guards at our back and he flicked his eyebrows up in anticipation. I looked at him ruefully and concentrated on counting bad guys. For such a large cave complex, I only counted twenty two, but there could have been a hundred men in the unexplored sections of the complex.

Our escorts were quiet, only nodding to friends they encountered along the way. I was beginning to wonder where they were taking us when that fact became evidently clear. We found ourselves in a narrow corridor that dead ended at a cul-de-sac, barred off from the rest of the tunnel by an iron gate.

I looked over at Santino again. He looked calm and ready.

One of the Gauls opened the gate and led the entourage inside. Once inside I noticed the room's sole occupant was a young blond girl. She was youthful and cute, but had a series of nasty cuts and bruises all over her thin body, most of which was visible thanks to the little clothing she wore. Judging from the description her mother had given us, I decided this girl had to be our target.

Madriviox walked to where she lay and roughly hauled her off the floor. He pulled her up into a choke hold, tearing off what little clothing she had left with his free hand, tossing it to the floor. I looked away, noticing another dozen of her kidnappers approach our position from down the hall. They leaned against the walls or milled about casually, their posture indicating they weren't preparing to spring a trap on us, but that they were aware Santino and I might not be welcome after all.

I hated it when the bad guys were competent.

Madriviox pointed towards me and barked something out in the guttural language of his homeland. One of his men nodded and offered me his sword. The only weapons I had on me were my rifle, my sidearm, a large bowie knife on my belt, and the small throwing knife I always kept sheathed behind my belt at the small of my back. I grasped the sword handle and looked at it dumbly. I wasn't sure what they expected me to do.

"Kill her," Madriviox ordered, the small girl limp, complacent and broken in his arm.

"Excuse me?" I asked, looking into the terror stricken eyes of the young woman.

"I said kill her. She is beautiful, but we have had enough of her. There are always more women."

I looked at the sword as though I didn't even know what it could do. I knew I wasn't going to kill her, but how could I continue our ruse if I didn't? My mind raced, but I was unable to think of a solution. I guess we hadn't thought this one through. We were getting cocky. Four years of successful missions, even infiltration missions just like this one, each going off without a hitch had made us arrogant.

"No," I said before looking up, nothing else to say.

The man *tsked* me. "Too bad. I keep that fifty percent now. We would have given you to the empress soon anyway."

With a snap of his fingers, his men turned on us, pointing their swords and spears threateningly at Santino and me. I looked around, hoping for a way out, but found none. I dropped the sword and ejected the magazine from my HK416, *Penelope*, before handing it reluctantly to one of the Gauls. He looked at it curiously before shrugging, passing her to one of the other Gauls who also looked at it skeptically. He banged it against the wall and I winced at the abuse. Santino did the same and we surrendered our knives as well.

"A pity," Madriviox continued. "I hoped to use you for a few months, but we will go to Rome now. The empress will be pleased. As for you," he said, whispering in the small girl's ear. "I let you live. Keep them company tonight. It may be the last time they see a woman."

"Hey, Gender Confused Moron," Santino chimed in, "you realize Agrippina's got lady parts dangling between her legs, right?" He crossed his arms confidently before smacking his forehead in realization. "Oh wait, I got that one wrong again, didn't I?"

Madriviox glared at Santino, my friend's small joke sparking a wave of chuckles amongst his own men. He barked an order that stopped them mid laugh, and they filed out of the area as quickly as they could. Anger swelled around Madriviox as he dropped the girl and watched as she crawled to a corner before curling up into a ball, trying to hide her shame. With nothing left to say, he sent me another sharp look before exiting the cell, locking the door behind him.

Santino and I walked over to the bars and rested our heads between them.

"How did we let this happen?" Santino asked. "We were just tricked by a bunch of illiterate Vikings." He shook his head. "Agrippina was one thing, but this is pretty pathetic."

"Don't sweat it," I assured.

"And why not?"

"Because they broke the first two rules in the 'How-to-be-a-Good-Bad-Guy' Handbook."

"Do tell."

"First," I said, holding up a finger. "They let us live."

"Always a bad idea," he agreed.

"Second, they didn't search us very well. We still have our pistols, and I still have this." I held up a small brick of plastic C4, more than enough to blow open the lock.

Santino chuckled. "Clearly they don't watch enough TV."

"Clearly. Still, we should wait till nightfall." I thought for a second. "Is your UAV picking up our signal down here?"

Santino pulled his computer from his bag and consulted it. "No. Guess the rocks are blocking it."

"Figures," I muttered. While it wasn't exactly a shit show, the mission was quickly turning into one of our worst. "See if you can pick this lock so we can bust out of here real quiet like."

"Me? What are you going to do?"

"Just do it," I told him perhaps a little too hastily.

I ignored his hurt expression and moved towards the cowering form of the young Roman woman. It occurred to me that I could have simply told Santino that I feared his scarred face may frighten the young woman, but my patience with his whining had worn thin long ago. I pulled off my bag, which the Gauls had also stupidly left us, and pulled out a thin blanket. I knelt beside the girl and tried to wrap it around her, but she recoiled from my touch, forcing me to back away. The poor girl was so frail and beaten; I wasn't sure how to interact with her. I tried holding the blanket out innocently, and was happy to see her gingerly reach out and take it with a shaky hand. I took a step back and enticed her to wrap it around herself by mimicking the gesture over my own shoulders. It took her another few seconds before she understood what to do.

"What's your name?" I asked her gently, crouching a safe distance away.

She didn't say anything. She just looked at me out of the corner of her eyes as she trembled, the blanket covering everything from her nose down.

I reached my hand out but didn't touch her. "I'm not going to hurt you. I'm here to bring you back to your mother."

The girl's eyes widened at the revelation, and her trembling slowly subsided. Quietly, through chattering teeth and eyes streaming tears, I heard the girl whisper, "Julia."

That was the name her mother supplied me.

"Try and get some sleep," I told her. "We'll take you to your mother in a few hours."

She didn't react outwardly, but her tears finally stopped flowing and her eyes closed before she quietly went still. She was already asleep. The poor girl was exhausted. I reached out and tucked her exposed arm under the blanket, careful so that I didn't disturb her. She may have been kept awake for days, probably for reasons I never wanted to think about it.

I joined Santino by the bars again. "What do you think? Four hours?"

"Three," he corrected. "Most of these guys already look drunk enough as it is, and it's getting late. What I don't get is how they expected these bars to hold us. You blew up a coconut just by snapping."

"I figure they're either too smart or too dumb for their own good," I deduced. "Either they've figured out we faked it somehow or else they're just too dumb and drunk to think we can do the same to iron bars. Either way, we win."

"Right," Santino agreed. "I picked the lock by the way."

I looked at the bars to see they were already slightly ajar. We could leave at any time.

Santino waited for some form of acknowledgment from me, but when one didn't come, he crossed his arms, leaned his right shoulder against the bars and looked at me. He was never one for awkward silences.

"Sure you don't want to talk about what happened back at the tavern? We've got plenty of time to burn."

"No," I said. "There's nothing to talk about, especially not with you."

He flicked his eyebrows into the air and looked away. "Well, that was rude," he mumbled. After a second he looked back at me and seemed to perk up. "Hey, here's an idea, why don't you feel free to blame *me* for all of your problems."

"I'm not," I countered, amazed at how angry I now was. "It's not your problem."

"You're damn right it's my problem because your problems always become my problems."

"What's that supposed to mean?"

"You know what it means, Jacob. Everything you've done since I've met you has affected my life in one way or another, and you know what, some of it ain't good."

I stared at him, the frustration dripping from his tone paining me more than I thought it could. He was my best bud, after all. We'd had our share of disagreements and arguments over the years, sure, but he'd never said anything quite so personal before.

Different perspectives and ideas on how to run an op, definitely, but never something with so much disguised meaning behind it. But it was more about what he had left unsaid that was the most upsetting, the implied lack of faith in the decisions I've made and frustration at the actions I've done.

Santino, Helena and I had grown so close over the first few years of our joint friendship that it seemed so insane to me now that, suddenly, I was losing them both.

I turned and pressed my back against the bars. I stood there a while before smacking the back of my head against them once, and then twice.

"What's wrong with me, John? How did I lose Helena? How am I possibly losing you?"

Santino pushed himself off the bars and walked towards the center of the room. "Hey, don't go all weepy-eyed on my, Jacob. You know you can't get rid of *me* that easy. Helena, on the other hand, well, she is a woman, and they do things in mysterious ways and all that, so I can't really be much help there. That said, you do have a way of pushing all your personal shit on others, whether you know it or not."

"How so?"

Santino took a step forward to answer, but the sound of his boots clinking against the stone floor jarred the sleeping girl awake. She bolted to a sitting position, her eyes terrified at the mere sight of us. Neither Santino nor I knew how to react, but we were lucky enough that we didn't have to when recognition finally spread across her face. As soon as the realization took full effect, she slumped against the wall again and was out cold.

Santino tiptoed his way back to the gate, an effortless endeavor for a man whose sole purpose in life was to remain as much like a ghost as a man could without actually being dead.

He lowered his voice to a whisper. "Who planned this operation?"

"We did," I answered.

He didn't say anything. All he did was continue to look passively at me.

"Okay, okay," I relented, "I did. I planned it. So what?"

He raised an eyebrow at me knowingly. "And the one before that?"

I sighed. "Me."

He threw me a smug grin. "Think about it, Hunter. You..." Our cellmate stirred again despite our hushed voices. The poor girl. I couldn't begin to imagine what she had gone through. Santino turned his attention back to me. "Mind if we drop it for now?" He flicked his head towards the girl. "For her sake?"

"Yeah," I answered distractedly. "Okay."

I spent the next few hours trying to get some rest, but my mind kept wandering back to what Santino had tried to say and sleep never came. Thoughts of a Helena who never wanted a thing to do with me kept coming to mind, scenarios where she and Santino simply walked out of my life, not with each other, just... at the same time. That they would just leave me alone to deal with a life under Agrippina's constant pursuit alone was disturbing. The idea kept invading my mind but just when I felt sleep take a more permanent hold on me, gunfire erupted from within the cavern. It drifted into the small cell in muffled tones at first, the crisscrossing corridors breaking up the movement of the sound waves, before growing louder. I stood up and moved to the bars again, Santino joining me. Julia seemed unconscious, hiding beneath her blanket in the corner.

"Helena?" Santino asked.

I tried to concentrate on the gunfire. "I don't think so. She's only supposed to rescue us if we don't check in after nine hours. Besides, it doesn't sound like her P90."

"Then who?" Santino asked, perplexed.

"Well, if I had to guess, I'd say it was..."

I was interrupted by a very large figure rounding the corner to the corridor, moving towards us with an ominous slowness as dust billowed around him. He held a torch in one hand and a very large gun in the other, and his identity became instantly known. He was wearing his own set of night ops combat fatigues and his face was covered by a black balaclava, only a narrow slit for his eyes visible.

He looked between Santino and me before pulling off his mask, revealing the face of my favorite Frenchman. "*Bonjour, mes ami*," our friend Jeanne Bordeaux said, nodding to each of us in turn. "Perhaps one day you will rescue me for a change, no?"

II
Planning

Mission Entry #2
Jacob Hunter
Valentia, Transalpine Gaul - April, 42 A.D.

The reason I ended my last entry so abruptly was because Santino, Helena and I had to take care of a little business.

Hostage negotiation, if you will.

The original plan called for Santino and me to infiltrate a band of thugs responsible for the death of an equestrian Roman family and the abduction of a young girl. Our insertion had gone smoothly, but when we arrived at their hideout, our cover was blown and we had to improvise. Jeanne Bordeaux, formerly of the National Gendarmerie Intervention Group (say that ten times fast) and a former Praetorian squad member, came to the rescue.

When Helena was on supply run duty a few days ago, part of her orders had been to get in contact with him, tell him what we were planning, and ask if he'd help out. She reported that he said he'd think about it. I guess we were lucky he was a quick thinker, and I was happy to see him. He was another connection to our lost home and his mere presence was a reminder of better times.

When he arrived, Santino had joined him in clearing out the rest of the cave while I helped our charge, a seventeen year old girl named Julia. She'd been stripped naked by her kidnappers and all she had to cover herself with was a blanket I gave her. I was as careful and gentle as I could be with her, but she wouldn't budge from her corner so I had to carry her out. Luckily, Santino and Bordeaux had done a good job clearing the cave complex. On the way out, I noticed the leader of the group, Madriviox, dead with a neat little hole through his forehead.

He got what he deserved.

We immediately returned to the tavern we'd left from. Helena is comforting and talking to the girl while Santino has run off with his barmaid again. Bordeaux is at the table with me, and with him here, we can move on to the next phase of my plan.

Until next time.

I put my pen between the pages and wrapped a rubber band around the small leather bound journal, capturing the pen within. Having spent a few years working at my college library, I knew it wasn't the best thing for the binding, but I was lazy and it made finding my spot again just that much easier. Not to mention finding a pen. I dropped the book into a bag and turned my attention to the large man seated across from me.

To say the man was large was like calling the Himalayas a series of rolling hills. He was taller than me, significantly broader across the chest and shoulders and had the build of a professional wrestle. His sharp nose and angled chin gave him a look I always associated with the French, and his bright blue eyes, scruffy light brown hair and short facial stubble made him a pretty good looking guy.

He'd joined the Papal Praetorians after his wife had been killed in a terrorist attack outside the Vatican. Her death still haunted him deeply, and was not something he discussed very often. It was a defining moment for him, an event that brought him into my circle of friends and subsequently to Ancient Rome. Once Claudius was defeated, he no longer had a reason to remain an active combatant, and made the decision to explore the territory he had once called home – France. While it was only Gaul these days, a territory that had very little in common with its modern equivalent, he had said it was where he felt he belonged.

Two years ago, Santino's UAV, which was almost always active and broadcasting, had picked up a data package from him. He must have uploaded it to his computer and set it to idle transmission. When the UAV came into range by a stroke of pure luck, it had automatically connected and received the email. We had been on the run at the time, just passing through yet another random part of Europe, so we didn't actually notice it until we were out of range again.

He hadn't written much, just a simple message that he was happily married to a widowed woman of German ancestry, and had bought a tavern near the one we were now in. It was why we chose to come to Valentia in the first place. He had finished by saying he was living a quiet life of relaxation which, for the first time in many years, was completely devoid of war. He had also written that his wife was pregnant and that they were expecting a child.

"Sorry, Jeanne," I said, forgetting my manners. "The journal was Helena's idea. A way to record what we're doing. Just in case."

"Not a problem, *mon ami*," he said while sipping some wine. I always got a kick out of the fact that despite being perfectly fluent in both English and Latin, he always insisted on throwing out a few choice French words as well. He was a typical stubborn Frenchman. "Although, I am curious as to what it is you're doing. Exactly."

"We'll get to that," I reassured him, "but first, how have you been? Are you a proud father yet?"

That forced a smile to his face. "I see you got my message. I had been wondering. And yes, I am actually. My wife and I had twins two years ago. Here," he said as he reached for his bag. He pulled out a digital camera, which he held out to display a photograph of two young boys. They were good looking kids, but they seemed too big somehow, out of proportion with their surroundings.

"How big are they?" I asked, still squinting at the camera.

Bordeaux gave me a knowing smile. "I know. They are going to be huge!"

I gave the pictures another look, eyes widening. "If that's what the kids are like, what about the mother?"

He smirked and manipulated the camera to show me a picture of a lovely woman with fiery red curly hair, and a pale complexion. Her round face and doe eyes made her more cute than beautiful, but there was no denying her attractiveness. He switched to a different picture that showed the two of them standing next to one another and I was finally able to see her with some perspective. She might have been taller than I was. I looked away from the picture to his smiling face.

"*Oui*," he said in response to my silent question. "I have my own little Amazon now."

"'Little'," I said in amusement. Helena had always been jokingly referred to as an Amazon by the legionnaires we'd spent time with five years ago because of her height and prowess at war.

"I didn't know they made women that big. She could be a star in the WNBA, a model or both."

"I got lucky," he said, pulling back the camera to look at the picture, a broad smile on his face. "I am quite happy."

"If you don't mind me asking," I started, curious. "What did you tell her about you? About all of us? I mean, how did you explain the camera? What about marriage? How did you work that out?"

Bordeaux put away his camera and leaned back in his chair, linking his fingers together as he laid them on his abdomen. "Well," he began. "It was not easy at first. I told her there were things I simply couldn't explain and that she would have to trust me. It was for her own safety after all. But once I gave her some of the warm clothes I'd brought, not to mention the medicine and first aid supplies I had, she realized my differences were all for the best. She loved me the day I gave her a pain killer for a headache."

"Must be nice to have such a loving woman," I remarked dryly.

He tilted his head back and looked at me oddly before continuing.

"It... is," he said slowly. "But it was not easy. It took a long time for her to bring herself to really trust me. As for the marriage, I knew finding a priest was out of the question, so I took her rights. It's what she wanted. She hasn't forced me to worship some random pantheon, but I respected her wishes. We have been spending the past few years discussing the ideas and concepts of Christianity, and she likes them, and I know my kids will not be trapped into worshiping a set of gods they think might actually smite them."

"I'm happy for you, Jeanne, I really am," I said, shaking my head at the table. "I know you were hurting after the Vatican attacks and it's good you were able to find someone else you can be happy with."

"*Merci*, Jacob, but you sound almost jealous. Shouldn't you and Helena be madly in love still? In fact," he said, glancing around the tavern, "how come I don't see any smartass kids with a good right hook running around?"

I laughed. "After four years? I wish. And Kids? You're kidding right? Besides, we've already got one. His name's Santino!"

"Oh, right," Bordeaux said with a laugh. "Still, I hear the tension in your voice. Is something wrong?"

"I really don't know." I sighed and leaned back in my own chair. "I feel like I've had this conversation a dozen times already in the past few days. Helena's just been acting distant lately, and every time I try to get close, she just pushes me away. I don't know why. I haven't cheated on her or ever given her reason to think I have, but every time a barmaid or other female comes around, she gets immediately jealous. I don't know. Sometimes, I wonder why I try anymore."

He pulled his cup from his lips and pointed it at me. "You try because you love her. If you didn't, it wouldn't bother you so much. And she loves you, or else she wouldn't be afraid to talk to you. If she really didn't care, she would throw all her problems at you at once, and make you figure them out. Many relationships are torn apart because people are simply unable to talk to each other. It's all about trust. If you don't trust each other, and you won't talk to each other, then perhaps you don't belong with each other. But if you do, and you do, you'll be just fine."

"Thanks, Dr. Love," I said with a half-smile. "But it really couldn't have come at a worse time. We're going to have our hands full for the next few months."

"Ah, the plot thickens."

"Yeah, basically," I muttered, taking a deep breath. "Ready?"

"*Oui.*"

"Okay. First thing's first then. What do you know about what happened to Caligula?"

"I heard he was poisoned at a dinner party and that no suspects were ever named. Agrippina is in control until Nero is old enough to become emperor."

"Sure it's easy to believe the national propaganda," I said, "but the truth is, I know who killed him. It was Agrippina.

He was clearly taken aback. He didn't know her like the three of us on the run did. "How do you know?"

"Trust me, I know. She was also responsible for Santino and me being captured that day we infiltrated Rome."

"Interesting," Bordeaux said, stroking his chin. "Why didn't you say anything?"

"Who are they going to believe? Me or the new empress of Rome?"

"Ah," he said. "I really should not be surprised. Her taxation policies are strangling many families here in the provinces and her forced enlistment draft is completely unnecessary. She has made many enemies amongst the Gaulic aristocracy from what I have heard."

"I know, Jeanne. That's not the worst of it. She's placed puppet administrators all over the empire. They fear for their lives because of how Agrippina disposed of their predecessors and do little to counteract her overaggressive policies. The Senate hasn't fared much better. It's been gutted like a Christmas turkey."

Bordeaux shook his head. "She started off so well."

I almost smiled at his comment. "That's exactly how Caligula started as well."

He angled his head. "You don't think she's been affected by the orb, do you?"

I shrugged. "Who knows? I've recruited some feelers over the years to get an idea of what's been going on in Rome but I haven't heard anything about her mental state. I just think she's a piece of *merde* head of state."

Bordeaux smiled at my well-chosen French expletive. "What makes you think you have the right to do something about it? Just because she's a bad administrator doesn't mean it's your responsibility to remove her."

"That's an excellent question," I said, collecting my thoughts before I continued. "It's an interesting moral dilemma, isn't it? Do I have the right? And I'll tell you my answer in a word: yes. It's my fault she's in the position, so, yes; it's my responsibility to fix it."

"Hunter, no one blames you for bringing us here."

"I blame myself," I snapped before staring at the table in embarrassment before returning my attention to Bordeaux. "Sorry. This shit has really been weighing on my mind lately."

"I understand," he consoled. "What's your plan, then?"

"Nero."

"Nero? He's a child."

"You have to look at the big picture. Nero was one of the most despicable tyrants to ever grace the annals of history. He may have been a half decent administrator, but he murdered thousands, and his vainglorious attitude drove him to focus his imperial power on his own glory, not Rome's. Those same feelers I hired have reported that even at four years old, he's a monster. Torturing animals, abusing his staff, demanding anything and everything; he's become the same spoiled brat he was always meant to be."

"Sounds familiar," Bordeaux joked lightly.

I smiled for his benefit, but quickly lost it. "It gets worse. In our history, Nero was betrayed by his Praetorians when factious portions of the empire rebelled against him. His Praetorians did this because by then, it's what they did. They controlled who became emperor, starting with the assassination of Caligula and their support of Claudius." I sighed, realizing once again it was our interference that led us to this point. "But four years ago, Vincent had a plan to mold the Praetorians into the ardent defenders of the Caesars they had been under Augustus. He succeeded."

Bordeaux nodded. "The Sacred Band."

"Yep. In fact, the entire Praetorian Guard is now more devoutly loyal than maybe even the Pope's Swiss Guard." I threw a hand in the air in frustration. "Damn it, to be fair, I thought it was a good idea at the time with Caligula showing such promise. Now? It couldn't have backfired more. Augustus was almost eighty years old when he died, and there's no saying Nero won't last that long either. Who knows what will happen to the future after eighty years of Nero"

"So, what are you going to do? Kill him when he's four and can't fight back?"

"Who said anything about killing?" I asked, mostly sure he was kidding. "No, I'm going to kidnap him, hold him for ransom and stage a coup that will put a proper ruler on the throne. It's the least I can do for Caligula since there's no one to blame for his premature death but me."

Just as Bordeaux opened his mouth to respond, a wailing woman burst through the door and made a bee line toward Helena and Julia. The older Helena still had her arms around the young girl's shoulders in a consoling manner, but was quickly abandoned when mother and daughter rushed into each other's arms. Both were crying tears of happiness as the mother clutched Julia by the head and kissed her forehead and cheeks over and over.

It was a tender moment and I noticed Helena with a happy but pensive smile on her face, a few tears running down her cheeks. She looked over at me and her smile faltered just slightly, but she composed herself quickly and looked back at the reunited family.

But their reunion only lasted a few minutes. The mother moved to where Helena sat and planted a few kisses on her cheeks, and made her way over to Bordeaux and me, offering us similar thanks as well. When she reached her hand out to offer me some money, I pushed it away and told her payment was not necessary. The mother hugged me again and gave me another series of kisses before Julia came over to stand beside her mother. She kept her distance from us, but there was a small smile tugging at her lips. It was more than I expected from a young woman who must have gone through so much.

With a last few goodbyes, the two women took their leave of the tavern and were on their way, hopefully back to the relative safety of the Italian peninsula.

"I see why you do this," Bordeaux commented as he watched them leave. "Is it always this happy?"

"Sometimes," I answered honestly. "Other times, we aren't doing things nearly so heartwarming and usually our business transactions end with us getting paid. We've actually accumulated a good amount of wealth over the years. Need a loan?"

"No, I'm fine." He laughed. "Do you deny payment often?"

"Rarely. Maybe I'm getting soft in my old age."

Bordeaux snorted. "Wait till you hit fifty, then you can complain. I'll be there in a few years," he informed with a humorous shudder.

I laughed politely and waited to continue our conversation when Helena sat down between us and scratched her long, unkempt hair.

"How have you been, Jeanne?" She asked. "Are you a daddy yet?"

So Bordeaux went through the process of showing her the pictures of his family where she commented about their size just like I had. Her gaze lingered on the picture of his family.

"You have a beautiful family, Jeanne," she said. "You should consider yourself lucky."

Bordeaux glanced side long at me as he heard the same strain in Helena's voice I'd used earlier. "*Merci*. I already miss them horribly even though I have only been gone a few days."

"We're sorry we had to borrow you," she told him, "but Jacob thinks this is important. We won't take up much more of your time." She looked over at me sternly. "Will we?"

"No," I said, giving her a look of my own. "I'll try to be quick." I looked Bordeaux square in the eye. "I need you to get the band back together."

"What?" He asked, not understanding the Blues Brothers reference.

"I mean, I need you to find Wang and Vincent and get them to join us in our mission. God knows we could use their help."

"You have yet to tell me what this plan of yours even is. Who do you have in mind to replace Agrippina?"

"Vespasian," I said immediately. "He was a fine emperor after Nero, and he's our best candidate now. He's young, only in his thirties, and word is that he's just finished up a campaign in Britain and is returning to Germany to campaign there." I paused. "You should know that in our timeline, Vespasian should still be in Britain for another few years and there never was a campaign of this scale planned for Germany. Probably ever. Things are already changing thanks to the few years of respite we gave Rome after saving them from crazy Caligula, but delivering to them bellicose Agrippina."

"So, how do you plan to do all this?"

I chuckled. "Well, I haven't actually thought that far ahead yet. I like to let things unravel as they happen. I think it was MacGyver who once said something about how well thought out plans hinder the ability to be flexible and adapt to possible snags."

Helena rolled her eyes and held out a hand in my direction. "You see what I've had to put up with? All this time he's been going on about his grand plan to save the universe, but he doesn't even know where to begin."

"Actually," I said as I gave her another look, annoyed at her interruption and tone, "I do know where to begin. Step one is to contact Galba and come clean."

"Galba?" Bordeaux said loudly. "Are you serious? He hates us. What good is that going to do?"

"We think it's necessary to get him involved."

Helena scoffed, but Bordeaux ignored her.

"Why?"

I glanced over at Helena who looked at me expectantly. "Well, some of us buy more stock in this than others, but it may mean less trouble later if we get him involved now."

Bordeaux's expression indicated he was confused.

"This is all just theory," I said, trying to clarify things, "but it makes some sense. It goes with the line of reasoning that surrounds Agrippina's ascension to the throne. In the original timeline, when Caligula was killed, Claudius took over, but in the timeline we now find ourselves in now, Claudius is dead, so when Caligula was killed, who would be the next candidate for the throne?"

"Agrippina, I guess," Bordeaux answered. "Especially since Caligula named Nero his direct successor."

"Right," I confirmed. "I believe, however, that it was just Agrippina using her wits to manipulate the situation, while others," I gestured to Helena with a hand, who looked frustrated, just as she did any time I gave Agrippina any credit, "as well as Santino, believe that some kind of fate is at work here. Our involvement hasn't changed anything. Agrippina ended up running things because she more or less had a hand in it during our original timeline."

"So what does that have to do with Galba?"

"Between 69 and 70 A.D. there was a civil war after Nero's suicide. Four men vied for the position and Galba was one of them, as was Vespasian. Otho and Vittelius are the other two, but they were small potatoes. The idea is that if we were to place Vespasian on the throne without dealing with these other people, fate dictates that sooner or later the other three men will step forward and try and take control themselves. What the outcome would be, I have no idea, but there's no guarantee it would be a better result." I held out my hands so that my palms faced one another, inches apart, and wiggled them left and right, never touching. "Fate will... I don't know, realign the timeline back on its original course or something."

"So, you think getting Galba on your side now, and having him support Vespasian, will help stop any future conflict between the two?"

I rolled my eyes. "It's a theory. We'll probably have to do something about Otho and Vittelius sooner or later, but I don't know much about them. They were pretty insignificant in the whole affair anyway. For that matter, so was Galba, but at least we have a relationship with him, even if he doesn't trust us."

Bordeaux leaned back in his chair again and ran a hand across his face. "I think I understand, but what did you mean by 'come clean?'"

I looked at Helena, who held out a hand. A 'this was your idea' gesture.

I cleared my throat before continuing. "I intend to tell Galba everything. Where we're from, why we're here, how we're here, Agrippina, Nero, and about his role in the 'Year of Four Emperors'. I'm still working out how I'm going to tell him he ends up losing but I'm hopeful we can get him to realize that by helping Vespasian now, he will be helping Rome in the end."

Bordeaux's jaw hung ajar and he looked to Helena, probably wondering if I had gone crazy. She tossed her hands above her shoulders, breathed an exasperated lungful of air and looked around the room distractedly. I hadn't even convinced her yet. Perhaps Santino was on to something. Was I creating a problem where there wasn't one and pushing it on everyone around me?

"Doesn't that go against everything you've always said we shouldn't be doing?" Bordeaux asked calmly. "It's obvious you're not against interacting with the timeline anymore, but telling Galba, someone who belongs in this part of history, about his own future... wouldn't that have serious repercussions?"

"I'm honestly not sure. We're still here though, and we've changed a lot of history. If even one of our many ancestors failed to get together, we should have winked out of existence by now. At least if we consider the grandfather paradox a viable time travel thesis. Granted, we may have yet to directly affect our pasts, but we're all descended from Europeans, so there's no way we haven't interfered with one ancestor or another by now. That said, I don't know what will happen if we tell Galba, but I think it's better we tell him rather than Vespasian."

Bordeaux leaned forward, propping himself up on his massive forearms which now rested on the table and once again looked to Helena for support.

"He makes a good point," she relented. "As much as I don't like it, it is our fault things have turned out the way they have. And I don't like the fact Agrippina is even still alive, let alone an empress."

I frowned at her use of the empress' name. Normally, she always referred to Agrippina as "the slut", "the whore" or some other negative slur. Helena hated her for more reasons than I could count but especially for how she treated me. If she was no longer angry at Agrippina for that, had her opinion of me changed as well?

We were going to have to talk sooner than I thought.

"I think I understand," Bordeaux said. "If Nero is the terror you say he is, it would be in the empire's best interest, and, yes, I guess we owe it to Caligula."

I nodded whole heartedly. "So, do you need anything from us before you go? We still have quite a bit of our supplies left."

Bordeaux sat back up in his chair. "I received word from Wang a few years ago. He actually sent me a conventional letter. I'm not sure how it made it to me, but it did."

I nodded. The Roman postal service was at least as good as any modern equivalent, just slower.

"He wrote that he was living in Greece," Bordeaux continued, "and that he was doing his best to remain inconspicuous, not easy for him as you could imagine. He's been using his medical background to improve medicinal knowledge in Athens for years now, and he's excited about his new treatments.

"I'll look for him first, and then move east to find Vincent. I've had no word from him at all, but he said he'd be making his way to Jerusalem. He should be there by now. I'll need Santino's UAV to help in my search. You should know that it could take quite a long time to find them, but I can try and meet you back here in four, maybe five months."

I stood. "I appreciate it Jeanne, I really do. With everyone back together, things should go much more smoothly." I offered him my hand, which he grasped. "We'll find Galba and work on Nero. By the time you get back here, we should be in position to contact Vespasian and make a deal with Agrippina."

"No problem, Jacob. I've been meaning to take my family on a vacation."

"Just be careful, and work as quickly as you can. We may need to alter the plan at some point."

He gave me a smile and tightened his grip on my hand. "Like there was any doubt of that."

Pulling on his bag and traveler's cloak, he leaned over and gave Helena a kiss on the cheek before he left, leaving the two of us alone. We watched him go but Helena quickly spoke up.

"Do you really think this is going to work?"

"Why not? If Agrippina can stage a coup, so can I."

"What if it's not necessary?"

I sighed. "If we don't..."

Helena reached out and snatched my hands, the first sign of attention she'd shown me in months. "Damn it, Jacob! You don't know what to do! You just don't! You're doing exactly what you said Vincent did four years ago. You're messing with people's lives. You're *changing* the past, not fixing it. We don't need to do anything because it will work itself out on its own." She leaned in closer. "We can just leave it be. Retire. Let history play itself out without our interference. We can go anywhere, find someplace quiet and live out our lives. We can even bring Sant..."

I couldn't take it anymore. I yanked my hands away from hers. "When did you stop trusting me?"

She leaned back and folded her arms across her chest, her expression still upset.

"It's not a matter of trust, Jacob. I simply don't want us throwing away our lives for nothing."

"Open your eyes, Helena! We screwed up. We altered the timeline and we need to fix it. There's no mystical force out there that's going to set it straight for us. You think God's going to help out? You know as well as I, that's not how He works. The only way to fix anything is to do it ourselves. If things turn out for the better, so be it. At least my conscience will be appeased."

She didn't interrupt me as she sat there, her arms still folded, her expression unchanged, so I pressed on. "Put everything aside except Caligula. What about him? He's proof everything we do here can change history. Without a competent emperor doing competent things for the next fifteen years, things will go from bad to worse."

She almost laughed. "Anything can happen in fifteen years. Even if you are right, that's a long time for someone to avoid an accident, fail to make enemies, do something stupid, or have a change of heart."

"And you're willing to just let…" I cringed at the word I had to use, "*fate* right all our wrongs for us?"

"Call it faith, Jacob. One man can't change the fate of the entire world on his own."

I came up short with my next reply. It was a profound sentiment, one that made almost too much sense, but as much as I wanted to believe her, I couldn't.

Just as I opened my mouth to answer, Santino meandered into the tavern with his young barmaid on his arm. She left him with a kiss and made her way back to her duties while he moved over to our table.

"Can you try to trust me just a little bit longer, Helena?"

She didn't answer.

Santino sat down and put his booted feet up on the table. "So? What'd I miss?"

"Bordeaux decided to help us," I reported while Helena looked away. "He's going to find Wang and Vincent and meet us back here in a few months."

"Let me guess. He bought into your whole, 'save the universe' plan, eh?"

"Actually, he did. I've always liked him."

"You like anybody who agrees with you."

I glanced at Helena. "Yeah, I guess I do. But who wouldn't?"

"So, what's the plan?"

"Screw things up even more," Helena mumbled under her breath, and I couldn't help but wonder, somewhere in the deep recesses of my mind, if she was right.

***

On the second morning after our meeting with Bordeaux, we headed north, following the Rhone River before turning east, looking for the Rhine. The past few nights with Helena had been awkward, but so had the past few months. No further attempts to discuss our issues had arisen, but our bed had been shared like two boyhood friends forced to sleep in the same bed by an overbearing mother. Once on the road, the three of us traveled in silence, the distance between us greater than ever, but we were professionals. We spent the time analyzing all the available intelligence we had on Rome's military situation.

Word on the street was that Vespasian had been appointed to the rank of legate, and sent to serve under another Roman during the campaign in Britannia with the *Legio II Augusta*. The rumors indicated that he had performed well in Britannia, better than expected, and it hadn't been long before he was granted another commission, and an army of his own to command in Germany.

Everything was going according to my knowledge of Roman history, except pretty much nothing.

Most of what I knew about Vespasian was based on Suetonius, a risky source at best, but I was pretty sure he was supposed to retire and disappear from public life for a number of years after campaigning in Britannia, an operation orchestrated by Claudius in the original timeline, only to be recalled into the military to deal with the Jewish revolt in the east in 66 A.D. Agrippina, apparently, had other plans for him. It was a shrewd strategy. There hadn't been progress in Germany since Julius Caesar had crossed the Rhine, who returned almost immediately and hadn't ventured very far. The only noteworthy news in the area after Caesar was the Battle of the Teutoburg Forest, where three legions were annihilated under the command of Quinctilius Varus. If Agrippina had plans to expand the empire, going there was the logical, though dangerous, choice; and appointing Vespasian was another.

We'd also heard from passing Romans, whose tongues were quite loose after a few drinks with a scantily clad Helena, that Galba had been assigned to Vespasian's command team. After The Battle for Rome four years ago, Galba had gone back to Germany to retrain the nearly destroyed *Legio XV Primigenia* after it had helped Caligula reclaim his imperial power. Later, he had been made governor of the Iberian Peninsula, another historical consistency.

I wasn't sure why he had chosen to serve under a relative upstart like Vespasian, but I had a bad feeling it had something to do with our involvement. As far as I knew, until 69 A.D., Galba's life was fairly mundane, but since our arrival forced him into a civil war, and a bloody battle outside the gates of Rome, maybe we had piqued his interest in war a bit and now he was itching for a fight.

Sometimes I wished Vincent were here, for the sole reason of discussing the finer points of Roman history, but sadly I didn't have that luxury. Hopefully, in another few months, I would. Either way, Galba was to retake command of the *XV Primigenia* and serve alongside five other legions under Vespasian's overall command, six legions in total, twice as many as Julius Caesar had when he invaded Britain.

It was clear that Agrippina's intention wasn't simply to invade Germany. She was planning on conquering and setting up shop. Six whole legions, along with their full compliments of auxilia, was an army that could conquer the world. It was also an army that could take control of Rome. All we had to do was get Vespasian to understand his potential historical significance, convince Galba to back him, and somehow force Agrippina to step aside so Vespasian could take over.

Easy.

***

It took us about a week and a dozen pointed fingers later, but we soon found our way to the enormous legionary barracks that was the army's camp.

To say it was huge was an understatement.

It sat on the west bank of the Rhine River and was called Vindonissa. It had been built around the birth of Christ and has since been called home by the *Legio XIII Gemina*, and if history was at all accurate, the *Legio XXI Rapax* should have just moved in. Along with Galba's *Legio XV Primigenia* and Vespasian's

Legio II Augusta, that accounted for four of the six legions meant to embark on the campaign.

It would be a difficult nut to crack as all that firepower would make sneaking in a challenge. Santino's UAV would have been helpful for advanced recon, but it was no longer available so we'd have to reconnoiter the camp the old fashioned way.

Like all legion forts, it had been constructed far from the tree line, a defensive strategy that ensured an attacking force would have to abandon the natural cover provided by a tree line to enter missile fire range.

General George Washington, before he was a general and when he was still a Redcoat, had made the mistake of not clearing out the tree line around Ft. Necessity before a battle during the Seven Year's War. The blunder had left much of his force dead, and he and his remaining men were just barely able to hold the line.

No insult to George Washington, but Romans would never make that mistake. Their camps were so efficient and practical that no matter how many legionnaires were present, the fort would always be built around the same basic principles, just scaled up.

Camps worth keeping around, like this one, generally had far larger walls around their perimeters and were built with stone instead of wood. The higher walls would make our infiltration route more difficult, but once inside we'd instantly know our way around. The only possible snag was that we didn't know exactly where Galba's tent would be. Vespasian, as the overall commander of the entire army, would be staying in the *praetorium* this time, not him.

But the *praetorium* was always situated directly in the middle of the camp, set halfway along the *via principalis*, and it didn't take a huge leap in logic to assume Galba would be nearby. As one of Vespasian's legates, he was only one step below Vespasian in the chain of command, and the army's generals would be posted near each other. All it would take is a legionnaire who valued his life more than his pride to tell us where Galba was.

Simple.

We set up our own camp about two miles inside the tree line and camouflaged our tents as well as we could. We buried them beneath a rock outcropping that jutted out over the landscape, creating a nice little space for our tents beneath. We secured large bushes around the perimeter and draped a camouflage net over everything. The site was practically invisible, and I was confident a scouting party would never spot it.

Once our hideaway was concealed, we spent a few hours resting before using the cover of night to scout the Roman camp from the trees. Using a mixture of infrared and night vision optics, we were able to identify and chart the movement of guards upon the walls. We timed their patrol route and noted which directions they paid attention to at all points along their patrol.

At daybreak, Helena used a camera with a telephoto lens the size of a soda pop bottle to take panoramic shots of the camp and its surrounding. While she was taking her pictures, I retrieved my small journal from a cargo pocket and took some time to sketch the landscape with a few pencils. While using both sketches and photographs may seem redundant, utilizing them together was a practice indoctrinated in snipers, recon marines, and other units for decades.

We returned to camp in the early evening, having shifted our recon position a handful of times, arriving to a freshly cooked dinner delivered by Santino. He had shot, cleaned, and cooked a deer while Helena and I were away, and by the time we joined him, he was already packing the leftovers in salt, preserving them for a lifetime.

As we ate, we pored over the images taken earlier, quickly remembering that we were no longer dealing with amateurs. Legionnaires were professionals. They weren't a peasant army roused by a belligerent warlord in a time of fickle bloodlust, but career soldiers. Warriors. This was their job. And they were very serious about their craft. It took us an hour before we even found a possible loophole in their defensive network.

We were able to note a single weak area – a blind spot along the north wall where patrolling guards left an opening, dead center of the wall. The segment of the wall in question was particularly dark and was left unguarded for about three and a half minutes – more than enough time to scale the wall and sneak inside.

Helena and I spent the rest of the evening preparing for the operation to come, while Santino complained about having to stay behind and play spotter. He wanted to see "Ol' Triple Chin," as he had dubbed Galba for his jowls and multiple chins, but we didn't have a ghilli suit for him. Helena and I were both trained snipers, and camouflage with the use of a ghilli suit was our stock in trade, not Santino's. While he may have been able to sneak up on God Himself, his kind of stealth was different from ours. He was a master at hiding in plain sight or in a crowd, but the art of camouflage was, as my trainers had said, less about avoiding detection and more about simply being undetectable at all.

Ghilli suits allowed us to be one with the environment. They were handcrafted and modular so that Helena and I could tailor them to mimic whatever environment we wanted. We'd spent most of the past few days doing just that, adding bits of grass and local fauna to them, crafting the perfect disguise.

By the time we finished them two days after finding Vindonissa, it was too late for Helena and I to delve into the conversation I knew we needed. We mostly kept to ourselves, but by 0200 on the third day, I tried to purge all thoughts plaguing my mind as we launched the operation by crawling our way through the low grass of the meadow toward the camp, back in sniper-mode.

Focused and meticulous.

We made the first leg of our journey smoothly and without incident in a little under an hour. We didn't have to worry about anything like random search lights since Roman torches could barely reach out past their palisade. Additionally, as luck would have it, tonight's moon was a waning crescent, about as far from full as it was going to get.

When I pushed my arm out again to inch myself forward, all it came into contact with was air. I looked out from under my hood and saw the ground fall away steeply. We'd made it to the trench. I tapped my toe twice in quick succession against the soft grass, letting Helena know we'd made it to the first major impediment. She gave my ankle a gentle squeeze to confirm she understood, and I slide forward.

Navigating the trench was easy, just down to the bottom for a few meters, then back up. We'd noted the previous night that the ditches appeared freshly dug, possibly as simple upkeep to ensure they were kept clear. But it also left the soil loose and littered with freshly dug grass, just enough for our grassy ghilli suits to blend right in.

The trip took about ten minutes. When I bumped my head against something hard after crawling up the other side of the trench, I knew we'd reached the palisade. Glancing up, I peeked through my hood of grass and took in my surroundings. The wall of the Roman fort stood immediately in front of me, at least thirty feet high.

I sent a double click to alert Santino that we had arrived by tapping my radio's push-to-talk button twice in rapid succession. We waited for what seemed like an hour before I heard Santino's faint voice in my ear.

"Clear. Four minutes on my mark..." he paused "...mark."

Helena was already rising to her feet, turning her back to me as she shrugged out of her ghilli suit. I pulled it off her shoulders and packed it into her backpack while she did the same with mine. We wore our night ops combat fatigues with our olive drab MOLLE vests over them. We were lightly armed, but Helena also had a small grappling hook dangling from her vest, which I dutifully retrieved and prepared to toss over the wall. I made a few quick circles in the air as I spun the hook, releasing it on the fourth. It went sailing over the wall and silently made contact with the rampart's floor thanks to its rubber tips. I pulled the rope until it was taut; giving it another tug just to be sure it was secure. Satisfied, I started my ascent, Helena right behind me.

A short climb later, I bounded over the lip of the wall, landing quietly onto the rampart. I sidestepped immediately to the left so Helena could land behind me. When she did, we gathered up the rope and I reattached everything to her rig.

I risked a quick look out over the camp, seeing for the first time an endless sea of torches illuminating an incalculable number of tents, all lined up in neat little rows. In that moment, I couldn't avoid a slight sense of unease tickle the back of my mind at the fact that I hadn't brought Santino instead of Helena, because this was when we could have really used him. I could see guards aplenty scattered through the interior of the camp and there were thousands of residents randomly going about one bit of business or another.

We'd anticipated as much, but the idea of sneaking through the forest of tents below us was unsettling. Santino could have walked down the *via principalis* stark naked and gone completely unnoticed, but I had to be here since I was the only one with enough facts to talk to Galba and Helena's ghilli suit didn't fit him. It hadn't been out of the question for us to craft his own ghilli suit out of locally made materials, even if it wouldn't have been up to the standards of our modern ones, but none of us had voiced any concerns during the planning stage about his absence. Four years ago, I probably wouldn't have considered bringing Helena on such a dangerous mission. She'd been a green rookie, chosen for the Pope's Praetorians because of a falsified record, but four years of operating with Santino and me had honed her into an effective military machine.

I tried to push it out of my mind as Helena placed her hand on my back, indicating she was ready to move. I reached behind me to tap the side of her leg to confirm I was ready as well. When we reached the first guard, I took aim with my air pistol fitted with tranquilizer darts, but didn't fire. I knew enough about Roman camps to know that if this guard didn't meet up with his partner, now at the other end of the wall, an alarm would go up almost immediately. Instead, we took advantage of our dark camouflage and quietly shifted positions to the inner edge of the rampart, and crawled our way behind him.

At one point, I thought I would have to shoot him when I saw his head snap around in our direction, but it turned out he was merely swatting at an insect. He turned towards the center of the wall to meet up with his buddy a few moments later, and I let out a slow breath through my balaclava. I glanced at Helena, only my eyes revealing my relief. She returned my look with a flick of her own green eyes and a gentle nudge to urge me forward.

When the guard was out of sight, I pulled Helena's grappling hook and rope from her MOLLE vest once again. I placed the hook on the rampart's wooden floor near the corner and tossed the rope out over the inner wall. The corner was pitch black so we had no insecurities about standing out against the lightly colored stone wall. I maneuvered myself out over the wall and fast roped to the bottom, taking stock of our surroundings after touching the ground, waiting for Helena to join me. Our corner of the camp seemed deserted at the moment, but that could change at any moment. When Helena's boots hit the grass behind me, I turned to see her jerk the rope to dislodge the hook, stepping aside to ensure it didn't fall on her. After it landed, I picked it up and secured it to her rig for the last time, and we moved off into the small city.

There might have been a thousand rows of tents before us, each containing eight sleeping men, and I had no idea how many tents there were per row. To find our way through, we simply picked a narrow avenue in one of the denser areas of the camp and slowly made our way toward the center, looking for a potential legionnaire to interrogate.

We didn't have to wait long before our first candidate appeared.

A man stumbled out of his tent nearly on top of us, muttering about how he really had to use the bathroom. Helena moved first and tackled him to the ground, covering his mouth in one quick motion. I knelt beside him and pushed my small boot knife against his throat.

"Galba," I whispered into his ear. "Where's his tent?"

The man's eyes were filled with shock, wide open and unbelieving, as though he were witnessing an apparition before him. He trembled and I heard the sound of running water beneath me. I glanced down to see that the man had urinated himself. Helena looked down as well, just in time to shift her knee out of the way. She looked back up at me and rolled her eyes.

"*Galba?*" I whispered with some force this time, driving my knife deep enough to draw a droplet of blood.

The legionnaire shook his head vigorously, his eyes wide with terror. Helena moved her hand just slightly. "Two tents behind the *praetorium*, three in the direction of the *porta decumana*."

I nodded. "Thanks. Your helpfulness won't go unrewarded."

Helena covered his mouth again and I shot him with a tranq dart before he could do something stupid. She looked at me with wide, annoyed eyes, not finding my parting words nearly as humorous as I did. We waited a few seconds for the affects to take hold and I removed the dart. I rolled him near the entrance to his tent with the shove of my boot. A random passerby wouldn't suspect any foul play, just another drunk passed out on the ground, and he'd probably be too out of it when he woke up to even remember us.

I flicked my fingers towards the *praetorium* and we carefully stalked our way through the camp. It took us about fifteen minutes, but we were eventually in position to cross the *via principalis*.

Luckily, traffic wasn't heavy, but there were guards posted sporadically. If not for a few parlor tricks Santino had taught us about creating diversions and dividing and conquering, this operation would have been over almost before it had begun.

But we were lucky, and our insertion seemed complete when we found ourselves in front of the tent the legionnaire had indicated was Galba's. I glanced at my watch. 0330. We had a few hours before the army started its daily hustle and bustle. I followed Helena as she reached the tent's entrance and gave the camp one last look. Nothing seemed out of the ordinary so I patted her on the shoulder and followed her inside.

I stepped into a large open space, littered with mobile furniture and storage containers scattered throughout in a haphazard manner. After a second to take in my surroundings, I went directly to the bed. Looking down, I saw the fat face of the ugly man I knew to be Galba. I never did figure out how his head always looked so fat while his body stayed in the tip top shape of any legionnaire.

Helena and I exchanged nods, and I bent over to clasp a gloved hand over his thick lips.

His eyes shot open, but he didn't flinch, try to escape or utter a noise. In his eyes I saw immediate recognition, even with our concealing facemasks. He was one of the few people who knew who we were. I held a finger vertically over my covered mouth and waited for him to nod in understanding. When he did, I slowly removed my hand.

"You," he growled. "I should have you arrested and crucified. I've recently received word from the empress that you have officially been charged with the murder of Caligula." He narrowed his eyes at me angrily.

I cocked my head to the side and looked at Helena. Her indecipherable figure shrugged. That was news to us. I'd always wondered why she hadn't pegged his murder on us years ago, but I guess it was better late than never for her.

Interesting timing, though.

I pulled off my mask, revealing a face I knew was familiar to him and stood up straight.

"Servius. I need you to listen to me."

"Listen to you?! Why should I do that, you traitorous murderer?"

I leaned down and whispered, "Servius, do you really think we killed Caligula?"

Galba looked at the foot of his bed before looking back at us, shifting positions so that he was sitting up and crossed his arms over his chest. It gave him the appearance of a chubby, stubborn two year old.

"No," he said. "I don't. You are many things, but I always considered you loyal, and since you didn't try to usurp power for yourself after his death, I see no motive."

Helena removed her own mask and pulled her very long hair from beneath the back of her vest.

"Listen to him, Galba," she said. "You may not want believe what he has to tell you, but you need to trust us."

I looked over at Helena, who had cleaned up since our time in the tavern, and was back to the ravishing green eyed beauty I'd always known her to be.

"So you brought your woman," Galba commented as he looked around. "Of course you did. Where is the funny one? I actually liked him."

I'm sure Santino will be ecstatic.

"Servius," I pressed, "what I'm about to tell you will sound ridiculous, outlandish, and frankly impossible, but I need you to keep an open mind."

"Why do you keep calling me that?" He asked nervously. "My name is Lucius, not Servius."

"No, it's not," I said sternly. "Your real name is Servius Sulpicius Galba. You only took the name Lucius Livius Ocella Sulpicius Galba from your step mother and her family, who loved you dearly and raised you as one of their own." I saw his eyes widen in surprise. "Now, let me tell you another story. One about you, me, Rome, its future, and how I need your help to ensure its very survival."

III
Galba

Mission Entry #3
Helena Van Strauss
Vindonissa, Germania Superior - April, 42 A.D.

My turn.

It seems only fair that someone other than Jacob have the opportunity to tell our story. He's always been too secretive for his own good. Stubborn and arrogant too. But while that stubbornness was one of the many reasons I fell in love with him all those years ago, it's also what brought us here today.

In a place I don't want to be.

I sit here writing this entry from within Galba's tent, at the very center of a fortress filled with tens of thousands of armed and dangerous men, all of whom wouldn't hesitate for a moment to cash in on the Whore's reward for our heads. To someone like me or you, this may seem crazy, but to someone like Jacob, it's completely normal.

The man I love is on a mission, and when he's on one, it's best to stay out of his way.

The man I love.

I've found it harder and harder to regard him in that way for maybe six months now, ever since his plan became less theoretical and more like an obsession. I don't feel wrong in questioning my feelings for him when his fixation suddenly became more of a priority to him than I was. And I don't mean that in a jealous way. What I mean is that he no longer seems to care about anything I have to say, if he even bothers to ask.

He doesn't seem to care about anything.

If only he hadn't been like this before, I wouldn't worry about him. At the very onset of our arrival here in ancient Rome, Jacob had placed all responsibility for bringing us here on himself, refusing to admit otherwise and pulled away from the only people he could trust. I was already in the process of loving him by then, but I couldn't bring myself to act on it until I knew for certain he wasn't a self-obsessed megalomaniac. I hadn't known him for more than a few months then, knowing that even the most gentle of people can have a dark side.

But I was lucky. Jacob changed and committed himself to working through his issues, but now he's doing it again. I feel like I'm losing him to inner demons that have always persisted in his mind and always will... but even though I know I have to be there for him... I'm not sure I can.

As for Galba, well, he hasn't taken the news we came here to tell him very well. Not well at all. When Jacob first began his story, Galba seemed fine, pacing around the room distractedly stopping only occasionally to glare at me as if all this is my fault...

Which irritated me.

Men have always underestimated me, beginning with my father, and I've never understood why. Why is it that I always had to prove myself just to gain an inkling of respect? Even Caligula and Galba, and every other legionnaire I'd met, all shorter than me, had underestimated me. They thought I was weak but they learned. I broke a man's nose and almost killed another, all to prove I was just as special as they were.

Like I said, they learned.

During the Battle for Rome, I was just another one of the guys. They even made me a set of legionary armor for me that actually fit. It was sweet. Galba spoke to me directly once, and after my near death experience, Caligula himself even came to sit with me. It was cute, and I really appreciated it. His acceptance was honestly the first time I've ever felt truly appreciated.

Galba just slumped across his desk.

Jacob hadn't been kidding when he said he was going to tell Galba everything.

He started with Galba's backstory. It was the only thing he knew he could say that would prove he knew more than he should, or could. Then he told Galba how everything should have played out, with Caligula going crazy and Claudius taking over. Jacob continued with Nero and the atrocities he would let happen – how he would let Rome burn, blame it on the Christians and build a giant palace on the spot where homes were destroyed. Then, he told him about his own attempt to take control upon Nero's death and how he had failed and died, the first of three, before Vespasian took control. Jacob finished by telling the tale of Rome's fall, followed by as much European, Muslim, Asian, and American history as he could in the last hour. He mentioned the Dark Ages, the medieval period, the Renaissance, the discovery of America, the unification of European territories into their own sovereign nations, and more history than I ever knew existed.

I had to give him credit. He was a good teacher. He was as patient with Galba as I could see him being with his young students trying to grasp a new concept. It was adorable actually.

I'm trying to catch up here, but I think I heard him mention the third world war that was going on in 2021. He made sure to mention the technical advancements and the terror they brought. Chemical, biological, nuclear warfare. He mentioned Nagasaki and Hiroshima, and the utter destruction that was unleashed on God knows how many Japanese...

It just occurred to me that if Jacob is right, you may have no idea what I'm talking about.

Sorry.

I made sure to watch Galba's posture during the presentation. As I said, he paced at first, but by the time Jacob got to the fall of Rome, he'd stopped to stand near his desk. With William the Conqueror, he was still standing, but had his fists on his desk as he leaned heavily on them. When Jacob got to steam power, airplanes, electricity, the moon landing, and the internet, Galba was seated at his chair, his hands clutching his ears as he hung his head, trying to wrap his mind around everything Jacob had just unleashed upon him.

Now he was slumped on his desk.

The poor man.

He's had his whole world upended. He's just been told how everything he's worked for was all for nothing, and that in the end, his entry in the Oxford Classical Dictionary was only a few lines long, at least that's what Jacob once told me about the man. Very few even remembered his name anymore. I know I hadn't heard of him. And he's just been asked to help Vespasian and try to forget the fact that history will remember him as little more than a footnote.

Okay, I'd better wrap this up.

Galba mentioned Agrippina and Nero were on their way to oversee the preparations for the invasion, and I know Jacob will want to take Nero as soon as possible, but mark my words, if I get within arm's reach of Agrippina, I will dig her throat out with my bare hands. Despite everything, I'll never forgive her for what she did to Jacob. I owe him that much.

Caligula as well.

They deserve their vengeance.

I glanced over at Helena, who had been feverously scribbling in my journal while I told Galba the longest story I've ever had to tell. She was shaking her hand after dotting her last period with an odd vigor, an angry expression on her face. She returned my look, and even though she quickly averted her eyes back to the journal, she slowly looked back at me, her expression softening. I gave her an earnest smile, which I was surprised to see returned. Seeing it, my own smile widened and I wanted nothing more than to embrace her, tell her how much of an asshole I'd been and that it was time to work through our problems.

Every muscle in my body urged me to do it, but I was distracted by the shape of Galba slowly rising from his chair. He got up and moved towards the tent's entrance and opened the flap to peer out into the morning darkness. Dawn was just around the corner, and I knew we'd overstayed our welcome. I had just summarized an entire world history course in a little more than an hour, but the story needed telling. Maybe Galba would let us hang out here until nightfall again if he decided not to kill us.

His head sagged forward as he closed the flap, making his way back to his desk.

"What you've told me," he paused, sitting slowly, "is very hard to accept."

That was probably an understatement.

"To think that all of what Rome has built will one day fall, only to be replaced by a religious cult that worships a single deity is difficult to imagine." He smiled just slightly. "But, if it is as you say and this… Pope, as you call him, is so powerful; it is not hard to believe that he would of course be ruling from Rome."

He paused again to take in a deep breath. "I have seen what you can do. Your ability to channel the sun's power to create your own light. Your weapons. The manner of your clothing. Your night seeing devices. All of it is logical were I to only accept your story." He looked me squarely before continuing. "I *knew* you were not from some far away land or mythical island, or even descended from gods. This... makes sense. I know of Archimedes, and some of what you describe seems based on his principles. It would only be a matter of time."

"You're right, Galba," I heard Helena speak up. "You Romans were the foundations from which our society grew. It's something to be proud of, not mourned."

"But what of this alternate... story? Where Claudius is a great emperor?" Galba wondered aloud. "The thought of it seems so foreign to me, the bastard that he was, but the way you say it, even though you lived through it, is as if you don't even believe what you experienced yourself."

"You have to look at it from our perspective," I clarified. "I remember learning about Rome when I was just a teenager, and how Caligula had gone crazy, died a few years later and left Rome in Claudius' very capable hands. Having seen it unfold differently *is* a foreign concept to me, exactly as you say. I still think I dreamt it up on occasion."

Galba sat heavily in his chair, his eyes locked with some random object on his desk, lost in thought. I glanced over at Helena again, and while she looked concerned Galba might not go for it, she stayed supportively silent near the entrance to the tent. She pulled the flap to the tent open momentarily to peak outside and gave the camp a quick inspection before looking back at me, tapping her watch.

I looked back at Galba. "Sir, we need to hurry this up."

He looked up quickly, startled. He took a breath. "I need time to think on this. Vespasian is young and inexperienced. I only just heard of him three years ago when he was an upstart tribune in a legion I cannot even remember. When he was given a legion and promoted to the rank of legate prior to the invasion of Britain, I was even more surprised. And now you stand before me, asking me to support him as the next emperor of Rome?"

I held both of my hands in the air, trying to remember that thirty kids would probably be more difficult.

"He is young, yes, and while he wouldn't have been emperor for close to thirty years from now, we can already see the beginnings of what made him so great. Look at where you are," I concluded, sweeping my arms out in an expansive gesture, taking in the camp.

"Indeed," he muttered. "I won't lie to you. A few hours ago, the only thing I felt towards young Vespasian was anger, resentment, and, yes, jealousy. This would have been my command if not for the audacity of Agrippina."

That piqued Helena's interest. "What do you mean, 'the audacity of Agrippina'?"

Galba looked embarrassed. "She approached me. Romantically. I was flattered or course, but I am already married." He paused. "My mother slapped her."

I whistled through my teeth, interested because the exact same thing happened in the original timeline. Agrippina made an advance on Galba, he denied her, and his mother slapped her. It only added to the theory that specific events continued to play themselves out, even if the timeline is altered slightly.

That thought in mind, I never could imagine what the lovely Agrippina saw in a man like Galba.

"So, instead of giving you command, she gave it to Vespasian?" Helena asked him, still standing guard by the entrance.

"Yes," Galba replied sourly. "Besides, he's the 'Hero of Britain.'" If you believe the stories they say about him, he managed to subdue the entire island with a single legion in a week. I will admit he has surpassed everyone's expectations, even mine, while all I've done for the past three years is stew in Iberia."

"So, what about it?" I pressed. "I understand how you feel, but after everything we've told you, will you help us?"

"I need time to think," Galba said. "Come back in a few days. By then, Agrippina and Nero should be here, and if I decide to help you, perhaps I'll help you take him. Honestly, I understand what you say about him. I've seen him occasionally over the past few years, and he is nothing if not a spoiled brat."

I smiled. "You see? I wasn't..."

I was interrupted by the blaring of Roman horns off in the distance and the rumbling of tens of thousands of men waking from their night's slumber. Helena peeked outside, but signaled she couldn't see anything yet. My radio earpiece crackled to life.

"Uh, guys?" Santino's distorted voice whispered. "You've got incoming."

"What do you mean, 'incoming'?" I replied immediately.

"I mean there's a giant fucking boat sailing up the river."

"What does it look like?" I asked.

There was a pause. "Jacob. It's huge. What more do you want me to say? It's half the size of the river, maybe a football field long, and has a few buildings on the deck."

His description immediately reminded me of the Romans pleasure barges that were used as drifting palaces. I had watched something on TV about archaeologists discovering one in Lake Nemi in the 1920s. Prior to the find, society had no idea they even existed. When it was discovered, lost revelations about Roman technology and engineering were uncovered. With the discovery came the first evidence of an anchor being used on a ship, something thought invented much later. As were ball bearings, another something that wasn't reinvented until the eighteenth or nineteenth century. The ship also had heated and cooled running water as well. The discovery had been an archaeological treasure trove.

Another was later found, but each had only been the size of about two tennis courts, not a football field if I recalled properly. But those boats were constructed under Caligula, inspired by his own designs. I wouldn't put it past Agrippina to take similar designs and add to them, making her new ship a combination of the two and therefore far grander than those of her late brother. Still, I doubted it was the size of a football filed, but if this boat of Santino's was one of these floating palaces, it could only mean Agrippina had arrived earlier than expected. I relayed my information to Galba.

"That must be Agrippina," he confirmed. "I did not know she was arriving by her pleasure barge, but it doesn't surprise me. It is a grand spectacle."

"Why is she even here?" Helena asked, more anger than curiosity in her voice.

"Why else?" Galba replied nonchalantly. "She wants to be a part of the campaign."

"You're kidding, right?" I asked. "Who's running Rome?"

"I'm sure she has plenty of Senators completely loyal to her that she has left in charge. Besides, it wouldn't be the first time the head of state was on campaign with the legions."

I nodded as the sound of men rushing about grew louder outside, which meant our escape plan was blown. Galba seemed to understand.

"It seems you will have to stay here. We'll be busy all day with Agrippina arriving early, as Vespasian had plans to assemble the entire army to welcome her, but I do not believe he will have the time now." A small smile formed at the corner of his mouth at the small setback for Vespasian.

I nodded and moved over to his bed and sat on its edge. "Works for me."

Galba shook his head. "You do not understand. I may send couriers to gather materials I may need for a meeting or have them place correspondence on my desk."

"So where are we going to hide all day?" Helena asked with a glance around the tent.

I bounced on the bed before picking up the sheets that hung over the side and smiled. She rolled her eyes, but moved to sit next to me all the same, removing her vest and duty gear.

"Do you have a place where we can store our gear?" She asked.

In response, Galba opened a simple cabinet full of his legionary armor and gear. He removed his equipment and we replaced it with our own, removing our combat jackets and boots as well, placing everything neatly inside. Helena moved beneath the bed first, but I paused for a last few words with Galba.

"Um. I wouldn't mention we're here if I were you."

He looked at me slyly, at least as his slyly as his ugly face could allow. "After everything you have just told me, do you really think I would give you to her now?"

I shrugged. "Never can be too trusting."

Galba laughed. "That is a grand understatement. Will you need any food or water before I go?"

"No," I replied. "We'll be fine. Just remember to keep in mind what we spoke about today."

"How could I not?" He asked bluntly as he left the tent.

Hoping he was as good a man as I thought he was, I handed the MRE and CamelBak blindly to Helena beneath the bed and slid in alongside her. The sheets concealed us entirely, and thankfully, the bed was high enough above the ground that the space didn't seem too cramped.

"Well, this is comfortable," Helena commented, clearly anything but on the hard-packed earth. "We have to spend a whole day down here?"

"Hold on," I said, reaching out from beneath the bed. Grasping something soft, I pulled it below to discover a feather pillow and a woolen sheet. I handed them to Helena and reached up again to find another pillow.

"Such a gentleman," she quipped as she maneuvered the blanket beneath the both of us.

"I do try," I said to a response of silence.

I turned to look into her eyes, green as ever, and like always, appearing to look right through me. She was waiting for something, and I knew from her gaze that she could wait all day.

I decided I wasn't going to spend it in awkward silence.

"So?" I started. "Anything on your mind?"

She narrowed her eyes, directing a hint of anger at me. "And what could possibly make you think that?"

"Oh, I don't know. You're normally so talkative that it's sometimes hard to know when you're ignoring me."

"Very cute, professor."

I frowned. She may have meant her words to sound flippant or comical, but her tone didn't deliver the sentiment. She shifted so that she lay on her back and stared at the bottom of the bed, her attention distant and directed away from me once again. A minute passed before she finally opened up.

"You're not the same man I fell in love with."

Well that was unexpected.

"I'm not?"

"No, you're not," she said, shifting only her head, her gaze once again making me more uncomfortable than most of what she said. "Most of the Jacob Hunter I fell in love with is still there – the one who is caring, strong, intelligent, and the man who I still love. But you're also different now. It began a few months ago when you first outlined your plan to 'fix the timeline'. Now you're obsessed, indignant, and self-righteous."

"Self-righteous?" I blurted.

Just then a voice crackled in my ear.

"Uh, guys?" Santino's voice transmitted again through my ear piece. "You're on VOX."

I felt my face get warm. I must have accidentally left my radio set so that it transmitted everything I said, not just what was said when the "push to talk" button was held. I reached into my cargo pocket and switched the radio back to PTT mode.

I clicked the transmitter. "3-3, this is 3-1, over," I sent using our official call designations. While no one could pick up our com chatter here, old habits die hard.

"3-1, 3-3, go ahead," Santino replied automatically.

"Go to ground, 3-3. Hold your position. 3-2 and I are hunkered down in camp for the duration of the day, howcopy?"

"Solid copy," he said before holding his tongue for a few seconds. "Come on, guys. I'm already bored out of my mind. You expect me to just lay out here and wai…"

I switched off my radio, silencing him.

"That wasn't very nice," Helena chided.

"He'll live. I'll switch it back on in a few hours." I paused while I checked the radio again before turning back to Helena. "So… 'self-righteous'?"

"Exactly. The problem is your idea that we've somehow broken something and that it's our, and only our, responsibility to fix it. We have no idea how these so-called laws of time work. The future could be exactly as we left it, but that isn't even the most important part." She paused and took a deep breath, "The important part is that I don't even know *why* you think this is so important because you won't talk to me about it."

My brain immediately wanted to say one thing, but a distant voice in the back of my head made me stop. I turned inward and tried to find an honest answer for Helena. I knew she deserved the truth, but in this moment, I was finding it difficult to give her an answer. I couldn't just tell her all my theories were based off of science fiction television and documentaries on the Science Channel. She wouldn't accept that, and I suppose I didn't either.

What I did trust, however, was myself. I've always trusted the men I had under my command as a SEAL, but the only person I could ever absolutely rely on was me. Every single job throughout my life that had to be done, I did myself. Every one of those experiences helped build my confidence in my own instincts and abilities. It hadn't been easy as a kid, as it rarely is, but over time and through the vagaries of life I grew into a rock steady adult who trusted himself implicitly. Experience is the forbearer of all knowledge and I had been through a lot in my time, and everything within me had been telling me that something needs to be done.

"I feel it in my gut, Helena," I said wholeheartedly. "I really do. I know this is the right thing to do."

"In your gut?" Helena asked knowingly, her look suggesting she had known the answer all along.

I eyed her suspiciously. "Yes. It's never led me in the wrong direction before."

"Well, Jacob," she said coyly, "I've always trusted your gut too. I always have but only because my own gut lets me. After everything Agrippina's done to manipulate us, I promised myself years ago that I wasn't going to blindly follow anyone ever again, that I'd never be that little girl again who had no choice in who she was going to marry." She took a second before jabbing a finger against my chest, biting her lower lip as she did so. It hurt a little and I flinched away as she continued. "You're just lucky that you've always been good at making decisions because I've never had any reason to doubt you before."

"Except now," I said, understanding.

She nodded. "I want to trust you, Jacob, like I always have, but I just can't if you don't trust me in return."

Just like last time, I opened my mouth to answer immediately, only to close it just as quickly. Seconds later, I figured out what she was trying to get at. In all the time I'd known her, she had always been the person I could rely on more than anyone, even myself, but all I'd done over the last few months was push her away and internalize everything without ever seeking her input. Bordeaux was right. Trust and communication were two sides of the same coin. From her perspective, I no longer trusted her because I no longer sought to confide in her.

To her, it must have felt like a complete betrayal.

I shut my eyes to shield myself from the intensity of her inspection.

I'd spent the past five months diligently preparing for what we were about to do, but now I wanted nothing to do with it since all I'd seemed to accomplish was turn my closest friends against me.

I opened my eyes and looked into Helena's, noticing that she must have known I'd come to some sort of conclusion because her eyes seemed softer than I'd seen them in months.

"Helena..." I started, almost unable to get the name out, "I'm sorry. You know how I can get sometimes, and I took it too far this time. I regret that more than you can know."

She waited a few seconds before nodding. "I accept your apology, Jacob, but you're not getting out of this that easy. We're not actually 'talking' right now. We're simply discussing your inability to communicate. The only thing I want out of you right now is a truce. You stop pushing me away and I'll stop ignoring you, and maybe you can finally convince me all this is worth it."

I haven't underestimated Helena since the moment she nearly knocked me out upon our first meeting, and since the day we began our friendship, even before it blossomed into something more, I always knew just how formidable she really was. That impression had been pounded into my brain over the years with a hammer worthy only of Thor, but I never realized it quite so much as I did right now.

"Agreed," I answered finally. "Consider a cease fire in affect."

"Not yet," she said, a twinkle of mischief in her eyes. "I need something from you first. Consider it a gesture of good faith."

When I saw the smile on her face my heart dropped. "What?"

"How old are you?"

I turned away from her as quickly as could. "No."

She punched me in the back, yet another of her endless beatings that actually hurt. "Honestly, Jacob, you are ridiculous. We've known each other for years and I still only *think* you're in your early thirties, but I don't actually know. You won't even tell me what month you were born in. You're acting just like Santino."

"I don't like birthdays," I said bluntly but truthfully. There were too many sad memories associated with them.

"Just tell me the day. I don't even need to know the year." When I didn't say anything, she continued insistently. "Now!"

I rolled back over and sighed. "Fine. It's the day Augustus died, and yes, I'm in my thirties," I said grudgingly, even though I was only thirty two. Although, technically, there was a chance I was still only thirty one, since we left the future in July and arrived in Rome in September, bypassing my birthday month of August completely. I honestly didn't know. "If you can figure out the date, you'll know."

"August nineteenth," she responded almost immediately.

My eyes narrowed. "How did you know?"

She smiled. "You really don't think I pay attention to your lectures, do you? You're a surprisingly good teacher. Besides, you always seem in a bad mood that day, and yes, you're that bad it's memorable."

I chuckled. "I guess you aren't so bad after all. At least you're learning."

"Don't get too excited," she said. "We still have a lot to talk about."

While her eyes told me there was still more healing that needed to be done before she went back to truly trusting me again, she offered me a small smile before turning her head to look at the bed again.

"Go to sleep, Jacob," she whispered.

I watched her pull Galba's linen sheet to her chin, but before she fell asleep, as I was sure she would do in seconds, she spared one last glance at me. It was a neutral glance, but the gesture alone made me feel a whole lot better. I edged just a bit closer to my companion and fell asleep in minutes.

***

I woke up eight hours later rested, attentive and happy, even with the legions outside constantly reminding me of their presence. Pulling away from Helena as gently as I could, momentarily forgetting it normally took a thunderstorm to wake her up, I moved to the edge of the bed and stretched my arms and my legs. Satisfied I'd worked out any grogginess I might have felt, I reached into my cargo pocket and pulled out my radio. Turning it on, I pressed the PTT button twice in quick succession, and waited for Santino's reply.

I started to worry when his return clicks didn't immediately come but after a noticeable three second delay, he responded in kind. I chuckled. Even though he had only communicated by the click of static, I could still sense his frustration. I placed the radio back in my pocket and pulled out my MRE.

Reading the label, I was relieved to discover that it wasn't one of the dreaded meat patty variants. Perhaps we were finally rid of the vile creations.

With a small sigh, I opened the package that contained two entrees, an appetizer, a dessert, coffee powder, and juice mixtures. I reached in to pull out an entrée but hesitated just before extracting it.

Each and every time I opened one of the ready to eat meals, I was reminded of the fact that we were quickly running through the last of them. Every time we ate one, we lost just that much more of our old home, and ever after all the time I'd spent here, I was still home sick. I missed my sister immensely, my SEALS and friends as well, but most especially, I missed my TV. Helena thought I was addicted to it, and while she was probably right, I suspected she was just afraid I'd be a lazy boyfriend if we ever got home.

There wasn't much sense thinking about it. With each passing year, the idea of going home became harder and harder to believe anyway.

I opened one of the cracker packages and applied some jalapeño cheese spread. Taking a bite, I nodded pleasantly. For some reason, MREs had a stigma for tasting horrible, like tissue paper or something. I couldn't disagree more, suspecting such complainers actually ended up eating the tissue paper itself.

As careful as I was, I noticed Helena shift in her sleep beside me. Always a light sleeper, I could recall many occasions when I had been unable to fall asleep during heavy thunderstorms, our thin tents offering little protection from the bright flashes and loud thunder claps brought on by the storms, while Helena dozed peacefully throughout, never once waking.

She rolled over and looked up at me, her hands beneath her head.

"Morning," I said happily.

Her expression was groggy, but at least she didn't seem angry. "Shouldn't it be late afternoon by now?"

I looked at my watch. "Oh, right."

She gave me a small smile.

"Hungry?" I asked, holding out the cracker. She took a bite and her eyes opened wide, her palate never meant for spicy foods. She reached for the CamelBak and swallowed some water, which I knew would only make it worse. Finally, she snatched a cracker without any cheese and started munching, the redness in her face slowly residing.

I looked at her knowingly, offering a weak shrug. "Sorry?"

She returned my look with the same anger her eyes normally exuded, but I knew it wasn't real. At least I hoped it wasn't.

"It's too bad I fell in love with you and not Santino," she said.

I placed a hand against my chest. "Ouch. That one really hurt."

"Sure it did," she said, peeking into the MRE bag. "What else do you have to eat in there?"

I looked into the bag that held the individual servings of food. "Rice pilaf and turkey with gravy. Great."

"Ever wonder who comes up with these combinations?"

"No," I said, "and frankly I don't want to. Those sadistic bastards at the MRE packaging plant once loaded an entire crate of the stuff with nothing but cream cheese in each meal. I was eating cream cheese for two weeks. Two weeks!" I repeated angrily. "Cream cheese!"

"Obviously they're all insane sadists."

At least our conversation was back near our normal banter level.

"You have no idea," I said, tearing open the rice pilaf package and handing it to her.

I tore open the turkey and gravy and started digging in. Helena and I traded packages after a few scoops from each, and I used the MRE's small container of Tabasco sauce to spice up the rice, finished off the rest of our crackers, and split the black and white cookie desert with her. Never liking chocolate much, I gave her that end, and I ate the vanilla side. Even without warming it through, the meal had tasted good and had been substantial.

We policed our mess and got comfortable again. I looked up at the bottom of Galba's bed and picked at some splintered wood with a finger, hoping we were in fact doing the right thing. Helena had a point about one thing. No matter how I justified it, we were in fact messing with people's lives every time we took a breath in this world, and the only responsible thing to do would be to just flee into the shadows and never interfere with society again.

But that felt like giving up, and even if we stayed away from every human being for the rest of our lives, it still wouldn't matter. Even if we buried our heads in the sand like ostriches, we were still interfering with the lives around us. Even that deer Santino shot the other day could alter the timeline. That deer could have been meant for a starving family two months from now, but since it won't be there for the family to hunt and feed off of, the children in that family may die of starvation. Those kids could be the ancestors of Charlemagne, Joan of Arc, Louis XIV, Jacque Cousteau, Celine Deon, even Bordeaux, or any other countless soul who could possibly draw their ancestry back to the area around the Rhine River.

I tried to keep track of all the people we'd helped over the years, and the number sat at eighty five men, women and children. Each was a life we interfered with, but that number didn't include the few hundred we'd killed while helping them, not to mention the thousands upon thousands of men had who died on the battlefield outside of Rome four years ago, which included Claudius, and later Caligula, whose deaths alone could be more than enough to alter the future. After all we'd done, there was no telling what 2021 looked like anymore.

Maybe I'm not being fair to the rest of the world, but I think it's hard to argue that the decisions made by the various civilizations to call Europe home weren't amongst the world's most influential. Sure, Attila the Hun and Genghis Khan still needed to embark on their rampage through the area, and I'm sure nothing we do here will stop that from happening, but even with their intervention and... seeding, the emigrating hordes of barbarians weren't the only people to call this area home. What if through the results of our actions here we somehow produce a stronger, more enduring Rome, one that could hold off the invading hordes of Huns, Mongols, Goths and the rest of them?

The possibilities were mind boggling.

As for places like China and Japan, they didn't really catch up to the rest of the world until the likes of Marco Polo and his successors got involved a thousand years from now. Eastern civilizations may be older, and at one point or another more advanced, but where the western world progressed over the millennia, the east hit a plateau.

Even Islam's day might be over. I knew Augustus had sent a Legion to Yemen to conquer the area for their stash of incense and precious stones. He'd been hurting for cash after establishing his unilateral dominance over Roman politics and needed whatever resources he could find. The expedition had failed thanks to traitorous guides and a deadly Arabian summer, but now that someone like Agrippina was running the show, they might try again. Who knows? The prophet Mohamed may accidentally trip on a rock after receiving his visions from God because a Roman siege engine, hundreds of years earlier, knocked a stone onto his path where there originally hadn't been one.

Then again, maybe nothing quite so revolutionary will happen by 2021 and the only discernible difference would be that Betamax players will put VHS tapes out of the market in the 1990s.

Stranger things have happened

And probably will.

"What are you thinking about?" Helena asked from beside me, closer than we'd slept last night, but still not in my arms. The distance seemed like miles. "You have that far off look on your face again."

I smiled. "Just thinking... like always."

"Obsessing."

I hesitated. "Yeah, I guess. I just can't stop thinking about it, Helena. I simply can't be responsible for something that could potentially end western civilization."

"You're being melodramatic."

"Maybe," I admitted, "but even if only one life is changed because of all this, I can't help but feel like I've murdered them all."

She leaned up on her elbows and tilted her head to look at me. "Just stop it, Jacob. You're beyond melodrama now and not helping anyone with talk like that."

I shook my head before turning to gaze at her. "I'm really not, Helena. If just one person back home ceases to exist because of what we did here; it's no different than if I held a gun to his head and pulled the trigger."

"It's not like that and you know it."

"Maybe not, but it's no different than if I just stood by and did nothing while someone else did the deed."

Helena didn't have a quick response herself this time, but I could feel her mind churning. I couldn't guess what exactly was going on in there, and I wasn't sure I wanted to. She'd never been a deep thinker, relying instead on a clarity of mind that gave her answers to problems more easily than they came to most. I'd always respected her opinions because of it, at least I had until recently I suppose, but in this case I still wasn't sure she understood the situation well enough to render an appropriate perspective.

A few seconds later, she lowered herself to the ground and pressed her body up against mine. She propped herself up on one arm and looked down at me. "I suppose I've never thought about it that way, but I still don't understand where all this is coming from. You haven't voiced a thought on timelines or changing the future in years, so why now? Why this past year? What's changed?"

"Because now is the time to worry about it," I answered easily. "I've tried to keep it out of my mind in all that time to avoid going crazy, but I have to think about it now. The longer we wait, the more divergent things will become and the more difficult it will be to put back together. Now is the sweet spot."

She nodded, accepting that. "But you still don't know if the timeline even needs to be 'fixed' because you can't see the future, Jacob. You can't lay there and definitively tell me that we need to do anything to ensure the future remains as we left it. You just can't."

"And you can't tell me that we don't need to do anything at all with any conviction either," I retorted with a long, slow sigh, waiting for the right thing to say to come to me. "I need you to trust me on this, Helena, I really do. Listen. In light of our last conversation, I'm willing to give you the benefit of the doubt. If you *really* think we shouldn't do this, just tell me now. Tell me this is more about your intuition and not your feelings being hurt because I wouldn't talk to you. If you can do that I promise we'll leave, never come back, and find a quiet place to live out the rest of our lives, but I need to know now."

She was quiet for a very long while as she stared in the general direction of my stomach, her eyes contemplative. After a while, she laid her left hand on my chest and pounded it with a clenched fist in frustration.

"Damn it, that's not fair. You can't put everything on my shoulders like that."

She paused and let out a long breath, but I interrupted her before she could continue.

"Now you know how I feel, Helena."

She looked speechless once again, but she was able to continue after a short while. "I do trust you, Jacob, I do. I told you I've always trusted your gut, and I feel no differently now. I just wanted you to know that you don't always have all the right answers, and that's okay."

I smiled. "Well, now that I know that…"

She smiled back, the most beautiful smile I'd ever seen. "You're such a jerk, Jacob. Sometimes I wonder how I can still love you."

"Just lucky, I guess."

She smacked my chest. "You are that. More than you know, but if you go out of your way to ignore me again, you won't be for much longer." She continued smiling, and for the first time in months, hunkered back down in my arms, and in that moment I knew better than to ruin it by saying a word. As she got comfortable resting her head on my chest, I awkwardly moved my arm around her back to hold her. She noticed my hesitation and looked up at me.

"It's all right, Jacob. I'm not going to bite you."

"That's not always so clear sometimes," I replied, finally reaching around and holding her by the shoulder.

She blinked up at me, an oddly mixed expression on her face. She didn't need to say anything more either, and I knew that look only confirmed her feelings that while we were reconciled, we weren't done yet. She had no problem beginning the healing process with a little cuddling, but it was going to be a while before we shared the same level of trust and intimacy we had a few months ago.

We rested there in contemplative silence for a few minutes before I got bored.

"Want to play a game?" I asked.

"What kind of game?" She replied, curious.

"How about, I Spy?"

"Jacob," she said with a weary sigh, "there's not much…"

"I spy something… green."

"Grass," she said immediately.

"Damn. You're good."

She slapped my chest again, probably harder than she should have.

"Just go back to sleep."

***

It was during times like these that I really missed home. Hours cooped up indoors would never have been a problem for Child Jacob, Teenager Jacob, or even Young Adult Jacob, each of which would find ways to keep himself entertained for hours on end. From movies to video games, music and books, and the wonders of the internet; 21st century Jacob was a man-child who knew how to keep himself busy. Many a girlfriend hadn't been too thrilled by my ability to avoid boredom; they'd come and they'd go, but Jacob always remained – entertained.

I'd grown out of such reclusiveness well before I had joined the military, but sometimes I wondered how Helena would have dealt with such habits back home. In some ways I was lucky we'd ended up here in Rome. Something told me she wouldn't appreciate my MacGyver DVD collection as much as I did.

Instead, Helena and I boringly spent the next three hours lounging together on the floor of Galba's tent playing chess on my wrist mounted LCD screen that was attached to a small computer in my MOLLE rig. It was either that or solitaire, and Helena proved a worthy opponent, even though I managed to edge her considerably in the win column.

We also chatted about inconsequential things, memories of the homes we had five years ago and more recent ones.

Our favorite story surrounded Santino, when the three of us had stalked a band of thieves to their hideout and he had triggered a simple snare trap that caught around his ankle and sent him flying into the trees. Helena and I had been on his flanks and hadn't seen what had happened to him, but once we took care of the bandits, we realized Santino hadn't participated in the take down. He'd contacted us over the radio and politely asked for us to find him via his GPS tracker to give him a hand.

We'd found him dangling from a tree, his head bobbing a few meters above the ground. His predicament wouldn't normally have been a problem, but his knife had also fallen out of its sheath and imbedded itself in the ground just out of his reach. I'd picked it up and looked at Helena, and we both burst out laughing as Santino hung there with his arms crossed across his chest, a rare frown on his face.

Back when Santino had lost his favorite combat knife during our mission to rescue Nero four years ago, Helena had promised him she'd find him a better and bigger one. She'd come through on her promise months later when she purchased him a ten inch blade shaped like an Arabian scimitar during our time in New Carthage on the Mediterranean coast of Iberia. Santino had immediately fallen in love with it and claimed it would take either an act of God or, jokingly, an act of sheer stupidity to ever part him from it. Needless to say, we simply couldn't contain ourselves when we found him hanging from a trap even a toddler could avoid; his knife having accidently escaped him.

It was after a few minutes of laughter at his expense that I finally handed him his knife back, and he cut himself down, falling to the Earth with a loud thump. He had stood and brushed himself off, replaced his knife, and in typical Santino fashion, acted like nothing had happened. He'd thrown an arm over Helena's shoulder and my own, and led us towards the bandits' camp to pick up what we had been tasked to retrieve.

Like most good stories, we'd told it a hundred times, but it never got any less funny.

Unfortunately, further storytelling was interrupted by the sound of the tent's entrance flapping open.

I quickly pushed everything from my mind when the sound of footsteps inched closer to the bed. I freed my Sig P220 quietly from its thigh holster, the metal gun rasping quietly against its plastic sheath, and I felt Helena shift in my arms, just enough so that she wouldn't get in the way if I needed to do something fancy. I saw the figure fall to his hands and knees, and I knew it was either Galba or someone I'd have to deal with messily.

When the sheet was ripped away from the bed, I pushed my suppressor equipped pistol into the intruder's face. My finger on the trigger, I diverted my aim immediately when I noticed Galba's dark eyes looking back at mine. I sheathed my pistol with a slow breath through my teeth, Helena's head slumping against my chest, the adrenaline rushing out of her system as well.

"Galba," I hissed. "You nearly gave me a heart attack."

"Me too," Helena said.

I felt her breathing heavily and hoped she wasn't having another pain attack.

"I apologize," Galba replied. "Please, come out. It is safe, but we only have a short time before you must hide again. I presumed you would enjoy an opportunity to stretch."

I nodded and waited for Helena to move off of my arm, which had fallen asleep beneath her. Free from her weight, I hauled myself out from beneath the bed, my back stiff from hours of idleness. I turned and offered Helena a hand and we spent the next five minutes walking around the tent, stretching muscles that had been dormant for over eleven hours. Helena moved over towards the tent's entrance, her back to me, and raised her arms high over her head and stretched. A second later she snapped them down, clutching her side. I turned away before she could notice I was watching. She'd been trying to hide the fact that she was still afflicted by her abdominal pains since they'd begun, and I didn't want to make it worse by letting on like I noticed now.

By the time she turned around, I was already sitting on Galba's bed, stretching forward and gripping my bootless toes, not paying her any attention. She came over and sat next to me while Galba poured some wine into three cups, handing us two of them.

He plopped into his chair heavily and raised his glass. "To the empress, Agrippina. May her wisdom know no equal." He took a long gulp and refilled his glass while Helena and I exchanged bewildered glances, taking polite sips.

Helena winced at the dry vintage, still unable to truly appreciate it, before asking, "Is there something you want to tell us, Galba?"

He scowled in her direction, not used to being treated like an equal by a woman, only to tolerate it because he knew what she could do. "Yes, I suppose there is," he said, finishing off his cup, failing to elaborate.

"Well..." I began, swirling my left hand in a circle after he didn't say anything for a few seconds.

He jerked, as if roused from a deep sleep. Looking at his empty cup, he glanced over at the wine jug before setting the cup down and massaging his scalp. "It appears," he began quietly, "that Agrippina has interesting aspirations for the upcoming campaign, and that she hopes to be more involved than we originally thought."

I glanced at Helena again, but her lips were tight and angry, her eyes unfocused and distant. It was her "Agrippina" look.

I looked back at Galba. "Maybe you should start at the beginning."

He looked up, his body sagging forward. "Agrippina came ashore this morning, strutting down the gangplank with a look of authority in her gait. She was wearing legionary armor, her attire speaking volumes as to why she is here well before she uttered a word."

I could only imagine how much Helena must be fuming. Female legionary armor was her shtick, and Agrippina had just stepped on her toes. The first thing I thought of, however, was actually Elizabeth I at Tilbury, Essex riding her steed wearing silver armor over a white dress, rallying her troops in preparation for the Spanish Armada, even though it had already been defeated at sea. Unfortunately, Elizabeth I had the chops for the duty, whereas it seemed to me Agrippina was just playing dress up and using legionary armor as an excuse to show as much skin as possible.

Galba refilled his goblet, but didn't drink from it. "She looked every part the military general. She even had a scarlet cape wrapped around her shoulders. Vespasian, myself, and the other legions' legates, along with more bureaucrats, advisors, legionnaires, and sycophants than the gods could count were there, ready to receive her. When she made landfall, she immediately called for a council of war in Vespasian's *praetorium* without delay."

I leaned back on Galba's bed, propping myself up on my elbows and squeezed my eyes shut, trying to concentrate. I had a suspicion as to where this was going, and it was bad. In the original timeline, Agrippina had showed interest in the legions when she was married to Claudius, and I wondered if she was going to take it another step now.

"Once inside the *praetorium*, she outlined her plans for the German campaign," Galba continued. "At first, I thought little of it. They actually made sense. Besides, both Caligula and Tiberius visited their battlefield commanders when they were emperor, so I was initially hopeful, even thankful Agrippina was claiming a personal stake in the campaign. It meant we'd have the backing of the Senate, and it would definitely inspire the men."

I tried not to think about Agrippina riding a horse, each leg dangling over the side, with the only thing covering her goods being her armor. Unfortunately, it was hard not to. The legions would love it and certainly inspire them.

"It wasn't until she announced she would be assuming overall command, that I started to worry, as did my colleagues. Legate Gnaeus Hosidius Geta, my friend and one of Vespasian's co-legates in Britain, was so bold as to ask her if she had lost her sanity. She had her Praetorians carry him outside where he was beaten and crucified. His replacement should be here within the month." He paused as he looked guiltily into his cup before giving into temptation, swallowing its contents in one big gulp. "She will be with the army at every turn in the campaign and will, as is granted by her title, be commander of the army with Vespasian acting as her second."

"You can't be serious," Helena grumbled.

"Of course I'm serious, woman! I do not need two of you talking down to me today..." he mumbled that last part, the alcohol already taking effect. "She is ready to take command and has two of her Praetorian cohorts and her Sacred Band with her to ensure a seamless transition."

That was the first good news I'd heard yet. If I could get in contact with Gaius, Marcus, or even Quintilius, the Sacred Band's *primus pilus*, perhaps I could get a clearer picture surrounding Agrippina and how to move forward after taking Nero.

"Other than her announcement, there is little else to report. We have plans to start the campaign in May, and to push all the way to the steppes of Sarmatia within two years."

I whistled. That was an extremely ambitious plan. Rome had tried a number of times, but had never been able to conquer Germany, and while tentative progress would be made north of the Danube River by the time Trajan came to power, they didn't hold it for long. Ambition aside, I really couldn't see the logic in it. Germany was a recalcitrant and angry land. Its occupants wouldn't sway to Roman rule easily. The only benefit the Romans would receive out of such an operation would be a strategic foothold against invading Huns in a few hundred years.

I take it back. If the Romans could hold the line in Sarmatia against that invasion, preventing the Great Migration, disallowing the thousands of Goths, Ostrogoths, Visigoths, Vandals, and other "barbarian" tribes into the Roman Empire, things may turn out differently. That event had always been one of the underlying reasons for "the fall of Rome", but as interested as I was in testing the theory, I couldn't let that happen.

It would defeat the purpose of everything I was trying to do.

"So what's her itinerary for the rest of this week?" I asked.

"She'll be staying on her barge, docked right next to the camp. We'll be drilling the boys hard in the upcoming weeks so there will be little for her to do. Even though she wants to command, she doesn't seem at all interested in the army's readiness. I imagine she will be spending much of her time there with Nero."

"So, he's here?"

"I have not seen him as of yet," Galba replied, "but Agrippina always keeps him close. I cannot tell you where he may be aboard the ship, but I can tell you that it is a labyrinth. It has many levels and its interior is honeycombed with passages and rooms. If you're planning to board her, you will be searching for a long time."

"Leave that to us," I said, "We're really good at sneaking around."

"Yes," Galba said slowly, "you are. Just don't be fooled by Agrippina's beauty a second time."

I grimaced at the reminder. When Agrippina had tricked Santino and me into rescuing Nero four years ago, I had been doing my duty to an innocent child and his grieving mother. Most of me was at least, but I couldn't deny that a part of me had been blinded by Agrippina's little seduction act she pulled when convincing me to go. The woman practically threw herself at me, and I almost went for it. I may have never gone on the rescue mission at all had she not been so beautiful and alluring.

"Don't worry about us, Galba," Helena said. "Just ensure no one tips her off that you've been talking to us." She finished her statement by jabbing a finger at him.

He smiled, directing it towards me. "I've always liked your woman," he said, taking another pull of his wine. "Beautiful, angry and direct. Good qualities to have in a lover. If only all of us were so lucky." He finished his thoughts with another long gulp of his wine, streams of the liquid messily running down his mouth.

"Maybe you should slow down a bit, Galba," I said, indicating his cup. "I think you've had enough."

"Bah!" He said, swinging his empty cup wildly. "I'm sure Vespasian won't care. I wouldn't be surprised if he's in his tent doing the same thing right now."

Galba stood, swaying in place after getting up too fast, his hand flying out to grasp his desk for stability. I looked at Helena and she returned my look with an amused smile. I rolled my eyes and stood to help the Roman collect his bearings.

He shrugged me off. "I'm fine... I'm fine. Now. Back under the bed. I will bring you some food tonight, but then you must leave."

"What about my plan?" I asked as he turned to leave.

He reached up and gripped the cross bracing that held the tent together, just above the entrance. He hung there for a few seconds before turning to face me. "I will help you but not until the campaign is under way. Hopefully, you can then draw Agrippina away from Germany and let the professionals handle the war. Then we can use Vespasian's triumphs to help convince the Senate and people of Rome he's a worthy successor."

I smiled. "Hey, that's a good idea. Wish I would have thought of that."

Galba didn't return the smile. "I've had plenty of time to think today, and will have plenty of time still to come. You have not made my life any easier with your words; I just hope I don't come to resent you for it."

I gulped, hoping he didn't either. Galba turned and stumbled out of the tent, leaving Helena and I alone once again. Standing halfway between the entrance and Helena, I turned and looked at her. She gave me a shrug, moved over to the cabinet where she had placed her P90, retrieved it and started to clean it.

I dug out my radio and switched it back on.

I clicked the PTT button and spoke into my throat mic, "3-3, 3-1, over."

Santino's voice came back almost immediately. "This is 3-3. Where the fuck have you been?"

I smiled. "Sorry, 3-3. 3-2 and I have been…" I thought for the right words, something between the truth and something to push his buttons. "been busy."

"Aw, that's cute. Now, want to fill me in on why you turned off your damn radio?"

"Sorry again," I repeated, "3-2 and I needed to lie low for the day. Our conversation with Triple Chin took longer than expected." I still had to smile at our use of call signs and code names. There was no way anyone could pick up our transmissions, but it was still a good practice. "But, the mission was still successful. We've also learned that target November is staying onboard the barge."

"What's November doing here?"

"He's with The Whore," I answered, looking over at Helena, who looked up from her cleaning to give me another grin. That designation was her idea. "Apparently, she has big plans for the legion. We'll talk about it later."

"Roger. Don't forget to keep me updated this time," he said, his voice bitter.

"Copy. 3-1 out."

I finished the conversation by switching off the radio. Rechargeable or not, it was still best to keep it off when it wasn't needed.

I moved over to the bed, arriving just as Helena replaced her P90 in the cabinet. I pulled up the sheet on Galba's bed for her to crawl under and I followed quickly. Beneath the bed, we settled into our familiar position, with less awkwardness than last time. It was getting chilly, and Helena's body warmth was definitely appreciated.

"What do you think?" I asked.

"I think Galba's turned into a drunk." She said pointedly.

I sighed. "That had occurred to me, yes. Last night, I could have sworn I smelt alcohol on his breath as well."

"Anything in history to suggest he was an abuser?"

"No," I replied, frustrated. "Looks like another life we've fucked up thanks to our medaling."

She didn't look convinced, but at least her face remained supportive. "Jacob, you have to stop blaming yourself. It's not your fault."

"But it is. It's still my fault we ended up in ancient Rome in the first place, in case you forgot. My fault I touched that stupid blue orb. My fault Caligula and Claudius are dead and it's my fault we're under this damn bed!" I almost yelled the last part, but settled for punching the bed's wooden frame instead. It hurt like holy hell and I clutched my hand and bit my lip to keep from yelling out. Once the pain subsided I turned my head away from hers and frowned. "My fault."

Helena reached out gently and griped my hand, bringing it to her mouth to give it a kiss. She wrapped her other hand around my cheek and gently turned my head towards hers. "No, it wasn't," she said sternly, her eyes drilling into mine.

When she looked at me like that, I could almost believe it wasn't my fault.

Almost.

"Besides," she pressed. "Don't you remember saying something about how you wouldn't change anything about our past five years together? And don't even think about considering the last four months in your answer."

I smiled at her, but I guess I had said that. If not for being transported to ancient Rome, Helena and I may never have clicked. We might have served our entire careers together in the modern world never having found that moment that brought us together. Most modern military regulations frowned on any kind of relationship between members of the military, but when we found ourselves trapped in ancient Rome, most of those regulations were thrown out the window.

She was right. I wouldn't trade her in for anything.

"Sorry. I guess I've been thinking too much lately."

"You're always thinking too much."

"True," I said while she shifted in my arms and closed her eyes to get some sleep.

I tried to follow suit, clearing my mind of just about everything, letting thoughts of time travel, Agrippina, the abduction of a child, and the memories of a bygone home drift away into nothingness.

***

If I could be thankful for one thing in that moment, it would be my ability to fall asleep on a whim. It didn't take much, and while continuation of sleep was never guaranteed for me, the act of putting myself into a state of dreaming unconsciousness was something that came easily, all in thanks to a handful of men who had beaten it into me, barring any unforeseen lightning storms, of course.

Basic Underwater Demolition/SEALS training, better known as BUD/S was many things. It was a test, an evaluation, a training program, and a lesson in bitter punishment, but what it did best was turn a graduate into a man eligible to wear the SEAL Trident, but only eligible.

The Trident would come later.

But the one thing I hadn't anticipated upon completion of the program was that BUD/S was also a wonderful sleep aid clinic.

Trainers would drill into us the idea that sleep was a luxury, and to expect it every night would lead to weakness. Days had blurred together, with late nights and early wake up calls. Our alarm clocks consisted of flashbang grenades, the sound of gunfire or the excruciating belittling of an instructor, and I learned to sleep whenever I had time for it. Over the weeks, my body began to instinctively process that sleep far more efficiently than ever, allowing what little sleep I earned to rejuvenate my body more than a solid eight hours had before.

I learned a lot in BUD/S, and our instructors made sure to deprive us of whatever daily accommodations we normally took for granted to ensure we would appreciate them more in the future. Even food was withheld, at least for us officers. The enlisted men could eat as much as they wanted in the time they had, consuming as many calories as their body desired, but those of us privileged with rank, only got one serving per meal.

I had already graduated from Officer Candidate School, and had thought that Special Forces training for the SEALs would go easier because of it. Boy was I wrong. Officers had to endure more hardships, face tougher challenges and be brought even closer to the breaking point than anyone else. A common foot soldier who lost his cool got himself killed, but an officer could get everyone killed. The instructors made sure to stress that point thoroughly which, when combined with everything else, resulted in the dozen officers in my class dwindling to only a few on graduation day, a testament to the BUD/S drop out record, which they were damn proud of.

Of course, it could have just been the warm, female body lying next to me that did it.

Either way, I awoke a few hours after nightfall and patiently waited for Galba to return. When he did, he came through on his promise of bringing us some food. Helena and I ate quietly and listened to Galba update us on what was happening in the camp.

He reported that camp morale was high. No surprise. I still remember the first time we walked into the *XV Primigenia*'s camp five years ago and how the men reacted to Helena's presence. Sure there had been a few bad apples, but most went well out of their way to impress her, and efficiency in the camp comically improved. I could only imagine their reaction to Agrippina.

The legionnaires didn't seem overly concerned about her taking overall command either, but then why should they? They were in awe of the beautiful head of state, and had no doubt her ability to command was equally matched by her appearance. It made me sick to my stomach. The next time I saw her would be too soon, *too damn* soon as far as I was concerned.

An hour later, Galba went to bed. It was still well before midnight and we were unable to go anywhere for another hour or two, so Helena and I donned our combat fatigues and gear, sat against the cabinet and waited.

For situations just like this, I'd taught Helena how to play evens/odds a few years ago, so we wasted our time playing that. The game was one of random chance, yet she still managed to beat me nearly every time.

Sometimes I swore she could read my mind.

I'd always suspected women could do that.

At 0200, we decided the coast was as clear as it was going to be, so after a day cooped up in Galba's tent, we ventured out into the clear night sky. It was an unusually muggy night, warmer than it had been in days, an indication of spring's early arrival. I sent Santino a quick message to let him know we were inbound and slipped out of the tent. We retraced our steps back to the wall, scaled the fortification quickly, maneuvered around the guard easily, slipped over the outer wall, and donned our ghilli suits. The rest of the trip was slow but likewise uneventful. When we reached the tree line, we removed our camouflage and looked for Santino.

He was nowhere to be seen so we crept around the edge of the woods, our rifles scanning for potential threats, when a dark figure emerged from a shrub. Santino's face was obscured by his night vision goggles, the only part of him visible being two small, green circles around his eyes, a result of the backlight from his NVGs. The eyes were very unsettling, and the bad guys reacted to it fearfully every time.

"Old McDonald had a farm," he said.

"What?" I asked, perplexed at the comment.

"Old McDonald had a farm," he repeated more insistently.

I looked over at Helena, but she didn't seem to have any idea what he was talking about either.

"What the hell are you babbling about?" She asked.

Santino stood straighter, and pulled up his NVGs to reveal his frowning face. "Old McDonald had a farm. What's the counter signal?"

"We don't have one," I replied. "Never have."

"No counter signal?" He said sadly. "What kind of spy movie is this?"

88

***

Santino hadn't sat idle while Helena and I had vacationed in Galba's tent, a fact he couldn't help but bring up over and over again. He'd crept along the tree line during the day towards the Rhine and taken a few photos of Agrippina's pleasure barge. As I suspected, Santino's initial report was confirmed to be mere hyperbole, but the size of the ship was still impressive. It was extravagantly large but still buoyant on small inland rivers, and the Rhine easily accommodated its presence. It was a wonder of Roman engineering.

After scanning the photographs, our first objective was to plan our insertion.

Over the years Santino, Helena and I had taught each other key skills one of us possessed but the other didn't. Helena had taught Santino how to be an effective spotter, teaching him what to look for in shapes, colors and movement in objects to help discern their threat level. She would place small, nearly invisible objects for him to try to find from a distance, and record how many he could. It was a training method used during sniper school, but Santino's lack of patience made him a tough student.

As for Santino, he had taught me some of the finer points in tracking, scouting, and silent movement, as well as some pointers on knife fighting. I had become pretty good at sword play over the years, but what he taught me was how to go head to head with nothing but a dagger or a boot knife. We'd received dozens of cuts on our forearms as a result and I had grown a resounding fear of ever having to put it to use. Hollywood had done a disservice to the fighting style because it wasn't easy and it was extremely terrifying.

Finally, I had tutored Helena on underwater demolition work. SEAL training emphasized a multitude of underwater combat techniques, and rigging ships with explosives was an important one. It wasn't an easy job, and I figured it might be worth having someone else who could assist me with it one day. We had waterproof explosives in our supplies, but knowing where and how much to use took a skilled hand, and the psychological battle alone deserved respect.

The prospect of maneuvering beneath a hulking ship, with nothing but the deep dark water beneath you was one that broke plenty of spirits in BUD/S. Helena and I had spent many warm summer days swimming in the rivers and lakes of the Roman Empire, sometimes frolicking, but most of the time performing extensive training.

With those skill sets in mind, the plan we developed was simple. Phase one called for Helena and I to slip under the boat and plant enough explosives to do nothing but distract the barge's inhabitants. All I wanted to do was cause enough damage to confuse and distract those on board if we had to cut and run. If I knew Roman's like I knew I did, their engineers would have constructed the ship so that a few holes wouldn't sink her.

To put it simply: the Titanic would not have sunk had the Romans built her.

Santino would spot for us during phase one, but for phase two, Helena would hang back and provide sniper support while Santino accompanied me aboard. That put those who were best at their particular jobs in all the right places. We'd probably sneak around for the better part of the morning, but when we found Nero, we'd take him. If we found Agrippina, maybe we'd stop by for a chat.

We still had another day of recon before Helena and I began phase one.

IV
Frogmen

Badass Entry #4
Lt. Jonathon Archibald Santino III
Vindonissa, Germania Superior - April, 42 A.D.

This journal is lame

The story is pathetic. The plot is slow. There's no nudity. The writers are just... well, you know... pathetic mostly.

We need some more testosterone around here. Good thing I'm around.

Still, I love those guys. They'd do anything for me, and I'd throw myself in front of a bullet for either one of them... so it's nice that there aren't many bullets flying at us these days.

Besides, they seem to have nothing but nice things to say about me most of the time.

Anyway, they've got the story pretty much caught up at this point, so I'll get to the point.

Helena's journal entry was only a few days ago, but it seems that since then, Jacob convinced Galba to help us with this crazy mission of his. We've also learned that our primary target, Nero, is also here. Jacob wants to capture him and hold him ransom to get Agrippina to step down – at least that's what he tells us when he decides to tell us anything at all. Honestly, I've never been a fan of the whole capturing a child part of the plan, but I know who Nero is.

He's bad mojo. Or, at least he will be.

But whatever.

Helena and Jacob are getting ready to plant some demo on Agrippina's barge before he and I infiltrate it tomorrow.

Agrippina.

Man. Now there was a fine piece of ass. Beautiful. Big boobs. Great body. She threw herself all over me a few years ago, and damn was it worth it. Too bad she's a freak, and I wouldn't touch her with a ten foot cattle prod these days, and probably shouldn't have then.

Whatever. It was worth it.

Hey... Jacob gave me this journal to jot down some thoughts while he and Helena complete phase one of the mission. I told him it wasn't a good idea, but he said the journal would appeal to a broader audience if it was written from multiple perspectives.

Joke's on you, buddy.

Wow!

Sorry. Just peeked through my binoculars to check in on the lovebirds, and I just caught an eyeful. Not of Jacob (thanks every god that's ever existed) but of Helena. Hey, it's my job to spot for them and Helena really shouldn't expose herself out in the open like that. Remember what I said about Agrippina? Throw in an actual human being with a soul, and you got Helena. I still can't believe that dork got that lucky. She's way too good for him.

Shit. Looks like I went on a bit too long here. They've already slipped into the water. I blame Helena.

By the way, if this does get made into a movie, you all know who the real star should be.

Me.

Good luck casting this thing, by the way.

Especially me.

Look me up in a few thousand years. I should be hitting my prime right around then.

Who better to play me, than me?

I looked out over the Rhine and tried to locate where Santino had positioned himself on the opposite bank of the river. He'd left an hour ago, and had hopefully set himself up in a good position to cover our advance to the ship. We weren't too worried about phase one because the chance of detection was minimal, but it was always good to have backup. I imagined he had to be getting pretty bored by now. Maybe he was even writing in the journal.

Somehow, I imagined his entry looking something like: *me Santino. Me like boob. Where knife?*

I smiled at the thought. I suppose I wasn't giving him enough credit. For all I knew he might write a beautiful ballad.

In haiku.

Yeah right.

I put Santino out of my mind and resisted the urge to look over at Helena, who was still busy changing into her swimwear.

We were going light, not even bothering with our wetsuits, so we'd changed on sight. I used the time to place myself in line with her and where I thought Santino was situated. I didn't want him catching a peek of something that didn't belong to him.

I had already donned my own swim trunks. They were a black, two- pockets affair, and were embarrassingly short. Any less of a man might have felt insecure wearing them, but I didn't have a problem at all. They were standard issue at BUD/S, and were comfortable and liberating. They were all I wore along with a diving knife strapped to my left calf. I also had a pair of flippers, diving goggles with a snorkel, a head-mounted flashlight, and a small, single use SCUBA device, the kind used by lifeguards on the beach. My last piece of equipment was a small rucksack that contained the demo.

Satisfied I'd given her enough time to change, I turned to find her pulling a sports bra over her head. Before she secured it over her chest, she turned away in an act of mock embarrassment, only to laugh it off a second later. I returned her smile and shook my head, but my expression quickly turned south. It always happened when I inadvertently noticed the two scars prominently featured on her body. Both a result of my blunderings.

The first one was on her left leg and was the more obvious of the two. It started on the outside of her thigh, just above the knee, and traversed all the way around the outside of her leg, ending on her hamstring, just below her butt. She'd received that injury during our escape attempt from a terrorist controlled outpost on our first mission back in 2021. During the escape, I had accidently flipped the commandeered truck I was driving, hurling her from the vehicle and through an open window. She'd have the scar for the rest of her life.

The second one was on her lower back, to the right of her spine. It was only a few inches long, but what made it worth mentioning was the mirror scar on the right side of her abdomen. When I closed my eyes I could still see the rebel Praetorian stabbing her with his *gladius*, cutting her clean through. It came back to me regularly in nightmares and I've never truly forgotten who was to blame for it.

I remembered the entire scenario vividly like it had just happened yesterday – me rushing to her side only to reach her too late, with barely enough time to exact some measure of revenge by decapitating her would-be murderer. She'd fallen into my arms, sword and all, and I'd cradled her as I felt life fade from her mesmerizing eyes. She'd touched my cheek and apologized, but it wasn't her fault, it was mine. I had promised her I wouldn't leave her side in that battle, but I had, and she'd almost paid for it with her life.

I would die before I let something like that happen again.

So, as she stood there wearing nothing but a sports bra, tiny athletic shorts, and a combat knife strapped to her calf, I wasn't thinking at all about how perfect she looked in the dim moonlight but instead about how I had almost gotten her killed.

Twice.

I was so wrapped up in the memories of my near failure to preserve her life that I didn't notice her place a hand on my shoulder. The first few years had been pretty rough for me and I never could bring myself to forgive my lack of action, even though Helena had never needed me to. She'd never blamed me for either injury, not once asking for an apology, but I couldn't let myself off that easy. Those two events bothered me more than any other in my life.

I tilted my head to look at her, and saw nothing but a look of pure love and compassion. She always knew when my mind wandered back to that moment and how to bring me back from the brink – even after everything that's happened between us lately.

She smiled again. "Feel better?"

"Yeah," I replied, mostly certain I was. I held out my hand and gestured out over the water. "After you."

Her answer was to put on her flippers, pull down her mask, fix her snorkel to her mouth, and quietly slip into the water. I followed her in.

The water was chilly. Even though it was only April, it had been a warm winter and it had been quite warm since our arrival here a few days ago. I couldn't complain. The water at Coronado during BUD/S had been just above freezing, and cases of hypothermia and frost bite had not been unusual. Comparably, tonight's water temperature was practically boiling.

Besides, the slight chill helped keep me focused.

Nearly fifty meters from the ship, I pulled ahead of Helena as we swam just below the surface of the water, the ripples left from our snorkels acting as the only indicator of our presence. About twenty meters out, I angled myself downward, and with only a slight splash on the surface, began my descent into the murky depths. I spat out my snorkel and pulled the small oxygen tank from my belt. With a quick breath I shoved it between my lips and was able to breath normally again. We only had about twenty minutes of air in the things so we'd have to be quick and efficient.

A few seconds later, I was quick to notice the lumbering behemoth that was the bottom of the pleasure barge loom into view. I switched on my headlamp and directed my attention towards the hull, Helena's light providing additional coverage. Maneuvering my body so that I was lying parallel with the ship, I felt along its surface with my bare hands. The wood seemed smooth and clean, no effects of mold, decay, or shoddy workmanship visible. I gave the hull a knock with my fist, and determined it was solid and thick.

I glanced over at Helena as she floated next to me, her body perpendicular to the ship and her head a few feet away from my own. She pointed at the ship and flipped her hand in a questioning gesture. I shook my own head to ward off her unspoken question and hooked a thumb towards my bag, floating behind me.

BUD/S wasn't called Basic Underwater Demolition/SEAL for nothing. I learned everything I know about swimming, the open water, demolitions, and how to combine all three effectively there, and what I didn't learn there was drilled into my head as I attended countless other schools for the next two years before I was able to join the Teams. Once we could do all that, and so much more, we became Frogmen.

Prior to the Vietnam War, there were no SEALs, instead, there was the Underwater Demolition Team, or UDT. Their legacy dated back to World War II when they were known simply as Frogmen. When SEAL teams were developed during the Vietnam War, the two teams worked side by side until the UDT was finally decommissioned in the 1980's. Since then, in respect to its roots, SEALs were known as Frogmen as well.

I took an unnecessarily deep breath as I floated, confused as to why Helena hadn't understood what I was doing. We had gone over these procedures a dozen times before. She should already know that I was using rudimentary methods to determine the ship's structural integrity. I had a few devices back home could determine the hull's thickness and density, but our supplies had unfortunately forgotten those toys.

It wasn't a problem. The ship was obviously constructed out of wood, and considering the kinds of explosives I was using, it didn't matter what kind. I held out my hand and extended three fingers before gripping an object Helena held out in front of her, one of the smallest demo pieces I'd brought. The object was cylindrical in design, and had a dial and two buttons. One button activated a timed countdown, while the dial determined the amount of time before it blew. The second button activated that device's remote detonation function. It allowed us to blow the charges on command if desired. Safe and simple, perfect for this kind of work.

After placing the first demo charge on the hull, utilizing an underwater adhesive Helena had applied to it before handing it to me, I gave it a quick tug to make sure it was secure. Satisfied that it was, I used my hands to guide my body across the hull and my flippers to propel me forward. I glanced at my watch. We still had about twelve minutes of air left to secure four more charges.

We had only traveled along the very tip of the bow, a fraction of the boat itself, by the time we finished planting four of the five planned bombs in a square pattern. I glanced at my watch. Four minutes left. We made our way to the center of the grid, and I held up two fingers indicating I wanted our middle sized charge, the biggest one I'd asked for yet. I placed the bomb against the hull on instinct alone, securing it as quickly as I could. I made a final adjustment to its placement, a feeling of lightheadedness growing inside me.

I must have used up my air supply quicker than I thought.

Taking as deep a breath as I could manage, I pulled the canister out of my mouth, and pushed off from the bottom of the ship, torpedoing myself away from it. I saw Helena was already a few meters out ahead of me, her air having apparently run out just before mine had. I put my snorkel back in my mouth and secured the oxygen tank to my belt as I kicked with all my might.

Just as I cleared the boat, my more experienced swimming legs allowed me to overtake Helena easily. I grabbed her hand as I swam past and pulled her forward behind me, making sure we stayed submerged as long as possible. I felt her start to surface after a few seconds, but I held her down.

Usually, people instinctually tried to find air as soon as they think they've run out. However, as a general rule, most of the time they actually have a few more seconds than they think before their heart stops pumping. Learning how to avoid panic and utilize those extra seconds could save your life, but the only problem now was that I wasn't sure if Helena knew that, and another five seconds later I felt her slow down behind me.

She was blacking out, and I had to surface now before she finally ran out of air. When we finally broke the surface she sputtered and coughed water from her lungs and fell beneath the surface again. I wrapped an arm around her chest and secured her above the water.

She sputtered out another lungful of water.

"What the hell are you doing, Jacob!?"

"Sorry," I said. "Bu take a look at the ship before you *really* get mad at me."

I was facing away, but her head was looking directly at it. I knew she would see what I already knew would be there, small shapes that were really two men standing along the railing, looking out over the water. We'd noted them during our reconnaissance, and they may have spotted us had we surfaced earlier.

She coughed up a little more water. "Oh. The guards. I forgot."

"That tends to happen when you're passing out."

"You can let go now, Jacob." she said as she regained control of herself. "I can make it back on my own."

I didn't argue with her, and slowly released her into the river. I shifted into a backstroke so I could keep an eye on her until I was satisfied she could manage, but, true to her word, she was now moving easily under her own power. I spit some water that had made its way into my mouth at her playfully and turned towards where I estimated Santino was, resisting the urge to challenge her to a race.

I felt fantastic. Reinvigorated. Something about pulling Helena through the water to outrun the prying eyes of guards aboard a pleasure boat had riled something deep inside me. My heart was pounding, but I wasn't out of breath, wasn't fatigued. It was an exhilarating feeling, one I didn't want to let go of. All these years of mundane missions and solving little problems seemed so insignificant against what we were doing now, and my body reflected that.

Tomorrow couldn't come soon enough.

Once we passed our point of entry, I scanned the opposite tree line for sign of Santino. I almost thought we'd passed him when I saw two quick pulses of a dim red light emerge from the trees. Angling my body, I headed towards the source. As I crawled out of the water, Helena wearily behind me, I moved into the trees and shrubs, and found Santino lying in a shallow ditch, one of his eyes buried in a spotting monocular.

I knelt beside him and looked over his shoulder at the enormous barge in the distance.

"Any indication they noticed us?" I asked.

"No," he whispered. "Just as you two surfaced, it looked like one of them may have caught sight of something, but he didn't seem suspicious. One of his buddies came up to him a few seconds later and they started bitching about something. It didn't seem like you were the topic of interest."

"Good," I replied, glancing at Helena.

She was lying on her back, her left forearm draped across her forehead, her right hand resting on her bare abdomen as her chest rose and fell heavily. It didn't seem like simple fatigue, and I wondered if she was recovering from another pain attack.

Santino noticed as well.

"Gee, Strauss," he started. "And here I thought I was out of shape. Lay off the donuts next time, okay?"

She stared him dead in the eyes before looking up at me with a smirk. We'd carried each other a few times over the years after one or the other had gotten hurt, and that had always been one of our inside jokes.

I looked down at him and patted his shoulder. "We'll see how well you do tomorrow, tubby."

Santino rolled his eyes. "Of course you can talk, Frogman. You're happier in the water than you are on land. Us surface dwellers," he pointed to himself and Helena, "prefer sucking oxygen and walking on solid ground."

I looked down at Helena, hoping for some support.

She shrugged. "He is right."

I rolled my eyes and plopped myself down on my ass. It wasn't the first time the two of them had taken sides against me. Despite the relationship Helena and I were in, and the friendship Santino and I shared, I was definitely the oddball in the group, and I regularly found myself on the opposing end of many arguments and opinions.

I sighed. I did love the water.

"Let's just get some sleep," I said. "You two ladies are going to need your rest tomorrow."

Santino grinned at my comment while Helena mumbled under her breath, "Who are you calling a lady?"

***

Twenty four hours later, we were preparing for our amphibious assault on Agrippina's pleasure barge.

I glanced at Helena as she dug a small trench from which to provide sniper support, grinning at the string of expletives that flowed from her mouth as her shovel hit roots, rocks, or other impediments that slowed her down. Turning away, I joined Santino near the water and donned a light reconnaissance rig around my chest. Instead of my normal MOLLE rig, a bulky platform meant to carry a lot of gear comfortably, our recon rigs only had enough space to hold a few rifle magazines, a pouch for our NVGs, a radio, and a few other small items within waterproof pouches, such as the detonator for the demo we had placed last night. We secured oxygen tanks around our left ankles and knives around our right. Santino had his mini scimitar on his leg, while I just had a standard issue boot knife. To round out our equipment, Santino had his grappling hook and cord while I had the air pistol, secured in a holster attached to the right side of my vest. Our goal wasn't to inflict casualties, some of those Praetorians may be our friends, but we still had our HK416s.

Just in case.

Flippers and goggles in place, recon rigs secure and ready to go, Santino slipped into the water and swam toward the barge. I took a second to kneel next to Helena before I followed, and put an arm on her shoulder. Her eyes were already buried in her scope, but she tilted her head to look at me. I moved my hand to brush the side of her cheek.

She frowned. "Don't get yourself hurt, Hunter. I've just started liking you again, and I won't be there to bandage you up this time."

I looked at her for a few more seconds before very tentatively leaning in to plant a soft kiss on her lips. She didn't recoil, and I held us there for a few seconds before finally backing away. She seemed content with our kiss, smiling up at me, so I quickly made my getaway and slipped into the water. I caught up with Santino effortlessly and together we made our way to the ship, gliding just below the surface of the water, our snorkels providing only the slightest disturbance in the water.

It was only a few minute swim to the boat and I sent Helena a double click over the radio to let her know we arrived, and waited for her return signal to indicate it was all clear. Santino and I waited, gently bobbing in the calm waves alongside the boat, struggling to stay in contact with the ship while minimizing our presence in the river. We could have equipped our oxygen tanks and waited beneath the water, but we decided it was best to save them in case we were under fire during our extraction. Our only consolation was that the water was calm and that we didn't have to wait with five foot waves crashing over our heads. It was something I'd done before and would rather avoid if I could.

We waited for another five minutes before Helena finally sent confirmation that the guards had moved their patrol to the opposite side of the deck, opening up a ten minute insertion window before they completed their patrol and returned. Wasting no time, grappling hook already in hand, Santino prepared to throw it over the railing. Neither one of us had ever thrown the thing while chest deep in water before, so we had developed a technique yesterday that we hoped would work. We had no way to practically test our method, so his first try was going to be dry run number one – pun intended.

The first step was for me to secure myself to the ship as firmly as possibly. I pulled my boot knife from my ankle and raised it over my head, clutching the handle with both hands. I brought it down in a stabbing motion with as much force as I could muster, and managed to drive the entirety of the eight inch blade through the soft wood of the ship, all the way to the knife's hilt.

Satisfied the knife wouldn't budge, I held onto it while placing the rubber soles of my wetsuit against the hull, securing myself to the ship. I was now the perfect platform for Santino to toss the hook from. I sent him a nod, sputtering water from my mouth as I did so, and he quickly moved to my back and climbed onto my shoulders, securing his crotch uncomfortably against the back of my head, his thighs squeezing against my skull.

I immediately regretted not bringing Helena.

Thankfully, before I had to endure the discomfort much longer, Santino sent the grappling hook flying over the railing of the ship, about twenty meters above the surface of the water. He stood and climbed. I followed, the weight of my soaked gear threatening to pull me down, but I barely felt it as adrenaline coursed its way through my body. I stubbornly pulled myself upward, one hand after another. I reached the railing, and with one last exertion, threw myself up and over it, landing quietly in a crouch. Santino already had his rifle at the ready, automatically waiting for me to secure the hook and rope to his back.

I gently squeezed his right shoulder, the signal for him to lead the way. As I followed him, I also sent Helena the all clear signal. She returned it. Only two minutes had passed. So far, so good. We followed the Romans' patrol route around the starboard side of the ship, their return leg keeping them on the port side.

The deck of Agrippina's pleasure barge looked like any random high class district back in Rome. In the stern stood a building that looked like a smaller version of the Parthenon. It was rectangular in design and had columns holding up the roof all around the exterior of the structure. It had to be a temple. Romans were a very superstitious lot, and never went anywhere or did anything before paying tribute to any number of their gods, going well out of their way to ensure they didn't piss them off.

The second of the two structures, which we were just passing on the starboard side, sat in the bow of the ship. We paused at its corner and looked out over the plaza that dominated the area between the two buildings. The deck was lined with marble in an intricate design of shapes and colors, intertwined in a rather artistically impressive motif. Columns stretched along the port and starboard sides of the plaza, connecting the two structures, and benches dotted the edge as well.

Since the ship's arrival, we had observed day time parties where scantily clad men and women cavorted about, dancing and eating on the deck. Word had it that Agrippina's court in Rome acted in a similar fashion, harkening back to the debaucheries of Tiberius' time as Caesar not too long ago. Agrippina made the rare appearances, but most of the time she was in the camp. Not once had we seen a small boy.

The parties were irksome affairs. Any military commander worth his pay grade would never taunt an army with such shows of frivolity. Flaunting wealth and privilege in front of excessively underprivileged foot soldiers, paid in many instances with little more than salt, was an idea born from a mind steeped in madness. It was only because of their discipline and the threat of a centurion's olive branch that the legionnaires hadn't rebelled outright.

I shook my head as I remembered the gluttonous, drunken attendees of those parties. They were amongst the foremost reasons for Rome's eventual fall. Corruption and apathy had spelled Rome's downfall equally as much as the inefficiency of their military or the invading barbarian hordes, and certainly more than Christianity, despite what Edward Gibbon said. It was because of those ineffective leaders, leaders who spent more time drinking and finding new ways to stab their peers in the back, that the barbarian invaders had been able to extinguish the flame that was the glory and civilization of Rome, driving Europe into a time of darkness that regressed society hundreds of years.

I tried to push those thoughts to the back of my mind when Santino held up a clenched fist, signaling me to stop. The night was dark, and despite torches secured to the pillars, we were hidden deep in shadow. We had confirmed only one patrolling pair atop the deck, so we figured getting inside the ship would be the easy part, but we had no idea what we would encounter once inside and Galba's description of its honeycombed interior didn't inspire much confidence.

Santino kept his hand up for a few seconds before flicking his wrist, indicating it was clear to move out. We rounded the corner of the second building, which resembled the *curia* in Rome: plain and unremarkable. There was nothing left between us and the interior of the ship, so we slipped through a door and quietly descended a small flight of stairs.

We were greeted by complete darkness, forcing us to utilize our NVGs. Securing mine in front of my eyes, the world instantaneously brightened in a sea of green. A random memory surged into my mind, about a cheap night vision scope I had when I was a kid. Cheap was a relative term, because I saved my allowance for what seemed like forever to buy the thing. I vividly remember my mom reluctantly placing the order when I was thirteen, and every last penny of my hard earned four hundred dollars disappeared that day.

Needless to say, the NVGs had been garbage.

Its picture quality had been poor, manual focusing was required, bright flashes would wash out images, and it projected a small red beam that always gave away my position when my friends and I would shoot at cars with our BB guns. It probably hadn't been the smartest thing to do, but it was fun, and boys will forever be boys.

But the goggles I had now would have made my thirteen year old counterpart piss his pants. These NVGs cost close to four *thousand* dollars, focused automatically, compensated for bright flashes, projected crystal clear images, and gave off no ambient light. There were the two, small, green circles around my eyes, a result of the green backlight displayed within the goggles, but they were hard to notice unless you were really looking for them.

I smiled in the darkness as another memory jumped to mind, of the time my SEAL platoon volunteered to play bad guys during a training exercise with a deployed Marine Force Recon unit. I remember sitting in compete darkness at one point, waiting for the scenario to end after I had been "killed" by a Blackhawk's miniguns. It had been two in the morning, but I was wide awake and sharp, and I hadn't noticed a thing until I heard the heavy panting of one of the unit's K9s breathing heavily against my cheek. It was then that I finally noticed the small green glows around their eyes as the Marines traveled back and forth down the hall, searching for anything suspicious.

Those green eyes spooked me and probably will for the rest of my life.

The Marines themselves had been almost invisible in the darkness, little more than two green circles bobbing in midair. It wasn't until after they'd left and the scenario had ended that I realized there had only been one entrance to the hallway, and that the Marines had spent at least ten minutes walking back and forth over my out stretched legs before I even noticed them. Those guys had been ghosts, and even though I was a Navy man and had inherited an intimate rivalry with Marines, after that moment, I had nothing but respect for that particular bunch.

I shook my head again to get myself back on task. I really had to kick the bad habit of letting my mind wander while on a mission. Santino glanced back at me, having to turn his entire head to do so. If NVGs had any drawbacks it was how they diminished your peripheral vision and decreased your depth perception. Minor annoyances, but it beat grasping around in the dark with our hands stretched out before us like two of the three blind mice.

Catching his look, I nodded, an exaggerated gesture as well. He turned back down the corridor and started moving. Like the caverns we had found ourselves in back in 2021, we didn't know where to go, but like then, I wasn't worried. Even if he didn't know where he was going, Santino had a sixth sense that guided him instinctually. It was an interesting and almost supernatural ability, but it had served him well over the years. He was a born tracker, hunter, and scout, and he rarely missed a thing.

He didn't really understand it either, but he theorized it was a skill he developed over the years as a kid. He'd grown up in one of the seedier areas of New York, and every day had been a quest just to stay alive. Gangs, pedophiles, rapists, and murders had been everywhere, and only a kid with a will to survive could make it home unscathed. He'd told me that not once over the years had he been beaten up or hurt because he had become adept at simply avoiding contact with those around him. He'd gotten really good at it, and had honed his skills by later tracking those he'd just as soon avoid.

However he received the ability, I was just glad he was here. It made my job easier. I technically could have been replaced by Helena on this mission, but Santino had to be here. All I had to do was follow him and cover his ass.

***

Galba had been mostly right. While I wouldn't describe the ship's interior as a honeycomb, it was certainly complex. Constructed similarly to ships of the future, it was constructed around long hallways and stairwells that took us between decks, offering a familiar environment to work in.

After discovering our first staircase, Santino descended three levels and headed aft. His logic probably centered along the notion that Agrippina's stateroom would probably be near the middle and rear of the ship, the boat's most secure part.

We passed room after room but saw nothing that appeared to be an entranceway to a room meant for an empress. We were just about to the stern stairwell when I saw a dim light coming around the corner of an adjacent hallway. Santino motioned for me to halt, and quickly flicked his hand towards the left side of the hall. He remained to the right, edging inside a door frame while I moved to the left, doing the same.

The candlelight grew brighter, and my NVGs grew dimmer to compensate for the increased illumination. When the figure holding the candle rounded the corner, my goggles compensated as well as it could, but the sudden brightness washed out my vision. I could still make out the target as a man, but his face was behind the flame, making it impossible for me to ID him. Santino, on the other hand, opted to act first and ask questions later, leaping on the man like a panther from a tree limb. He body checked him into the wall and pushed his forearm into the man's neck, cutting off his air supply.

Frightened by Santino's attack, the man dropped his candle and the flame went out as it fell to the deck. My goggles refocused immediately and brightened. I saw the man's eyes roll into the back of his head as Santino slowly choked him into unconsciousness.

And then I recognized him.

Before Santino could finish the guy off, I leapt on him, just as he had just done the hapless passerby. I pulled his arm away from his target's neck, and the man fell to the floor, flinging his hands to his throat as he attempted to coax air back into his lungs.

"What the hell?" Santino asked, confused at my intervention.

I held up a finger, signaling for him to hang on and wait.

I knelt in front of the man, letting him gaze into the floating green dots that were my eyes. There was no way he could have recognized me, but it was impossible to mistake the technology.

"Hu… Hunt…?" He croaked, unable to sound out the word.

I smiled. "Burning the midnight oil are we, Varus?"

***

"What in the name of Mercury are you doing here?" Marcus Varus asked as he ushered us into his decent sized stateroom, referencing the god of travelers.

If I had been the key to transporting us through time to ancient Rome, then Varus had been the lock. While it had only been through a twist of fate that we found ourselves in ancient Rome, without Varus, it may never have happened at all. Remus' orb only worked with his direct descendants, or so we assumed, and as it turned out, both Varus and I shared that in common.

"What?" Santino asked. "We can't stop by and visit a friend?"

"I am hardly a friend of yours, brute. I remember the dinner four years ago and what you did to me," he finished, sneering at Santino's grinning face.

I smiled, despite the cruelty of the joke Santino had played on poor Varus.

It was a sad fact, but the truth about Santino's jokes was that they were sometimes more childish and cruel than clever, especially when he was intoxicated. It had happened at one of our last dinner parties, the last happy one we had attended before the party that resulted in Caligula's death.

It was also the wildest one we had attended during our short time spent in Caligula's service.

I wouldn't have described it as an orgy, but it wouldn't have taken much to escalate it to that point. We'd been taking the whole, "when in Rome," saying literally, and it had been fun. We'd feasted and drank till everyone had eaten more than they should have and were damn near plastered drunk. Helena and I had been making out on a couch in the corner, Caligula had two floozies with him, and every other patron was either singing, dancing, drinking, kissing, or leaving to get extra frisky with their dates. Caligula, after all, had some standards, and he wouldn't have people fornicating in front of him.

Even before the party, Varus and Santino hadn't ever really gotten along. Varus was a squirmy intellectual type and Santino enjoyed nothing more than to bully such targets. He did it with me, occasionally, since I actually had a brain, but he knew Helena would kick his ass if he took it too far, so he generally directed his attention elsewhere.

In his typical, juvenile way, Santino had decided to "de-pants" Varus, but it had apparently escaped Santino that Romans didn't wear pants. But that hadn't deterred him. Cleverly, Santino effectively fused two stereotypical bullying rituals into one devastating attack. By grabbing the hem of Varus' toga and pulling it over his head, he'd not only technically de-pantsed him, but had simultaneously performed an atomic wedgie as well. It wasn't really a wedgie, but the fact that he had been able to yank the toga over Varus' head and shoulders dictated the title.

But sadly, as was tradition, Varus hadn't been wearing any undergarments, and he'd flashed the entire party as he spun around in circles, trying to dislodge his robes. Helena and I had laughed along with everyone else, too drunk to know any better. After fixing his toga, poor Varus had been bright red and fled the party in shame, his wife chasing after him after she'd taken the time to smack Santino with a single slap that knocked him to the ground. I hadn't seen Varus for almost two weeks after that, until Caligula's last party, and we hadn't had a chance to talk since either.

I could imagine he was still pretty angry about the whole thing.

"Yeah, about that," Santino said quietly, almost apologetically. "That was pretty funny, right?"

I knew Varus wanted to kill Santino, but his trembling quickly subsided. He was an intellectual after all, and Santino was obviously much bigger and stronger than he was. I supposed I wasn't giving Varus as much credit as he deserved because he was in good shape, lean and probably pretty strong to. He also wasn't a bad looking guy, as no ancestor of mine would be, of course, and his wife was very attractive.

Without comment, Varus moved toward his bed and I followed him, making my way carefully so that I didn't knock over the stacks of papers and notes strewn about the floor in a chaotic mess. The room was a disaster, filled with all kinds of random documents and manuscripts. I noticed a vacant chair in the room and headed towards it, accidentally knocking over one of the stacks in the process. Varus sent me a look of disinterest.

"Sorry about Santino, Marcus. You know how he is. I'm also sorry we didn't get a chance to talk after Caligula's death." I paused. "I know it's been four years, but I am sorry for your loss."

The room was eerily silent, and even Santino was respectfully quiet. Varus and Caligula had been very close, probably the closest friends each of them had, and I knew Varus had taken his death pretty hard.

His relationship with Caligula had always interested me because it was a case of historical ambiguity. As a student, I'd spent much of my focus researching Caligula and his family tree, but not once had I encountered a man remembered as a confidant of Caligula's with Varus' name. That either meant his name was lost to history or it had been stricken by someone who didn't want him remembered. Of course, there was also the chance that he was supposed to die that night we'd gone back in time and became even less remembered than Galba had been.

I'll never know.

"Thank you, Hunter," he replied sadly. "I still miss him."

"He was a great man, and could have been greater. He died well before his time."

Varus nodded, accepting my words, but it took another moment before he snapped himself from his thoughts and started rummaging through his papers again, tossing random sheets over his shoulder.

"It is interesting that you reveal yourself now, Hunter," he said distractedly, forgetting our conversation had even happened. "I actually have something for you. Something I think you will find most interesting."

"Umm, okay." I said, looking at Santino, who had taken his goggles and mask off and offered me a shrug.

Varus had a one track mind, more focused than obsessive, but even so, I found it humorous that he didn't even seem remotely curious as to why we were here.

Taking a moment while Varus searched for whatever it was he was looking for, I decided to check in with Helena.

"3-2, 3-1, over."

"This is 3-2, go ahead."

"We've made contact with target Victor. He has important intel so we're waiting him out. Hopefully he can provide directions to November. Howcopy?"

"Solid copy, 3-1." She paused. "Be careful. 3-2, out."

I glanced towards the door and found Santino already posted next to it in a crouch, his knife held in a reverse grip at the ready. I turned back to face Varus, who was still rummaging through disorganized papers thrown behind his bed.

I frowned. It wasn't like Varus to be so disorganized and messy. For as long as I'd known him, his toga had always been perfectly clean and wrinkle free, his face always shaven, and the few times I had visited his home in Rome, I was always impressed with his neatness and organization. He was a taciturn fellow, contemplative and scholarly, a man who had a place for everything and preferred everything in its place.

He was clearly in over his head with something.

I bent over and picked up a handful of his notes, written on a thick, stiff writing medium known as papyrus. Tilting them toward the candle light, I tried to discern what was written.

After living in the future and spending years in the past, I had become fluent in both Latin and English, the latter of which I was sadly finding myself using less and less as time went on, as I almost always conversed in Latin these days, even around Helena and Santino. It was depressing to think of it as yet another piece of home that was slowly slipping away, knowing one day I would probably abandon English altogether. If I ever had children, I hoped to pass it on to them. Maybe they could use it as a secret code or something, but that's all it would ever be to them.

It must have been even worse for Helena, Bordeaux and Vincent, whose native languages had been completely unused in the ancient world.

Unfortunately, the text was in neither language, and while some of the letters appeared familiar, most did not. I'd taken a year of Greek in college, and had brushed up on it a bit these past few years, so I could at least identify it when I saw it.

It wasn't Greek either.

"What language is this?" I asked Varus.

"Hm?" He mumbled, pulling himself up from the bed. He had been lying on his stomach with his knees bent like a child's as he searched behind the bed. "Oh, it's Etruscan."

"Etruscan?" I asked rhetorically, lost in thought. "You mean like…"

"Found it," he said happily, holding up a clutch of papyrus in his hands.

"Found what?" I asked, not quite sure if I wanted to know. My plans were complicated enough. I didn't need him adding anymore variables into the equation, and anything dealing with Remus' orb would be a big one.

"Do you remember the document I discovered with Remus' orb?" he asked.

He looked at me and didn't continue. He seemed to be waiting for an answer to a complicated question. I wondered if he actually thought I could forget.

"Uh, yah. Its kinda hard not to," I replied, trying to keep the sarcasm from my voice.

"Right. Good. Then you will be happy to learn that I have completed a rough translation of most of it."

"Really?" I asked in abrupt interest. "What does it say?"

"Sadly," he said, suddenly squeamish, "I have found nothing that describes the orb's origin. Nothing I have translated so far has offered any insight into what it's used for or where it came from, but there is still more to translate. However, it could take my entire life to finish it, and I am sorry to admit that what I have translated is not fully reliable."

"So you basically founding nothing then," I pointed out, perhaps a bit too obnoxiously.

"That is inaccurate," Varus countered. "While I have yet to understand its true purpose, I was able to discover that the way in which you used the orb to arrive in Rome was not how it was intended to be operated."

Before I responded, I had to remind myself to keep my thoughts succinct. Varus still thought we were from a distant land, but still from this time period, and that's how it had to stay. While he was probably the only Roman I could truly trust, even more so than Galba, he was too close to Agrippina. I couldn't let that information fall into her hands. All it would take was for her to think that maybe Varus had more information than he was letting on, and that he needed a little more *coaxing* before he gave it up to her.

"What do you mean by that?" I asked. "It seemed to have worked pretty good last time I checked."

Varus waved a hand at me in an irritated fashion. "You listen, but you do not hear, Hunter. I'm surprised. After our first meeting, I had thought you to be more than just a mere barbarian, unlike that savage over there," he said indicating to Santino.

Hearing attention directed at him, Santino's head snapped around with a big grin on it.

"Think," Varus continued, tapping temple. "You are right that it did indeed perform a most fascinating function, in this case, bringing you to Rome from wherever you are from, but did it not seem almost... random? Crude? It seems to me that your arrival was little more than blind luck. What good does it do Remus to have a handful of advanced people find their way to Rome five hundred years after his death?"

"Well, maybe something went wrong with his plans," I offered. "He thought he could use the orb somehow but something happened, and he never got around to using it."

"Exactly. But for what then? Do you remember the message and how it referred to only those of his own blood possessing the ability to use the orb? If that were so, then at the time, only he and Romulus could wield its power. So why didn't they?"

I cupped my chin in my left hand and thought about it. Varus' logic was sound, but he didn't have enough information to create an effective hypothesis. From his perspective, the orb didn't work through time. He had no idea what the thing really did. But, it did make me think about one thing, something I hadn't thought of before. If Remus knew how to wield the power of the orb, which he clearly must have, then why, when Varus first touched it years ago, the first person to do so in possibly five hundred years, did he not get sent back to the days of Remus, instead of me showing up, also not in the days of Remus? Or why didn't he go to the future?

"I've got nothing," I said. "What do you think?"

"I believe your experience was merely an accident of circumstance," he answered. "It is a transportation device, yes, but I do not think the way you used it was the way it was supposed to work."

"Then how?"

Varus shrugged. "That, I do not know, but I am convinced it is meant to be used in a different way. Unfortunately, I have not seen the orb in years. Once it was brought to me during the battle outside of Rome, I had it taken to Galba's *praetorium*. It was gone when I went looking for it after the battle."

"Someone stole it?" I asked.

"I believe so. It has put me in a very limited position. However, I have transcribed the odd mantra found at the bottom of the manuscript and I want you to have it. I am confident that it will be important one day."

Varus held out the scroll of papyrus he had found, and I tentatively accepted it. Unrolling it, I noticed a small paragraph written out twice.

"What does it say?" I asked.

"I do not know," he answered. "It reads as gibberish to me. Many of the words have no Latin equivalent that I have been able to discover, and the rest of it speaks of mathematics and calculations, something I am certainly not well versed in.

"But as you can see, I have provided the original Etruscan and then transcribed it phonetically for you at the bottom. I still need time to work on a proper translation, but I fear I may never succeed. At times I almost wish Claudius was still alive. He was the only other man I knew who could read Etruscan, and his vocabulary far outweighed my own."

Gears in my mind churned at his words. I'd almost forgotten that in the original timeline, Claudius had been one of a handful of people who could still read and write Etruscan. Something about that seemed important, but I wasn't sure what. I shook my head and returned my attention to Varus.

"But why me? I thought I was just another annoying plebian."

"Hunter, you insult yourself. After that night you risked your life to save my own, when we had only known each other a few hours, it would be unthinkable of me to still perceive you as such. You're a good man, and now that Caligula is gone, certainly the only man I would ever trust with this information. If there's anyone who can discern this mystery, it is you."

"That's... nice." I paused. "I guess. Look, Varus, we need to talk," I told him as I rolled up the small piece of papyrus and placed it in my waterproof pouch. "Don't you find it strange that we're here?"

He blinked. "Well, yes, it does seem odd that you would be sneaking aboard Agrippina's ship."

I rolled my eyes. It was always the smart ones who were always so dumb.

"We could really use your help, Varus. Can you tell us where Nero is?"

"Nero?" He repeated. "No, I cannot. I haven't seen him in months, very few people have. Agrippina keeps him very secluded."

I looked over at Santino who remained focused on the door.

"We have intelligence that he's onboard," I said.

Varus looked confused. "I suppose he may be. Agrippina hardly lets him out of her sight. If he were here, he should be with her."

"Can you take us to her?"

"Yes, but why?"

I sighed, there was no way I could explain the whole thing to him quickly. "It's a long story, but I'm satisfied Agrippina is going to lead Rome into ruin, and if not her, it will be Nero. I'm planning to blackmail her by capturing him and put someone else on the throne."

Varus looked relieved. "You are!? Thank the gods. I cannot stand her, and Nero is almost as bad. Such a spoiled brat. He's horrible!"

"Shh, keep your voice down," I whispered. At least he took the news well. "What's your gripe with her anyway?"

He opened his arms wide to encompass his small room. "She is the one who has tasked me with all of this. I do not know how she even knew about it, but she does, and she is determined to take advantage. She constantly comes to me, hoping for answers, taking up hours of my time discussing my translations which should be meaningless to her..." His voice trailed off, as though there were more to the story.

"What?" I asked.

"She is relentless," he moaned. "Every week she comes to my home and whispers seductively in my ear. Her intent is obvious, but she only uses her sexuality to frustrate and aggravate me. It was nice at first, for she is very beautiful, but after years of forced servitude in her employ, I would now prefer her dead or gone. My wife has not been happy with her antics and it has placed considerable strain on my marriage."

"We'll deal with it," I reassured, "but our main concern now is getting her away from Germany. We need the professionals to handle the war, not some amateur with great legs."

"I agree. Her decision to come here was rash and not agreed upon by many of her military advisors back in Rome."

"Fine. Whatever. Can you take us to her room?"

"Yes. Follow me."

Santino relinquished his position by the door and fell into step behind Varus as he lead the way out of his small room, throwing Santino one last look of annoyance before stepping through the door. Following his lead, we traveled up one floor and took a right turn at the rear of the ship. He led us to a large door only a short walk away from the stairwell.

"This is her room," he whispered, indicating the only door along the rear wall. "Be careful."

"Don't worry about..."

Before I could finish, a candle flickered around the corner and a man dressed in legionary armor came face to face with the three of us. No longer confined to the *pomerium*, the sacred boundary around the original borders of Rome, the Praetorian before us was allowed to wear full combat armor – *gladius* and all.

His face expressed shock and hesitation, but Santino's did not. Acting on pure instinct, he leapt on the man, just as he had done Varus minutes ago, and wrapped his arm around the Praetorian's throat. Santino's face was intense as he choked the man unconscious, dropping him to the ground when the man's struggle ceased.

He brushed himself off, smiling.

"Barbarian," Varus muttered.

I looked over at him. "Marcus, I'm very, very sorry about this."

"About what?" He asked in confusion.

Before he had time to wrap his large brain around what I meant, I pulled out my air pistol and shot him in the thigh with a tranquilizer dart. I caught him as he fell, his legs buckling underneath him.

"Like I said. You'll thank me later."

His eyes glazed over and his eyebrows narrowed, but he'd figure it out in a few hours when he recovered. The Praetorian saw him working with two people who clearly didn't belong onboard. If he wakes up and discovers Varus was working with us, Agrippina might crucify the poor guy. Instead, by shooting him, hopefully the Praetorian will think Varus was working against his will.

I rested my friend on the ground gently and quietly reloaded the air pistol and shot the Praetorian in the arm, reloading again. Santino smirked at me. "Varus is not going to be happy."

"He's a smart guy. He'll deal with it."

"You really are a sadistic bastard aren't you? I bet Helena has a real good time with you in bed."

I looked from the snoozing Praetorian to Santino. "Shut it."

He chuckled. "Let's get these two inside."

I nodded and gently opened the door leading into Agrippina's room. Removing the dart from Varus' leg, I pulled him into the room and set him down next to the entrance. Santino did the same with the Praetorian. Shutting the door, I turned around and took in Agrippina's room in a glance, which wasn't nearly enough time.

Her room was decorated like an art museum, with sculptures, paintings and murals arrayed all throughout its interior. There were red and purple fabrics draped across the walls and furniture, oriental style rugs on the ground, and enough window space to allow natural light to brighten up the room. I pulled off my goggles, letting my eyes' natural night vision develop, and took a closer look around.

I looked specifically at the displayed art, quickly noting a common theme. Every piece seemed to prominently feature the same character: Venus, the Roman version of the Greek goddess Aphrodite. As to see why Agrippina would choose her, I had not a doubt in my mind. Of all the classical deities, Venus was the only one I could see Agrippina really relating to. She was seductive, vane, prone to anger and was a rash decision maker, personality quirks she shared with Agrippina. I wasn't an art history major, but I recognized many of the paintings and sculptures from mythological context alone.

I saw a painting of Venus emerging from the sea upon her birth, naked and riding an open sea shell. It was eerily similar to the painting by Botticelli, but completely original. Another depicted the story of Vulcan, Venus' husband, who learned she was having an affair with the god of war, Mars. Intending to catch them in the act, he trapped the pair in an inescapable net during one of their sexual encounters. The story concludes with Vulcan calling all the gods and goddesses to view the spectacle, hoping they would take his side and punish Mars. Unfortunately for the lame-footed and gimpy Vulcan, all the goddesses were too in awe of Venus' beauty to look upon them, while all the gods simply joked and laughed at Vulcan's expense, wishing they could take Mars' place, naked and entangled with the loveliest creature that ever existed.

I'd always found that story amusing.

One piece depicted of the Judgment of Paris, when he chose Venus's gift over Minerva's and Juno's, thus sparking the Trojan War. Another showed Pygmalion sculpting a model of Venus to create an image of the perfect woman, only to fall in love with the sculpture. Yet another displayed Venus' rescue of either Aeneas or Paris at the hands of either Diomedes or Menelaos respectively during the Trojan War. The final painting was another image of her wearing nothing but the *cestus*, a girdle forged by Vulcan that made her even more irresistible to humans and gods alike.

Her *cestus* always seemed redundant to me, since she was already supposed to be the most beautiful woman, mortal or god, in the eyes of all people, both male and female. It was always my impression that those who looked upon Venus saw in her what they considered perfect beauty. She was supposed to resemble the pinnacle of womanhood, a paradigm, a true ten on any bar hopper's scale, and since every person's opinion of beauty was different, so would she have to be as well.

I squinted at the closest picture, the one with Venus wearing the *cestus* and noticed two things. First, in each piece of art, Venus was always completely naked, showing no shame, not that a goddess would have any to speak of. There were plenty of art pieces I remember from home that portrayed her naked, but most tried to maintain some semblance of dignity by covering up her goods with a fig leaf or something. The artists of these works were unaware of any such concept and left nothing to the imagination.

The second thing I noticed was that Venus' face looked familiar, and it didn't take long before I realized the model for these pieces was none other than Agrippina herself. I almost laughed at the vanity of the woman. By using herself as the model for the goddess of love, the most beautiful woman the world will ever know, she was practically claiming that mantel for herself.

But I had to admit, she made for a pretty convincing model.

"Are you seeing all this?" Santino asked, his eyes wide like a kid's in a candy store.

"Yeah," I replied.

"That's Aphrodite isn't it?"

"Yeah," I replied, pleased at his insight, even though since we were technically in the Roman era, Venus was probably more appropriate.

"She's... naked, and... smoking hot."

"Oh, yeah," I said, still drinking in the details.

"Think I can..."

"No," I said sharply, playing the part of his mother refusing to buy him something from the store. "Keep your hands to yourself."

"Damn," he replied, disappointment obvious in his voice. "That sculpture over there would go great in my bathroom, right next to my gold plated toilet."

I looked at the sculpture in question. It was an image of Venus, wielding a sword and wearing armor fit for an Amazon. Some Amazonian armor allowed the breasts to hang out, so as not to constrict their movement, but according to at least one ancient writer, mothers of new born girls would use a special tool to cauterize the area where the girl's right breast would grow, preventing its development completely. The absence of a right breast was thought to enhance the strength of the right arm and shoulder, making them more formidable warriors. While it was an interesting story, something told me modern science could probably disprove that theory.

Venus had never really been portrayed as a war-like goddess. That was more Minerva or Diana's territory, but according to Homer, she *had* fought in the Trojan War, and was even wounded by the Greek king Diomedes after he was divinely influenced by Minerva's powerful touch.

That said, despite her nakedness and warrior-like demeanor in the sculpture, I think the reason Santino really wanted that particular piece for his imaginary bathroom was because she was squatting and her face appeared as though trapped in a very tense moment.

This time, I couldn't help but smile at my friend's crude sense of humor.

I surveyed the rest of the room. It was large, almost the size of a tennis court, and at the far end of the room, set flush against the farthest rear wall of the ship, was a gargantuan bed. It was bigger than any I had ever seen and sat atop an elevated platform. Along the rear wall was a large open window as long as the room was wide, cut in a way that produced a number of long, wooden bars that ran horizontally along the window, a security measure that would keep both animal and interloper from entering.

Such windows dotted the exterior of the ship at various locations and elevations.

Draped with a fine lace netting that served as both decoration and bug control, the window allowed a large bright swath of moonlight to fall on the bed's lone sleeping figure.

In the time it took me to process the imagery, and hold my small conversation with Santino, the two of us had walked about half way through the room. Reaching that point, I was able to identify the sleeping form as Agrippina. A very naked Agrippina. Lying on her back, her arms were sprawled out alongside her head in a sensual manner and her legs were spread just slightly.

I couldn't believe how much sexual energy permeated the room. The place was sexier than the most high end strip club on the planet. The level of sensuality was so intense that I found staying focused difficult.

"Watch the door," I told Santino, taking another step towards Agrippina.

"What? Not this time, buddy. Agrippina's legal."

"Just do it."

He looked at me sourly. "Just don't do anything stupid," he mumbled.

I pulled up short, pausing for a moment to reflect on his comment. Usually, that was something I would say to him, not the other way around. Did he really believe I was going to do something I'd later regret or was he just being himself? Santino wasn't one to provide deep insights or clever observations during adult conversations, but he had been known to offer insightful commentary in very specific moments in the past. Often, such comments would call for considerable reflection later on.

I shook my head and made my way to the raised platform that held Agrippina's large bed. It was situated four steps higher than the rest of the room and turned her sleeping area into a type of throne to receive dignitaries from. It seemed appropriate for her, but I wasn't about to remain at the foot of the steps and allow her to pass judgment on me.

I crept into the room slowly, each step I took landing first on the outside of my foot before rolling flat. Even in a wetsuit, the practice of walking on your outsole was still the best practice for silent movement, and after another twenty paces, I reached Agrippina's platform. I could see her nude form in front and above me, but I could not yet see her face, as it was turned toward the bulkhead behind her. I glanced one last time at Santino, who had dutifully taken up position by the door, crouching, and waiting for trouble.

I climbed each step carefully, hoping to avoid a creak in the wooden floorboards beneath my feet. With one last step, my silent climb was complete, and I inwardly thanked all those tireless Roman engineers and carpenters who managed to build a set of stairs that didn't make a sound.

Agrippina was now fully visible, her chest and abdomen smoothly dancing to the rhythm of her soft breaths. Her eyes fluttered deep in sleep and I wondered what a woman like her dreamt about. I stared at her, a great many ideas drifting into my mind, but I dismissed them and reached out a hand to cover her mouth. I didn't want her screaming before I questioned...

Something was wrong. Light shimmered and rippled across her prone form, a blue hue that made her skin appear like the serene flow of an ocean. I'd assumed the illusion was perpetrated by the light of the moon rebounding off the river and washing against her through the window, but now I realized that wasn't possible. Her bed was below the window, resulting in the light from outside passing over her to hit the floor just behind me. The shadow left by her nose was also off, as though the light source was coming from within the room, just off to my right.

I turned and saw the source, hiding behind one of the many sculptures that cluttered the room and blocked the light source from view from anywhere but Agrippina's raised dais. Situated upon a Corinthian pedestal was the blue orb that had brought us through time and space to this Godforsaken realm of shit. I almost laughed as my first thought was of poor Varus, slumped unconscious within the same room that held the orb, it being so close all along, but yet so far at the same time. I couldn't imagine Agrippina allowed many visitors into her room, and certainly not Varus.

It wasn't far away, only a few steps out of reach, and like the first time I encountered it, a light shone forth from it in all directions. Just a little smaller than a volleyball, its surface did not seem solid. Like a planet, what seemed like clouds swirled around the orb, giving it its shape and definition but simultaneously giving me the impression that were I to pick it up, my hands would sink right through the clouds before touching the true physical object beneath.

But past experience told me this phenomenon wouldn't occur, and that by grabbing it, my hand would encounter a solid surface. That is, until it swallowed your hand and sucked your entire life inside out, shitting you out into the most undesirable hellhole in all of history, completely ruining your life and the lives of...

The sight of it filled me with anger and I realized I'd brought my rifle into my hands from its slung position along my back and had it pointing in its general direction. I looked at *Penelope* dumbly, wondering how it had gotten there. I shook my head and repositioned it so that it sat against my back again. I reached out toward the orb and took a step closer to its glowing aura at the same time. It was within reach now, but I didn't touch it. Instead, I guided my hand around it, feeling the warmth it exuded sooth my sudden surge of rage.

I could no longer contain my curiosity. Here it was. The thing I had been hoping to find for years, but hadn't planned on even searching for until we'd first fixed the timeline. I bent over to peer into its magnificence, inspecting it on a level I never had before, but saw...

"I had hoped you would come searching for it, Jacob Hunter," a high pitched but soft spoken voice said from behind me. The orb seemed to dim at the interruption and I twirled on instinct the instant I heard the first word. Agrippina was awake and had turned her eyes to look in my direction. With her arms still resting beside her head, she was as seductive and alluring as the orb had just been, but I ignored her beauty and went straight for her mouth with my hand. I expected her to scream, but she was calm as I rushed at her, as if waiting for me to just get on with it and kill her, not even caring.

I held my hand against her mouth, pressing so hard that her head sunk deeper into the pillow beneath it. Again, she didn't react, merely moving her arms from beside her head to rest them against her thighs. She twisted her body so that she lay on her side and closed her legs, using her right hand to draw a sheet across her lower half. She didn't bother to cover her breasts.

She gazed at me casually as I held her there, and I continued to wait for her to struggle, but she did nothing, and I just stood there. A bead of sweat dripped from my nose to land against her chest but still she did nothing. Slowly, carefully, I removed my hand from her mouth and placed it on her shoulder, pointing at her with the other hand.

"I don't have time for games, Agrippina. I need answers, and I want them now."

"A pity," she said, looking away from me and toward the window once again. "Games are so much fun in these dull times. Without them, men grow bored and fail to realize how fun this world can be."

"I told you I don't have time for this," I growled, my hand moving on its own towards her throat. "This is life, where there are no rules and no one gives a damn what game you're playing. All I want is to do what's right, and to do that I need information."

She chirped out a quick laugh and my hand involuntarily tightened. I glanced at it, deciding to loosen it.

"By whom, exactly, are you doing right, Jacob Hunter?" She asked. "Certainly not by me or else you wouldn't be here trying to usurp my rule and disrupt all the fine plans I have put into motion."

I forced the surprise from my face and tried to suppress my frustration. She was only baiting me. There was no way she knew what I was trying to do.

"Perhaps this is for your Amazon?" She continued. "Is all this an attempt to do the right thing for her? No, I do not think so, for she was always so angry and I assume still is. You would have brought her so that she could exact some measure of revenge if you were truly trying to appease her feelings." She blinked up at my slowly. "Perhaps you really should have sent her, so that I could service her in ways you are so obviously incapable of."

"No more games," I growled, my hand tightening once again as my head inched closer to hers. She moaned under the pressure of my grip. I couldn't tell if she was recoiling from the pain or enjoying it. "Now tell me, where is Nero?"

"My Nero?" She blinked innocently. "He's back in Rome, of course. Why? Did someone tell you something to the contrary?"

I blinked. "You knew we were coming."

"Of course." Her voice was a silky purr. "I was not jesting when I said that it was good that you had come in search of the orb."

She was fishing again. After everything she'd done, she knew we'd cause trouble for her one day. I had no doubt that over the past few years much of her time had been spent imagining ways that we would strike at her. Taking Nero from her was an obvious one. All she had to do was make an offhand remark to her generals the other day that he was onboard, just in case we were around to hear about it. She'd probably done it a hundred times before.

She had always seemed a patient woman.

And she was very good at her games.

I was growing more and more frustrated with every passing second. Questioning her directly wasn't going to get me anywhere, so I let my anger expedite the process. I reached out and flipped her over so that she rested on her stomach. I stepped on the bed and placed my right knee between her shoulder blades.

"My, my," she said softly. "I had hoped you would get rough with me."

I ignored her as I retrieved my boot knife and pulled a lighter from my pouch as well, making sure she could see what I was doing as I held the flame against the blade. Before the knife could cool down, I tore away the sheet that hid Agrippina's legs and backside and pressed it against her right butt cheek.

Jack Bauer had taught America the finer parts of home torture for the better part of a decade on TV, but the CIA had given me far more substantial knowledge on the subject of human intelligence gathering much later in my life. It had amazed me how many clever household items could be used to inflict pain on someone, and there had been a few I swore I'd never utilize. In fact, I never thought I'd have the gumption to use any of it, but I supposed I'd make an exception in Agrippina's case.

And the exception was well worth it. I took a certain amount of pleasure from her moans as her supple backside burned. Her breathing grew more labored and her body perspired as she writhed against my knee. I removed the knife and saw a neat little crease on her otherwise flawless behind, a superficial wound, one that would heal easily.

"Do you want to tell me where Nero is now?" I asked.

"He's not here," she said, her voice only slightly belabored.

My anger got the better of me again as I relit the lighter, holding it beneath the knife until it was all but glowing. I waited so that Agrippina could see what was to come, but with her silence came my knife and the sizzling sound of her skin burning. Light wisps of smoke floated from the new wound, and I smelled the slight odor of charred flesh. Her moans were intense this time. Raw. She'd reached the limit of her masochistic nature.

Good.

I removed the knife and saw her second wound was at least at the second degree burn stage. It had to hurt like hell. She'd have trouble sitting for at least a few weeks, and I only wished I could be there to see her suffer.

I leaned close to her ear. "Where is he?"

"I told you!" She gasped through the pain. "He is not here."

I decided to pull back. There was something in her voice that told me she was telling the truth. I flipped her back over, and leaned my knee into her stomach this time as I pressed my boot knife against her throat and leaned in close once again, my nose inches from her own.

"He's not here?"

She shook her head, even the small motion causing my knife to nick her throat. I left it where it was.

"He's back in Rome?"

She nodded this time and tears began to fall lazily down her cheeks. "Yes."

There were ways to determine if someone was lying or not. The CIA had taught us those as well, and everything about her tone, inflection and eye contact told me she was telling the truth this time. She was still human after all, even with all she'd done, and therefore vulnerable to the pitfalls of human psychology.

I paused before deciding to shift tactics again, realizing that I didn't need Nero anymore. Agrippina was right here. Maybe I could coerce her on my own, but I tried to settle down first. I removed my knee from her stomach and climbed off the bed, leaving my knife where it was. I looked down at her and decided I had a few questions that needed answering first.

"What are you doing here? Really?"

There was still fear in her eyes, but her sobs slowed as my voice softened.

"I was looking for you," she mumbled, her tears evaporating.

"Why?" I asked.

"Because I wanted to see what you would do when you saw the orb."

I looked at her curiously. "Testing a theory?"

"I was," she said easily, "and you didn't disappoint me."

I watched without action as Agrippina placed her elbows on the bed beside her and scooted herself back so that she came out from underneath my knife. I barely even twitched, let alone tried to stop her. She sat up and tossed her hair away from her face and reached out to grab my forearm. Again, I didn't react as she pulled me down beside her like a grumpy child in need of a good scolding. She sat so close that her breasts were pressed up against my arm.

"There are so many things we must discuss, Jacob Hunter," she said softly, her expression as innocent as they come. She was a completely different person now; all her sexual promiscuity, confusing mannerisms and air of superiority completely gone, replaced by a rational human being. Suddenly, I doubted everything I had heard from her earlier tonight, no longer certain I shouldn't trust her now. All I could do was sit patiently, stupidly, and wait for her to continue.

She angled her face away from mine and smiled at no one but herself. "Gaius was always the family favorite, destined for great things and bestowed with many opportunities, but I was raised by the same parents who bore and nurtured my brother – the same family who insisted *all* their children be well schooled and educated. But unlike my doting sisters, my schooling did not end when it was time for us to take on our more womanly responsibilities.

"Knowledge is power, Jacob Hunter. I believe you know this to be true. Uncle Claudius was always so insistent that we girls harness our minds as well as our bodies, advice I followed and they ignored, and the study of language became a passion of mine. Claudius often said that understanding those whom others cannot gives you power over both. 'Keep it secret,' he used to tell me, 'never let on that you are already two steps ahead of them'."

Agrippina sighed and turned her head back to gaze at me.

"He was such a complex man, always letting on like he was less capable than he really was. I never understood why. But regardless, the important thing to understand is that of all the languages I understand, Etruscan is the one he personally taught me. Few men can speak it, you know, but I believe you know another. Marcus Varus. He's the one unconscious on the floor there by the door."

My heart skipped a beat. How could she know it was Varus who lay crumpled at Santino's feet? It was too dark and she had been facing away from us when we had come in. I opened my mouth to speak, but she pressed a long, slender finger against my lips. Her fingernails were well groomed, and her skin smelled of fresh flowers.

"Not yet, Jacob Hunter. You may speak soon, but first you must understand that I know a great many things about both you and the orb. The past four years have opened my eyes to a great many wonders, most beyond description. I have learned how glorious a tool the orb can be, but also how dangerous it is. It can have a powerful effect on the mind. Some are strengthened by its power while others are corrupted by it. Only time will tell which."

She looked down longingly and took my hand in her own. "You are drawn by it. It calls to you, beckoning you to use it. I know this because I feel it too. I have experienced its longing for the past four years, and when I imagine your separation from it, I feel a great sadness. You see, we share a bond, you and I. The orb speaks to us. It is something not even you and your Amazon can share." She paused a moment and drew my hand to her knee, gliding it smoothly along her thigh so that it rested against her hip. She scooted closer, if that was even possible. "I came here to see if you still had a connection with the orb and... with me. It fills me with such joy to learn that you still do."

"You came...?" I started, but she cut me off.

"Yes. I came here for you. I want to help you. I want you to help me. To use the orb together and make Rome everything it was meant to be and more. We can do great things, you and I."

I felt a distinct soreness in my eyes, a burning sensation that meant I hadn't blinked in quite some time. I squeezed them shut and wondered what had brought on such a trance, knowing it wasn't Agrippina. There was nothing sexual about her current demeanor at all, despite obvious actions to the contrary. I looked at my hand pressed firmly against her shapely thigh and felt nothing at the sensation. I had touched Helena in that manner hundreds of times, each as exciting as the last, but I felt nothing now. I looked into Agrippina's eyes, and failed to feel the slightest urge to lean in and kiss her. I suspected in that moment that Agrippina felt the same.

There was something oddly off about the whole scenario. It almost felt like she was right, like we did share some kind of bond. I glanced at the orb and glared at it. There sat a perfectly good rationale in of itself. I pulled my hand away from Agrippina's leg and pressed it against my temple, trying to think as I squeezed my eyes even tighter.

After a moment, I rose to my feet, pulling away from Agrippina, her hand still lazily attached to my own. She wasted no effort keeping me close, but clung to me until I was too far away for her to hold on. I felt disoriented and nauseous, so much so that I almost fell down the steps but a sudden adrenaline surge steadied me. My mind started to clear and Agrippina's spell, or whatever it was, faded away.

The orb's blue glow dimmed.

I sheathed my boot knife and retrieved my rifle from behind my back. I held it out in front of me and straightened my posture as well as I could. I felt drained, and my head was still swimming in confusion, misunderstanding and sudden fatigue. It took everything I had left to even look at Agrippina.

"I said no more games," I said breathlessly. "Stay where you are and I won't hurt you, but that orb is coming with me."

Agrippina frowned and reached around to caress her burned behind. "So you've chosen that path then." She sighed and looked away. "Unexpected, but if that is your choice, there is something else I wish you to know."

I looked down at her warily. "What?"

She met my gaze, her deep blue eyes sparkling in malice and a type of cruel enjoyment.

"I want you to know that just prior to the battle outside of Rome four years ago, I issued a bounty for your Amazon."

"What?" I asked, not completely understanding.

She blinked innocently. "I offered five thousand *sestertii* to whoever brought me her head. At the time, I didn't even know why, really. Silly decisions like that come to you when you are young, I suppose."

"You... you..." but no words came to me. My head swam again and, this time, I succeeded in stumbling down the stairs. I managed to keep my footing but a sharp pain in my chest doubled me over in pain as realization of her words hit me. I held myself up with my hands on my knees and fought off the anger building inside me, demanding my body cooperate and allow me to breathe again.

I failed, and a mental image of Helena's severed head popped into my mind. Her mouth hung lifelessly ajar and her green eyes were aimed at the sky, without color and dripping with blood. I smacked my temple with the palm of my hand, trying to forget the image ever existed, and yelled out like a man possessed – completely failing to maintain my demeanor.

She had all but killed Helena herself. On that already bloody day, not a single enemy Praetorian would have passed up the opportunity to cash in on Agrippina's lucrative reward. Helena's death had been a guaranteed thing, and only through the grace of God had she survived. She had been no more than a mere pawn in Agrippina's sick and twisted game of life, a game with no moral boundaries, common sense or consequences, a game where people died on a whim. Her whim.

Nothing prepared me for the hatred, the pure vehement evil that course through my veins like the mightiest of rivers in that moment. Not the death of my mother, the bloodshed that sparked World War III, the sense of frustration over marooning us in Rome, or the feelings of guilt over failing to protect the woman I love all those years ago.

Agrippina's naked form gazed down at me calmly. I stared at her with tear stricken eyes as I shouldered my rifle with a shaky hand, chambered a round, flicked off the safety, and shifted my aim towards her stomach. In that moment, if I was going to kill her, I would ensure it was long and painful. I paused, allowing the fact she was going to die seep into every synapse in her brain, but she didn't even seem to care. She just sat there, exposed for all to see; convinced she sat in control of everything.

"Every game has an ending," I choked, looking into sultry blue eyes I could barely see. "And yours is over."

I pulled the trigger.

Three rounds of deadly vengeance seemed to crawl towards Agrippina as they cut through the air. The concept of time no longer held sway over reality as it once did and I could almost see the distortion of air around each bullet as they sliced through the air at a leisurely pace.

That's when I noticed that the bullets would miss.

My mind was overclocked, racing so furiously that I didn't even notice how my aim had faltered. Somehow, a previously unknown assailant had pushed my rifle to the side milliseconds before I had fired, angling my shots to hit Agrippina's bed sheets a few inches from her thigh. My attacker then came at me in a dive from a location I had previously thought empty, his momentum and mass hitting me with such force that we tumbled deep into the room. Time began to progress normally again and I rose to my feet, slinging *Penelope* around to my back and got a good look at my attacker.

He was wearing a tight, black, body suit and a mask that covered everything but his eyes. His outfit was so completely un-Roman that at first I thought it was Helena, but I knew it couldn't be. The person before me was clearly a man, a head shorter than I, and very skinny, but judging from the force of his tackle, made of solid muscle. The man had to be a Roman, one whose fashion sense conflicted with everything I knew about his culture. The man looked like a ninja as he adopted a fighting stance with his knees bent and his arms out in front of him protectively.

Who was this guy?

Agrippina had brought her feet up underneath her and was kneeling on the bed now, her eyes analyzing every move we made as she wiped blood from her neck and wiped it on her bare thighs. She smiled at me and spread her arms wide. "You didn't expect all your questions to be answered so quickly, did you, Jacob? That, as you would say, would spoil the story."

I narrowed my eyes and tilted my head at her odd word choice but was distracted by my attacker trying to circle around me. I dropped into a combat stance of my own, knees bent and my left leg behind my right, fists up. We circled each other as I stared into the man's eyes, eyes that were as calm and calculating as Agrippina's.

He made the first move.

He ran straight for me, leaping into the air and kicking out with the tip of his foot. I easily blocked the kick to the left and hoped to land a quick jab to the side of his neck when he landed. But instead, the man used my poor judgment to fall immediately into a crouch and roll beneath my jab. He ended up behind me and swept my legs out from under me, dropping me onto my back. I fell for the maneuver like a pathetic rookie, the punch I had intended to land meeting nothing but air. I hadn't expected anything like that from my opponent. The man was fighting like a martial artist, knowledgeable in any number of forms and disciplines.

Taking the initiative once again, the man leapt from his crouched position, hoping to grapple with me on the ground, but I was prepared for him this time. I rolled onto my toes, and pivoted so that when he landed, I planted a kneeling side kick into his rib cage, knocking him two feet away from me and onto his back. I stood up and looked for Santino. I found him dealing with his own attacker. They seemed deadlocked, but then Santino managed to draw his scimitar, and I knew that fight was already over.

But my own attacker didn't waste time wondering about his partner, and used my distraction to jump to his feet and rush me with a superman punch to my chest, knocking the wind from my lungs. I doubled over and he sent a knee flying into my nose. I stumbled backwards as I felt it break upon impact. My head spun as blood sprayed from my nostrils.

My opponent was relentless, following up with a side kick into my chin, sending me flying through the air again. I fell a few inches away from Santino's sculpture this time, a foot closer and I would have been skewered by Venus' sword. I looked up, the world still spinning, and I saw my attacker loom over me. His eyes didn't suggest he was taking any pleasure from the fight, or that he was predicting a premature victory. He just stared at me coldly, revealing nothing, and I felt a knot grow in my stomach. I looked to his left hand and saw three blades gripped there, my vision evidently playing a cruel trick on me.

I couldn't focus enough to even stand. I was defeated and I knew it. I moved my hand to my radio, hoping to send Helena one last message when my attacker made his first real mistake.

He forgot about Santino.

My friend also knew better than to waste time in a fight, and I watched as my opponent was amongst the living one second and then had a knife sticking through his throat the next. Santino pulled it back and the man collapsed. He reached down and hauled me to my feet by my recon vest and yanked me towards the door.

"What about... about... Agrippina?" I asked, choking on my own blood which streamed like a fire hose from my nose.

"Jacob, just shut the fuck up," he said. "We need to get the hell out of here." He clicked his radio with his free hand, his other arm busy holding me up. "3-2, 3-3, we're extracting hot. Prepare to offer cover fire."

"Roger, 3-3. Where's 3-1?" I heard fear in her voice through my earpiece. I was usually the away team's radio man.

"He's fine," Santino answered, glancing at me, "but, well, you better get a Band-Aid ready. 3-3, out." He pulled his hand from the PTT button and gripped his rifle with it. Our fight had been noisy, and we had probably awoken half the ship. Men and women were already peeking out from behind their doors, trying to get a glimpse at what was causing all the commotion.

A trio of Praetorians rounded a corner just as Santino and I were about to begin our ascension to the deck. Santino raised his rifle in their direction and fired with one hand, putting ten rounds in the wall next to their heads. They jerked back and took cover around the corner.

"Can you walk yet?" He demanded. "I'm tired of hauling around your fat ass every time the fight gets interesting."

"Yeah," I said as I slapped my cheeks a few times. Feeling my head clear, I reached into one of my pouches and extracted the demo detonator. I'm fine."

"Good," Santino said as I depressed the button, setting off the explosives I'd placed last night. They went off in violent succession, pitching the ship forward at the initial explosion. Santino and I carefully made our way up the stairs three at a time as the ship shook around us. My head was still foggy, but I kept up. We reached the deck and made our way to the bow of the ship, encountering the two man Praetorian patrol immediately. They were in the process of picking themselves off the deck after the explosion, but I dissuaded them by pulling out my air pistol and firing my last few darts at them in rapid succession. Santino and I took off in the opposite direction, where we were met by even more Praetorians streaming onto the deck from below. Santino turned and sprayed the wooden planks in front of them with half a magazine's worth of bullets as he ran, forcing them to back off.

"Get your goggles and oxygen tank ready," I instructed as we passed the temple, still trying to shake the last bit of grogginess from my head. "Dive deep, put your flippers on, and make a break under the ship and back towards Helena."

Santino didn't bother answering, but grabbed his oxygen tank from his lower leg as he leapt over the rail all the same. I followed suit with a slightly more graceful dive than Santino's cannonball form, vaulting over the railing like a track and field high jumper, pulling on my goggles as I fell. The particular dive kept my back to the ship so that when I arched my body, the natural curve of my spine automatically sent me torpedoing through the water and underneath the ship. Santino, on the other hand, had to reorient himself and move beneath the ship under his own power. I put my flippers on and waited for Santino before I swam as fast as I could towards Helena's position. With luck, the Romans would think we'd fled in the opposite direction.

The swim only lasted a few quick minutes, my anger still fueling my body. All I felt was rage, but was surprised to find it wasn't directed at Agrippina, but at me. We beached ourselves and found Helena, where she reported there was no activity that made her think they were coming in our direction. We watched for a few minutes while those aboard scurried around the deck, trying to ascertain the damage. Realizing those onboard had enough to deal with, we abandoned the scene and walked a few minutes inland. We retrieved our tied up horses, along with our gear, and headed southwest into the Alps.

We rode at full gallop for an hour before the peaks of jagged mountain ranges dominated the landscape in front us. Another hour at a slower pace and we were safely surrounded by an endless jigsaw puzzle of mountains, hills, and trees. We found a nice rocky outcropping, just as we had before, and set up our camp. We camouflaged it perfectly and with an hour or two of darkness left, I went inside while Helena and Santino debriefed each other. I was too frazzled to think about what had just happened.

Entering the tent, I threw off my recon rig, rolled out my bed roll, and knelt on it, my back to the tent's entrance. I sat on my heels, and rested my forearms against my legs, my palms facing up. I tried and failed to rationalize everything that had just happened.

People always looked at modern military personnel as passive, stoic, unemotional killing machines, men and women capable of killing on nothing more than the orders of another. All they saw were the apathetic victors, the heroes in the photographs or the caskets of the fallen, brave and daring volunteers each, who risked their lives for the sake of others.

What they didn't see were the times those emotional barriers came down. In many instances, these public barriers were little more than façades meant to assure those we were protecting that we would never fail them. The news media may offer the public a glimpse into the lives of a handful of vets dealing with PTSD or, in many a sad case, failing to deal with it, but what they rarely ever see is raw emotion, the eventual byproduct of trying to rationalize every despicable action perpetrated on another human being.

Everyone dealt with it differently. Some cry alone, others suffer panic attacks, while others talk to no one but themselves before passing out from exhaustion. It always happened behind closed doors, usually when they were alone... alone with no one but their conscience. Others never reacted, managing their emotions by disconnecting with reality and moving on like I always had. I'd always been able to push those feelings into some dark recess of my mind, never thinking they'd come back to haunt me someday. Somehow, I'd always been in that latter group, able to distance myself from emotion, but tonight, I just felt empty.

Helena came in a few minutes later.

She zipped up the tent and moved to kneel opposite me.

"Santino told me what happened," she said consolingly.

"I was going to kill her, Helena. No remorse. No more questions. Just... murder her."

"The orb was there. It..."

"It had nothing to do with it," I snapped. "I could tell when it was influencing me, and it wasn't then. It was just that the things she said, the things she implied... Agrippina wasn't lying to me, Helena. There's something about her and the orb that can control me and I don't know what to think anymore. I don't know what to do to protect myself from it."

"Jacob, you won't always have all the right answers," she said carefully, "no one does. We talked about that. It isn't some indelible personal deficiency you alone possess, but what separates you from everyone else is that you know how to survive. Adapt. What's more is that you have me. And Santino. We can help you so that you'll know what to do next time."

I shook my head. "It's not that simple. Besides, I'm not nearly as perfect as you think. Look at how I treated you and Santino only a few months ago. The orb can take advantage of emotions like that – pride, arrogance and anger, and warp your will with them. What if... what if I turn out like Caligula or Claudius if I keep exposing myself to it?"

"Don't do this to yourself, Jacob," she said, her voice filled with emotion. "You're your own man, and as good a one as I've ever known. Don't lose yourself over something you can't control or even understand yet. Stick to your gut and stay focused. You don't have to be perfect. Everyone makes mistakes! Everyone! You just have to learn from them."

I felt anguish tear my heart to pieces as feelings of rage and dread continued to engulf me. "I can't control it, Helena. If I go near the orb again, I don't know what I'll do. It may affect my judgment beyond my ability to handle. What if it gets someone killed? What if it gets you killed. I can't watch that happen again. I ... I can't... I..."

Helena shot to her feet and moved in to surround me in an engulfing hug. She sat off to my side and threw her arms around my chest and back, digging her head into the side of my neck as I sat there in denial. I tried to fight down my fear but only felt anger rise up again instead. I started to shake, uncontrollable convulsions that threatened to throw Helena off of me, but she held firm, refusing to let me go in my moment of pain and panic.

"Please don't do this, Jacob," she whispered. "You're not the only one who can't stand the idea of losing the one you love."

I heard her words and drank them in, but was unable to repress the fury swirling within me as I found myself being dragged to the floor of our tent by Helena, tremors continuing to course through my body. She turned my head to rest it against her chest, and I felt an overwhelming desire to sleep. I shut my eyes, forcing any potential wayward tear back behind the shoddily erected barricades my subconscious struggled to rebuild, and felt the sweet escape of sleep overpower me as Helena rocked me in place.

My last thought before unconsciousness was that maybe Agrippina *was* right. Maybe she really did have all the answers. Maybe the only thing I needed was to accept her offer and work with her. Maybe with her, my life would be complete, or... or at least find meaning again, and the sense of emptiness deep within me would be filled. The responsibility I'd heaped upon myself would be gone and I could dictate a new path to the future without the need to reorient the timeline.

Who would care?

I thought of little else as my mind slowly spiraled on a downward course toward oblivion, but a physical presence reminded me not to trust random thoughts influenced by emotion. The warm, familiar form of Helena next to me reminded my subconscious to think more clearly and rationalize everything, the same as her comforting voice always did when I was awake.

It was unfortunate then that at that very second, when my mind finally collapsed in on itself, that the last thing I remembered was the sweet scent of Helena's presence associated with the horrifying idea that maybe Agrippina was in fact right. It was a furtive thought that threatened everything I had come to understand and hope for, but was perhaps an idea worth investigating.

The only question left was how I would feel when I awakened.

Part Two

V
Byzantium

Mission Entry #5
Jacob Hunter
Byzantium, Thracia - June, 42 A.D.

If you are at all knowledgeable about geography, you should already know from the heading that we went east. As for the mission to capture Nero, all I have to say on the matter is that it was a failure. He wasn't even there.

No – that's not all I'm prepared to say, actually. There's more.

Finding Agrippina hadn't been a problem for us that night, but what really threw a wrinkle in our plan was that we found the blue, time traveling orb as well. It was the same one I knew we'd have to find some day, but was also the one thing I hadn't been prepared for. There had been, and still are, too many unanswered questions about the thing, so many, in fact, that I hadn't even wanted to go looking for it until we were satisfied the timeline was back on track.

And still don't.

But I'd found it that night and it had influenced me in ways I hadn't thought possible. There's just something about it, some kind of draw that I can't resist. Something that makes me think things and do things I wouldn't normally do. I've yet to determine whether it affects others as well, but I haven't really had many opportunities to test the theory. But regardless of whether it does or doesn't, I can vouch for how it affects me:

Negatively.

To the point that it almost made me do things I would later regret.

Then again, I did do things that night that I regretted anyway. Things I don't want to discuss nor feel the need to record here I've suffered through enough self-inflicted pain over the episode already, and the only reason I had been able to deal with it all was because we egressed the fuck away from Agrippina that night, and have been on the run ever since.

Like I said, we went east.

We knew Vincent was somewhere in the Middle East, probably around Jerusalem, so we decided to follow Bordeaux's trail. We hoped to meet up with them a lot sooner than originally planned, but when we arrived in Athens, he'd already left with Wang.

Having already missed them, we'd decided to spend a few days there, where we learned firsthand how much of an influence Wang had been on local doctors and the Greek medical profession in general. Greece had always been on the cutting edge of science and medicine, even after the Romans conquered them, but their knowledge palled before Wang's – a simple combat medic from the 21st century.

We'd asked around concerning his whereabouts, and many of his former partners told us his story:

Wang had arrived early one morning a few months after he'd left Rome, claiming he had walked all the way from the Orient and that he possessed knowledge far beyond their own. They were skeptical, of course, but with his help, Greek doctors had been able to synthesize all kinds of new drugs, the most popular being more effective pain killers. Others, such as diuretics and cough drops, were popular as well.

They'd given us a few test samples, and I remember smiling at the small objects that mimicked those in gross demand two thousand years from now. Obviously, Wang didn't have the material or equipment needed to make the kind of pills you take every day, but he had done his best. From what I observed, the pills, which were more like wafers, consisted of mashed together herbs and plants that had been dried, crushed and formed into little consumables, held together by God knows what.

It had worked though, and the headache I'd been suffering from that day had been gone in minutes.

Unfortunately, the doctors also informed us Wang had left two weeks before our arrival in the company of a very large Gaul and his, likewise, very large family. They had seemed comically sad that Wang had left them and had indicated no one knew where he was going, just that they had gone east.

So, after a quick tourist stop at the Acropolis and Parthenon for some pictures, we moved on to Byzantium, the ancient city later known as Constantinople, which would even later be named

Istanbul. What name you know the city by is any man's guess, but I do know its Greek name – Byzantium – should still exist in your timeline if you dig down deep enough through your history books.

It was a good place to lay low for a while.

I needed to get my head together after the incident with Agrippina, and I knew Helena and Santino could use rest as well. After four years on the run, constantly taking risks and making enemies, we needed a break. Byzantium would be a good place to blend in and keep ourselves off Agrippina's radar for a few months.

East was the last place she would think to look for us.

There was nothing of value for her here.

Byzantium was also the best place to wait for Bordeaux as he made his way back with Wang and Vincent. They'd have to cross through Anatolia, you may know it as Turkey, but I doubt it, and the best place to cross from east to west was over the Bosporus, the narrow straight that separated the Black Sea and the Sea of Marmara (or simply Propontis as its known these days – the "before sea").

It's been a little more than two months since Santino's last journal entry, which I feel the need to comment on as elegant in its crude simplicity, and it may be a while again before the next one. I was too hasty and arrogant when I first decided to act on my plan a few months ago. Santino, Bordeaux... Helena... they were all right. They were always right. I don't know why I even listen to myself anymore.

I need perspective.

I need time to regroup and think.

I sat back and thought, leaving my journal to rest upon the table where it lay.

Taking time to regroup and think was a hell of an idea, but even after a few days here in Byzantium and months on the run, I'd done little in the way of thinking. It had taken me the entire time we were here just to convince myself it was time for another journal entry, and I now realized it had in fact been long overdue.

What had happened aboard Agrippina's barge and later with Helena in our tent ate away at me at times, but never so much as it did that night. I had let my guard down with Helena and allowed myself to succumb to the one emotion I couldn't afford to feel: fear. We weren't going to accomplish anything that way, but there were times when I couldn't help but dwell on that night. The orb and its power had been disturbing, yes, but it was an obvious problem. What was truly unsettling were the things Agrippina had said.

The image of her kneeling on her bed as blood dripped from her neck and was smeared all over her thighs was burrowed into my mind, but her words were all I could focus on – *You didn't expect all your questions to be answered so quickly, did you, Jacob? That, as you would say, would spoil the story*, she had said. And she was right. It was exactly something I would say, but how would she know that? And before even that, she had said something about choosing a particular path. What path? Was there more than one?

Her words had a distinctly predictive nature to them, as though she knew more than she let on. As if she knew the course of events that night before they even began. The thought shouldn't have been a surprise considering her possession of a glowing, time traveling ball, but I was convinced she couldn't use it. I had seen Claudius hold the orb in his own hand without any indication he could use it like I could and Caligula had had ownership of it for months after the reclamation of Rome. In neither instance had there been any sign they had any idea how it worked, let alone been able to operate it. As far as I knew, Marcus Varus and I were the only two people in the entire universe that could use it.

My only conclusion was that I didn't know what to think, but that I'd damn well better figure it out soon. Not only that, but that we now had two immediate objectives, neither new, and neither overtly specific. First, we had to destroy the orb; both of them, actually, since technically there were two. The second had yet to surface, but we had to find and destroy it just as surely as the one in Agrippina's possession. Second, we had to continue our goal of usurping Agrippina. The more I thought about her the more convinced I was that she had to be removed for the sake of *everything*. She knew too much about the orb, and that was bad enough. At worst, she was displaying signs of corruption from its presence, although it was taking far longer with her than it had with either Caligula or Claudius.

Helena was probably the last piece of redemption I had to work on. The last, yes, but that didn't mean I had to wait to work on it. We'd been so close to bridging the gap that had formed between us over the past year, but little progress had been made since Agrippina. I'd been distracted, introspective, much the same as I had been prior to my time on the barge, only this time I had cause and wasn't unaware of it. I thought Helena understood this time, thus her own distance, but I couldn't be sure.

The only problem was that I had no idea where to start with either goal. Santino and Helena weren't ready to discuss it, both preferring to stay out of the game as long as possible. They'd been avoiding me more than usual lately, and I hadn't done much to promote conversation either. Helena, I knew, was worried about me, having voiced her concerns on a number of occasions. But while I wasn't nearly as distant as I had been before, I wasn't ready to talk quite yet.

Santino, on the other hand, was simply more inclined to let things play out and see what happened. It was a character trait he'd developed during his time with Delta, whose original mission parameters were often discarded in lieu of more timely developments that threatened to dramatically alter a mission.

I sighed and crossed my arms, still disgruntled over the whole affair. Everything was so muddled in my brain that I couldn't think straight. Every time I felt I was on to something, another something would pop into my mind and distract me. Whether it was our direction for removing Agrippina or realigning the timeline or finding the orb; the past few months had been filled with foggy internal monologues about what to do and how to do it, but with no results to show for it.

But that's why we were here. It was to be a time to relax. If there was ever a time to get a handle on my life, it was now. It was time to grow up and find perspective.

Luckily, we couldn't have chosen a better spot.

I picked up my journal and wrapped a rubber band around it with my pen inside, and gave my surroundings a thoughtful look. Byzantium, as the ancient city was presently known, was a Greek city that was everything but the shinning beacon of Christianity it would become as Constantinople, or the exemplar of Islamic dominance it would be as Istanbul. Byzantium, as I'd come to notice, was many things, but it was nothing like I remembered from when I visited Istanbul as a kid.

Istanbul had been a beautiful city, despite how much I once despised it. I hadn't hated it based on any modern religious connotations, but because Constantinople had once been the capital of the Byzantine Empire, the eastern continuation of the Roman Empire, and I had hated anything that fucked with my beloved Romans.

At least I had before I found myself living in their hellhole of a world.

Now, I couldn't care less. Good for the Ottomans.

Like its modern equivalent, Byzantium was rich and prosperous, and the area I was now in reflected that prosperity even if the city as a whole was only a precursor of what it would soon become. Located on the only waterway that connected the Black Sea with the rest of the Mediterranean, and situated on the far ends of both western and eastern cultures, Byzantium had become one of the largest trading hubs in the Roman Empire. Anything that could be bought or sold went through Byzantium, and the city turned a tidy profit because of it.

Istanbul, circa 2021, however, was huge, spreading all the way to the Black Sea along both eastern and western banks of the Bosporus, a narrow waterway that connected the Black Sea and the Mediterranean Sea, and inland for miles in both directions. The ancient city of Byzantium was tiny in comparison. Currently the city's territory consisted of only the small peninsula at the southern tip of the Bosporus, formed by a narrow waterway that juts into the western shoreline for a few miles, known as the Golden Horn, used as a deep water harbor since the city's founding.

The city was nice and compact, and with the addition of the Golden Horn, easily defensible, as was proved regularly, even though it would eventually fall. Nothing lasted forever. Although only a few square miles in size, the city still boasted areas both opulent and dingy. Santino and Helena had voiced concerns that its small size wouldn't make for a suitable place to hide, but I had my suspicions otherwise. I figured that due to its location and importance as a trading port, the population density would be extremely high. When we arrived, I was quickly proven right. The amount of people who crowded the streets was vast, and every last one of them seemed to congregate around the dozens of city markets, where any number of goods and items could be found.

To make matters worse for my companions, I'd convinced them to take up residence in one of the seedier areas of the ancient city since logic dictated it was the best place to remain inconspicuous. It was rank and dirty, but it suited our purposes. Located near the southeast side of the city, it was fairly close to the water. In fact, our small two room apartment had a fantastic view of the Propontis, even if our neighbors were less than desirable.

It had only taken Santino a number of hours before he realized the majority of the building was used as a brothel.

Our shady neighbors, downtrodden conditions and beds that smelled like mold and fermenting bodily fluids were minor inconveniences we needed to get used to, a fact lost on Santino. It had been nothing but complaints from him about how we could have easily afforded better living accommodations which, I had to admit, was true. In fact, we'd accumulated enough wealth over the years to set us up for quite some time in one of the finest establishments in *any* city.

We brought our wealth with us in two supply containers, both about the size of a small bed, along with the few remaining MREs, spare clothing, ammunition, explosives, tools and repair kits, medical supplies, and other survival gear – what moderate amounts we had left. We also placed the few extra rifles and pistols we had, including Helena's M107 .50 caliber Barrett sniper rifle, the rest of the ammunition and other miscellaneous supplies in a third container, burying the ones that were left over.

Yet another lost part of the place we'd come from.

We'd loaded everything into a wagon, drawn by Helena's horse and my own, and went east. We didn't run into any trouble along the way, but that was because we had left our cocky attitudes with Agrippina and assimilated completely into Roman culture. Our rifles, combat fatigues and boots were all stowed away, replaced by tunics, woolen trousers, Greek style dresses for Helena, and sandals for footwear. We kept our pistols handy, but had brought our swords out of retirement, reluctantly realizing we may have to use them to maintain our cover.

We were on vacation.

Basically.

Our few days here had been relaxing so far, reminding me of our first few days spent in Ancient Rome. Like then, life seemed so peaceful, but with the nagging feeling that we were being watched. Then, we had been under the watchful eye of Caligula's Praetorians, but now it was out of a sense of paranoia. While no one knew we were here, and the Roman Empire was vast, I couldn't bring myself to trust a single person I interacted with.

With that thought in mind, I dropped a few coins on the table to pay for my meal as I left, and didn't pay another soul in the restaurant any attention. I'd had lunch in one of Byzantium's upper class districts, where the sun seemed brighter and the chances of getting stabbed in the back slimmer. The food had been adequate, not quite at the standards of the 21st century, but the outside patio was pleasant and great for people watching, something my mother, sister and I had done all the time back when we were kids.

The immediate area was a public bazaar of sorts, where small booth-sized shops sold food, clothing, jewelry, weapons, and all sorts of other knickknacks. I had observed men and women of all ages, ethnicities, and cultural background mingling in the busy streets, doing this and doing that, nothing of real consequence.

The laughter and happiness of these simple people was contagious, however, and I was suddenly transfixed by a couple purchasing some new clothing for their young daughters The girls tried on their new dresses, squealing in delight, giving both mother and father tender, warm hugs. It was a touching sight, and maybe I was just feeling old and nostalgic, but I could have sworn I felt something like jealousy as well. Whatever the case may have been, I was just glad to have the opportunity to relax and spend some time alone for once. I hadn't been very good company for the past few months, and having been in such close proximity to Helena and Santino for so long hadn't done much to raise my spirits.

I listened to the clinking noise of my coins striking wood as I gathered up my bag. Turning to leave the establishment, I decided to go on an afternoon walk through the bazaar. I was wearing simple woolen trousers that went to my knees, with a likewise simple linen tunic that draped past my waist. It was a very comfortable outfit that breathed well in these warm summer months, and my open-soled sandals completed the casual outfit.

Slung over my shoulder was a locally made bag I had purchased from one of Byzantium's shops my first day here. Its design was similar to modern day messenger bags, like the one I had used during the Battle for Rome, that I was compelled to buy it the moment I saw it. Unlike modern day bags, this one started its life as a single piece of canvas, cut and sewn to produce a bag, a flap to cover it, and a non-adjustable shoulder sling. It was very basic, and lacked the pockets and compartments I was used to, so I put to use the sewing skills my mother had drilled into me as kid and managed to attach three pockets on the outside of the bag, each large enough to hold a single M4 magazine, as well as a number of internal pockets. I made pockets for my small flashlight, multitool, two spare magazines for my Sig, and I even crafted a small interior holster for the pistol. I also carried the monocular scope off of *Penelope*, a small first aid kit, a basic survival kit, a pair of socks, and my radio. I even had the small computer system, minus the eye piece, in there as well, just in case I picked up Santino's UAV, should Bordeaux return early.

Each item was secured and easily retrievable, and gave me slightly more confidence that I'd survive each day.

With my bag of goodies secured over my left shoulder, I began to wander through the market, occasionally stopping at random kiosks to peruse the selection.

The first stall I passed by was selling what I called "meat-on-a-stick". My first day wandering through Byzantium had landed me here, and I'd purchased one of the chef's heavily spiced mystery meat sticks for lunch. It had a distinctly Indian taste to it, heavy with curry, cumin, coriander, or some such, but I had never gotten around to asking what the meat was. The owner had been very persistent that I try it, and always one looking to sample new foods, especially when on vacation, I'd given in and purchased the freshest looking one I could find. Tentatively biting into it, I was pleasantly pleased with how spicy and flavorful it was, and offered my compliments to the chef. As I ate, I asked what it was that I was consuming, only to be told it had been one of the many rats infesting the area.

The interruption in my chewing had lasted only for a moment before I shrugged and kept on eating. I couldn't deny that the rat was in fact delicious. I purchased one the next day as well, but today had opted for the sit down restaurant just down the street.

I smiled and waved as the owner tried to flag me down again, but I politely waved him off, saying I'd be back tomorrow. I hoped he wasn't so insistent on my business because I was the only dumb sap who ate his food, but I liked it, so I didn't care.

As long as I didn't contract the Bubonic Plague, I'd be happy.

I continued my tour around the market, listening to men and women haggle and bid on an assortment of items. I passed by one jewelry stand in particular and my eye caught something bright, sparkly and probably expensive. I walked over to an elderly woman who appeared to be the patron of the small establishment. She seemed small and frail beneath her multicolored shawl, but her beaked nose and eyes like a hawk said otherwise, and I knew not to act like an ignorant tourist around someone like her. She could probably sell a steak dinner to a vegan, and I had to be careful I didn't buy something I didn't want.

What I did want, however, was a necklace that I knew would look lovely on Helena. In the four years we'd been on the run, not one gift had been exchanged between us. Not a Christmas or birthday, except mine, went uncelebrated, but we rarely had enough time to go shopping. The only gift exchanged had been Santino's knife from Helena, but that was more out of necessity. Santino would have gone crazy without one.

I decided that considering the circumstances, it would be a nice gesture if I bought her something. Start the healing process, as some would say.

But I had never been the best shopper for women, although I had tried my best. I tended to stay away from clothing, since I found women's clothing sizes beyond complicated. I had no idea what the sizes meant. It didn't make sense that their sizing numbers didn't correspond to inches and I could never understand how someone could be sized with a negative number. So, I'd long ago decided it was best to stick with jewelry. It was more expensive, sure, but it was much easier to pick out. Besides, women loved the stuff, and having to shop for a sister, a mother, the random girlfriend and countless aunts during my early adult years, I'd developed a pretty good eye for what was tacky and what wasn't.

The little old lady eyed me suspiciously when I approached her booth, possibly measuring me up as a potential scam. I gave her as friendly a smile as I could manage and politely pointed to my object of interest.

"May I see that piece over there, please?" I asked in Latin, mostly sure she'd understand. "The one with the rubies?"

The woman continued to eye me as she blindly retrieved what I asked for. Her hand went right to it, and she tentatively passed it to me. I smiled and bowed my head slightly in thanks before examining it.

The band itself was very simple, a mere cord of some kind. It felt more durable than it looked, which was good because it looked very delicate, but that only enhanced its elegance. As for the rubies, there were two of them. Each about the size of a nickel, they were roughly cut, at least by modern standards, and dangled beside one another from the cord, encased in a pair of solid gold bands. They looked of good quality and alone would make the necklace a nice buy, but what really interested me hung between the two rubies.

It was a simple crescent that enveloped a five pointed star, attached by its points to the interior of the crescent. The crescent itself was slender and made of gold, while the star was of simple design and roughly cut from some kind of green gem. What made it so interesting was that the crescent and star was the symbol for Byzantium, long before Christianity or Islam had adopted them.

Christianity's main symbol was, of course, the cross, but the five pointed star was one as well, associated with the magi and the birth of Jesus Christ. Islam, on the other hand, had adopted the crescent as their symbol under the Ottoman Empire, and a small star was sometimes placed next to it as well, which is what differentiated the Islamic symbol from the symbol of Byzantium, as the latter's star was of near equal size to the crescent, and placed within it.

The crescent and star symbol held no religious connotations amongst Islam, but was simply adopted by the Ottoman Empire after their conquering of Constantinople in 1453 under Mehmed the Conqueror, probably just because old Mehmed had a good eye for historically rich symbols. Even his choice of the name, Istanbul, had a local legacy, being the Byzantine word for "the city". Many Islamic countries presented the symbol on their flag, some with or without the star, but many Muslims argued that the symbol was meant only for national pride, not faith.

Religious and cultural connotations aside, the necklace was simply beautiful, and I knew Helena would love it. At least she'd better after I spent a few hours going over those exact cultural and religious implications.

I looked down at the diminutive woman and held out the necklace, reassuring her I hadn't stolen or damaged it.

"How much?" I asked.

She tapped her chin with a finger before flashing all five fingers followed by just her pointer finger.

"For you!" She yelled at me. "Sixty *sestertii*."

That would put the value of the necklace at a very approximate three hundred American dollars. She had to be kidding. Considering inflation rates after the past two thousand years, that price was way too high.

"Forty," I said, finding the whole haggling experience enjoyable. I was getting pretty good at it these days, but unlike Madriviox and the Gauls in Valentia, something told me this old woman wouldn't be quite as naïve.

"Fifty five," she countered.

"Forty five."

The woman looked at me coyly, perhaps for once seeing me as a true buyer and seller of goods, instead of just some dumb tourist.

"Fifty," she finished with a smile, knowing that was as good as I was going to get.

"Fine," I said, fishing around for some money. Two hundred and fifty bucks in this day and age was a hefty sum, but we had the money these days, and Helena was worth it. At least I hoped the gift would remind her that I still thought she was. Or maybe it would convince *me* that I thought she was.

Locating the small money purse at the bottom of my bag, I noticed something was wrong. My Sig was missing, as was my flashlight. Thinking they might have simply fallen out, I looked around my feet but found neither. I looked up and saw a small boy with short black hair look back over his shoulder and make instant eye contact with me.

And in that instant I froze, unsure what I should do.

The boy had stolen valuable equipment that could prove detrimental in countless ways should it fall into the wrong hands. It was also evidence of our presence in the city, information that could reveal our location to Agrippina and invite trouble. However, chasing after the thief could also cause a scene, alerting any agents Agrippina may already have stationed here.

If I ran, I could also hurt someone.

If I stayed and alerted Santino maybe he could…

Just stop it. What the hell is wrong with you?

Just make a decision, Hunter.

Just do something!

I looked up and snatched the necklace from the woman, who had kindly wrapped it in a piece of silk cloth, and tossed her the appropriate amount or coinage, plus a few extra *denarii* for being such a kind host. Dropping both money purse and necklace in my bag, I turned back to find the boy gone. He must have taken off as soon as he realized he was burned.

With the midday crowd still mingling about, I almost lost hope of tracking the little kleptomaniac down. I wove through the crowd, pushing people aside, hoping to catch up with him near one of the two exits to the square. I still couldn't see him, so I jumped in the air, using peoples' shoulders to help propel me higher. Most gave me dirty looks and a few threatened my sexual organs, but I ignored them and kept moving. I wouldn't have been so adamant to catch him had he been just a normal pickpocket and taken my money, but I couldn't just let my pistol and flashlight float around the Roman Empire.

Leaping over a woman who had been trying her own "meat-on-a-stick" entrée, I finally spotted him fleeing from the square down a dark, narrow side street. As he ran, he spared a single glance in my direction, throwing me an upraised middle finger as he went.

There were many origin stories surrounding the genesis of that particular crude gesture, one of which theorized it went back as far as the Greeks, where it was specifically used as an insulting gesture. In Roman writing, the middle finger was known as the *digitus impudicus*, the impudent finger, and was commonly used as an insult. Seeing it used by a child in the days of the Roman Empire was annoying, but entirely humorous as well.

I ran as fast I could, feeling my legs begin to burn, a reminder that it had been weeks since I had last worked them out. I lost the kid again when he rounded a corner, but I was gaining on him. Unless he found someplace to hide, he was as good as caught. Turning the corner, I saw another right angled corner a few dozen meters in front of me that would take me to another major throughway.

I ran towards it, but just as I about to rush out into the adjoining plaza, I heard a shuffling noise behind me.

I stopped and turned around to see a large trash heap filled with thrown out clothing, furniture, food, and dead animals. Wonderful. Moving towards the dump, I wrinkled my nose at the putrid stench and noticed a spot in the pile that looked recently disturbed. Muttering in annoyance, I plunged my hand through the trash. When I felt something that could have been hair, I pushed deeper, grabbing what I thought felt like clothing and yanked as hard as I could. I was rewarded with the face of a kid who knew he was in big trouble.

For nearly a minute we simply eyed each other.

I estimated he had to be only twelve or thirteen years old, with short black hair and a dark complexion. He had a round face with bright blue eyes, but still looked more Roman than Eastern. As if on cue, the kid smiled at me and held up my stolen pistol and flashlight.

Grunting in annoyance, I lifted the kid out of the garbage, and put him down next to me. I retrieved my stolen goods and put them back in their proper spots in my bag. I looked down at him and gave him as stern a look as I could, until I realized I must have looked too much like my father when he went about scolding me, and my expression immediately softened.

"The only mistake you made," I began, "was turning back to look at me. Had you not done that, you would have made it."

The kid cocked his head to the side, his expression confused, probably wondering if I had lost my mind. The last thing a kid like him would think is that I would give him a lesson on how to better pickpocket people.

"And you never stop running," I continued, almost lecturing. "You run around the city twenty times before you finally duck into a safe spot. The quicker your pursuer loses track of you, the quicker he starts looking through the areas you've already been. The more distance you cover, the more places he needs to look."

The kid continued to stare, seemingly unwilling to say anything for fear that I might snap and break his neck.

"Who are you?" He finally asked, his voice still a prepubescent high.

"I'm nobody, kid," I said, a small smile forming at my unintentional reference to *The Odyssey*.

After Odysseus had poked out the eye of the dreaded Cyclops, Polyphemus, he told the creature that his name was "Nobody." When Polyphemus then went to his brethren, to tell them of Odysseus' horrible misdeeds, his only response to the question, "who did this to you," was "Nobody."

Of course he later yelled out from the safety of his ship that his name was, in fact, Odysseus, sparking the ire of Polyphemus' father, Poseidon, thus exacerbating all the troubles that already plagued him. But at least in that moment he had been a rather crafty devil.

"Nobody?" The kid asked. "Who do you think you are? Odysseus?"

I was shocked. How could I stay angry at a kid who knew his Homer?

"It warms my heart to discover that the youths of today are still keeping up with their schooling," I said sardonically and I couldn't help but laugh. Adults from all time periods in history must have used that line on the youngsters in their lives, never quite realizing just how bleak the future had been for all those jaded old people who lived hundreds of years before *them*. "So, educated youth, what is *your* name?"

The kid continued to look as though he were waiting for me to erupt at any moment.

"Xenophon," he replied, cautiously.

"That name has quite a bit of history behind it," I commented. "Mind explaining how a street urchin like you came by such a lofty name?"

Xenophon had been a fairly popular name throughout antiquity, but one particularly popular man named Xenophon had been a Greek explorer who traveled throughout the Persian Empire sometime around the fourth century B.C., dictating his experiences as he went. He was most famous for his time spent as the leader of the Ten Thousand, a mercenary group who fought through Mesopotamia to reach their home in Greece.

"I know all about Xenophon and his travels, old man," the child said squeakily and angrily. "I am not a stupid child you can pick on."

"Hey. Weren't you the one who just pick pocketed me? I have every right to insult you." I paused, and gave the kid a little shove. "And how does some common street criminal know his Homer as well as his history? Shouldn't you be hanging out with Aristotle or somebody?"

The boy opened his mouth wide and raised his hand as if to yell something back at me, but a third voice interrupted him.

"Who's your friend?" A voice that could only be Helena's asked.

I looked to my right, noticing her approach but did a double-take at what I saw. She wore native garb colored in dull yellows, oranges and reds, complete with a thin, see-through veil over her face. It had a distinctly eastern flair and style to it, one that reminded me of something from an episode of *I Dream of Jeanie*. I had fallen hard for Jeanie when watching reruns of the show as a kid, her scandalous attire and overt sexual undertones always getting my blood flowing, and Helena's sudden association with my childhood crush brought on such urges even now, and it didn't help that I knew Helena was available in ways Barbara Eden had never been.

"Who? This?" I asked nonchalantly, trying to play it cool as I glanced down at the thief. "Just some young punk who tried to rob me."

"I see," she said.

Ever since Xenophon had laid eyes on Helena, he hadn't been able to look away. His posture was sagged, his shoulders were slumped and his head was lulled longingly to one side as he stared at Helena strutting toward us. The kid's eyes never stopped moving. There was too much to see. His eyes darted from ample cleavage to legs clearly visible beneath the sheer fabric that hung tightly around her thighs and into Helena's eyes, which were gazing at the boy in a way that would melt any man's heart. The kid's mouth hung wide open and his tongue dangled from it. I rolled my eyes, then reached out and shut his mouth, snapping him from his trance. He shook his head and tried to focus.

I chuckled. I knew he had to have been experiencing one of those dreams meant only for the movies. The ones where the girl walks in slow motion, her eyes locked with your own as she slowly removes her clothing, purring that she wants you. It was always a great gimmick in the movies because few men could honestly deny not having had one of those dreams at one point in their lives.

Helena walked over and put her hands on my right shoulder, resting her chin upon them and tilting her head to give me a kiss on the cheek before scrutinizing Xenophon.

"So, dear, what should we do with this young thief?" She asked.

"I'm not sure," I replied, turning my head back towards Xenophon. "I hear authorities further east would cut off his hands for such a crime."

"Oh my…" Helena purred.

The boy scoffed, unimpressed at my threat and turned to simply walk away, but before he could take another step, I reached out and grabbed his shoulder, pulling him to a stop.

"Heel," I ordered.

I reached into my bag, and felt around for the last piece of gear I had brought with me. Finding what I was looking for, I pulled out my Balisong knife, more commonly known as a butterfly knife. I'd found it on a dead South American mercenary during an Op that took my SEALs and I deep into Brazil. Taking prizes from dead enemy combatants was frowned upon in the modern military, but it wasn't a trophy, it was a tool, and I had no problem admitting it wasn't the only thing I'd taken from the dead.

Philippine designed Balisong knives were pretty flashy in their presentation, especially when opening and closing. A skilled handler, which I'd become after a bit of practice, could manipulate the blade in a way that made it appear like they were twirling it in fancy patterns, known as "flipping".

So, just to scare the kid a bit, I pulled it out and twirled it in a figure eight pattern a few times before allowing the safety latch to catch the two handles together, securing the knife in its open position. I looked him in the eye, waiting for him to meet my inspection before I shifted my look toward his hand, Helena still casually hanging from my shoulder. I gently gripped his arm and tapped the blade against his wrist. I nicked him on my third tap, drawing a bit of blood to pool around the injury, and I felt Helena's hands tighten upon my shoulder. I ignored her and continued looking the kid in the eye, noting as he winced at the quick jolt of pain.

But on my fourth tap, I released his hand and went through an intricate pattern to close the knife. Once it was closed, I tossed it in the air and caught it in my other hand, holding it there for a few seconds before tentatively extending it towards the boy. Xenophon gazed at it with glazed eyes, not knowing what to do, so I shook it a bit to grab his attention. He held out his hand cautiously and took the knife from me, looking at it in wonder. He held it in both hands, opening it carefully before closing it again.

"Why?" He asked.

I cocked my head to the side. "Honestly, I haven't got a clue. Just take it and get the hell out of here, kid. And leave the pick-pocketing to the professionals from now on."

Xenophon smiled and quickly ran off to find someone to show his new toy.

"Why did you do that?" Helena asked from my shoulder.

I shrugged her off, stepping around to face her.

"Like I told him, I really don't know." I sighed. "Maybe I'm just getting soft, but at least he knew his history."

"If only we could all show such promise," she joked as a thought came to her. "You do realize you just gave a piece of modern technology to a child... not to mention that it was a sharp knife."

"I think he can handle himself," I said. "Besides, what's the worst that can happen? Some inventor doesn't make his millions from the patenting of his precious little knife two thousand years from now?"

"Well, yes, as a matter of fact."

"I…" but I couldn't think of a response. Maybe I actually didn't care what happened to the timeline anymore. Was there even a reason to care? "…whatever. Let's just go."

She nodded silently, but her look said enough. We turned and walked out onto the main street in the direction of our apartment. She tried to hold my hand as we walked, but I pulled away and looked off into the crowd. A hurt look crossed her face.

"Are you all right?" She asked.

I didn't look at her. "I'm fine."

"Still upset about what happened on the barge."

Her comment came out like a statement rather than a question.

"It's not just that," I replied honestly. "I mean, yeah, that part weighs the heaviest, but it's not everything. It… it doesn't excuse the way I treated you before it ever even became a problem, nor how I've treated you since."

"Sometimes people just need their space and that's okay. This is one of those instances, but how many times do we have to go over this? Everyone makes mistakes. Even you." I felt her fingers attempt to intertwine themselves with mine once again. Her hands were so soft and welcoming that I accepted the gesture this time. Her fingers slotted between my own and she squeezed fiercely. She leaned in close. "*Especially* you. At least you *seem* to be learning from them."

I smirked at the quip, knowing without seeing that she was smiling as well, and allowed myself to relax. I brought our joined hands to my lips and kissed her hand gently, looking down at her as I did so. She was in fact smiling and decided to use that moment to snuggle her head against my shoulder. Despite everything, I decided that, for the moment, it was best to keep my mouth shut and let it be just that: a moment.

We strolled casually through the streets of ancient Byzantium, the surrealism one would expect gone after years saturated in a surreal world. There truly was nothing right about the life we had been thrust into, but if one thing felt natural it was having Helena on my arm. To quote an empty platitude – life's too short – something I should have realized long ago because in this moment, life certainly felt complete, and I allowed myself the opportunity to absorb it. The sky was blue, the sun warm and no one was trying to kill me. That alone was reason enough to…

Suddenly and without warning, Helena shoved me into a door frame with enough force to knock the wind out of me. I stumbled forward a step as I caught my breath, but before I could ask her what the hell she was doing, she tackled me into the door again, planted her lips on mine, and started making out with me like a drunken prom date.

Without another thought, I closed my eyes and drank in long lost smells and tastes that had eluded me for far too long. They were intoxicating, possessing my mind with happier thoughts than I deserved, but there was something particularly different about how Helena was currently kissing me. It lacked the passion and intensity she normally brought with her, as though it were all just for show. I opened my eyes and noticed how her own weren't focused on me, but on the street. I decided to roll with it and wait for her to make the next move.

Nearly a minute later, she tugged on my tunic to pull me from the door, making it appear like we were passionately switching positions, with me pressing her against the door this time. She continued raining kisses on me, but with less vigor now, just enough for me to speak.

"Not that I mind, but…"

"Shhh," she whispered, as her teeth tugged at my lip. She moved her head to the side of my neck and spoke softly into my ear. "I noticed two men down the road staring at us. Don't worry, I didn't make eye contact, but I knew they were looking at us. I figured we could play dumb and duck in here."

"How very James Bond of you," I said, the first joke I'd told in months.

She pulled away from my ear and planted another long kiss on me, this one with the feeling and intensity I'd come to expect over the years.

She pulled away again. "I swear, if we ever make it home, we need to watch those movies because I never have any idea what you're talking about!"

I chuckled at her ignorance of movie gold.

"What about your two marks?" I asked.

She glanced over my shoulder again, scanning the passing traffic as she nipped at my neck. Besides a pair of giggling teenage girls pointing at us and a mother shielding the eyes of her two young children, no one else seemed to be paying us any attention.

"Looks like they're gone," she reported, pulling me out of the doorframe by my tunic and dusting off my shoulders. She wiped the corners of her mouth and looked at me naughtily. "Let's save some of that for later, Lieutenant."

I always loved it when she called me by my rank. I smiled and inhaled deeply, trying to determine what part of my mind had convinced me that I couldn't trust this woman.

I wanted to know so that I could have Wang surgically remove it after we found him.

I fought for an answer to a question that demanded one, but could find nothing. There wasn't a rational part of my mind that could explain away the fact that I had been simply too dimwitted to trust her. The only things I'd needed were a few kisses, a rush of adrenaline and the use of my rank to turn my whole life around. It made me wish Helena had taken the initiative on her own earlier, but I trusted that she knew better than anyone when I needed space and when I was ready for help.

I reached out to grab her shoulders and pull her close again, but out of the corner of my eye, I noticed two men who could only be the ones she'd spotted earlier. One was staring right at us while the other scanned in the other direction as though he was covering his friend. I tried to look away but like an idiot, and unlike Helena, I couldn't help but make eye contact.

The man reacted instantly, yelling to his friend as he rushed towards us through waves of busy locals.

Aw, shit.

"Come on!" I yelled, pulling Helena's arm as I took off.

Her confusion lasted all but a second as the men approaching left subtlety behind with their first step, and Helena fell into pace with me immediately. She only made it a few meters before she stumbled, her loose outfit flowing over her feet and tripping her up. In response, she tore off the outer garment, revealing a shorter silken skirt beneath that flowed loosely along her upper thighs. One of her first lessons in survival had been to always be prepared, and it was nice to see she came ready to bug out quickly if needed.

The two men were dressed like any other locals but something in their faces seemed familiar as well. Their eyes were cold.

Calculating. Roman. Praetorian. I knew I had the means to stop them at any time with my Sig, but that would defeat the purpose of us lying low. I pulled out my radio instead.

"3-3, 3-1, over."

Nothing.

"3-3, come in."

"No, Santino?" Helena asked, sidestepping a small child and his mother before returning to my side.

"Guess not," I said, tossing the radio back in my bag.

"Never around when you need him, always around when you don't."

I didn't answer, but kept running as I followed just behind her. We'd moved well beyond the bazaar and into a more residential area of the city, but there were still hundreds of people milling about in the streets going about their daily business. I didn't waste time looking behind me as I tried to maintain a good pace while simultaneously avoiding civilians. Helena grabbed my hand and yanked me down a side street with nothing but a single vendor stall. As I ran by, I pulled it to the ground with a small exertion of strength. It toppled easily and would maybe buy us another few seconds.

The anger of an angry merchant was a price I was willing to pay for them.

Helena pulled out in front of me again and I saw her hop onto an empty crate, followed by a jump to a second story balcony, before making a final leap, just far enough to get a grip on the ledge of the roof. Hauling herself up effortlessly with a simple exertion of strength, she waited for me to join her. Having passed the first crate, I kept running until I reached the wall that dead ended the alleyway. Instead of turning right down another alley, I leapt and planted my foot against the wall, pushing myself off with all my strength. I found a handhold on the frame of a window and hauled myself up, Helena helping me scale the wall and onto the roof.

I took a moment to analyze the terrain, noting that the rooftops around us were of different height, but mostly at our level. Like many homes in the Middle East during the modern age, they were close together and easily traversable. I looked back to see the pair pursuing us trip and fall as they ran full bore into the vendor stand, tangling themselves in the stall's wooden beams and cloth canopy. I considered taking them out with my pistol when Helena yanked on my sleeve and I saw other figures on a rooftop a few homes away from us. They were dressed in the same black ninja suits as the men who attacked Santino and me on Agrippina's barge. Helena's attention had shifted to the right, and I noticed another group of four there as well.

This was idiotic. Running from ninjas across the rooftops of Ancient Byzantium?

Who comes up with this stuff?

I was so fucking sick of Ancient Rome.

"Come on," I said, pulling Helena again. "Got anything in that bag of yours that won't draw any attention?"

"No," she answered.

"Great. Time to go hot then," I said, pulling out my suppressor equipped Sig P220. I planted my feet, turned and took a knee, observing at least a dozen black clad ninjas running towards us from three different angles. I unloaded half a dozen rounds at the center group before popping off my remaining rounds at the group coming in from our left.

I stood and ran, unloading the spent magazine into my bag as I went. When I turned again, there were a handful of bodies dead or dying on the roofs, but those who remained had spread out, making them very hard to hit while on the run.

I swore and shoved my pistol back in my bag, realizing I needed speed over firepower now. Distracted, I didn't see a low lip jutting out over the edge of the building we were currently traveling on. Just before I made my small leap to the next building, my toe tripped on it and I went sailing through the air. Thankfully, I cleared the small gap but landed roughly on my shoulder. I did a quick roll, got to my knees, and allowed Helena to help me up.

She shook her head, but for once didn't comment on my klutziness.

We ran from our pursuers, leaping over a number of small gaps between rooftops, but we were quickly running out of real estate. I could see the eastern walls of Byzantium and the Bosporus beyond them. We needed to get back down to street level, but we couldn't just leap off. We were far too high. We needed another route down.

Perhaps it was best for us to continue on high ground. If we had to get into a firefight, it was better to be up here than down in a killzone like a narrow street. Then again if we were at street level, maybe we'd be able to lose our pursuers like Xenophon had attempted mere...

Helena grabbed my hand with one of her own and pointed with the other. "Get ready to jump!"

I followed her upraised arm and spotted a building to our right, on the far side of the street, with a second level doorway and a balcony. If we timed it just right, Helena and I should be able to jump to the top of those stairs and make our way into the home.

"Are you crazy??" I shouted.

She didn't answer as she stumbled again. When she recovered, she sent a painful glance at her feet, and I realized why she wanted to get off the roofs so quickly. Her weakly constructed sandals had come off and she'd been running on bare feet for quite a while. Every step she took left a series of small blood stains behind her, a painful trail that was easily followed.

I didn't have time to think of a way to help.

Ten steps remained between us and the jump. I risked another glance over my shoulder to see our ninja buddies still behind us but gaining. With four steps to go, Helena stumbled again, her feet unable to continue supporting her. I snagged her arm and brought her in close. One step remained, and with a surge of energy, we were flying through the air, our legs kicking beneath us as we fought for distance. Below us, residents looked up at a pair of flying morons who had just jumped off a roof, most of the men's attention on Helena. On our way down, I realized we had over jumped, and we'd have little time to stop ourselves before slamming into the door.

I came down first, still holding Helena's hand. My knees instinctually buckled into a roll, Helena's body reacting similarly. I hit first, but the heavy wooden door only bucked under my weight. In typical fashion, the damn thing must have been dead bolted into the frame, and I felt something crack in my chest as well as in the door frame. Helena slammed into it a half second later, her added mass and momentum enough to smash the door open on its already broken hinges. She let go of my hand and managed to swiftly roll inside, while I had to scamper on my hands and knees, trying to follow.

Once inside, I kicked the door shut, plunging us into darkness. I stood, but my first step failed to meet solid ground and realization dawned on me that I was about to fall down a flight of stairs. Helena, unfortunately, had risen to her feet on the third or fourth step down, oblivious to the fact that I was about to fall on her. I was already on my way down before I could think to warn her, and gravity did the rest.

We fell together, tumbling over one another and banging ourselves against everything that got in our way. The nausea-inducing tumble ended when I hit the floor first, summersaulting head over heels before my back slammed against the opposite wall, the back of my head following suit. My body collapsed on its own accord and I slid on my butt so that only my head rested against the wall. Stars sprang into my mind and my vision darkened, but I could still make out the shape of Helena as she barreled her way towards me. I tried to move out of the way as she landed hard on her side, her left hip thwacking against the floor loudly. She started to roll, hitting my shins first before her momentum propelled her up and then down onto my chest. She landed on me perpendicularly, her lower back resting on my abdomen.

My head throbbed as blood trickled down the back of my neck and I found it difficult to breath, Helena's presence upon my chest only hindering the process. Instinctively, I placed one hand against her shoulder, the other against the side of her hip, and pushed her off me with little thought of how her own body would react.

My breathing eased almost immediately.

I finally allowed myself to look at Helena, concluding she seemed mostly fine. Besides her bleeding feet, any additional cuts and bruises seemed minimal, and none of her limbs appeared broken, but I couldn't know for sure.

Her clothing hadn't fared nearly so well.

Most of her outfit had been made out of a thin silk-like material – not overly durable – and had been torn to shreds during our run, leap and fall down the stairs. At least she'd had the sense to wear her modern undergarments beneath, her sports bra and tight short shorts basically all she had left.

She began to cough uncontrollably where she lay, doubling over in pain on the ground. She curled into a ball and clutched her side before a spasm forced her to uncurl and arch her back so violently that I feared she'd fold in half in the wrong direction. Every muscle in her body seemed contorted and close to bursting from her skin at the exertion. For a moment I thought she was experiencing a seizure, but the muscles at the small of her back loosened and her body relaxed. She curled into a fetal position again and wrapped her arms around her stomach to stave off the pain, the latest painful throes of yet another of her attacks ebbing away.

I crawled as fast I could to her side and flipped her onto her back, hoping beyond hope that she was still conscious. When she opened her eyes, I saw them full of pain and, as ever, directing pure rage at me and me alone.

"How… in the name… of God, have you survived… your life, Jacob?!" She yelled through her agony, punching me square in the jaw to punctuate her words. "You have to be the biggest klutz on the entire planet, from now until the goddamned future and everything in-between!"

I held a hand to my sore jaw and forced myself to keep from smiling. A moment later, I held out my other hand, indicating that she shut up when I heard a banging noise above us. Our leap of faith had to have thrown off some of those chasing us, but it seemed like someone had come to inspect our house.

Helena got the point quickly and I helped her to her feet as she fought off the last of the pain. Together, we shuffled over to a dark corner of the house. I heard voices from the level we had just vacated and hoped for a miracle that there was only a few of them. I retrieved my Sig from the floor, my bag having spilled its contents everywhere, and quietly reloaded it, thanking God I'd left a bullet in the chamber so I didn't have to make any noise pulling back the slide. Helena retrieved a small knife from her own bag.

"Let's try and take these guys alive," I whispered, my adrenaline pumping once again. "Find out who the fuck they are."

She nodded and scampered off to hide beneath the stairwell, waiting for the men to come downstairs. I waited as well, crouching in the shadows directly to the left of the stairs. I tried to take a deep breath to calm my nerves but winced after just a quick one. I needed to get my chest taped up soon or I'd be having serious trouble breathing pretty quickly.

The voices upstairs stopped, and I heard them shuffle towards the stairs. Not a second passed before the first set of black footed men descended to our level, passing Helena without a thought as to what lurked beneath the stairs. The man stopped on the landing and waited, scanning the dark room with eyes that hadn't had enough time to develop their natural night vision. As a result, he failed to notice my presence mere feet from him in the dark corner, and I made my move.

I sprung from my hiding place and grabbed him by the neck with my arm. I brought my hip into his body and tossed him to the ground. I placed a hand against his face and smashed the back of his head into the floor to keep him quiet. I snapped my head around to see Helena grab the feet of the second man before he could reach the bottom of the stairs. He tripped and fell, knocking his head into the wall as he went. He crashed onto the floor and Helena was on top of him in an instant. She rested her knife against his neck, and I was just about to order her to cut his throat, just to scare my guy a little, when he cut me off with the use of my name.

"Hunter! Wait!"

I looked down at the man I had subdued and wondered who the hell he could be. I reached down to pull his mask off to reveal a very familiar face.

"Gaius!" I practically screamed, looking down at one of my closest Roman friends. I looked over and saw Helena pull off her own victim's mask to reveal my other friend, Marcus.

I was stupefied. What the hell were they doing here?

I turned back to Gaius. "What in the name of almighty Jove are you doing here?!"

Gaius looked scared shitless as he coughed in pain. "That, my old friend, is a very long and interesting story."

***

Relative to the rest of the day, our trip back to our apartment had been rather dull.

Once our initial confusion had worn off, Gaius and Marcus had been quick to assure us that they were not our enemies. According to them, they hadn't had any idea they were chasing Helena and me until I pulled my gun on them. They hadn't been much more forthcoming than that so far, indicating they needed the relative safety of our apartment before they could explain themselves.

I agreed, and the four of us had made our way back to Santino and the safe house. Before we left, Helena spent a few minutes rummaging through the lady of the house's collection of clothing. She hadn't found much, but she'd managed to pilfer a black robe for herself. The last thing we needed was for her to walk down the streets in her underwear. That would draw far too much attention.

After donning her new outfit, I helped her limp along to the house. I bandaged her feet with the limited medical supplies I had in my bag, but each step had to be like stepping on glass for her. We also had to take a moment to wrap Marcus' sprained ankle, a result of his tumble down the stairs. Finally, even though I needed it for my own head, I offered Gaius the disposable cold pack from my med-kit. The only thing we couldn't fix was my cracked rib. It would have to wait, even though every breath I took felt like someone was sticking a knife into my lungs, and every step hurt more than the last. After the time it took us to find our way home, it wouldn't have surprised me to discover that my lungs had been shredded to pieces, but a lack of blood in my mouth quelled those fears.

What I couldn't divine, however, was if any of Gaius and Marcus' comrades were following us. The two Romans claimed to be on our side, and I really wanted to believe them, but it was hard to trust anyone these days. If only we had Santino's UAV to provide rear reconnaissance. Instead, I had to settle for surreptitious glances over my shoulder as we rounded corners and pushed our way through people. I hadn't noticed a tail so far, but that didn't guarantee our trip wasn't being watched.

Twenty minutes later, our apartment was within sight. We passed by the waiting wenches hanging around outside and in the hallways and stairwells, each giving Helena an annoyed glance as we passed by. These particular whores would have rated very low on any man's scale, and they knew if Helena tried to bust in on their action, they'd be put out of business quickly.

At the end of a long hallway on the third floor of the building, we found our door, opened it, and went inside to find Santino leaning back in a wooden chair, his bare feet on the table, apparently spending his time counting something on the ceiling. He turned his head to see what the commotion was, but because Helena and I weren't the first ones in, he flew into action when he didn't immediately identify Gaius or Marcus.

In one swift move, he fell off his chair, and rolled under the table, flipping it on its side to rest it in front of him. The next thing I saw was his HK416 pointed in our direction, which he kept duct taped to the bottom of the table for this very reason. Helena had her P90 hidden under Santino's bed, and I kept *Penelope* over the door inside the apartment's sole bedroom.

"Get down," Santino yelled from his defensible position.

"Stand down," I ordered, but all the same, stepped out of his line of fire. "It's Gaius and Marcus."

"Gaius and Marcus?" He asked no one in particular. The two men entered the room, shutting the door behind them in silence.

Our apartment was small and rectangular. The wooden table sat just across the small open space from the door, with a fair sized bed to the right of the entrance. The only other furniture in the room was a single wardrobe between the bed and the door. To the left of the entrance was a small room with another bed.

I hauled Helena over to Santino's bed, sat her down and began the process of removing her blood soaked bandages.

"I recall telling you a long time ago that you weren't allowed to get hurt anymore," I told her, pulling out an iodine pad to clean her wounds.

"Right," she answered. "You said only you were allowed to get hurt."

"You're breaking the rules," I quipped, holding her foot still as she winced at the cold sting. "Again."

"Jacob, if I only let you get hurt, you'd be dead a thousand times over by now, probably from your own damn clumsiness."

"Good point," I conceded, spraying some antiseptic on her wounds and wrapping a gauze bandage around it. I finished her left foot first before starting work on her right. Meanwhile, Gaius helped Santino turn the heavy wooden table back on its legs. Santino gave him a proper handshake, grasping his forearms just below the elbow, while giving Marcus a friendly bear hug, lifting the smaller Roman off his feet. Marcus had saved Santino's life the day Caligula had been poisoned, and they'd bonded immediately.

I finished with Helena's second foot as Santino poured steaming cups of tea for each of us.

"I'd stay off your feet for at least a day," I recommended to Helena, giving them one last look over.

"A whole day?" She asked, feigning disappointment. "What ever will I do for a whole day with nothing to do? In bed?"

"Don't get any ideas," I joked with a sly smile, before turning to Santino. "Hey, Santino, toss me Wang's medical kit."

He nodded and went to retrieve the enormous bag Wang had put together years ago. We had more medical supplies than we knew what to do with, but those were stored away. Wang's bag, however, had everything we could ever need at moment's notice, and everything was organized so that I could find whatever was needed by touch alone.

I pulled out two giant rolls of gauze, dropped the bag to the floor and handed them to Helena. I took my shirt off and noticed a large bruise starting to swell exactly where my breathing hurt.

"I think I cracked a rib," I told her. "Wrap me up good and tight."

She gave me a very annoyed look. I hadn't mentioned my injury earlier and she must have been getting very tired of patching me up these days. She reluctantly rested the end of the gauze against my chest and started to wrap.

"Next time you want to talk about me getting injured, you'd better think again," she said matter of factly.

"I just wanted to…"

My response was cut short when she pulled the gauze tight around my chest. This time it felt like Santino had shoved his scimitar through my rib cage.

"Never mind," I wheezed. "I'll just shut up now."

Helena nodded curtly, offering me a *humph*.

Ignoring the increasing pressure and pain Helena was inflicting upon my chest, I tried to ease myself into a comfortable sitting position. Santino pulled his chair near the bed while she worked on me, and Gaius and Marcus joined us as well. We all just stared at each other, everyone wondering the same thing.

"So what the hell are you guys doing here?" Santino asked, never one for awkward silences and always speaking what was on everyone else's mind.

Both members of Agrippina's Sacred Band squirmed in their chairs, before Gaius, the slightly older of the two, stood and paced around the room. Only a year or so younger than me, his face was hard, like any Roman soldier's and seemed far older than even my own, which had seemed to age a decade in the past few years.

His chiseled features, small nose, inquisitive eyes, dark hair and perpetual five o'clock shadow gave him a look that belonged on the cover of a Harlequin romance novel, even if he was only five and a half feet tall. Like Marcus, he was short by modern standards, but his height was ideal for his kind of work. Marcus had a similar complexion, but his face was round and more akin to cheery expressions.

Gaius was still pacing, so I gave him some prompting.

"Why don't you start with…" but I winced again when Helena adjusted her wrapping to go around my right shoulder.

"Sorry," she apologized.

I gave her a doubtful look before turning back to Gaius. "Why don't you start with why you're dressed like that and why you and your buddies seem so… not Roman."

"Well, Hunter," he said nonchalantly, flipping a hand over his shoulder, "you have *you* to thank for that."

"Me?" I asked.

"All of you," he answered, never one for nonsense. "Agrippina had some interesting ideas for her new Sacred Band after you fled Rome. Ideas she learned from you. She had these black suits fashioned after your own combat clothing, although obviously not as advanced, and ordered us to develop a new fighting method that made us more spies and assassins than soldiers. We even work in pairs, just like you do, as well as in a larger group of eight people. An *octetus*."

I assumed an *octetus* was the term for their new squad, taken from the Roman term *octet* – eight legionnaires who shared a tent in a legion camp.

"We may not have your rifles or gear," he finished, "but we have groomed ourselves into a formidable group."

"So," Santino mumbled, pinching the sides of his forehead, "Agrippina has some grand idea for better bodyguards and makes you figure out for yourselves how to do it?"

I raised a hand in the air. "What part of that was confusing?"

Santino shrugged. "Just inefficient is all. And lazy on her part."

"Basically, you are correct," Gaius clarified. "She gave us very loose orders to develop something more akin to your method of waging war. Subterfuge, infiltration, stealth… assassination. We were to become something she could use more indirectly than a legion. We borrowed heavily from what you taught us during our days in the *Primigenia's* camp, but also hired out experts from Persia, Egypt, Germany, India, and as far as the Orient to teach us whatever techniques they knew."

"Very thorough," I complimented.

"What about you two?" Helena asked. "Why is it that of every member of the Sacred Band, you two are a part of this new group of thugs?" She paused to tie off my wrap as tightly as possible. "There, Jacob. I also recommend that you stay off your feet for a day or so," she finished as she slid off the bed to sit next to me, her shoulder touching mine.

Gaius and Marcus looked at each other before Marcus spoke up from his chair.

"We are not embarrassed to admit that we are… well… in awe of you. From the day you defended Caligula with your life, owing him nothing, we both knew you were something special. Our only regret is that we know we'll never be as good as you are."

"You two handle yourselves just fine on your own," Santino offered. "You're handier with a blade than I am, and that's saying something."

"True," Gaius answered, now leaning on the back of his chair, "but you have abilities we don't even understand. That is why when Agrippina called for volunteers for her new unit, we left our command positions and spent the next few years after you left training. Our entire force was ready only a year ago."

"So if you're not Praetorians, then who are you?" I asked.

"We have no name," Gaius said with a slight shake of his head.

"Right," Marcus picked up, right where his friend left off. "We are still technically members of the Sacred Band, and will serve alongside the Empress should we need to go to war, but unofficially we are on special assignment. We have no new title, and while we no longer carry the rank of *primus prior*, we are still Praetorians."

"Interesting," I said.

It really was. Here was another deviation from the timeline. Rome had always employed assassins, thieves, and spies, but never had there been an official group of well-trained ones, specifically not on the payroll of the empire. As far as I knew, they'd never had anything akin to something like the CIA or the Hashishin employed by the Ottomans. Not only that, but they were using fighting techniques we had taught them, and being the crafty Romans they were, had built upon them, probably creating something pretty impressive. A head of state with these men at their disposal, especially since they were so devoutly loyal, as the Sacred Band most surely was, would have quite an asset at her disposal.

No one said anything for some time.

"I think the real question," Helena said slowly, "is what are you doing in Byzantium, if you're not trying to kill us?"

That *was* a great question. I shifted my look from her to the Romans, waiting for their response. Both men glanced at one another once again, looking very worried. Gaius sighed, moved around his chair, and retook his seat.

"We're looking for the orb," he said.

"Whoa, whoa, whoa," Santino said, punching out open hands with each "whoa", "you mean the blue one? The one that got us here?"

"You mean as opposed to the red one?" Helena joked, inciting Santino to smirk at her.

"The one that there are actually two of," I reminded.

"That is correct," Gaius continued. "We seek the orb stolen on the battlefield just after Rome was retaken in Caligula's name. No one is sure where it is, but one of our tasks is to find it and retrieve it for the Empress. She has given us substantial free reign to track it down and obtain it, however we see fit."

"You mean steal it back?" Helena scoffed.

"That was not to be our first approach, no," Marcus answered. "We hoped to purchase it legally."

"That is correct," Gaius said. "We have a lead here in Byzantium, and the two of us along with the rest of our *octetus* have been asking around the city for any further information."

"So we ask again," I said, insistently. "Why were you chasing us?"

"We were not lying when we said that we didn't know it was you until you fired on us," Gaius assured. "We work in eight person squads and there are three *octeti* here. The way we work is with one pair from each squad blending in with a crowd, while the other six shadow them on rooftop in this clothing. These are permanent postings. Our two crowd operatives were chosen for that roll because they are well versed in numerous languages, while we are not. Additionally, to keep our chain of command succinct and efficient, those two are in command of the *octetus*, and are privy to more information. They must have either been given secondary orders by the Empress to capture you, or they recognized you from your Wanted posters scattered around the empire. When we saw them chasing you, all we saw was a man and a scantily clad woman, and followed as best we could."

Everyone looked at Helena and smiled. She blushed, and pulled the edges of her robe near her breasts tighter together, not that she was showing much before anyway. She looked around awkwardly before settling on the floor. Santino reached out and nudged her knee playfully, but she ignored him.

"Please understand," Gaius said, rising to his feet again. "We do not have much time. We need to get back or our unit will become suspicious."

I stood as well.

"Gaius, listen to me. I don't know what Agrippina has told you about the orb, but it's dangerous. It's the reason we're here in the first place. You know this. You were there the night we arrived. We..." I checked myself before continuing, looking at my friends first, remembering that whatever we decided tonight would affect them both as well. Maybe Helena was right and I was learning.

I turned to Santino first, whose expression was blank, no emotion either serious or juvenile evident, but when I looked at Helena, all I saw was how tired she was. Not from the day's exertions, but from years spent on the run, with no hope. Her face had to be a mirror of my own.

I felt it too.

She gave me a supportive smile.

I turned back to Gaius. He was waiting respectfully, but expectantly.

"We want to go home," I said in a dour tone. "We've overstayed our welcome. Had Caligula survived, we might have found a place here, but instead, we're public enemy number one, with nowhere to go. All we can do is run, and we can't do that for much longer."

I looked at my hands, palms up, and felt for the first time just how much I wanted to go home. To see my sister again. My SEALs. Hell, even my father. I had to imagine there was still hope left, time to fix what we'd broken and somehow find a way back to the world we had left. A way to control my future. But, as I stood there, that hope was becoming harder and harder to recognize. For all we knew the orbs were useless and the future, unrecognizable.

Helena got up from the bed, standing on the sides of her feet gingerly, and waddled over to where I stood. She moved to my right, gripped my hand in both of her own, and gave it a squeeze. I looked at her and saw nothing. I didn't need to. I turned back to Gaius.

"We need your help," I told him, wrapping my arm around Helena's waist. "If you find out anything about the orb, please, come to us first. We need to at least try and make it work. If it doesn't..."

I couldn't even think of what else to say. If it didn't work, we had no other choice but to destroy it, therefore eliminating our chances of ever getting home.

Gaius looked thoughtful, as did Marcus, but they didn't even take a second to consider what I'd said. Instead, Marcus moved toward the door, while Gaius approached Helena and me. He stopped an arm's span away, reached out, and gripped Helena's right arm and my left. The small Roman stood well below my chin and Helena's nose, but I thought no less of him because of it.

"My friends," he said, "we know you had nothing to do with Caligula's death, despite Agrippina's thoughts otherwise, and have wanted to help you ever since. If we find it, we will tell you."

"Just like that?" I asked. "No strings attached?"

He cocked his head to the side. "No, no strings. Why would there be? But yes, 'just like that.' Marcus and I have heard reports of your deeds over the years, and while we would like nothing more than to have you continue your kind work, we understand how much you must miss wherever you're from, especially with the Empress searching for you. We want to help."

With that, he stuck out his forearm, which I slowly gripped just before the elbow.

"Thank you," I told him, still shocked by how easy that was.

"You are welcome, Hunter."

Santino's face remained blank, even though I knew he wanted to go home just as much as any of us, but Helena's was filled with emotion as she tried to contain just how happy she was at the news. To show her thanks, she leaned forward and kissed Gaius on the cheek, smiling as she pulled away, as was Gaius, who had finally received that kiss I knew he'd always wanted. Every Praetorian and legionnaire alike had had a bit of a crush on her, despite concealing it behind all that "Mother of the Legion" garbage they'd used four years ago.

Marcus didn't seem too happy by the door.

Gaius let go of my arm and moved to join him.

Before they left, he glanced over his shoulder.

"Do not leave the city and don't wander about it. We will find you."

And with that, they left.

Helena and I stood there, transfixed by the possibility of going home. We still had some history to fix and rewrite, but maybe we could really go home after all.

172

"Santino," Helena called, waiting a second for his attention to focus on her. "Maybe you should follow them and gather as much intel as you can."

"What? Gaius just said to stay put." He looked exasperated as Helena's expression failed to sympathize, and he continued. "Why am I always the one who has to go do this... go do that? I'm a person too, you know!"

"Because Jacob and I are too hurt to do it," she answered.

"But it sounds dangerous," he whined, stamping his feet. "I thought we were on vacation."

"Aren't you the one always claiming that you can sneak up on God?" I challenged, playing along with whatever Helena was thinking.

That got his attention. "You're goddamn right. Fine. I'll see what I can see."

He moved over to his wardrobe.

"What to wear, what to wear?" He wondered to himself, before automatically grabbing his night ops combat fatigues. He quickly slipped them on, pulled over more local wear, found his gear bag and left without another word.

I watched him go. "Why did you tell him to follow them?" I asked Helena. "We can trust them."

"I know we can," she said as she maneuvered herself to front of me and look up at me with large eyes, "but he'll be gone for hours. *Hours...*"

I looked down at her and watched as she slowly dropped her robe to the floor. As the heavy fabric pooled around her ankles, I tracked my gaze up her long legs, past her strong abdomen, and up into her eyes, strangely feeling those same butterflies I'd felt the very first day I'd met her. I saw every single scar on her body, the two major ones, as well as the other smaller ones she'd accumulated over the past four years, and couldn't care less. In my eyes, the woman was perfection personified. A true Aphrodite. I looked into her eyes as she unraveled her long hair, shaking loose her mane in a tumble of confusion. I hadn't seen her so exposed and with that look on her face in maybe a year.

"Wow," I managed to croak, still trying to reboot my brain. The only thing going on in there was a giant, red "Error" message flashing brightly and insistently.

She wrapped her arms around my neck, and pulled herself close, pressing her midsection against my abdomen.

I placed my hands on her hips and held her back just slightly.

"Helena, wait. Are you sure you want to do this? I mean, we still need to…"

"Will you shut up and take hint," she said, shaking her head inches away from my own. "I'm here, Jacob. Right now, and I'm not going anywhere. If you want to help yourself, now would be the time to start."

"I know, Helena, but you're the one who…"

"Jacob, just shut up!" She said stubbornly as she jumped off her bandaged feet and into my arms. Her grip tightened around my neck and I felt her long legs wrap tightly around my waist. She secured herself against my body and pressed her lips roughly against mine. She worked them against my own for a few minutes, and I felt more tension than I could ever hope for fall from my shoulders in droves. When she finally pulled away, she looked at me with her wonderful eyes and smiled brilliantly.

"I need this, Jacob, and you need this too. After everything we've been through, for now, let's just focus on this. We have all the time in the world to worry about the other stuff."

I returned her smile and finally reached down to cradle her by her backside, carrying her to our very small room, kicking the door shut behind me. I crossed the room in two short steps and gently laid her on the bed before removing my locally made trousers, revealing my favorite smiley faced boxers beneath. Helena rolled her eyes at them, especially since they'd accumulated quite a few holes over the years, and got to work removing the remainder of her own clothing – what little she still had left. It took her ten seconds, which seemed like a million years, but my patience was rewarded as she was now wearing nothing but a smile.

She leaned back against the bed, crossed her legs and held an arm across her chest to cover her breasts, beckoning me forward mischievously with a forefinger. I returned her smile with a goofy, Santino worthy grin, and practically flung myself at her with just enough restraint to protect my damaged chest. I planted my arms along either side of her waist and pressed my lips against hers with more vigor than even she had a few minutes ago. I felt her working her hands along my back towards my shorts, but just as she gave them a quick yank, I remembered something.

"Oh," I said, rolling off the bed, temporarily pulling up my boxers again. I made my way to the door and retrieved my bag. "I bought you something."

"Really?" She asked, surprised at the novelty of the idea.

"Sure," I said nervously, just hoping she didn't hate it. I pulled out the piece of silk cloth containing the necklace and tentatively handed it to her, tossing the bag under the bed. "I, uh… I hope you like it."

She accepted the present carefully, looking at it for a second before looking back at me.

"You bought this before I ran into you today?"

"Um… well, yeah." I replied, scratching the back of my head, trying, and failing, to play it cool. "I guess I wanted to surprise you."

She smiled at my awkwardness and went to work unfolding the flaps of cloth. Gently parting the final fold, she paused. Her face wasn't sad, angry, happy, or even surprised. She just sat there and stared at it, maybe wondering what to do with it. I started to wonder when she'd last been given a gift before realizing she'd probably never received one from anyone but her family before. I felt a twinge of guilt and sadness at the prospect. I was never able to really understand just how closed off and devoid of love her life had been before we met.

I was just about to say something reassuring when she looked back up at me, her mouth opening in a joyous grin. I almost thought she might cry, but she held back.

"It's beautiful, Jacob," she said, a brilliant smile blooming on her face as she looked back at it. "I… I love it. How much did it cost?"

I almost laughed. "Too much, but I figured you were worth it."

"Aw, that's sweet," she joked, before holding it up to the light, glancing at me deviously. "How much do you think it will go for back home?"

This time I did laugh. "I'm sure a museum will pay handsomely for it. Hell, with all the authentic crap we can pawn off back home, we'll probably be set up for life."

She smiled, and held it out to me. "Will you help me put it on?"

"Sure," I said, fiddling stupidly with the clasp that was apparently too complex for my fingers to operate. Finally getting it open, I reached around her neck, and secured it with more success than when I'd tried to open it. I pulled back and admired my handiwork. It fit wonderfully, dangling just within the nook between her breasts, the Byzantium symbol centered perfectly. With her necklace dangling seductively, she reached out and gripped my boxers, pulling me into bed beside her.

"I think it's time we finally picked up where we left off," she said cutely, finally finishing the job she started earlier with my boxers. She balled them up and threw them at my face. I smiled at her playfulness and caught them out of the air, throwing them aside

"You mean it's time to pick up where we left off months ago, right?"

"Of course," she replied, pulling me closer. "What would we do if we picked up any time before then? Sulk?"

"Golly you're so clever," I joked. "No wonder I haven't been able to resist you all this time."

She laughed and pushed me aside, climbing atop me and positioning herself on my hips. She reached out and grabbed my hands, guiding them along her hips until they cupped her backside. She let go and used my vulnerability to slap me lightly across the face, smiling as she did so.

"*That* wasn't very cute, Lieutenant Hunter."

I laughed through the sting of her assault and flipped her off of me and onto her back again, a playful squeal coming for her lips. She smiled at me as I gripped her hands and pinned them behind her head.

"Nope," I said. "It's because you haven't called me that in the past year."

"Well, Lieutenant," she said as she managed to free one of her hands from my grip. She placed it against my abdomen and slid it south, finding exactly what she was looking for. Her eyes flicked up, her mouth seductively ajar. "Then today is your very lucky day."

VI
Dealings

Mission Entry #6
Jacob Hunter
Byzantium, Thracia - July, 42 A.D.

We haven't baked any Welcome Home cakes quite yet, but we have a lead on the orb. Well, one of them anyways. The other is still with Agrippina.

Our old friends Gaius and Marcus ran into us during our stay here in Byzantium. They're on assignment to retrieve the orb that was stolen from Varus after the Battle for Rome. It turns out they're a part of those black ops boys that attacked Santino and me aboard Agrippina's ship as well. Apparently, they're some kind of Roman Special Forces outfit, trained and stylized to mimic what those of us from the future can do.

To combat us.

At least Gaius and Marcus still had their loyalties straight.

It didn't matter. What mattered was the orb. Once we have it, all we need to do is figure out how it's supposed to work, and we can go home. If we can't, we have no choice but to destroy it, along with the second one as well. Better we end its potential for trouble now, instead of waiting for something even worse than me to come through next time.

I just wish I knew how it worked exactly because all I have are theories.

Theories I'm not even ready to go into yet.

All we want to do is go home. We're so sick and fucking tired of Rome, and all its "glory and splendor," but we can't just leave. Not yet. We can't leave with Agrippina's claim to the throne lingering. Nor can we leave without Bordeaux, Wang, and Vincent... if they even wanted to go.

Our first priority was to get Agrippina away from Germany and all the chaos she's wrought there.

Oh, have I not mentioned that yet?

Well would you believe it? Agrippina's decision to take control of Vespasian's legion wasn't a great one after all.

No surprise there.

To Vespasian's credit, there was no way he could have foreseen the devastation she'd bring with her. Needless to say, she's a horribly inept commander, one prone to brash decision making and poor generalship. Not that it would have been easy campaign, anyway. Throughout Roman history, Germany had been one of the few provinces Rome had actively campaigned against that never completely fell under their control. Through stubbornness and determination, Germany remained relatively independent throughout Rome's existence. And despite initial gains by the legions over the past few months, making its well past the Rhine region, months of fighting had resulted in little progress at the cost of thousands.

Ironically, Agrippina's strategy mirrored that of the blitzkrieg, *developed by more modern Germans a half century before I was born in the original timeline. It called for a massive invasion force to simply push hard and fast in the direction it wanted to go, smashing everything in its way, striking so precisely and swiftly that the enemy had no chance to counterattack.*

That might have worked for Hitler, the douche that started our second world war, but he had access to tanks, trucks and planes, vehicles that could move far quicker than any Roman. Plus, he had a well-established infrastructure already in place to help logistically supply and feed the massive army that had exploded out of Germany in a manner of weeks. The Romans had no such infrastructure to work with. Germany was a hinterland for all intents and purposes, and Agrippina's blitzkrieg went against almost every rule in the Roman playbook.

A legion's strength did not come from the flexibility and discipline of its fighting men alone, but in their logistical genius as well. Romans built roads, constructed farms, erected forts – created infrastructure – as they campaigned both slowly and deliberately. Legions could move quicker than any other infantry based army in history, but they were also methodical. As they traveled, the land they walked on inherently became "Roman." They were always ready to receive reinforcements, supplies and dispatches from Rome itself, because they protected their asses.

Agrippina made no such preparations, and I had no idea why generals like Vespasian or Galba hadn't challenged her decision making. Probably because they feared her three cohorts of

Praetorians, not to mention the Sacred Band (which never left her side). They could overwhelm Agrippina's small bodyguard unit if they wanted to with the help of their <u>entire</u> legion... but it would cost them more than they'd want.

Maybe even their own lives.

I'd offer more on the campaign, but we only have sketchy information at this point, and no details pertaining to the battles themselves. I just wanted to point out how important it is to draw Agrippina away from the legions and let men like Vespasian and Galba take over. I wasn't sure how to do that, but I had a hunch that if we were to go after one of her precious orb's she might have something to say about it.

So, we needed the orb, and that's where Gaius and Marcus come in. Over the past few weeks, we've had intermittent contact with them via a series of dead drops we've established throughout the city. Their dispatches assure us that they're close to locating the seller of the orb. Once they do, they'll let us know and we'll go from there. Hopefully, we can just buy it, but something tells me it won't be that easy.

Oh, I guess I should also mention Helena and I are finally... finally... back to normal. More or less. We... made up a few weeks ago, and she's become a wonderful stress reliever. On another positive note, she hasn't lost an ounce of that craziness she brings with her to the bed...

What the hell am I doing?

Go read a romance novel.

As I put down my pen, I promised myself that was the last time I ever mentioned Helena and I in the journal. The thing was supposed to be a historical record of what was happening with us in case we never make it home, not a novel, and hopefully, once I got more details on the orb itself, it will become a technical manual for how the troublesome thing works. With some luck, if someone finds both manual and orb should we be unable to destroy it, they'll be smart enough to leave it well enough alone and get rid of it.

Still, it was probably nice to give it a more personal touch – make it more interesting for the ladies. They loved a good romance story. I wasn't quite sure if what Helena and I had was "good" or not, but I, at least, thought it was special. Besides, if we let Santino write the whole thing, we'd run the risk of alienating anyone above a fourth grade reading level and I still wanted a movie deal out of the whole thing.

Closing the journal yet again, I secured it and tossed it to Helena. She was sitting on our bed, keeping herself busy with something while I'd been writing at the table. Santino sat opposite me, balancing his knife on a fingernail. I watched him flip it in the air and catch it by its grip.

We were bored.

After our run in with our black clad nemeses, the three of us had limited our time outside of the apartment to a minimum. It was frustrating, because I couldn't visit my lovely lunch location, and I knew the meat-on-a-stick vendor had to miss me. The only time we went out was to get food and supplies, alone, and we never went to the same place twice. We did whatever we could to keep our identities hidden, knowing Agrippina's ninjas, for lack of a better term, were probably out there looking for us.

Night time was a different story.

Between midnight and dawn, against our Roman friends' advice, the city was our playground, and we took to it like Batman in Gotham City. Like modern day free runners, we'd climb, run and leap our way around the rooftops and walls, patrolling the city. We kept to the shadows, but we weren't perfect. It was only a few nights after Gaius and Marcus came to our room that we started hearing rumors on the streets about mysterious ghosts that scampered around on people's homes and disappeared the moment they were noticed.

High praise.

But we weren't just having fun. We were training and reconnoitering the city, working out bodies that had sat idle for far too long and looking in every nook and cranny we could find. We planned every escape route back to our room and every hideaway we could duck into at a moment's notice. If we had to run from those ninjas again, we didn't want to end up cracking anymore ribs in the process.

There was also the possibility that we would need to obtain the orb through less scrupulous means than a simple monetary transaction. If things went down the way we suspected they would, it would be at night, some place secluded, and there was absolutely no chance we would pull it off without a hitch. Statistics never lie, and since we've been in Rome, nothing has ever gone the way we planned.

It was currently 2330, and we were getting ready for our next nocturnal prowl. Boredom had been the only thing on the menu for the past ten hours, and now we were getting antsy. It was hard to explain the adrenaline rush that came with anything we did, but back home, as a SEAL, my time spent in the field had been some of the most exhilarating of my life. The amount of terror, anger, testosterone, and bullets that flowed freely during those missions had made my blood boil, and after every successful mission, the only thing I wanted was more.

I loved and hated what I did. It reminded me of a quote from the Roman poet Catullus who wrote: *I love and I hate. Why do I do this, you ask? I know not, but I am tortured by it.*

Living in a world consumed by war left few options to find fulfillment. One could sit back and wait for the inevitable or one could fight, waging an ever-losing battle to protect those who couldn't protect themselves. It was a bleak reality, and even though I despised killing, even when necessary, I couldn't deny the rush I felt every time the bullets started flying.

It invigorated me like nothing else.

Doing what we've done here in Rome was no different. Running around on rooftops, trying to avoid detection and spooking small children who just happened to be glancing out their window was just another way for me to get my kicks. Helena and Santino felt the same.

Santino had been in the military a few years longer than I had, and being a member of Delta was the ultimate adrenaline rush. The guy would walk into enemy territory and meander around like he was a local, trying to gain intel as he went. Exposed and alone, it had to be the most nerve wracking job on the planet.

Helena, on the other hand, had lived a life of luxury and opulence, even though it had hardly been a life worth living at all. Her first taste of combat, and the rush that went with it, came with our first operation back in 2021. She hadn't been involved in the infiltration part of the mission, which had its own kind of tension, but she'd told me months later, after we had gotten to know each other better, just how much of a rush it had been. She'd shot two wild drivers with two fantastic shots, and those, combined with a half dozen more conventional shots earlier in the night, had been the first kills of her life.

She hadn't been happy with what she'd done, but she did admit a certain amount of pride in her endeavors. She'd participated in an operation meant to capture or eliminate a man responsible for the deaths of hundreds of thousands, and had single handedly protected the lives of her teammates. Now that was something to be proud of. She'd grown hard over the years, perhaps in some ways, too hard, but at least she'd found a way to keep on loving me.

Without that, I had no idea where I'd be in this world.

Probably dead.

***

The boredom was *killing* me.

So much so that as my mind sat idle, unconsciously reminiscing about countless things, it was unable to register the fact that my chin was about to slip off the hand that supported it. A few seconds later, when it finally slipped, my mind had no explanation. I looked around, thankful that neither Santino nor Helena were paying me any attention. Helena had her back to Santino and me, slipping on her combat fatigues, while Santino tried to flip and catch his knife again, only to let it slip through his fingers. The knife implanted itself in the wooden floorboards and he snapped his fingers in defeat before retrieving it. He put it back in its sheath.

We were bored *and* antsy.

Then, all of a sudden, we heard the sound of overly seductive women trying to ensnare their next meal ticket. Not soon after came a series of insistent knocks on our door.

I immediately reached for Santino's HK416 beneath the table.

We weren't expecting company tonight.

"Wait!" Santino said emphatically, leaping from his chair and over the table in the direction of the door.

He walked carefully towards it and put an ear against it. I looked at Helena, who had put on her combat fatigues and was now leaning against our wardrobe, her arms crossed. She looked at me and shrugged.

Santino reached out tentatively and returned the knocks, two quick ones, pausing briefly before a third one. Almost immediately, a reply knock sequence came back, four knocks with a pause in between the first and second ones. Santino whistled the tune to "Hail, Britannia" with each knock.

I rolled my eyes while Santino opened the door. Gaius and Marcus rushed through.

"See," Santino said as he closed the door behind them. "These guys must watch their spy movies."

I ignored him and picked up my chair and moved it to the other side of the table, offering it to one of the Romans. I moved over to sit on the bed and Helena joined me while Santino sat with our visitors at the table.

"So?" I asked. "Any new developments?"

"Yes," Gaius answered. "We've found the seller and have already arranged a meeting with him."

"Great!" Santino exclaimed. "We'll get the thing tomorrow, have one last meat-on-a-stick, and be home in time for the Fourth of July."

"It's not that simple," both Gaius and I told him at the same time.

I looked at Gaius. "Wait... why not?"

"You did not think it would be as simple as approaching the dealer and purchasing it, did you?" Marcus asked.

"Well, no," I replied. "Things are rarely that simple."

"And they certainly won't be now," Gaius intoned. "Had we been the ones to track down the supplier, it may have been, but we were not. Another *Octetus* did. However, we were able to later inform the dealer that another buyer is present in Byzantium. You. He now expects to auction it off to both parties two nights from now."

"I assume the other buyer is one of your fellow Praetorians?" Helena asked.

"Correct," Gaius answered. "However, he has yet to be informed of this, and I do not look forward to telling him. He is an angry man."

"So we'll have an opportunity to bid for the orb two nights from now," I said, mostly to myself. I rubbed my chin with my hand before directing my attention back at Gaius. "You should know that if we are to participate in this auction, we will come ready. If we see any of your friends sneaking around, putting one of us at risk, we will kill them."

Gaius and Marcus exchanged glances.

"We know," Gaius answered, "but we also feel that we owe you this opportunity. Even at the expense of our partners."

"Honestly," Marcus interjected, "we have no feelings of friendship toward those men anyway. Very little of the original Sacred Band is still in active service, as most of Agrippina's new band replaced those whom Caligula enlisted. We have trained with them, yes, but in that time, Gaius and I always felt something off about them. Most of Agrippina's new Sacred Band seem... odd, in some way."

"In *what* way?" I asked.

"They're ruthless bastards," Gaius answered for him. "Before Agrippina, Caligula's Praetorians were honorable men. Men with valor and principals. Men from the legions. But Agrippina's recruited her new Praetorians from prisons and the streets, looking for criminals, cutthroats, and thieves."

"If I were you, I would be more afraid of being killed by them than by anybody else," Helena offered.

"One would think, yes," Gaius agreed, nodding approvingly at her. "But the empress is not stupid. She still has many loyal and honorable men in high places that keep this new breed in check."

Made sense.

"Where and when's this auction going down?" Santino asked, back to business.

"Two nights from now, an hour past midnight, outside the hippodrome at the southeast side of town," Gaius answered. "The dealer asks that each party only bring one representative, but with the range of your weapons and your communication abilities, that should not be a problem for you."

I smiled. "We'll be fine."

"Good," Marcus said, getting to his feet. "We have to go. We can't be gone long."

"Wait," I said, leaning back over the bed and grabbing a gear bag from behind it. I picked one up at random and rummaged around inside before I found what I was looking for.

"Take these," I said, holding out two small devices, each the size of a wallet. "If you find yourselves on the rooftops during the transaction, attach these to your clothing and open the shutter like this..."

I demonstrated how to open and close the shutter, which kept a rectangular bulb at the top of the blocky device hidden when closed.

Both Romans accepted their gifts, turning them over in their hands questioningly.

"Thank you, Hunter," Gaius said tentatively, "but what are they?"

"Here," I said, holding out a pair of NVGs for them to wear. I nodded at Santino, who doused the candles we had burning, plunging the room into darkness. "Put these on."

I couldn't see the Romans now that the lights had gone out, but when they managed to successfully place the goggles over their eyes, I heard one of them stumble into the door, while the other almost knocked me over, surprised at their newfound ability to see in the dark.

"This... this..." Marcus started.

"Is amazing," Gaius finished, his head glancing about wildly as he tried to drink in as much detail as he could. I waved in his direction, and he quickly came to his senses.

"Now," I said, "as you observed earlier, with normal eyesight, this device appears to do nothing. Now, watch with the night vision on."

I opened the shutter on one of the infrared strobe beacons, and waited for the reaction. I couldn't see a damn thing, but with the help of NVGs, the infrared strobe must have been flashing as brightly as lightning for the two Romans. Infrared strobe beacons were worn by pilots in case they were shot down, and carried by soldiers either for rescue purposes or simple identification at night.

Exactly how I intended Gaius and Marcus to use them.

"The strobe emits a very bright light with those goggles on," I explained. "If you wear these, we will be able to see you, and we won't shoot you."

"At least we'll try not to," Santino said in the dark.

I sighed and waited for Santino and Helena to relight the room's candles, while Gaius and Marcus removed their NVGs and handed them to me. I traded them for the beacons.

Both men still looked stunned.

"You continue to amaze us, Hunter," Gaius said. "If this sphere is able to send you home, wherever that may be, maybe you will consider letting us come with you?"

I thought about it. Both men were bright, capable men, but the immense cultural shock that would come with living in the 21st century might be too much. If anything it would be an interesting experiment, I guess, but I suspected the combination of hamburgers, women in thongs at the beach, Ferris Wheels, and football would be too much for the Romans to handle.

Besides, I wasn't even sure they could make the trip at all.

"I'll think about it," I told them.

They smiled at my consideration and left without another word. I closed the door behind them and turned to face my companions. They waited patiently for me to retake my position next to Helena on the bed.

"So, what do you think?" Santino asked.

"I think it's the best chance we've got," I replied. I looked over at Helena.

"I agree," she said wearily, probably still unhappy that we were once again purposefully risking our lives.

I squeezed her knee in support.

"But remember," I said, "no matter what happens, we can't go home yet. Not only do we need to contact the rest of the team, but we still have to deal with the other orb as well. Whatever happens, we destroy this one first."

Both of them nodded, and mused silently for a few minutes.

"It's gonna be just like old times," Santino said.

I nodded silently in agreement. This had to be a military operation like we'd never performed while in Rome. Everything we'd done down here had been off the cuff, haphazard, performed with an overconfidence developed from our vast technological superiority and unique skill sets. We'd never gone into a mission with anywhere near the level of detail as had become routine for operators back in the U.S., but this time, everything had to go off perfectly. Agrippina's ninjas were too unpredictable for us to go in halfcocked. We needed to set the stage, write the rules and make sure each participant stuck to our script. It's what we were trained to do.

No more playing dress up trying to fit in with the Romans like cocky ass clowns.

The thought made me nervous, but another emotion worked its way through my body as well. It was the feeling of excitement mixed with fear I always felt before a mission back home. It was the feeling that reminded me to get ready for the danger, for the adrenaline rush was sure to come.

I hadn't felt it so intensely in years and I couldn't deny that I liked it.

I really liked it.

***

Two nights later, I was doing exactly what snipers did best. Waiting.

But at least I felt both comfortable and safe in my sniper hide – a place on a field of one's choosing that offered elevation, a clear view of an area and plenty of room to dish out some punishment. Hides could be anything from holes in the ground to bombed-out deli stores, a simple rooftop or even a five star luxury suite.

As long as it kept a sniper hidden and in a position to kill bad guys, it was a hide.

The comfort I felt was like slipping into a pair of old shoes that I had loved so much but had temporarily misplaced. Although I had kept up on my target shooting over the years, practicing when the opportunity arose, finding time to seek out, locate and customize a hide was something I hadn't done since I was still a resident of the year 2021. It surprised me how happy it made me because it wasn't something I'd relished back then. Yet, as I lay here now, I felt safer than the times as a kid when I'd sneak into my parents' bed after a scary dream.

Helena and I had gone scouring the rooftops for suitable hides as soon as Gaius and Marcus had left a few nights ago, while Santino scouted the ground near the Hippodrome. Helena and I decided on two separate locations that provided overlapping fields of fire, elevation, room to maneuver, and clear sightlines across most of the city. I was situated atop a five story house, seven hundred meters east north east of the Hippodrome.

Interestingly, it was a house I'd visited before. At least, I've been to the area where it would have stood two thousand years from now. It wasn't a house then, but a beautiful park situated near the eastern coast of the city. Although I couldn't recall the name, I still remembered my ten year old self trying to escape my parents' constant watchfulness, hoping to explore the beautiful and serene park, my younger sister dutifully at their side.

She'd always been the obedient one.

While much of that trip was a blur in my mind, the one thing I remembered was how it became one of the most defining moments of my life. On our first day in the city, a lifelong love of art, literature and history was born in my mind as my family and I toured the Hagia Sophia. It was then, and will be again soon, one of the most unique buildings in existence with its curious amalgamation of Christian and Islamic architecture and art. I'd spent hours exploring every nook and cranny that morning, sticking my nose in places it shouldn't have been and driving my mother insane wondering if she'd lost her son only a few hours into the trip. My father hadn't been happy when he'd found me wondering in a crypt that had been roped off from the general public, but the damage had been done.

I was hooked.

Unfortunately, the building wasn't around quite yet. We'd arrived about five hundred years too early, which, even though I would have loved to see the building in its prime, was a good thing. Based on where I had positioned myself, the building would have blocked my view of the Hippodrome completely.

Stationed about eight hundred meters due west of the Hippodrome was Helena. Her hide was higher and much more remote, consisting of some kind of tower used for God knows what. The roof was spacious enough for her to lay prone and keep her M107 Barrett sniper rifle atop her gear bag beside her. She secured her hide by attaching small, fisheye cameras to watch the tower's only entrance at the base of the building. Each camera emitted an infrared beam that, when crossed, would alert Helena by flashing her eyepiece and displaying whatever the camera picked up.

We were pulling out all the stops for this one. We wore all of our combat gear, had assault rifles loaded and ready to go, and brought bailout bags in case we needed to flee the city and leave the rest of our gear behind. Our eyepieces, gun-cams, forearm mounted touch screens, and mini-laptop computers were all up and running for the first time in maybe two years. Solar energy had kept the devices going, but without Santino's UAV, we couldn't use the GPS system to perform aerial recon, or keep an eye on where we were in relation to one another. At least the fisheye cams had micro-transmitters built in that could send a signal a few dozen meters, more than enough to reach us from their security positions. I had five of the fisheye cams guarding my own ass, the numerous routes to my position creating a unique security situation for us to overcome.

I sighed and tapped the trigger guard of my sniper rifle distractedly. I hadn't needed to do something like this in over four years, and I was out of practice. It wasn't the waiting that bothered me, or the impending death I was soon to dish out, but the thoughts of failure and the possibility I might get one of my friends killed. It was a foreign feeling for someone who, as a SEAL officer, had rarely ever used his sniper rifle while on mission. As a SEAL Team platoon leader, my role was to provide guidance and leadership for my men, not to go lone wolf with a sniper rifle and play Rambo.

That's not to say I hadn't fired it on a mission before. I was a fine shot, one of the best, although my affinity for it was something of a mystery. Helena's skill at shooting came from experience, honing her skill for as long as she's been able hold a rifle, and is the finest marksman I know because of it. As for me, I'd shot an old .22 rifle to get my shooting merit badge in the Scouts, but other than that, I had never even picked up a firearm until I joined the Navy.

Patience and math were two of the most important ingredients that produced a successful sniper. Patience I had, but math was never my best subject. Sniper school taught me how to read the fluttering of a flag, the billowing of dust or the subtle shift of a mirage to determine wind speed, direction and range, but it was too bad it still took mathematical formulas to calculate them, and I'd been forced to grudgingly learn them. I could calculate them with little trouble now, but as I progressed through sniper school, I quickly learned that I rarely needed the math, and found myself able to determine what I needed naturally and by instinct alone. As long as I knew the ranges, which I could lazily, but accurately, find with a laser designator, I could dial in my scope and nail exactly what I was targeting.

Even then, I generally found the ranges easy to guestimate.

And Helena still did it better though, and she was quicker, too.

Natural shooting ability aside, *Penelope* wasn't up for the kind of work I needed to do tonight. She was sitting next to me, of course, but what was currently resting against my shoulder could best be described as her much older and more badass brother. The United States Navy SR-25 Mk 11 Mod 0 Sniper Weapon System looked and felt like a bigger version of a M4, which made it instantly comfortable in my grip. Whoever planted the cache of weaponry that traveled back in time with us must have done his homework, because the weapon was the same model I had used with the SEALs.

Created specifically for Navy SEALs, and constructed to our own specifications, the Mk 11 version was considered one of the most accurate semi-automatic sniper rifles on the market. Combined with a twenty round magazine and an effective range of around one thousand meters, the rifle was an effective killing machine.

I'd only used it on a few specialized occasions before, times when I'd been called to participate in specific sniper support roles for other branches of the military. During those missions, I'd command four to six other snipers from the platoons in my SEAL Team. The most memorable mission of that kind occurred two years before I activated the orb and traveled to ancient Rome and three years after World War III began, when America was sick of defending its expansive southern border with Mexico and did what any self-respecting superpower would do after spending years on the defensive.

We invaded.

175 years after the original Mexican War, America slowly but surely progressed its border south. After massive bombing

campaigns by the Air Force, a Navy blockade, Special Forces missions, and the steady progress of Army and Marine divisions, America's primary target was in sight. Mexico City. It was for the invasion of the country's capital that I received a special call from SOCOM, requesting myself and five of my finest snipers to gear up, head south and expect to be gone for at least two months.

We arrived off the AC-130 to no fanfare or jubilation, and were quietly given two Humvees, two drivers, and two gunners from the Army. We had been amongst the most low tech mechanized infantry on the battlefield, but easily one of the most effective. The ten of us were tasked with performing sniper support for the advancing invasion force and to cause as much trouble as possible. There were other sniper teams there, of course, but I never encountered them. We received our orders directly from the Army's commanding officer in the field, a full bird colonel whose name I never learned.

The use of SEALs in this manner was nothing new, at least not relatively. Taking small task forces from Special Forces outfits and plopping them in the middle of a war with units from other branches of the military had grown popular during the war in Iraq. SEAL Teams weren't big enough to hold any territory on their own, so we didn't try. Instead, we'd be integrated into a conventional military unit, but were mostly left as an autonomous fighting force. The tactic wasn't popular at first, at least by the conventional units we'd join, but it turned out spectacularly. It gave my SEALs free reign to do whatever it was we needed to do without constricting anyone else's operational parameters, while giving them the benefit of our expertise as well.

The siege of Mexico City had been long, hard and bloody. We were there two months longer than expected, lost one of our gunners, a driver, and one of my snipers in the process. Mike had been a good man. He'd been a SEAL for ten years, but still respected my command decisions while I respected his experience. He'd been a victim of bad luck, a simple case of the wrong place at the wrong time. A mortar had hit two feet from his perch, and broadsided him with its devastating arsenal. Mortars were some of the most inaccurate weapons out there, at least the shoddy ones being used by the poorly trained militias we'd been fighting, but if you were unlucky enough to find yourself in its blast range, you were as good as dead. We'd packed up his body, conforming to the code that we never left a man behind, and pushed on.

We used our Humvees as mobile sniper platforms and raced around the battlefield, providing cover as the main body of the invasion force slowly made its way through the densely constructed city. Snipers had been around since World War I, but the fast reaction force we acted as hadn't been something we were normally used for. It wasn't until a Marine sniper developed the process during Operation Iraqi Freedom in 2004 that it had found its place on a battlefield.

It was efficient and effective. The Humvees themselves provided a certain amount of elevation that we'd occasionally take advantage of, but were mostly used to get us from A to Z. We'd make our way into parts of the city, ditch our rides, find some high ground, and with our gunners and drivers as a security force, take up shop in a local hide and get to work. I'd accumulated one hundred and two confirmed kills with the SR-25 Mk 11 during those four months, but my final tally was probably closer to two hundred.

I sighed as I continued to peer through my scope. Those were memories full of pride in my performance and that of my SEALS, but also ones filled with pain and terror at the hellish environments we'd found ourselves in. Four months spent operating mostly at night, the days too dangerous to traverse, surrounded by smoke and fire and the fear of poisonous gas. All that time spent catching maybe a few hours of sleep every few days, constantly on the run, hunting, being hunted, killing, but never, not once, had I let fear hinder me

But I felt fear now, and I didn't understand it. I suppose it couldn't help that while I felt deep bonds with my SEALs, I actually loved one of the women at risk on *this* mission. I simply could not let anything happen to Helena again. Wang wasn't here to play medic this time. We might not get so lucky again.

I took a deep breath, forcing every distracting thought from my mind, held it, let it out slowly, and repeated twice. I was no help to my friends with my emotions in turmoil, so I forced myself to calm down. Thinking, in of itself, wasn't a bad thing. It helped my patience by letting the time pass interestingly, but it could also cloud the mind and obscure judgment. I needed to be sharp.

I shrugged my shoulders as I lay prone, trying to get comfortable. I loosened my grip and relaxed the muscles in my biceps, neck, and my thighs, absorbing myself into the roof, becoming one with my surroundings, practically and realistically becoming in tune with everything going on around me. I tried to visualize my place in a 3-D representation of the city of Byzantium, situating myself in a strategy video game like the ones I used to play as a kid.

Calm and comfortable, I looked through my scope again. It was equipped with night vision capabilities and its zoom was fully adjustable between 10-25x powers, making objects at extreme ranges feel like they were right at my fingertips. I shifted my rifle west, and pinpointed Helena's exact position, easy thanks to the infrared glowstick she had attached to her back. It wouldn't bother her, but it allowed me to check in on her quickly. I had a similar glowstick on my back as well, in case she wanted to find me.

Satisfied she was fine, I panned my scope at its widest setting, scanning a city that may soon become a war zone. The night was quiet, warm, but not muggy. Perfect. I looked at a torch mounted on a wall. The flames didn't even flicker. The wind was still, making shots a breeze, no pun intended. The dryness of the air kept bullets on target as even the slightest amount of moisture could alter their trajectory. I couldn't have asked for better conditions.

I glanced at my watch.

0130.

Showtime.

I shifted my perspective t down a street that ran southeast towards the Hippodrome, focusing on another brightly lit infrared glare through my night vision scope. That would be Santino, approaching the target site, acting as our buyer.

He was the obvious choice for the job, and not just because the other two choices were qualified snipers. After five years here in the Roman Empire, he had picked up Latin almost instantaneously, and was already fairly proficient at Greek. I had to admit, he was far more studious than I was on the subject, and had made good progress. For some reason he had a natural aptitude for linguistics, languages, and accents. Helena and I, on the other hand, still spoke Latin with our native intonations behind it. I had a distinctly Midwestern, American accent, whereas Helena still retained a hint of German. Santino, however, could now successfully pull off Spanish, Gaulic, Greek, and Italian accents when speaking Latin perfectly. I remember reading that there were hundreds, maybe thousands, of English dialects, just in America alone, and the case was the same in the Roman Empire. Santino was so good at it, he could even make himself sound like he was from Southern Italy, Northern Italy, or Rome itself, the latter's dialect possessing a very haughty emphasis at the ends of some words.

Santino...

One of the most asinine, dimwitted, and sarcastic ass-hats I knew was also a world class linguist, on par with any number of geniuses back home. Just thinking about his stupid grin and bad jokes pained my soul, but I couldn't deny that he had a knack for it. I guess it proves that people, like ogres and onions, have layers.

Even Santino.

But he wasn't showing any of that cocky bravado tonight.

Tonight, he was a totally different person.

I shifted my aim, a process snipers refer to as "glassing," and focused on the meeting area, a simple plaza near the entrance to the stadium, about the size of a basketball court. There were ten columns in two rows, running away from the entrance at ten foot intervals and benches within the gaps. Those columns may prove tricky to shoot around, but I'd deal with them when I had to.

There were torches along every wall that encased the plaza, walls that were the rear ends of residential homes. The entire city was so dense I could jump off my rooftop onto this building's neighboring rooftop, and run all the way to the plaza if I had to. Except for the main throughways, the streets were exceptionally narrow, a blessing and a curse as well. If potential targets decided to remain at street level, we'd have a tough time targeting them. Santino was well aware of this fact, so if he had to run, he knew to get to high ground fast.

As a final check, I pulled out my flashlight, equipped with a red lens, and gave my range card one last look.

Last night, Helena and I had done a little extra prep work that took the better part of the night. We began by scouting the hippodrome, plotting its most likely entry points and escape routes from it. Once we completed that task, we then identified the arena's surrounding landmarks: towers, temples and other high points. We marked them with a series of infrared patches to identify which landmark was which and, more importantly, which landmark belonged at what distance from both my hide and Helena's. A simple glance at each landmark's group of IR patches would correspond to a prearranged distance we had already measured. Two patches meant three hundred meters, eight patches equated to six hundred and fifty meters, and so on. Should an enemy pass by a set of these patches, I wouldn't have to calculate my distance from him; my range card would tell me.

We were ready to go.

I focused on the entrance to the Hippodrome, where a man was already standing in a hooded robe that concealed his face. It was dark, and I could see he was wearing very durable sandals beneath his feet. He looked like he was ready to take off if need be, something I could appreciate, but also took note of. He was exactly 625 meters away, so I twisted the appropriate dial on my scope to zero in my mark.

Santino was just rounding the corner, making his way between the rows of columns. He was wearing a long dark robe as well, which pooled around his feet. The worst thing that could happen to him right now was that he tripped over his cloak, which concealed his boots and combat fatigues beneath.

Santino stopped in front of the man and bowed slightly. His radio, hidden beneath his robes, was set to VOX so that Helena and I could keep track of the conversation.

"Greetings," Santino said, opening his arms in a wide gesture. He sniffed the air haughtily and looked up. "Such a fine night. I have always found the stars to be a wondrous backdrop when dealing in such unique items."

I rolled my eyes, as I continued to observe them through my scope.

Santino's cover was that of a roving Greek salesmen of unique goods and items, a cover Gaius had concocted when convincing the dealer to negotiate with him. Apparently, Santino owned a store in Corinth that specialized in obscure and expensive items, the kinds that would go great with whatever frivolous decoration the excessively rich already had. But while Gaius had provided the cover, Santino had developed the character all on his own. His beard was overgrown and bushy and he had slicked back his hair with some kind of product.

I suspected it was lard, but I didn't really want to know.

Finally, Santino had stood in front of the mirror earlier today and rehearsed his demeanor, facial contortions and dialect for hours, and by the time he was done, he'd become a completely different person. When we'd departed a few hours ago, Santino's Latin had a distinguishable Greek dialect, his eyes suggested he was a born haggler, his smile was nowhere to be seen, and he had the personality of a trader who thought he was much better at his job than he really was, even if had the repertoire and eclectic inventory to back it up. He was arrogant and cocky, natural for Santino, but also an unprepared nincompoop, someone who'd lucked his way through life... also probably natural for Santino.

I zoomed in my scope just a bit to get a better look at their figures.

"A fine night indeed, sir," the dealer replied. "I do enjoy these early morning dealings as well. I just hope you brought enough money to carry on as long as needed."

Santino placed his hands on his stomach and chuckled brassily. "We'll just see if your little item is worthy of a place amongst my wares."

"That will not be a problem, sir," the man said, and I knew he had to be smiling. "I feel you will be most impressed."

Santino harrumphed in dismissal, and looked around the stadium's entrance, waiting for his fellow barterer to show up.

The guy was late. If Gaius wasn't bullshiting us, then the other buyer would be one of his Praetorian buddies. There was no doubt he wouldn't show up alone, so I glassed the rooftops looking for anybody dressed in black.

It seemed clear.

I clicked my PTT button. "3-2, 3-1. Do you have a visual on possible tangos?"

"Negative, 3-1," Helena replied. "All clear so far."

"Copy," I transmitted.

I shook my head. Something felt off about this. Professionals like Gaius and Marcus' Praetorians wouldn't be late unless they had good reason, or were perhaps scouting the place as well. I felt safe almost seven hundred meters away, but even so, I manipulated the touch screen on my forearm to flip through the image from the fisheye cams on my eye piece. I knew it would have contacted me if they'd sensed any movement already, but it couldn't hurt to check.

I wasn't surprised when I found nothing. We were very far away and well hidden. My scope even had a honeycomb patterned cover over the front lens to reduce the chance of lens flares from incoming light.

Still, something didn't feel right.

I tilted my rifle to look down the road Santino had just been traveling on. I saw two men dressed in dark clothing make their way towards the plaza. As soon as they turned the corner, they became instant targets. They walked up to the dealer and waited, offering no form of greeting.

The dealer seemed nonplussed by the fact the other buyer hadn't come alone, but ignored it and began his transaction.

"Greetings to you all," he began. "Thank you for displaying interest in the item I have brought here tonight. I believe you will find it most fascinating. If you have any questions, now would be the time to ask them. If you will begin, sir...." he trailed off, indicating one of the Praetorians.

Both men remained silent, failing to offer their names.

"Fine," the dealer replied. "And you, sir?"

"Xanthias," Santino said. Xanthias the slave had been one of the characters in my Greek text books back in college. Like Santino, he had been a lazy bastard who never listened to his owner, Dicaeopolis. "I have but one question. Where did you acquire this item?"

That was the only question any of us wanted to know. We knew the rest.

"It was an inheritance," he replied. "My uncle obtained it four years ago. He was a legionnaire with the *XV Primigenia*, but died last year while on campaign in Britain. His personal items were returned to our family in Greece, and I found the item you will be bidding on tonight. Trust me, sir, it was completely legal. A spoil of war."

Spoil of war, my ass. This asshole's uncle must have stolen it from Varus sometime after the Battle for Rome. There had been six thousand men in that legion, along with an equal number of auxilia, and while they all knew me, I'd only interacted with an extremely small number of them. Most of them were good men, but there were always a few brigands in a group. I wondered if the man even knew what he was taking.

The dealer continued to chat when Helena's voice cackled in my ear.

"Contact. Eleven o'clock, your position."

My body automatically tracked my rifle towards the area Helena indicated, and I saw exactly what we were looking for. The two men wore tight fitting clothing, probably black, but I couldn't tell due to the green tint of my scope. Each man had a *gladius*, or Roman short sword, encased in a sheath strapped to their backs. Along their belts was an assortment of pouches, as well as a half dozen throwing knives held in place by what resembled shotgun shell pockets. One man had a compact bow across his back as well, along with a quiver of arrows at his thigh. The other man had no bow or quiver, but had an additional blade at his waist.

I looked around for other contacts and found them easily. I spotted nine other pairs, each similarly armed, and encircling Santino's position unnoticed.

"Eighteen count," I told Helena.

"Twenty two," she corrected. "Four more atop the hippodrome."

I glassed the entrance and high walls of the stadium and saw the four she was referring to.

"Confirmed, twenty two tangos."

"Wait one," she said. A minute later, I heard her voice again. "Confirmed, twenty two tangos."

I hadn't spotted anymore either. "Confirm positive ID on Georgia or Missouri?"

"Negative."

That wasn't good news. Either Gaius and Marcus weren't here, which unless my math was really that bad couldn't be the case, or they hadn't activated the infrared beacons I had given them. Either way, it could prove detrimental to the mission.

"Solid copy, prepare to engage on my mark."

She double clicked her radio.

I took a deep breath and let it out slowly. My forehead glistened slightly with nervous perspiration, but I forced myself to focus, grasping for all that training thrown at me over the course of my career. It wasn't my ass on the line. It was Santino's. It was my job to keep my cool when there were others relying on me. I continued to observe the interlopers, waiting for them to do something that would force me to end them.

"So," I heard the dealer say in my ear, "let us begin the bidding."

"Wait," Santino said. "Can we not see the object, first?"

"Of course. How silly of me."

The man maneuvered a simple satchel from his back and pulled out a spherical item wrapped in a dark cloth. He carefully unwrapped the package, revealing one of the blue time traveling orbs. As I looked at it through my scope, I half expected to feel some kind of connection with it like I had the last time I was near it, but I was happy to note that I felt nothing. It appeared inert, its color and texture appearing more like a blue bowling ball than the glowing magical device that got us here.

"It's a blue... ball," Santino said, unimpressed.

"Yes, but observe," the dealer replied.

Still holding the orb with the cloth in his left hand, he reached out with his right and poked it with a finger on his right. Immediately, the orb began to shine brightly.

Well, shit.

Did this guy possess the same blood line Varus and I did?

He had to. It was the only explanation for his ability to activate it.

Right?

How many more people were there that could control this thing?

I winced, expecting the jolt of intense pain that accompanied the time travel process, but felt nothing. When I opened my eyes I saw that we were still in Byzantium. I looked through my scope again, zooming it in as far as I could, and looked at the orb. Once again, I saw clouds swirling within it, like observing a hurricane from outer space, but nothing else. No shapes, objects, or human forms were evident within, and the only thing I could theorize was that there was no one on the other end of the orb, whether they were calling or answering.

I wondered why not.

I pulled back the power on my scope, resetting it for an accurate shot. Both Santino and his haggling opponent appeared shocked at what they saw. All three men stumbled back a step before regaining their composure.

"Most impressive," Santino said. "Quite the spoil of war, indeed."

"Yes, it is very beautiful. The glow will dim over time until it becomes opaque once again. Now, Mr. Xanthias, if you will, the starting bid is three hundred..."

"Enough of this," the Praetorian exclaimed loudly. "I claim this object in the name of the Empress of Rome, Augustina Agrippina."

The seller huddled his arms against his chest, resting the ball protectively against his body.

"You have no such authority," he countered.

"Indeed," the Praetorian said, pulling his sword from his belt. Without pause, he stabbed the dealer through the chest. Reacting out of pain and surprise, the man stumbled backwards, throwing his hands over his head as he fell. The orb flew from his grip and Santino, quick on his feet, reached out and snagged it. Still playing the Greek merchant, he took a few steps back, cradling the spherical object and holding out his free hand in a Heisman-like pose.

"Please, please, we can work something out. Name your price."

The Praetorian took a step towards him, pointing his sword at Santino's neck.

"This can end two ways," the man told Santino. "Both end with your death. All you control is its swiftness."

Santino didn't respond verbally, but his body language did his speaking for him. His posture straightened, his fear resided, and he was grinning from ear to ear. The two Romans, including the one holding the sword, shifted on their feet in surprise at how quickly the man before them had suddenly grown a spine.

"You really don't want to do that," Santino informed them calmly, already placing the orb in a bag of his own, cocky as ever.

"There's a very pretty lady out there who's got your number, and I don't mean that in a good way."

"What?!" The Praetorian growled, only slightly more lost than I was. He moved forward again, just enough to obscure my shot. "Hand it over, fool!"

Santino sighed and looked at the ground, shaking his head.

"Don't say I didn't warn you, buddy."

As soon as he finished his warning, he took a quick step to his left. He looked over his shoulder, glanced around and seemed satisfied with his new position. The two Romans looked at each other in confusion. Santino stood there, rocking on his feet, clapping his hands and snapping his fingers impatiently. Looking just as confused as everyone watching him by now, he glanced around again, then at his watch, before he smacked his thigh in realization. He took another step to the left and pointed his finger at the Roman like a pistol, snapping his hand back, mimicking the firing of a "gun."

Nothing happened.

Santino looked at his hand in confusion. He smacked his wrist with his other hand, and tugged on his thumb, as though he were unjamming it. Apparently satisfied at whatever he had been doing, he took careful aim once again and "fired." This time the armed Roman's neck exploded in a stream of arterial blood and gore. Behind him, the other Roman fell backwards as a small crater formed near his left shoulder blade. Both men crumpled dead before they hit the ground.

"What took you so long?" Santino asked, putting his ear piece in place.

"Sorry," Helena replied. "I didn't want it to look too easy."

"Women," he said. "Always making things more difficult than they really are."

I ignored their banter as I focused on Helena's precision shot. She'd angled it perfectly and aimed at one of the few spots on a person's body that allowed a bullet to penetrate with enough force while still remain intact so that it could successfully kill a second target behind the first. Her suppressor equipped DSR1 hadn't even made a peep from anyone else's perspective but her own, and I hoped the superstitious Romans actually thought Santino had shot their friends.

I quickly shifted my aim towards the rooftops. I saw the Romans hesitate for a few seconds, but it wasn't long before the seasoned warriors drew swords and nocked arrows to bows.

"You might want to start running, 3-3," I suggested. "You're about to have incoming."

I didn't bother to look and see if he heard me or not. Instead, I rested my crosshairs on the biggest threat I could find, a Roman with his bow loaded and the string pulled back to his ear. I was in the zone now, and I didn't hesitate, but before I pulled the trigger, his head exploded.

"Tango down," Helena confirmed.

It still amazed me just how good a shot she was. I gritted my teeth, but smiled.

If she wanted a challenge, fine.

Her bolt action rifle and five round magazines gave me a slight advantage over her. After every shot she had to manually reload another round into the chamber, whereas my semi-automatic SR-25 could fire with each pull of the trigger, and I had twenty rounds to fire before I needed to reload. I moved my reticule to the dead man's partner and put a round through his chest, ending his life before he even knew his buddy had gone down. The spent casing flew from my rifle's ejection port into a mesh bag I attached to catch them.

No sense leaving any additional evidence behind.

Four down, twenty to go.

They didn't stand a chance as Helena and I began to systematically take them apart. Another archer pointed his bow as Santino ran and I shot him in the shoulder, spinning him to the ground. I put another round in his chest to make sure he stayed down. His partner noticed his friend's death, having no idea what happened to him, the cough of my rifle barely passing beyond my building, and took off running. I tracked him as he ran past five IR patches, so I adjusted my scope instinctually for 550 meters and pulled the trigger as he tried to leap between buildings. The bullet caught him just as he launched himself from the rooftop. He went limp at the impact and lost control over his jump, plummeting between the buildings.

I saw another Roman by himself, 475 meters away, and shot him in the chest.

"Four tangos down," I communicated to Helena.

"Seven for me," she reported, much to my annoyance. "But we have another problem. Enemy reinforcements coming in from the west. I count at least fifty."

I shifted my body so that my rifle faced further to the west and saw just what Helena was describing. Fifty or so armed and dark clad men came running in our direction. There was only one anomaly amongst the group – well two actually. It seemed like Gaius and Marcus had decided to join the fight after all, because I clearly saw two IR strobes pulsating amongst the group as they ran toward Santino, who had finally made it to the rooftops. An arrow flew a foot from his head and I tracked its progress back to the source, removing the man with a shot to the stomach. I also saw one of the Praetorian runners, hot on his heels, only to be taken out by another surgical strike to the neck by Helena.

This was not good. Because of how Agrippina's ninjas had positioned themselves prior to Helena's first kill, Santino only had one direction he could run in. The problem was it threw off my ability to continue covering his withdrawal. Luckily, we'd prepared for that potentiality.

I clicked my radio. "I'm bugging out to Hide-3."

"Copy," Helena replied, for once too busy to transmit the double clicks.

I got to my feet, tossed the SR-25 into a large bag shaped like a bloated rifle, picked up *Penelope*, shouldered both rifle and gear bags, and took off from my position, heading southwest. Last night Helena and I located a third hide that we could use if the battle moved too far north into the city as it appeared to be doing now. Tall buildings were about to block my line of sight in a few minutes with Santino running in that direction. Helena's position to the west, however, was higher off the ground than any other point in the city and allowed her to stay put, but in order for us to maintain an effective field of fire, we had found a third hide on a tower near the coast of the Propontis. It was relegated to the secondary position because its line of sight into the courtyard in front of the Hippodrome was negligible.

I huffed under the weight of my gear but I didn't stop. I knew where all the big jumps were, having rehearsed the route a number of times last night, so I plowed through the darkness at top speed.

The only impediment along the way was a clothes line that held large sheets drying in the summer breeze, an obstruction that was not there last night. When I rounded the corner, I ran headlong into it, entangling myself in the white linens. It only slowed me down for a second, and I was just glad Helena hadn't seen it.

I tore them off and pitched them off the side of the building, forcing my head to stay in the game. The tower was in sight now, and I had been out of the fight for almost two minutes now. I hadn't heard anything over the radio that would make me worry about Santino, just Helena's constant updates on enemy KIA, but that didn't mean the situation *wasn't* deteriorating because of my absence. The intel Gaius and Marcus had provided indicated there'd only be twenty four Praetorians here, not seventy four, and those extra numbers were an obvious snag in our mission.

Approaching my last jump, I pushed my body as hard as I could, this last one being the longest. Making my leap, I reached out to grab the ladder that would take me to the roof of the tower. Missing the ladder or failing to grasp the handles would end in a quick death, but even my overwhelming klutziness wasn't going to get me killed now.

Luckily, the jump was more successful than I could have ever hoped for, and I secured myself easily. Taking a quick pause to catch my breath and with a quick exertion of strength, I pulled myself upwards, rung by rung. Reaching the roof, I retrieved my SR-25 and rested its bipod on the low wall encircling the circumference of the roof, and focused on the advancing Praetorians.

They were getting smarter. Word must have gotten around that something was killing them from afar, because they had quickly adopted defensive measures that included zigzagging, stopping intermittently as they ran, skipping, and others stole my signature move: rolling. I had eight rounds left in my original magazine and took careful aim at the advancing troops, who were now spread out and running from my left to right across my field of vision.

Eight rounds, four hits, two confirmed kills. Not a good start, but even for a sniper of my caliber, these targets were very hard to hit. Helena's breaking of concise, military radio protocol, resulting in a constant stream of profanities on her end confirmed she was having trouble as well.

I swiftly reloaded and followed a new target, vowing I was going to get this particular agile bastard.

Agile, yes. Creative, no.

He made a pattern of two skips, a zig, followed by a roll, the latter aggravating me more than anything else. On his third repetition of the pattern, I put a bullet in his right flank as he came to his feet from his latest roll.

This ain't the movies, pal.

The impact of the bullet pitched him left into his partner. I took advantage of the other man's stumble and put a round in his chest. 500 meters away, my third target was far less predictable. I had to recheck my secondary range card after it took five rounds to finally get him with a solid, but lucky, shot in the neck. Two more targets expended my remaining rounds.

Reloading my third magazine, another problem quickly became evident: I'd only brought four magazines with me. Eighty rounds ensured three to four rounds per target had there only been twenty some targets out there. With that many rounds per man, a drunken cat would have ended the night with rounds to spare, but with the way these guys were moving, and their additional numbers, Santino could be in serious trouble.

"Uh, guys?" Santino asked over the radio, his voice only slightly belabored from his run. "Why aren't you calling out dead bad guys like you were earlier?"

"You try doing this," Helena suggested in frustration. "Tango down."

"They're catching on to what's happening to them," I reported. "Where are you?"

"I'm almost to the Horn. I'm running out of room to run here."

This was very bad. If I took more careful aim to hit everything I targeted, too many bad guys would slip through and reach Santino, but if I fired erratically, I'd run out of ammo before I could kill enough of them. I only had a few magazines for *Penelope*, but at these ranges I'd be lucky to hit much of anything.

"I could use an exit route here," Santino urged frantically, rare concern emanating from his voice.

I tried to think as we quickly ran out of options. Plan "B" didn't exist and fear for my friend slowed my rate of fire as Santino ran for his life. If only we had an army that could counter Agrippina's, maybe we'd stand a chance. But where the hell was I going to find an army? It wasn't like nations left armies just laying around, waiting for someone to come around and find an excuse to use them. Did they?

"Head to street level," Helena recommended. "Lose them in the alleys. It's your only chance."

Santino didn't answer and I felt ashamed that I hadn't said anything. Helena's suggestion was obvious, and had Santino not already come to the same conclusion, I knew that he had to have been close. Yet, it seemed so utterly brilliant that I couldn't even fathom how such a thought would have ever come to me.

"What's next, 3-1?" Helena's voice called out again insistently.

I tried to think but couldn't. I didn't know what to do.

"Jacob!" She pleaded.

"I don't know…" I trailed off, not know what was about to happen.

The situation was turning into a clusterfuck along with my state of mind. I felt delirious, so much so that in my own confusion, I almost missed my eye piece flash in front of my eye, indicating my computer had received some form of update. Interested, I tapped the screen on my forearm and a brief text message appeared on my lens.

LOOK UP

Confused, I craned my neck up towards the night sky, wondering what the hell I was looking for. I saw the Big Dipper and the rest of the stars that made up constellations I had never bothered learning, but nothing out of the ordinary. Not until I caught sight of a star moving faster than it should have, pulsating a dull shade of red.

I blinked. Either my eyes were deceiving me, I was observing a UFO or the last thing I expected to see was stealthily hovering above us at one thousand feet.

Santino's UAV.

For the first time in what seemed like years, I laughed out loud uncontrollably, my moment of indecision almost forgotten. The UAV could mean only one thing.

Accompanying my discovery was the unmistakable roar of Bordeaux's Mk 48 LMG spewing forth dozens upon dozens of 7.62 caliber rounds of destruction. I yanked open the sheath on my wrist mounted screen and for the first time in months, saw an aerial view of my surroundings thanks to the UAV, along with six green dots scattered throughout, pulsating a bright green.

Bordeaux's team must have done some advanced intelligence gathering with the UAV because along with our green dots, were a series of smaller red triangles, about thirty five of them, indicating enemy troops. Thanks to the Blue Force Tracker II software installed on our computers, updating anything on the map was as easy as tapping the screen on our wrists. These red triangles were caught in a horseshoe created by the six of us, with Helena and me at the ends. Our reinforcements must have crossed the Golden Horn and entered the city from the north.

I watched as red triangles winked out of existence in quick order. Looking through my scope, I observed man after man fall to Bordeaux's hail of gunfire and the steady stream of two other rifles, until only Gaius and Marcus remained, their IR strobes still flashing brightly.

Another flash indicated a second data package, one that displayed a radio broadcast frequency. I reached for my radio and tuned it to the proper frequency, smashing the PTT button with vigor. "Bordeaux, is that you?"

"*Oui, mon ami*," he said, and my smile broadened at his continuous and somewhat pretentious use of French. "Who else would it be?"

I didn't reply immediately, the memory of only a few minutes ago coming back to me. How could I explain my apparent inability to make tactical decisions or form conscious thought into words when I needed to most? The only thing I could take solace in was that they hadn't heard our radio transmissions, the one that offered proof of my negligence. I put it into the back of my mind for now.

"You couldn't have picked a better time to show up," I commented. Are Vincent and Wang with you? You guys there?"

"We are, Hunter," came Vincent's Italian accented voice, despite being a native of Switzerland. "It is good to hear you."

"Wang?"

"Aye, Hunter," the Asian descended Brit said in his Welsh accent.

"God, it's good to hear from you," I said, unconditional happiness beginning to percolate amongst my dire spirits. Their presence was more than uplifting. Not only did I have new allies at my side, but the only other friends I had left in ancient Rome. Friends I hadn't seen in years.

"Look," I continued, my mind clearing as the stress of the situation ebbed and my blood pressure leveled, realizing we still had work to do. "We've got a lot to clean up here. Those two Romans out there with the IR strobes are Gaius and Marcus. Wang, find them and have them take you back to our apartment. They know the way. Keep it quiet."

"I live to serve," he joked. He'd always been a quiet jokester, not as overt as Santino but always one with a quick quip on his tongue.

Great.

"Bordeaux," I continued, "we need your help policing these bodies. We can't have any evidence of what happened tonight. Your gun show had to have awoken half the city, but let's just hope they thought it was thunder, or the gods, or something. You, Santino, and Vincent get on that. Dump the bodies in the Bosporus."

"Copy," he replied.

"Helena, let's get to work finding those IR patches scattered around and pick up the fisheye cams from Hide-2. Also, now that we have the UAV, we'll see if we can hunt down any remaining Praetorians."

"Sounds good, Jacob," she said, all semblance of radio protocol abandoned.

I think that just about covered everything we needed to do. During my transmission, I glassed as much of the city as I could from my viewpoint, and only saw a few innocents peeking their heads out into the very early morning sky, only to find nothing amiss, and go back inside. I packed up my things and secured my bags before I swung my legs over the low wall and descended the ladder.

"Seems like you're doing well as the leader of this group, Jacob," Vincent radioed.

"He's not our leader," Helena corrected quickly. "We just like to follow him because he's got a cute butt."

"Yeah," Santino agreed. "We... wait, what? No, no we don't. People'd just think it was sexist if we followed you because of *your* cute butt."

"Either way," Vincent pushed on, remembering even after four years it was best to just ignore Santino. "It's nice to have someone else do it for a change."

"Honestly, sir, I'm not sure I'm up for it," I said from the bottom of my heart. "Want the job back?"

"No thank you," he answered easily. "Bordeaux's already filled us in, and I'm not sure I could handle it. This is your plan."

"Thanks," I said with a quiet *I think*, "but things aren't nearly as simple anymore."

I had a lot to explain in the next few hours. Things weren't nearly as crazy as capturing a child anymore, but only because I had a sinking suspicion that our lives were about to get far worse, but for now, it didn't matter. What mattered was cleaning up Byzantium and getting reacquainted with my old friends. I didn't have much to fall back on in these times of need. Just one beautiful woman and an annoying best friend.

I needed all the friends I could get.

VII
Band

Mission Entry #7
Jacob Hunter
Byzantium, Thracia - July, 42 A.D.

No time to write.
Got the band back together.
Catch you later.

I couldn't help but be brief in my last entry since Helena and I were way behind schedule. Everyone else had to be back in the apartment by now, and I was way too excited to take the time to write much more.

We were so late because one of the ninja-Praetorians had managed to slip through our net, and it had taken us quite a while to chase him down. We'd found him a few hundred meters beyond the city, and Helena took him down with a well-placed shot to his back. We then had to dispose of his body, just like all the rest, and the task of hunting him down, dumping him and collecting our equipment had taken far longer than I'd anticipated.

I took the few moments Helena spent retrieving a small cache of indigenous clothing from its hiding place near our apartment to jot my down thoughts. It wasn't overly insightful, but I had been too giddy to form a compelling thought. Despite being caught off guard, the night had been a major success. We'd eliminated a numerically superior force, obtained one of the two time traveling orbs and had found our friends in the process. All I wanted was to get back to my room and celebrate, and I knew Helena did as well.

We donned our local clothing as quickly as possible and made our way inside our building and up the stairwell, sure enough encountering the night owls on the prowl. I went up first and watched in horror as one of the prostitutes walked toward me in the futile hope of soliciting my attention. I was just about to deny her politely when Helena bounded up the stairs and body checked the nasty creature into the wall, hissing an apology as she went. I apologized more diplomatically, but didn't break stride until I caught up with her at the entrance to our room. Helena opened the door and went in first while I followed, shutting it closed behind me.

We had a full house.

Gaius, Marcus, Santino, Bordeaux, Wang, Vincent, and two other people, one a young male, the other a woman in her thirties, were all present in our apartment. Space was tight, and everyone had spread out within the room as comfortably as they could manage. Bordeaux and the unidentified woman sat at the far end of the table, facing the door, with Gaius and Marcus across from them, facing the window. Between the table and the bed sat Vincent on the final chair in the room, while Wang and Santino sat on the side of the bed, already bickering about something.

I smiled at the two of them. They had become pretty good friends in that first year they'd known each other, but had rarely agreed on anything. Whether it was tea or coffee, cricket or baseball, football or... football, the only opinion they shared was of their hatred for 80's music.

The final soul in the room was a young man who leaned against the wardrobe, which stood against the wall opposite Vincent's position.

Every head in the room turned to face us, eager expressions on their faces.

But no one moved.

Everyone just sat in their seats, unsure of how to react or what to do now that we were all suddenly reunited. All we needed was a spark to set the room off, which occurred when Helena dropped the wooden log that secured our door with a loud clang. With that, the room erupted into excitement and confusion, and I felt a flood of raw emotion overwhelm everyone as conversations were restarted, smiles blossomed, and Helena and I moved around to greet our long lost friends.

I quickly shook Bordeaux's hand, as I'd seen him only a few months ago, but moved over to embrace Vincent and Wang, pounding each man on the back cheerfully, exchanging a few words with both. Helena likewise embraced her friends but also offered quick kisses on their cheeks as well. While Helena and I welcomed our friends, Gaius and Marcus moved their chairs near the door and Bordeaux angled the table so that it, the benches, the chair, and the bed formed a loose oval around the perimeter of the room. Once everyone was settled, Helena and I moved to sit upon the table as the silence returned, again no one sure where to begin.

And as if on cue, Santino spoke up first.

"Don't everyone start at once," he said, breaking the tension as he always did.

We all laughed, eliciting Bordeaux to finally speak up.

"Perhaps you should start with what you're doing here," he offered from his seat next to the unknown woman. "I thought we agreed to meet in Valentia a month from now."

Even though I knew it was coming, I found myself taken aback by his comment and at a loss for words. I honestly wasn't sure how to respond. The only reason we were here was because I had fucked up with Agrippina.

I looked around, noticing everyone had their attention focused squarely on me. They were waiting expectantly for an answer while Santino rolled his shoulders awkwardly. I noticed in particular the two new faces in the room, and realized I couldn't say what I had to say in front of them.

Helena, seated to my left, reached out and gripped my hand before answering for me.

"We had some trouble obtaining Nero," she said. "I take it you filled everyone in on what we were trying to do?" She asked, gesturing with her other hand at Bordeaux.

"They understand, *oui*," he answered.

"Good." Helena said. "We encountered Galba on campaign in Germany under Vespasian…"

"Wait, wait, wait," Vincent said, shaking his head. "Vespasian? In command in Germany?"

"It seems you're out of the loop, sir," I said, finally finding my words. "Things are changing."

"It seems so," he agreed, looking at the floor in thought.

"Anyway," Helena started again, "we found an opportunity to take Nero, who was in the company of Agrippina as she prepared to take control of the army. Or so we thought. She set a trap for us. Jacob got pretty banged up by the same people we encountered tonight," she pointed at Gaius and Marcus as examples, "and we had to flee the area and hide. Jacob decided Byzantium was a good place to stop since he knew you'd have to come through the area to get back to Europe."

Our three friends nodded their heads, accepting her story completely. I squeezed her hand in a silent thank you. She looked over and smiled, but it wasn't completely compassionate; I owed her something. Probably a back rub or some other equally fun punishment. She was a nice taskmaster like that.

"So," she said, letting go of my hand, "who are your friends?"

Bordeaux and Vincent looked at each other, but then Vincent offered his only remaining hand in Bordeaux's direction.

The big Frenchman nodded politely, and stood.

"This," he said, indicating the tall, attractive, redheaded woman who I knew could only be one person, "is my wife. Madrina."

Madrina smiled and stood next to her husband. Just as the picture indicated, she was enormous, almost my height. She seemed older than in the picture, but her pale skin, high cheek bones and cute dimples made her a very comely woman.

"Madrina," Bordeaux continued. "This is Jacob and Helena. The silly one over there is John, but just call him Santino."

She smiled at each of us as Bordeaux ticked off our names.

"It's a pleasure to meet you," she said in Latin but with a very thick accent that sounded almost like modern German. "I have heard a lot about all of you. Especially, you... Santino?" She looked up at Bordeaux curiously as she tried to pronounce his name properly, and he nodded, smiling.

It had been pretty close.

"I'll take that as a compliment," Santino said with his typical smile.

"I wouldn't," Madrina finished, before retaking her seat, almost embarrassed that she might have offended him.

Santino just kept smiling.

"I like her," Helena said, smiling at Bordeaux, but then turned to Madrina. "It's nice to meet you too. It'll be nice to have another girl around here for a change."

Madrina returned Helena's smile, and I feared their potential girl talk.

No man knew what happened during those little pow-wows.

"What about your children?" I asked.

"They are on their way home with some of Madrina's family that came with us," Bordeaux answered. "They should be in Illyricum by now.

"Wait," Helena said, looking at Madrina. "You aren't going home with them?"

Bordeaux and Madrina exchanged glances before the redheaded woman answered.

"They will be fine. My place is with Jeanne."

"We aren't going anywhere safe," Helena informed her.

Madrina looked up at Bordeaux, and wrapped her hands around his massive left arm.

"I know," she said while Bordeaux leaned over and kissed the top of her head.

Bordeaux had a family now, yet he was still willing to risk his life to help us. But why? Duty? The idea that if he turned his back on us, his absence may result in not only our failure, but possibly our deaths? Madrina, on the other hand, had no such sense. While she was his wife, she was also a mother. Did her willingness to aid her husband, possibly putting herself in harm's way, make her a bad one?

I wasn't sure I could answer any of those questions, particularly the last.

I wasn't a mother.

What I did know was that they must have shared a truly intimate connection. Madrina wasn't the first woman Bordeaux had shared such a bond with, but the first had been taken from him by hate filled men willing to sacrifice their own lives for seventy two virgins that probably only existed in their own minds. Having to watch Helena almost die seemed trivial in comparison. She had survived, Bordeaux's first wife had not. Madrina must have meant the world to him.

"Well this warms my cold, dark, dreary heart," Santino quipped, "and I agree with Helena that it will be nice to have another girl around here to look at..." Helena opened her mouth to counter him, but Santino plowed on, "...but who's the creepy-ass kid moping in the corner? I thought that was Jacob's job."

He finished his statement by hooking his thumb towards the young man who leaned nervously against our cabinet, near Gaius, and all eyes turned promptly. He was tall, by local standards, just shy of six feet, and had a mop of brown hair, not dissimilar to mine, only curlier. He had a thin nose and a well-defined jaw line and chin, and while his posture and body language revealed his tenseness, his deep blue eyes seemed sharp and discerning.

Noticing our attention on him, he shifted on his feet but remained silent. Vincent rose from his chair and moved to stand next to him, placing his non-amputated hand upon his shoulder. His left arm had been lost just above the elbow during the Battle for Rome four years ago, and it was reassuring to see him so alive and active despite its loss. While the older man's square jaw and hard eyes looked a few years older, his grizzled expression and well built, stocky build assured me he was still a man not worth messing with.

"This," Vincent said, looking at the boy, "is Mark."

"That's it?" Santino asked. "Just Mark?"

Vincent smiled and I noticed more than just humor in his expression. Mark was one of the last names I ever expected to encounter during the days of ancient Rome. Unless, of course, this kid was actually...

I looked up at Vincent, hoping to God he didn't do what I think he did.

"You didn't," I accused worriedly. "Did you?"

"What?" Vincent asked. "Interfere with one of the Gospel writers? Whisper a little information in his ear? Alter the course of Christianity as we know it?"

"You didn't," I repeated insistently.

He laughed to himself. "Hunter, you really *are* gullible. Of course I didn't. Although, I have to admit, I've been waiting years to use that one on you."

"You're worse than Helena," I told him, receiving an elbow in the ribs for it.

"What about me?" Santino complained.

"No one is worse than you."

"Damn right," he said proudly.

I turned back to Vincent, twirling my hand at him. "You didn't actually find out anything about..." I began tentatively, "...well... you know."

"Would you really want to know if I did?" Vincent asked, raising his eyebrows.

I glanced at my feet. "No, not really actually."

"Good," Vincent said, his demeanor becoming serious again. "This young man's name is actually Titus Marcellus Glabrio." He paused and surveyed the room. "He is my son."

Silence came over the room again before Santino, not missing a beat, said, "I must say, sir, I'm very impressed. At this rate, he'll be bigger than Bordeaux by the time he's five."

I stuck my finger in his direction, ready to scold him myself this time, but then Helena reached out and grabbed my hand, pulling it down to the table between us. She shushed me and shook her head.

I nodded. I guess everyone already knew Santino really couldn't be that stupid.

Vincent gave him an exasperated look, and continued. "He is not my biological son, of course. He is my stepson. My biological son, however, just turned one."

Helena beamed. "You found someone?"

"I did," he said, smiling back. "My wife's name is Culpurnia Glabrio. She is an attendant to the governor-general of Judea's wife. Her late husband, Titus' father, was in the legions and died over a decade ago."

"I'm so happy for you, Vincent," Helena said, unable to stop grinning. "You've waited for so long. It's wonderful!" She looked over at Wang and Santino on the bed, her smile faltering momentarily before it recovered with a more mischievous look to it. "I guess that just leaves you two…"

Santino and Wang looked at her before turning to look at each other. Their looks lingered a moment before they turned back to Helena again, noticing for the first time how close in proximity they were to each other on the bed. In response, they hastily shifted apart, their cheeks blushing. Neither man looked back at the other.

"Nice one, dear," I said, wrapping my arm around Helena in a hug.

"Thanks, honey," she replied, wrapping her own behind my back.

"Oi!" Wang said defensively, pointing a finger at her, "I had my hands full in Greece. I developed a dozen medications from sleeping pills to pain killers, using nothing but local resources and the primitive, backwater tools they had available."

"Noted," Bordeaux chimed in. "You're excused." He looked at Santino. "But what's your excuse?"

Normally, Santino would just brush off any jeers at his manhood with a juvenile joke or childish comment, but despite his endless fornications with random women over the years, I knew he had a soft spot when it came to relationships. I almost expected him to make a crack about how the team was slowly turning into *Praetorians: 90210*, but I guess he just wanted to join the club these days.

He looked around the room, hoping for some support, but finding none, finally pointed his finger accusingly at Gaius and Marcus.

"What about those two?"

The two Romans exchanged glances.

"What about us?" Gaius asked. "We are both married."

"To other people," Marcus clarified.

Santino looked around the room again, hoping for someone to help him out, before tossing his hands in the air and leaning back on the bed. "I fucking hate you guys."

"What's your son's name?" Helena asked Vincent as everyone had a good laugh at Santino's expense.

The older man smiled. "Brian Wilson Glabrio."

"Brian Wilson?" I repeated, narrowing my eyes and turning them on the floor, trying to remember why that name sounded familiar. "Not very Roman…"

"None of you know?" Vincent asked, looking around the room at vacant expressions all around, and then he shook his head. "I really must be that old. Brian Wilson was one of the founding members and lead vocalist for the Beach Boys."

"You've got to be kidding," Santino said.

"I told you years ago that I loved them," Vincent remarked.

"Yeah, but…" Along with Santino's hatred for 80's music came a misunderstanding for Classic Rock in general. He sighed, "…never mind."

"It's a good name, Vincent," I said, reassuringly.

"Thank you, Hunter. I miss him already and worry for his safety constantly."

"Why's that?" I asked.

"Judea has become quite volatile over the past few years," he answered, switching to English. "Many speak of open rebellion, but I doubt much will come from it. You know as well as I that it will still be many decades before that happens, but the environment is different now. Believe me when I say, it could happen within years."

"Yeah…" I agreed, lost in thought. The Jewish uprising in the Middle East was still another thirty or so years away.

Unless…

And then a light bulb went off in my head, but I set it aside.

"Don't worry, Vincent," I said, shifting my seat on the table. "I get the feeling you'll probably be seeing him sooner than you think."

"Yes… well," he said, taking his hand off Titus' shoulder, but not moving back to his chair, "I think it would do you well to explain what it is you're planning first."

"I will," I said, pushing myself up off the table, "but before all that, Vincent, mind explaining why Titus is here exactly?"

"He's…" Vincent paused, glancing at his amputated arm, "…he's my replacement."

"What?" Santino, Helena and I asked in unison.

"Exactly as I said." Vincent sighed. "I was old four years ago, and I've really started feeling it since."

"Children have that affect," Madrina offered from her chair beside Bordeaux.

"They do indeed," Vincent replied, offering her a smile. "Besides that, I cannot use my rifle as efficiently as I once could. That is why I have been training Titus here for the past two years. I had no intention of doing so at first, but once he discovered my rifle and managed to use it without any guidance, he demanded I tell him everything. I've been training him ever since, and he has become quite the warrior."

"You told him everything?" I asked in English.

"Not… everything," Vincent answered tentatively. "There are still a few gaps in our story."

"More riddles!" Gaius complained. "Will we ever know where you are from? Why is it that you still do not trust us?

"We do trust you, Gaius," Helena said, always the mediator, "but it's for your own safety. The less you know, the better."

"It's still my guess that they're from the future," Marcus told his friend, his arms crossed proudly against his chest.

"Again with this 'future' business," Gaius exclaimed. "That is the worst idea I have heard yet. They are obviously ancestors of the ancient Titans, rivals to the gods themselves!"

Helena and I exchanged knowing glances as they bickered for a few more minutes.

"For the moment, it's not important," I told them from the center of the circle. "What is important is that young Titus here understands exactly what he's getting in to." I turned to face the young man, his late teenage face showing no sign of fear or intimidation. "Well? Are you?"

Titus looked at Vincent, who nodded in support, before he looked me square in the eye. "I am prepared, Jacob Hunter."

"Fine," I said, but decided right then that no matter how things played out, one of the first things he needed to drop was the use of my first and last name conjointly. He'd better not keep that up. Agrippina was one thing, and Gaius and Marcus used to do it all the time as well, and it had gotten old long ago.

"Don't worry, Hunter," Vincent assured. "I'll still be with you every step of the way, just in a diminished capacity."

I nodded, assured, turning now to face Bordeaux and Wang. "What about you two? You haven't been getting all lazy and paunchy on us while you've been gone?"

I looked at Bordeaux first, but all he did was roll his enormous shoulders and I had my answer.

"Never mind," I said to him. "What about her?"

Bordeaux looked down at Madrina and smiled. "I haven't bested her in a fight yet."

"Sure you haven't," I said with a snort of amusement, turning to Wang. "And you?"

In response, he rolled up his sleeve and flexed his impressively ripped bicep, proving he was still in better shape than Bruce Lee ever was.

"Great," I replied. "Except for Santino, who's been packing on the pounds…"

"I have not!"

"… we're ready to go…"

"Finally!" Wang said, smacking his knees in anticipation. "The point."

I looked at him. "Actually, I'm not quite there yet, and I'm hurt that our little reunion here has been too much of a drain on your time."

Wang blushed again while everyone chuckled at him, but I scolded myself silently for snapping at him. I'd meant for my retort to sound like a jest, but it had come off pretty harsh. I looked at Wang and held up an apologetic hand. "Sorry, James. I'm just used to dealing with Santino all the time."

He smiled. "Well that's bloody understandable."

"Good. Now, speaking of Santino," I said, holding out my hand, "the bag please."

He nodded and picked up the small local bag which held the orb and tossed it to me. I watched the sealed bag as it flew through the air, and a familiar tingling sensation crept up my spine and into the back of my skull. I was just about to reach out and snatch it when a blur to my right reached out and snagged it first. I looked to see Helena holding the bag, a know-it-all expression affixed firmly to her face.

"Yeah…" I said, the prickle of anxiety fading. "On second thought, maybe you should go ahead and open it."

She smiled and sat back down on the table, while I moved to stand near the door. Gently, she reached into the bag and extracted the most annoying creation to ever exist on this fair planet. It glowed a dim blue, perhaps sensing its proximity to me, but nothing swirled within, and it appeared solid. I eyed it suspiciously, as though it were a conscious being intent on doing me harm. I slid further away, putting just that much more distance between me and it.

Everyone not privy to what we'd been doing tonight looked astonished. Except for Madrina and Titus, who just looked confused.

"You found it!" Wang proclaimed excitedly. "Does that mean we can go home?"

"Maybe," I replied, and everyone's head shifted from the orb, to me, "but not yet. We're not even sure how it works yet. The last time I used it, I saw the cavern we traveled to within the orb, but now, there's nothing. That could mean a dozen different things, but we can't just go about experimenting with it, hoping to make our way home. We could end up in the Jurassic Period for all I know.

"What about the other one?" Vincent asked.

"That," I said, "is the other reason we can't go home yet. Agrippina has it, and while we've caused enough trouble on our own, there's no telling what kind of damage she could do with it if she ever figures out how to operate it."

Gaius, Marcus, Titus, and Madrina all looked confused, but the rest understood.

"So what are we to do with it?" Bordeaux asked.

"Well, big guy, today seems to be your lucky day," I said as a confused look spread across his face, "because you get to blow something up."

***

Unfortunately for Bordeaux, it took another few days before he could act on my promise to let him blow up much of anything. He'd already been out of his seat and rifling through his bag for explosives when an insistent knock had sounded from our door. It had been four in the morning, but despite tired and drooping eyelids all around, the entire room sprang into motion at the interruption.

Hands went to rifles or swords, chairs were abandoned, and strategic positions were taken to best defend the room. I'd been the last to find cover, of course, so I had the unpleasant duty of answering the door, which I did very carefully, half expecting one of Agrippina's ninjas to be standing there selling girl scout cookies or something.

It turned out to be no more than a few of the prostitutes infesting our building. They'd seen the constant flow of men into the room earlier, and had recruited a force of eight to try and infiltrate our lines and make some serious money. I tried not to look directly at them as they crowded around my door like a swarm of insects. Most were hideously ugly, and I could feel the venereal diseases trying to claw their way towards me from across the hall, and I just prayed they didn't rush at me.

Before they could, I politely told them to get the hell away from us and slammed the door shut. That had been enough excitement for one night. We packed up the orb and turned in. Helena offered Bordeaux and Madrina our room, even though it offered little in creature comfort, because it was the only private space we had. Helena figured Madrina, at least, would appreciate the privacy while I only hoped the abnormally large couple fit on the bed.

The rest of us conked out in the main room. Santino took the bed, claiming it had been his all along so there was no need to give it up now. The rest of us laid ourselves out on the floor, using as many pillows and blankets as Wang and Santino could pilfer from neighboring rooms. Helena and I flipped our table on its side and pushed it parallel to the back wall, creating a basic barrier between us and everyone else. We didn't plan on doing anything frisky, but the added shelter was nice. I'd had worse accommodations over the years, my mind wandering back to the few months I'd spent in Mexico again, when my men and I would find our way to one forward operating base or another, and spend the night with a random Army unit.

Not the most ideal of living conditions.

The rest of the guys spread out as best they could, but had about as much room as sardines in a can. Helena and I were comfortable, but with that many men in one room, the collective snoring kept me awake until sunrise. Helena, as always, had been out as soon as her head hit my chest, and had slept like a rock through the entire night. Hours passed before I finally pushed her off me, frustrated that I couldn't join everyone else in sleep's soothing embraces.

At least Helena didn't snore, even though I always joked that she did.

So, when I noticed the first wisps of dawn peak in through the window, I decided then would be as good a time as any to adhere to my annual tradition of watching the sun rise. I hadn't missed a year since I started doing it back in high school, but something about this one seemed like it would be special.

I climbed out through our window and up to the roof.

Our building was situated perfectly for a wonderful view of the Propontis, and I sat there and watched as the sun rose from the watery depths to claw its way into the sky. With no trees, buildings, or other obstructions blocking my view, I almost understood how ancient man could believe the sun was in fact Apollo racing his chariot across the sky on his day-long journey.

I let the sun warm my face for a few minutes, relishing in the peace, quiet and tranquility the early hour offered. I felt calm, allowing the only negative thought in my mind to consist of the fact that this moment wouldn't last forever. I let everything else fall away, basking in the glow of blissful ignorance, but as soon as the sun sat above the water line, its mirror reflection beneath it, I forced myself to sneak back into our room.

I slipped into the little cubbyhole I shared with Helena, a smile on my face, and pulled her dozing form in close and finally fell asleep. Three hours later, my smile was gone when Bordeaux walked in from his room, cheery and happy after a good night's sleep. The rest of us weren't quite so receptive and took a moment to throw pillows and blankets at him for being so fucking happy, so early in the goddamn morning, while Helena slept on uninterrupted. Wang even threw his pistol at him, but the large Frenchman simply caught it in midair. He retreated back into his room, and two hours later, the rest of us awoke on our own accord, complaining about stiff backs and sore muscles, all except Santino, of course.

After one last meat-on-a-stick for breakfast, we prepared to leave.

I wasn't ready to tell everyone what I was planning quite yet since my plan was still percolating in my own head, but once our gear was packed and loaded into our wagon, we headed east.

Again.

The only two exceptions were Gaius and Marcus, who were heading back to the German front, so that they could report to Agrippina that we now possessed one of her time traveling toys. They didn't fully understand why they were going, and I didn't blame them, but they obeyed. They said their goodbyes and dutifully left, sad to leave, but completely willing to do their part.

Three days passed, and we now found ourselves well within Anatolia – modern day Turkey – a mountainous and desolate strip of land with few people and even fewer settlements. There wasn't much to look at, except sparse trees and a rocky, shrub infested desert that wasn't quite as barren as the region we would soon find ourselves in.

We set up camp after a grueling third day of travel and turned in for the night, but once again, I found myself unable to sleep. Helena lay to my left, deep in sleep, but there was nothing I could do. Even counting sheep failed. In a fit of frustration, I slapped my sleeping mat, not feeling the slightest amount of remorse over it because I already knew it wouldn't disturb Helena.

Sometimes I really hated her.

But not really.

With no sunrise to watch and no way to rejuvenate my body, I quietly got up and made for the tent's exit. With a final glance at Helena, I shook my head. She always looked so beautiful and peaceful when asleep that it was hard to imagine any harm could ever come to her. My lips tightened at the thought, but I turned and left the tent, suddenly troubled.

Our tents were arranged around a campfire, three modern and two old-fashioned. A few dozen meters away, Wang was situated in our temporary Listening Post/Observation Post on overwatch duty for the entire camp. He controlled Santino's UAV and could monitor the area around the camp in all directions. With him on duty, the camp was more than safe. I could have sought him out for a chat, but Vincent, who was due to take over for Wang in half an hour, was seated next to the campfire.

He was warming his hand over the fire, wearing a light fleece jacket and his night op combat fatigue pants. It was a cold tonight, so I had donned a fleece as well, but only wore a pair of black shorts over my legs.

A short and chilly walk later, I joined Vincent by the fire, nodding my greetings to him as I sat on a log awaiting its turn in the fire, feeling my shins and thighs begin to warm immediately. We sat there in companionable silence for a few moments, waiting as two patient men could, the quiet lingering for quite some time. After a while, he took an audible breath and stuffed his hand deep in a pocket and gazed up at the stars.

"Beautiful night," he commented.

I glanced upward to discover what could indeed only be described as a gorgeous night sky.

"Yes," I said vacantly. "It really is."

Vincent lowered his eyes to look at me and raised his eyebrows.

"What is it, Jacob?" He said, sensing my apprehension. "You'd never been very good at hiding the fact that you had something on your mind, and it seems four years hasn't changed that."

"Really?" I asked. "Helena seems to have trouble with it from time to time."

He chuckled. "Helena is a very gifted young woman, but I've been around quite a bit longer than she has."

"True," I admitted before letting out a long breath, closing my teeth repeatedly with a series of loud clicks as I gazed into the fire.

After a few seconds, Vincent laughed again.

"It's all right, Jacob," he said between chuckles.

"I don't think it is, Vincent," I said, shaking my head while I wrapped my arms around my knees. "Helena didn't tell the whole story back in Byzantium. There's more to it. Much more." I paused. "Bad more."

Vincent nodded but remained silent, so I pressed on with everything.

I started with Varus and our encounter aboard Agrippina's barge. I told him about my encounter with the orb and about how it had enticed me with its mere presence alone, beckoning me to use it, steal it, pick it up, something. I still couldn't fully explain exactly what it had done to me in that moment, but the memory of how I had tortured Agrippina was as fresh as ever. Vincent sat in silence as I detailed what I had done to her, and said nothing more when I began to close my tale by recounting the things Agrippina had said to me, things that had planted utter confusion and uncertainty in my mind. I completed my story by telling him how I had tried to kill her, and how I couldn't quell the emotional anguish I still felt from it. Vincent let me grieve for a few minutes, tears threatening to rain down upon our raging fire.

"Have you spoken to Helena about this?" He asked finally when I'd settled down and composed myself.

I found myself staring into the fire as he spoke and I forced myself to meet his eyes. "Mostly. Without her..." I paused, unable to find the right words, "...without her, I don't know where

I'd be right now, but she's the *only* person I've been able to talk to about it at all."

Vincent shifted on his log and removed his hand from his pocket.

"Then why did you feel the need to speak with *me*?"

That was a good question. I wasn't sure what I was seeking from Vincent. He wasn't my father, in either the religious or paternal sense, but he was the next best thing. Maybe I sought acceptance or absolution, or maybe I just needed someone else to talk to.

The older man sensed my apprehension and pressed his point. "You know I am not a priest. All I can offer you is little more than a sympathetic ear."

"I know, but I thought that maybe…"

"Maybe what, Jacob? That I'd listen to your sins, make you say a Hail Mary and two Our Fathers, and send you on your way? Helena is a wonderful, caring, empathetic person. What can I offer you that she can't?"

I threw my hands in the air and smacked my knees with them.

"A different perspective, maybe? Helena is many things, but not exactly impartial when it comes to Agrippina. The only reason she's accepted what I've done is because she thinks she'd have done the same thing, but she wouldn't have. She isn't affected by the orb like I am. No one else is. I… I could use a little direction here."

"You've been second guessing yourself," he said, not missing a beat after I'd finished. "Hesitating. Questioning what was once natural instinct. Am I correct?"

I glanced away again before meeting his eyes. "I haven't been sleeping well either, actually. I don't know what my problem is. It's like my brain just shuts down and refuses to cooperate. Is that normal?"

This time it was Vincent's time to stare off into the fire. "To your last question, I have no answer, but I have seen what you are experiencing before." He paused and closed his eyes. "In me."

"Sir?" I asked, wondering where he was going with this.

He stood and moved around the fire to sit on a log closer to where I was sitting. After a few seconds he closed his eyes and said, "Hunter, I'm going to tell you something I haven't spoken of publicly in almost thirty years. It happened just after I finished my required tour of duty in Switzerland, and found myself back in my home town of Kloten."

He stopped again, not a pause, but a complete shutdown of his thoughts. He worked his jaw, as if he were still contemplating telling me anything, and I began to wonder if he'd renege on his story, but then he continued.

"On the first night of my return," he started softly, with obvious hesitation, "I was reunited with my sweetheart of five years. We'd gone to school together and I was certain we'd be married just as soon as I finished my time in the service. I took her to dinner and a play that night, a small affair as the city was not big, but we had a fabulous time..." he trailed off, a small smile forming on his lips before he repressed it completely and his remaining hand balled itself into a tight fist, "...but that night was destined to become the darkest of my life.

"We were walking home through an alley, not dangerous, just dark, holding hands as we laughed and talked. But as we approached the main road, two men stepped out from around the corner. The first man pulled a gun on us and the second pulled a tire iron from his belt.

"My first thought was that I could defeat them both in a fight. Look the hero to my girl. So I focused on the man with the gun, hoping he'd make the first move. He ordered me to take out my wallet and throw it on the ground. In retrospect, he seemed nervous. He kept his distance and never came any closer. I was such a fool. While I planned my assault, ignoring his demand, the second man stepped forward and hit my girl on the side of her head with the tire iron."

He paused again, and tears streamed from hardened eyes that I never thought could ever convey such raw emotion.

"I threw them my money and they left, but she never recovered. I carried her to a hospital only to have the doctors tell me she was in a coma, and that they had no idea when she'd recover. Her parents arrived, only to blame me and banish me from the hospital, never allowing me to visit." He expelled a lung full of air. "She's still there, at least, she was before we came here. Her parents refused to take her off life support.

"I've been to see her on every anniversary of the incident, despite her parents' wishes, until the day we came here. Her sister was always kind to me and helped me see her, but I... I don't think I've ever told her how much I appreciated her for it."

"I'm sorry, Vincent," I said, placing a hand on his shoulder. "I had no idea."

"Very few do, Hunter, but the story is not yet complete. Two nights later, I tracked her assaulter down with the help of a friend in the police, and found him outside a bar along with the gunman, and confronted them. I beat them both to within an inch of their lives." He tightened his hand into a fist and looked down at it as he continued his tale. "I can still remember as my fists drove home against their faces, pulverizing teeth and destroying bone." His hand shook violently. "I spent two hours keeping them awake before pummeling them again, just so I could do it all over again. The one who hadn't done a thing ended up paralyzed, but both lived, and I didn't care. I was nineteen years old. I knew then and there I was a different person."

I was shocked. Beyond shocked. Vincent had always struck me as the most patient, calm and unflinching individual I'd ever met. A man who always did the right thing. He never doubted himself and always made rational decisions. I couldn't imagine him doing anything like what he was describing.

"What happened?" I asked, incredulous.

"I ran away," he answered sadly. "I broke down. The anguish I felt for her and the anger I felt at myself drove me into self-imposed exile. I wandered through Europe for over a year, working odd jobs, begging in the streets. I was a wreck. Then... one day, I came back. I saw my sweetheart in the hospital, visited my family and changed my life."

"What made you come back?"

"I just realized one day that I'd made the wrong choice. In a time of great need, I pushed my friends and family away when I should have kept them close, and nearly killed two men because of it."

It was at that point that I understood where he was coming from.

"Neither man had any family," he continued, "and no charges were ever filed. My friend in the police saw to that. It wasn't something I wanted, but it was the reality I had to accept. I decided to reenlist with the military for a few years before finally joining the Swiss Guard. My first thought was to become a priest, but I knew after what I'd done that I didn't deserve it. So, I did the next best thing. It allowed me the opportunity to utilize the skills I'd developed in the military and surround myself in one of the most holy of atmospheres."

He took in another deep breath. "I will tell you, Jacob, the only people who have heard the entirety of this story are the priests I confessed this sin to on a near daily basis, and you."

I sighed, weary of hard choices and tough situations forced on people who didn't deserve either. I didn't know why life decided to play such cruel tricks on the best of people, on anyone really, but Vincent's story reminded me I wasn't alone. There were others with their own demons to battle and burdens to bear.

I reached out a hand and placed it on Vincent's knee. "Thank you for your candor, Vincent, but what made you decide to tell me?"

"Well, I think you deserved to know anyway, but," he said with a look towards the stars, "you should know that I already knew what happened between you and Agrippina. Helena spoke to me about it early yesterday morning. She told me to be ready because she knew you'd come to me."

"She did, did she?" I asked with a smirk, not even close to surprised.

"She did," he confirmed with a nod. "Like I told you, Jacob, she's a very special woman. You'd do well to remember that. Don't make the same mistakes I did. Talk to her. Use her. She wants you to. We all do. When you've done that, you can come back, and maybe I can help a bit too. But she's the one you really want to listen to."

Our campfire had been entertaining me quite a bit that night, and I found myself staring at it once again, having never grown so fascinated by it than I was just now. Vincent's words weren't anything new. Helena had told me the same exact thing months ago under Galba's bed. There, we'd aired our grievances, but hadn't worked through them. That was also a mistake, and I couldn't start throwing everything new concerning Agrippina under the bed now, especially not when it was time to confront them now more than ever

"Thanks, Vincent," I said, turning back to him with a wry look on my face. "I knew talking to you would help."

He smiled and stuck out his remaining hand, which I grasped firmly.

"So did Helena. Just remember, we all have our good moments and our bad, and some are worse than others, but regardless of which decides to surface at any given time, it's how we handle them that define who we are."

I released his hand and stood up from my log.

"I'll remember that," I said, turning back to my tent, "enjoy the rest of your night."

"Easy for you to say," he said, rolling his eyes. "I'm getting too old for watch detail this early in the morning."

I laughed and left the older man to wait out his remaining time before taking over for Wang.

My walk back to the tent was a slow one, an air of dread wafting over my head and following me all the way to the tent. I stood outside for a few seconds, perhaps fearing what I may face once Helena finally awoke in a few hours, but then I forced myself inside and secured the tent closed behind me. Pulling off my fleece coat and boots, I felt the chill air hit me like a swarm of daggers, stabbing at me repeatedly until I found my way into my sleeping bag, which Helena was keeping nice and warm. I rested my head on the pillow just briefly before deciding to shift up close to Helena and wrap my arms around her, holding her close and tight. I brushed some hair away from her neck, and kissed it, knowing my subtle touch would do little to jar her awake.

But after only the one kiss, she shifted where she lay and hummed pleasantly to herself.

"That feels nice, Jacob," she said softly. "You must have had a good talk then."

"You know," I said, leaning up over her, "for a woman who could sleep through the apocalypse, you have an interesting talent for being awake exactly when I need you to be."

She squirmed in my arms, and shifted onto her other shoulder. She pulled herself close, pressing her cheek against my bare chest. "That's because I love you, Jacob."

"I know, Helena, and that's why I want to talk to you."

"Right now?" She asked

"Right now."

She pulled back and looked up, using her hand to tilt my head down so that she could kiss me. She smiled at me and pulled away, resting her head against my chest again and closed her eyes.

"I'm ready, Jacob. Always."

***

And we talked.

And talked.

We talked until dawn.

We spent hours going over how I felt about Agrippina and what happened aboard her barge. Helena was quiet at first, but our talk quickly became one of the most heartfelt conversations of my life. I almost broke down again, not out of anger or even sadness, but just out of plain happiness at how lucky I was for having someone like Helena. She didn't try to shower me with advice or attempt to justify what I'd done. She didn't try to explain that it was all the orb's fault and none of my own. Nor did she have suggestions for what to do in the future. She said none of the things most people hated hearing when seeking solace from another individual.

Instead, she mostly listened, requesting clarification only in places she didn't quite understand, asked meaningful questions that drove the conversation deeper, and most important, didn't allow her own overwhelming bias to get in the way. This was my time to vent and grieve, and she understood that.

In the end, the feeling of unease was still there, the thought that the orb may still hold some sway over me remained, but everything else felt better. I fell asleep against her chest that night, her near naked body embracing me warmly, comfortingly, having ended our conversation with a bout of lovemaking more passionate than we'd ever shared before. Sleep came easily that night, exhausted as I was, but something told me it would continue to come just as easily as the days rolled on.

When dawn turned to morning, we had only been asleep for an hour, and Santino had arrived at our tent to inform us that breakfast was ready. I had been amazed at how quickly Helena responded, but was more impressed at the response itself as she'd leapt to her feet and shoved Santino to the ground through the vinyl of the tent.

He had to have known it was her since she was the one who normally resorted to violence.

Especially in the morning.

Outside, we heard him say, with laughter playing in the background, "She's always like that in the morning."

Helena responded by violently punching at the vinyl again, probably still half asleep. I watched drearily as she swayed in place, her arms up as though she were preparing for a boxing match, wearing nothing at all.

"All right," Santino said, "I'll make it two."

Helena collapsed at the comment and crawled her way to return her head to my chest, and fell asleep before I could make a single comment.

I was out seconds later.

Three hours later, Santino came back and shook the tent more tentatively this time to wake us up. Reluctantly, Helena rose to her feet with the mental acuity of a zombie, only remembering to put on a shirt and a pair shorts after I threw them at her, and I watched her go with a grin on my face as she shoved Santino to the dirt as she passed him by.

***

We were on the road again by late morning, continuing our trek eastward, but just as the sun began its descent from its apex, and with only a sparse tree or lonely shrub in the area, I looked around, safe in my assumption that we were countless miles away from the nearest soul, and called for a halt.

Madrina and Helena were on wagon duty, while the rest of us guys were on horseback. Women drawing carts was the norm in the area, and we didn't want to deviate from common practice. At one point in our journey, I'd noticed the two women conversing quietly but intently, and Bordeaux later rode up to inform me that he hoped I hadn't told Helena any dirty little secrets, because they were about to become his dirty little secrets as well. I'd groaned and pulled my horse away from the smiling brute, hoping Helena didn't say anything I'd later regret.

Madrina pulled hard on the reins and the wagon halted. Seconds later, Wang and Santino dismounted their horses and pulled one of our gear containers from the back of the cart. They heaved it with little difficulty, as it was completely empty, except for one small thing.

"Where do you want it, boss?" Santino asked.

I surveyed the area again, noting a single palm tree fifty meters from the road, and pointed at it. "Bury it behind that tree, at least ten feet deep."

The two men nodded and carried off the container while Bordeaux and Titus followed, carrying shovels for the four of them. Vincent remained behind, his skills with a pistol for security far outweighing his ability to dig a hole. The two ladies and I lingered as well, and I pulled out my Sig Saur P220 pistol and started cleaning it. I smiled at it as I wiped a silky cloth across the slide. The P220 wasn't standard issue for SEALs, the 9mm P226 owning that honor, but I liked the P220's increased stopping power. I always gave *Penelope* far more credit and recognition than my trusty little pistol, but I had to admit, it had saved my life on a number of occasions as well.

I decided I'd take the time to give it a more thorough cleaning this time.

An hour later, a shadow loomed across my body and interrupted my tanning session. I peeked through an eyelid, but the sun's glare disrupted my ability to identify who it was.

"We are ready, Jacob Hunter," Titus said from above me.

I grunted. His continuous use of my full name had, as I predicted, become irritating. I waved a hand at him and stood, hauling a dozing Helena to her feet alongside me. I looked over at the shirtless Titus, who had removed his top along with the rest of the diggers to keep cool. I couldn't help but be impressed. For a kid of eighteen who had two thousand year old genetics, poor dietary habits like all ancient men, and no access to modern fitness equipment and training regimens, he was a model of physical excellence. No more so than the rest of us, of course, but he'd never had the kind of help we had. Vincent must have worked him hard over the past few years. He'd already proven to be a halfway decent shot over the past few days, and he dug as good a hole as any legionnaire. It didn't take much more than that to make me happy to have him around.

Even so, he was too damn quiet. Very contemplative and thoughtful, he never said what was on his mind unless directly asked to, and even then it was with obvious bashfulness. He was the complete opposite of Santino, and while I knew I should count my blessings for it, his polar opposite attitude was almost equally annoying. But he was still trying to fit in, I suppose. The rest of us were much older and far more experienced, so his timidity didn't surprise me.

Looking over at him, I offered him a smile and patted his dust-caked shoulder in appreciation. He returned the smile distantly, and turned to look at the remaining trio of men returning from the dig site as well – just as dirty and just as shirtless.

"My God, Santino," I said loudly as I spotted him, "put a shirt on. No one wants to see that."

Providing a visual aid for my joke, I held my hand out over Helena's eyes, blocking her view. She playfully tried to bat away my hand, acting the part of a curious child.

Santino looked at his stomach and over his shoulder, spinning himself around a few times. His sixpack glistened like a Men's Fitness magazine cover, but he was just as gullible as I was when it came to his ego. I'd been calling him chubby for the past year now, slowly progressing to calling him a fatass, and that child-like mind of his ate it up. Sometimes I wondered if he really was that stupid, or if he just liked to play along because he didn't care who the punch line was at the expense of, as long as it was funny.

I suspected the latter.

"Come on, Hunter!" He complained. "Just tell me what I need to work on! I've been good; no MRE snacks at all, I swear!"

"Don't ride him so hard, Jacob," Helena said. "I've always found paunch oh, so sexy."

I laughed and waited for Santino to stop spinning around and join the rest of us. Wang and Bordeaux had already found their way onto the wagon, sitting patiently as they waited for everyone to get comfortable for the show.

I only had to wait a few more seconds before Santino finally joined us, and I turned to Bordeaux.

"Ready?" I asked.

"*Oui*," he answered from atop the wagon.

"Do it."

I heard the subtle click of his small detonation box, before the follow up explosion nearly deafened us all. A cloud of dirt went flying in the air, along with thousands of tiny pieces of the cargo container.

Bordeaux had decided to use one of our original gear containers as a means of containing the blast in a way that also magnified its power. The containers were bullet and water proof, air tight, and could withstand mortar strikes. By placing an explosive within the sealed container, any explosion's power was increased exponentially. Inside, he'd placed the orb with a thin strip of C4 wrapped around its circumference, more than enough to destroy it alone. Burying the container was only further insulation to contain the blast.

As the shockwave passed, I realized I had my eyes squeezed shut, and felt Helena reach out and touch my arm.

"Are you all right?" She asked.

Peeking, I noticed we hadn't moved. "Yeah," I said with a sigh. "I guess I almost thought we'd be sent home."

She gave me a reassuring smile and rubbed my arm. "You knew it couldn't have been that easy. Come on. Let's see if it worked."

I took her hand as we headed toward the blast sight together, the remaining six members of our party following closely. Reaching the palm tree, which was now tilting at a forty five degree angle from the pressure of the blast, I inspected the neatly blown out hole that spanned at least thirty feet in diameter. The orb was nowhere in sight, and all I saw were blue dust fragments glittering in the sunlight.

"It worked," Santino commented.

"Of course it worked," Bordeaux said, annoyed that anyone would ever doubt his ability to destroy something.

I half smiled at his comment, continuing to gaze at the crater. It was a small victory, yes, but a hollow one. All we did was destroy something that didn't belong here to begin with. Six of us standing here right now were no less innocent in that light, but we weren't as easy to deal with. We'd managed to dispose of one of the many snags in the timeline, sure, but it didn't make our jobs any easier. We still needed to find the second orb and find a way to make it send us home before destroying it. That was the only way to ensure its destructive potential came to an end.

Unfortunately, it seemed like the only way we were going to get it was if we went through Agrippina first, and to get to her we needed to get through her Praetorians, and possibly her legions.

"So now what?" Wang asked, not taking his eyes off the crater as well.

"We keep heading east," I replied.

"Why is it so important we go there?" Bordeaux asked.

I sighed. It was time to discuss the plan.

The new and improved one.

"What does Agrippina have that I don't?" I challenged, walking out in front of the group.

"Power?" Wang offered, but I shook my head.

"Money?" Bordeaux tried to similar success.

"Boobs?" Santino asked while I ignored him.

Helena, Madrina, and Vincent were staying silent, unable or unwilling to offer any further guesses.

"An army," Titus said bluntly.

All eyes turned to him. It was the first time he'd spoken when not directly asked to do so. He looked calm in his answer, his face confident, and he had every right to be.

"Exactly," I said, nodding appreciatively at the young man.

"So what can we find in the east that will help us against an army?" Helena asked as she hugged herself, trying to stave off the cool dusk air and nervousness alike.

"What else?" I asked rhetorically with a shrug of my shoulders. "An army of our own."

VIII
Judea

Mission Entry #8
Jacob Hunter
Caesarea, Judea- August, 42 A.D.

So I bet you're wondering what we're doing in Caesarea. That, or perhaps you're wondering where the hell Caesarea even is? Maybe both. To answer the second question first, it's about as far east as one can get from Rome and still be in the Empire, just north of Jerusalem. The first question is a bit trickier. We're here because instead of fighting history, I'm going to embrace it.

Finally get my money's worth out of that History/Classical Studies double major.

This may take a bit of explaining, so bear with me.

Twenty years from now, Rome is about to experience a major outbreak of hostility among the Jewish people in the province of Judea. Unfair tax laws, offensive religious policies, the restriction of self-government, and simple hostile attitude will soon be enough to piss the Jews off to the point where they decide to move against their Roman protectorates.

Jews...

Anti-Semitism was nothing new, even if it was a term coined in the 19th Century by a German journalist named Wilhelm Marr, if I'm remembering my European Civ II class properly. It's also technically a misnomer. Semitic languages ranged from Arabic, Hebrew, Aramaic, to Phoenician, yet the hatred was aimed solely at the Jewish people.

Personally, I had nothing against them, but it didn't take a historical genius to argue that Jews were notorious for finding themselves on the bad side of many personalities throughout history, whether it be Muslims, Christians, Crusaders, Nazis, Muslims again, and more contemporary folk: Romans and Greeks.

Poor guys.

So, what was Rome and Greece's beef with them?

Well.

Jews are stubborn, at least in the sense that they adhere to ancient practices and rituals as though they had been developed only weeks before. Romans, however, didn't much like that, and were constantly annoyed at how uptight Jewish society was. They took issue with single deity religion and didn't like the idea that Jews were owed something they called the "promised land." I'm making light of the issue, I know, but while Romans were normally at ease with other cultures and their religions, any subservient society was still expected to know its place on the pecking order.

As for the Greeks, well... let's just say Jews, like any other culture, take a certain amount of pride in their society and did little to hide their superiority about it. Greeks, being the pompous windbags that they were, felt the same way. All that logic and philosophy went right to their heads. So, since Hellenistic (Greek) culture was dominant from Africa to Babylon and Saudi Arabia to Greece, Jewish culture was just a very small fish in a much bigger pond.

They simply never got along.

So, where does Agrippina fit in then?

Simple.

Despite her obvious shortcomings, she hasn't been a total failure as empress. She's actually done some good, most of which would have been done under Claudius anyway. She annexed all the right territories like Thrace, Noricum, Lycia, and Judea as well, and placed the childhood friend of Claudius, Herod Agrippa I, on the throne, just as Claudius would have done. However, Claudius had given Herod free reign to rule Judea, finally giving the Jews some semblance of autonomy, whereas Agrippina had not.

But the peace hadn't lasted very long in the original timeline anyway, and during the reign of Herod II, Roman procurators overstepped their jurisdiction and usurped more and more control for themselves, initiating a chain of events that led to the Jewish revolt in 66 A.D.

That's where Agrippina messed up.

Herod's nothing but a puppet ruler under her tenure. He has no real control. We've only been here a few weeks, and it's been as easy as sitting in a restaurant to learn just how many disgruntled Jews there are here. Some simply want Herod to have more power while others want the procurators gone. There are even some who speak of complete secession. These later fellas will soon be remembered as Zealots, the same as those who started the conflict in 66 A.D.

They'd be handy soon enough.

As I've said, I'm not an expert on the Roman-Jewish War of 66 A.D., but there was more to it than Roman and Greek dislike for the Jewish people alone. Besides the social upheaval, there was economic mismanagement, religious disenfranchisement, political pandering, and most importantly, the impetuousness of youth.

As it was in any society, the driving force behind any kind of social resistance or protest started with the idealistic young people. I've got nothing against voicing one's opinions, even if they do go against the norms of an institution, because the ability to protest and voice that opinion is a fundamental right that should be granted to all humanity.

Unfortunately, unlike the generally understanding America I left, the Roman Empire wasn't exactly lenient when it came to recalcitrant troublemakers. As a result, it brought down the wrathful fury of its legions upon the small province of Judea.

And here we are, twenty five years earlier, placing our faith in the theory that if you want to get shit done, you see the young people first. Sociologists would leap at the opportunity to be in our position right now. If we could rally the young people of today, who were in fact the same old men who were probably content to live under Roman rule and opposed the war in 66 A.D., in the original timeline, we'd be verifying a very interesting social paradigm.

So, we have some plans, and I must say, for once, not half-assed ones. We are ready this time, and I have the full support of my team.

Oh, sorry I was so brash in my last journal entry, but I was too excited to put any serious thought into anything. Vincent, Bordeaux and Wang were back and had a few friends with them. Bordeaux had his wife, Madrina, and Vincent his stepson, Titus. Madrina is a hell of a cook, and since Bordeaux would never risk putting her directly in harm's way, has become the team's central organizer. She handles the expenses, logistics, inventory, and makes sure everything runs smoothly, and she's pretty good at it. I guess raising kids does that to people.

As for Titus, Vincent has been training him to replace him for the past few years, as his lost arm had drastically hinders his combat effectiveness. Nineteen years old, the kid is strong, fast, smart, and a good shot. We've given him the spare combat fatigues meant for McDougal, along with our fallen commander's G36 assault rifle, and he's fit in just fine.

He's too quiet though. Never says a damn thing. And he still calls me by my first and last name. That's aggravating.

Okay. I'm not adding anymore spoilers. If you've read your history and already know what's going to happen, great, if not, you're just going have to wait like the rest of us.

"What're you smirking at?" Santino asked as he munched on a piece of bread.

"Hmm?" I replied distractedly, glancing up. "Oh, just taking a little pleasure in baiting my future readers. I'm going to make a movie out of this yet!"

Santino shook his head and waved his pita bread at me, trying to swallow his latest mouthful. Middle Eastern cuisine hadn't changed much in two thousand years, and I was happily enjoying pita bread, falafels, and a classic shish-ka-bob, complete with vegetables and meat.

"No, that's not it," Santino managed finally. "Something else." He tapped his chin in thought. "Isn't your birthday coming up?"

"Nope," I said honestly.

He was late by a week, and it hadn't been as horrendous as I'd thought it would be, now that Helena knew about it. Although, she did force me to admit how old I was, just so she could carve a number into the MRE dessert cake she'd given me. At least she'd unenthusiastically agreed with my theory that I was thirty one, and not thirty two due to the lost months during our trip through time.

It took some doing though.

"Then what? I haven't seen you this pleased with yourself in years. Helena wear something sexy to b…?"

"No," I answered quickly. I wasn't going to let him have the pleasure of forming the mental image.

"Just tell me! It's not like we're really doing anything right now. Just waiting. Like always."

I wrapped up my journal and dropped it in the bag I'd bought in Byzantium, and turned to survey my surroundings. Santino and I were sitting in a nice café on a balcony overlooking the Mediterranean Sea. We had a beautiful view, and even though it was at least ninety degrees Fahrenheit outside, the dry air made it bearable and the sea breeze, comfortable.

"This isn't exciting to you? Get your blood boiling?" I asked him, pumping my fists. "We're done sneaking around. Done not knowing what to do next. We're taking control for once. It's like we're on some grand adventure now instead of just half-assing it. I'm instigating an open rebellion against one of the most dominant world powers to ever grace civilizations, usurping an empress with my own emperor, pitting two political sides against each other, and possibly changing the course of world history!" I paused for dramatic effect. "And looking good doing it."

I brushed my hands through my newly cut hair to emphasize my point. I'd let it grow almost to my shoulders in Byzantium, but now it was back to my preferred length of short, but still longer than Navy regulations. It was much more comfortable this way and Helena really liked it too.

Santino had cut his hair as well, and had shaved his beard too. His new hairstyle was one popular throughout the empire these days, stylized after how Julius Caesar wore his hair: short, with tiny little curls for bangs. His freshly shaved face was also a local Roman grooming standard and set him apart from many of the local Jews who sported bushy facial hair. Combined with his stupid grin and myriad dashing scars, he had even more luck with the ladies these days, a fact he let few forget, especially Wang. Helena's little joke a month ago had spawned some kind of competition between the two of them, the only apparent objective being to sleep with as many women as possible.

Santino was winning, and whenever he wins at anything, he's generally pretty annoying about it.

Santino yawned. "Some grand adventure. All we've been doing is sitting on our asses for three weeks." He looked out over the Mediterranean. "Nice view, though."

"You're worthless," I commented. "Only you couldn't get caught up in all this."

"This isn't a Dan Brown story, Jacob. This is real life."

I tilted my head to the side. "You can read?"

He smiled. "I've seen the movies."

I sighed, resigning myself to Santino's mood. He *was* right. We *were* doing a lot of waiting these days, but political scandals took a long time to work themselves out.

"Will you two please stop bickering," the faint voice of Helena said in my ear piece. "Try and stay focused."

"*What?*" I said, pretending her words were somehow shocking and insulting. "No way. Are you telling me it's okay for you and me to bicker, but I can't even argue with my best pal?"

"Yeah, mommy," Santino chimed in, the both of us on VOX. "I'm just hanging with my besty. Gee, Hunter, you sure can pick 'em. Always the needy, clingy, bitchy ones."

I nodded my head in agreement. "You know what, John? You're absolutely right. Maybe I should listen to you more often."

He bobbed his head along with me. "Been sayin it for years."

"Of all the…"Helena said, anger now clearly evident. "You two know I can shoot you right…"

"Stop…" the drawn out voice of Vincent interrupted in an obviously annoyed manner.

Santino and I exchanged smiles and traded air high fives. Having everyone back together brought out the worst in us, and the past couple of weeks had been just like those first few weeks in Rome, with Santino cracking jokes, me backing him up, and Helena hating every moment of it.

Of course, back then all she would do is playfully punch me when I annoyed her. Now, she was denying me more recreational and… fun things.

But like Santino earlier, she had a point. Santino and I weren't enjoying lunch together to annoy her, as much as we wished we were, but to meet our contact. Because we had extensive knowledge of the current and near future socio-political atmosphere of the area, I knew King Herod was the key to our plans, as opposed to his Roman equivalent. That's why we were waiting for one of his top tier administrators to meet us for lunch.

To have a little chat.

I glanced around the café. It was just as nice as the one in Byzantium, but the view alone made it far superior. It added such grandeur to the spot, and the amount of space and open area available made the location much more beautiful than anything Byzantium had to offer. Most of the buildings were tan in color, and the flooring was constructed out of a creamy sandstone. Combined with the sandy beaches, the bright blue water and crystal clear sky, I could almost imagine we were in the Bahamas.

It looked like a grander version of any Middle Eastern city, just without the centuries of decay and war, long before infighting and squabbling would tear it apart. I'd never been to Dubai, but I could almost picture this place as a two thousand year old equivalent, just without the palm tree shaped islands.

The plaza where our café was situated was huge, easily the size of a football field. It had outside seating for hundreds, and it was beautiful. I hadn't known much about the city coming into it, except that its port had been recently renovated, but all in all, even Rome wasn't quite as stunning. Vincent told me it had taken Herod the Great twelve years to rebuild the city, and it was certainly worth it. The city boasted a theatre, a hippodrome, perhaps the finest port in all antiquity, and the entire city appeared to have been chiseled by the skilled hands of a sculptor, like Michelangelo, out of some kind of pure white stone. A material so wonderful it could have been a city sized chunk of ivory for all I knew. Arches, towers, turrets, multistory buildings, aqueducts, temples, small palaces... the city had it all, and it was breathtaking.

It's a shame that it was destroyed at one point and probably will be again.

The table I was sharing with Santino was directly in the center of the café, and sat right next to the low wall that separated patrons from the cliff that dropped off to the beaches below, only a few meters below us. Bordeaux and Madrina sat a few tables away, sharing their own meal, wearing local clothing that looked almost identical to the indigenous clothing of Middle Eastern townspeople in our own century. Vincent and Titus were near a vending stall for exotic weaponry not too far behind Santino, effectively pulling off a father and his eldest son out for a day of shopping. Wang was hiding in an alley, out of sight, ready to deploy as a quick reaction force if something horrible went down. Finally, Helena was posted in an abandoned lighthouse, very far away.

The shoreline behind me ran for about four hundred meters before jutting out into the sea at a right angle for another hundred meters. Helena's lighthouse hide was at the end of the little peninsula formed by the shoreline's shift seaward. Utilizing a little Pythagorean Theorem know how – the little math that I knew – that put Helena four hundred twelve meters out, not accounting for her elevation.

Santino and I were well covered, and I couldn't think of a time or place where I've ever felt safer. We were about to do something both smart and stupid, and it was nice to have the backup. I wasn't going to let the feeling shift to overconfidence like it had with Agrippina, but it was still nice.

Secure in my friends' presence, I was watching a flock of seagulls fly over the water when a long shadow fell across my face and I noticed Santino put his feet down in readiness. I turned my head to see a bearded man stop next to our table. He wore a long brown robe, with a thick sash dyed dark red, and the sleeves had two thick stripes running around the edges. He had dark features, craggy skin, dark hair, a salt and pepper beard, and he looked perturbed.

Santino pulled out a chair, brushed it off with his sleeve, and offered it to the newcomer.

The man turned to stare at Santino, his eyes steady and angry, and it only took ten seconds before Santino's wide smile faltered and another five after that before it fizzled away completely. He looked at the table in embarrassment. I found myself shocked anyone had the power to do such a thing. Clearly, this guy wasn't one to screw around with.

Satisfied Santino was now secure in his place at the bottom of the food chain; the bearded man took his offered seat, crossed his left leg over his right, and appraised the two of us intently. I didn't flinch at his perusal, doing my best to return his stare coolly.

"This guy doesn't look too happy," Helena's reassuring voice commented in my ear, no anger from earlier remaining in her observation.

I nodded just enough so that she could catch it through her scope. She was right for the second time today. This guy was a Zealot. He hated Roman authority and their overreaching disregard for anything Jewish. In the original timeline, almost twenty five years from now, men like him would form the nucleus for the uprising against Roman rule, resulting in one of the bloodiest rebellions in Roman history, and over a million Jewish casualties.

"You are *Vani*," he said, more of a statement than a question.

"We are," I answered. "My name is Burt, and this is my friend Ernie."

"I wanted to be Burt," Santino mumbled in English.

I shot my eyes at him. "Shut it."

It had surprised us to learn upon our arrival that our reputation had greatly preceded us. Even here in Judea, people had heard the stories of a mysterious band of do-gooders who went around helping those who couldn't help themselves. Everyone knew the highways of Rome weren't safe from the likes of Madriviox and all the other scum we'd eliminated over the past four years, and to hear of people who tried to help others was unusual.

Nearly every day since we'd been here, whether we were just walking through the markets or eating in a restaurant, stories of our endeavors circulated through Caesarea like they were headline news stories.

Humorously, most of the stories were outlandish versions of what really happened, especially when they revolved around Helena. Told mainly by the young men of the city, one story was that of a nine foot tall, black haired Amazon, whose outfit was always described in a way that reminded me of the armor worn by female warriors in any number of geek fantasy stories.

Not that I knew anything about those, of course.

Apparently, the woman could shoot lighting from her eyes, decapitate men with a blink, and disintegrate them with the snap of her fingers. I'd joked with Helena that it seemed society knew her better than I did.

Other stories weren't nearly so ridiculous, but each carried a morsel of truth to them, and once people started noticing dark figures flitting about their rooftops during the night these past few weeks, the rumor mill had fresh material to work with. Like we'd done in Byzantium, we spent our nights scouting and mapping the city of Caesarea. It was twice the size of Byzantium, but with our added manpower and the help of Santino's UAV, most of the work was done quickly and easily.

"My name is Matiyahu Ben Yosef," he continued a second later, which I translated as Matthias, son of Joseph. "Is it true that you... do things for people?"

"It depends on what you mean by 'do'," Santino answered with a shudder.

"I have also heard that you are honorable men," Matthias rebuked, standing from his chair angrily. "Men who value human life above all else. If not..."

I held out a hand and indicated he should retake his seat.

"We *are* honorable," I reassured. "Please excuse my friend. He is as loyal as a dog, but unfortunately not much brighter."

Matthias looked back down at Santino, probably wondering why the smiling idiot wasn't enraged by my insult. He slowly retook his seat, probably figuring Santino had a child's mind in a man's body.

"Fine," he said, resettling in his chair. "If you are indeed men of honor, as you so claim, I wish to purchase your services. From the stories I've heard, you are capable of a great many things."

"We do what we can," Santino said cheerfully.

I kicked him beneath the table. We didn't need him pissing this guy off with his stupid ass antics.

"What would you have us do?" I asked.

Waiting for him to reply, I took a second to scan the plaza, checking for foul play. I caught Bordeaux's eye, only to receive a shake of his head in return. Helena must have noticed my shift in attention because she sent an all clear double click over the radio as well. Looks like this guy was playing ball. We'd told him through a number of intermediaries to come alone and during the middle of the day, ostensibly for his own protection, but really just because we didn't trust anyone.

We knew he was the head of the local Zealot movement, and that his rhetoric and speeches had been fueling the rebellious spirit of the city for months. We hadn't known his name, just that he was looking for a way to topple Agrippina's stranglehold on Judea and establish Herod as the legitimate sovereign of the territory.

"There is a war coming," he answered. "Rome is unfit to govern the Jewish people. We are followers of Yahweh, the one true God. Our people did not endure years of slavery in Egypt and the perils of reaching the Holy Land, here, only to find ourselves enslaved now as we were then."

I nodded.

Twenty five years from now, many in this area felt that their customs, religious views, and culture were being constricted by Roman government to the point where they were losing their identity. This simply would not do for a sect of humanity like them.

That said, the Jewish population was close to, but not quite ready, for war. It could take another two years or so before the rebellion began if it were left to its own devices. We couldn't wait that long, and it seemed young Matthias couldn't either...

I paused

Matthias...

Ben Joseph?

"Before we continue, I have a small personal question," I interrupted, waiting for his nod before continuing. "Tell me, do you have a son?"

Matthias tilted his head back in surprise. "Yes, in fact I do. A young boy, five years of age. His name is Joseph, after my own father."

I smacked my thigh beneath the table. I knew his name sounded familiar, but it wasn't until he clarified he had a son named Joseph, that it clicked.

Joseph Ben Matthias.

Known as Titus Flavius Josephus later in his life, or simply Josephus, he was the primary source of information concerning the war between Roman and Jew in 66 A.D. He'd fought for the Jews, only to become a client to Vespasian, hence the addition of Titus Flavius to his name after he was captured. Historians either loved him or hated him. Most admitted he was an invaluable contemporary historian, but others felt he was overly biased towards his Roman protectorates. I now know I couldn't blame the guy. Living in Rome was a perilous affair, and if Josephus wanted to survive, he had known better than to annoy those who had retained him to record the events.

Either way, the thought was just plain cool. We'd met some pretty interesting and influential Romans over the years between Caligula, Claudius, Galba, and even Agrippina. While Joseph was still just a boy, the fact that we were very possibly interacting with his father was fascinating. It was almost as though fate, and I hated that goddamned word, was driving us toward as many historical figures as it could.

"Why?" Matthias pressed.

I recovered well, pointing my finger at him. "You speak of war, yet you have a son. If you are instigating something of such magnitude, maybe you should be thinking of him more than us."

"I *am* thinking about him," Matthias countered angrily. "It is for his very future that Roman rule must be questioned and dealt with. We are nothing but pawns in their political games. They care little for our values and practices, and desire only our servitude. They conscript our young men into their legions, over-tax us with little thought to our survival, deny us the freedom to practice our religious ceremonies, and of all the cultures in their vaunted empire, despise, humiliate and degrade ours more than any other."

I heard the vehemence and power in his voice as if he were orating upon a *rostrum* even now, espousing his views to his fellow Jews. Not only did I hear his words, but I felt his emotions as they bubbled to the surface, realizing just how feverishly he believed in his ideals.

The only thing I wondered was if he felt the same way twenty five years from now, in the original timeline, when things were quite different.

"If you are *Vani*," he continued, "defenders of the weak and champions for liberty, then you must understand our plight."

He made no indication that we should feel obligated to help him or that because of these supposed ideals, for us to not help them, would make us hypocrites in our own eyes. He knew he was dealing with powerful people and made no assumptions otherwise. He'd pleaded his case well, and knew without saying, that if we were who we said we were, we had no choice but to help him.

I glanced at Santino, then back at him.

"What would you have us do?" I asked.

"When the time comes... stand with us. Help us defeat the Romans."

I forced myself from sighing in disgust, because here's where I had to lie.

"We will help you, Matthias Ben Joseph. Contact us when you have further information."

Matthias showed no emotion, no suspicion, or even a smile in celebration. He merely stood, nodded and left. Santino and I'd been sitting at this table, at the same time, every day, for a week now, and he knew we'd be here tomorrow.

Now that he was gone, I allowed myself to release the slow sigh of personal abhorrence I had been holding in for too long.

I tried to reason everything I'd just done and soothe my conscience by remembering that this war was going to happen with or without our influence. One way or another, Romans and Jews were going to fight each other. Many on both sides were going to die. We were merely accelerating its beginning to serve our needs, but we had no intention of helping the Jews win. All we needed was for them to draw Agrippina away from Germany. We planned to fight with them until that happened, but once she arrived, we needed to take action, and that meant abandoning those we promised to help win their freedom.

I tried to reassure myself by remembering that despite our abilities, we were still a very small drop in the ocean that is the Roman war machine. They'd have little trouble putting down this rebellion with or without our help.

Fate, as it was, would get what it wanted.

"So?" Santino asked, his skilled eyes tracking Matthias' departure. "Now what?"

"Now," I replied, letting out another sigh as I got to my feet, "we go play the other side."

***

I glanced at my watch. 0130. Ten hours after our meeting with Matthias.

Santino and I were sneaking through the side streets of Caesarea, making our way to the home of the Roman procurator, Cuspius Fadus. Like foreign embassies in the 21st century, Rome kept little bastions of itself tucked away in the provinces it controlled, where provincial administrators and their families would operate and live in small compounds, tucked away and secure behind twenty foot walls and a local force of urban cohorts.

Nothing we couldn't handle.

Infiltrating a Roman administrative complex was child's play next to sneaking into a legionary fort.

Our intel confirmed lazy guards, gaps in their perimeter, and a complete lack of patrols, whether on rooftop or within the courtyards. We assumed there would be guard patrols within the halls of the buildings, but I wasn't expecting much. There was a fair chance that once inside we'd encounter very little, if any, resistance.

Bordeaux, Wang and Titus were on overwatch, tracking us with the UAV. They waited nearby, having gone to ground in defensive positions along bordering rooftops to provide cover fire should we need it. Helena, as always, was situated about three hundred meters away, playing the pivotal role of guardian angel. The past four years had instilled in me an inherent trust, along with a need, to know she was there. The rest of the guys were appreciated reinforcements, but without her doing what she did best, I wouldn't be so confident.

Finally, Vincent and Madrina were on bail-out duty. Madrina had the wagon we'd brought with us from Gaul loaded and ready to go, while Vincent controlled the rest of the team's horses. Should we need to get the hell out of Caesarea, it would be a quick matter of linking up with them and bugging out.

I lowered my arm and glanced at Santino, just in time to stop myself from bumping into him. He'd stopped at a corner and was peaking around, scanning for potential threats. His hand signal indicated all was clear, and he led the two of us into a small alleyway, dead ending with the halls of the embassy to our right, and other residential homes to the left and in front of us.

Using the shadows for cover, Santino reached into his locally made bag and extracted his grappling hook and rope. After performing a quick inspection of his equipment, an assortment of expletives spewed from his mouth when he discovered the rope had found a way to tangle itself in his poorly designed pack, a problem that wouldn't have happened had the mission called for our night ops combat fatigues and modern age gear, but tonight, we were going native.

Madrina was not only a logistical expert, a great cook and a pretty face, but a fine seamstress as well. Being pretty handy with a needle and thread myself, she and I crafted a few sets of clothing that very closely resembled what Agrippina's Praetorian ninjas wore. The outfits weren't overly difficult to craft, the material consisting of some kind of ancient denim/corduroy hybrid, and the end result was close enough to fool just about anyone who'd encountered the troublesome foe before.

Santino dropped another expletive when he had to backtrack his untangling and attack the rope from another direction.

"Ever get the feeling we overuse this plot device?" He asked, frustrated.

"You mean the grappling hook?" I asked back. "Nah, grappling hooks are way cool. Every good movie has them."

"Name one."

"Uh, ninja and pirate movies?"

I didn't have much to offer. It had been four years since I'd last seen a movie, and my once extensive vault of pop culture knowledge was quickly fading.

"Good enough for me," he said, finally deciding on the best route to untangle his mess. "Speaking of movies, put any thought into what you're going to do first when we get home?"

I actually hadn't thought much about it. Camp gossip had, as of late, been rife with little else but thoughts of home, but I tried not to allow myself the luxury of an, as of yet, distant hope.

"Probably take a two hour long shower I guess," I answered, not really needing to think about it much. "There's dirt on me that's been with me ever since our time in the *Primigenia*'s camp."

Santino ceased what he was doing completely to look at me. "Will Helena…"

"Shut it."

"And after that?" He asked, not missing a beat, already back at work on the rope.

I sighed. "I'm not sure. Since we were talking about movies, maybe I'll watch one. Helena has promised to sit through all the Bond movies with me, maybe we'll start…"

"Do you two ever stop talking?" Helena asked from three hundred meters away.

"Sorry, mommy," Santino said, finally getting the rope under control.

I sent him a thumbs up, more for the quip than his successful defeat of the stubborn rope, and backed up to give him room to throw it over the wall. Tossing it over, he pulled it taut and ascended into the little piece of Rome away from Rome.

Once upon the stone wall, the compound's lack of security became immediately apparent. The guard station to our left revealed two snoozing guards, derelict of duty and in serious need of a few lashes from a centurion's olive branch. We paid them little mind and moved deeper into the compound, making our way inside the small housing and administrative complex where the guards were negligible as well – as we knew they would be.

Santino and Wang had infiltrated the embassy yesterday, under the guise of rival store vendors hoping to defer to Roman law over a price gouging controversy. The two had spent their time mapping out the interior of both administrative and residential wings of the large building, and had identified the location of the procurator's room. The two morons even managed to get their fictitious case heard by him, who sided with Wang, stating that the quality of Santino's goods did not justify his prices.

Crazy bastards.

We moved quickly through the complex, only running into one real problem along the way. Just outside the procurator's room, a pair of guards who apparently took their jobs more seriously than the rest, stepped into view as we made our way down the hall that led to our destination. Using the cover of darkness, I hid behind a small column while Santino ducked under a marble bench, and we waited for them to simply pass us by. We had to wait another ten minutes before they finally passed by us again.

A ten minute window being more than enough time to make our way into the procurator's room, we carefully walked to Fadus' room, opening and closing the heavy wooden doors with a gentle touch. Moving into the room, Santino tapped my shoulder and pointed to the ceiling, indicating the open skylight above us. I tossed him nod, indicating I too saw the designated escape route we had noted the night before. We located two chairs, and moved them beside the bed, plopped ourselves down, and inspected our target.

It was hot outside, muggy, and the night air was stifling. Cuspius Fadus lay bare-chested upon the bed, only a light sheet wrapped haphazardly around his midsection, and the only other piece of adornment he wore was a pretty nice piece of arm candy, in the form of a naked, dark skinned girl somewhere in her twenties. This girl wasn't Fadus' wife, and while I never condoned adultery, I was pretty impressed with his catch of the night.

"Wake up," I whispered.

Fadus' eyes shot wide open and he bolted into a sitting position. The young girl awoke much slower, confused as to what had alerted her older lover before she noticed us. After another ten seconds, along with a very revealing show of her nude form, she finally realized her nakedness and went about securing the sheet over herself. She cowered beneath Fadus' arm for protection and eyed us nervously.

Fadus was in his forties, with black hair and a bit of paunch on his stomach, but still in pretty good shape. I assumed he didn't need his prestigious position to score with lovely young ladies like the one here tonight, but it probably helped. Like most of his fellow procurators, word on the street was that he was avaricious and bloodthirsty, the same qualities his successors thirty years from now possessed as well.

He was exactly someone Agrippina would choose and the people hated him for it.

"The Empress sent you, didn't she?" He asked. "You must be her new lapdogs she has been threatening everyone with."

I stayed silent, deferring to Santino's dialect magic, once again in character.

"We are," he confirmed, his Latin sounding distinctly southern Italian. "My name is Mario, and this is Luigi."

"What do you want?" Fadus asked, shaking his head in confusion. Whether it was from our presence or the names Santino provided, I didn't know.

Santino leaned in close, resting his elbows on his knees.

"It is the Empress' wish to settle an issue here in Judea. She regrets her appointment of Herod. Even though he holds little power, she wishes you to remove him."

"That shouldn't be too difficult," Fadus admitted. "I have received word that he will be in Caesarea for at least another week. With the growing tension in the city, I would think it a matter of little difficulty to send him back to Rome. Should hostilities occur, people will either blame him or expect him to resolve them himself. Neither option seems enjoyable to me."

"You do not understand," Santino said with a shake of his head. "She wishes for you to eliminate him."

"Assassinate him?"

"Yes. His presence has become a nuisance to Rome. The Empress receives constant correspondence from him and his people demanding a change in Rome's political and administrative policies concerning Judea, but as you are fully aware, the Empress is quite satisfied with her policies."

"Yes, she is quite confident," Fadus admitted, looking at his feet.

Even a career bureaucrat had to know some of her policies were bullshit and that people were not happy about it.

He looked back at Santino, his eyes suspicious. "Why are you coming to me unannounced in the middle of the night? Could you not have made an appointment with me tomorrow and come see me then?"

"We are asking you to assassinate a local head of state," Santino said slowly. "One does not normally ask such things in an official capacity... does one?"

"Well, no, I suppose not," Fadus admitted, pulling his arm away from his whore, and pushing her off the bed. Santino and I watched her impressive backside as she pattered across the room and out the door.

"What is the Empress' deadline?" He asked.

"You have two days. No later," Santino said hastily. It must have been killing him that he couldn't make a joke about the girl, her retreating bare butt, Fadus' promiscuity, or some combination thereof.

"Why don't the two of you perform the task?" Fadus asked. "From what I understand, you are most capable of such a deed."

Santino stood from his chair and I did the same. He looked up at the skylight and tossed his grappling hook over the ledge, and I was quietly thankful that the gadgets were indigenous to the time period, and wouldn't seem odd to a Roman procurator.

"Because the Empress wishes you to do it," Santino finally said, making sure he emphasized the point that any wish from Agrippina was more of a demand than a request. He let me head up the rope first, leaving Fadus with a final thought before he shimmied up behind me. "Do *not* disappoint her."

Fadus nodded his head vigorously and ignored our departure.

He was onboard, even if he didn't know it yet. No one crossed Agrippina these days. Doing so was certain death.

Once on the roof, I helped Santino out of the skylight, and hauled up the rope.

"Nice job, buddy," I complimented. "I thought you were going to crack when that floozy ran out of there."

"*Pfft*," he wheezed. "I am a professional, you know." He sighed. "But you are right. That girl had a fantastic ass. I think I'm getting lonely."

"Get over it. When was your last tavern wench? Last night?"

He let out another sigh. "Memories…"

I laughed and the two of us quietly snuck out of the compound, making our way to the team's prearranged rendezvous point.

"So," Santino said enroute, "now, now what?

"Now," I answered, "we have a little chat with Herod."

***

"Why am I here, Jacob Hunter?" Asked the annoying voice of, for once, not Santino, but of young Titus Glabrio.

I looked at you him in frustration. "Before I answer, may I ask you something?"

"Of course, Jacob Hunter."

I balled my hands into fists and started shaking them in annoyance as we walked. "Titus, when have I ever called you Titus Glabrio? In fact, when has *anyone* referred to *anyone* with anything but their first *or* their last name?" I paused, recalling old memories. "And why the hell am I the only one you do it to??"

Titus continued looking out in front of him as we walked, ignoring me completely. I thought I saw a small smile creep onto his face, but I couldn't be sure. Something about his attitude was suspect, and I wondered if Wang or Santino might have had something to do with it.

"So why am I here?" Titus asked again, ignoring my tirade completely.

"Because I thought you'd be less annoying than Santino," I growled, "but now I'm not so sure."

"Then why didn't you bring Helena? My father tells me you two are very close, but you don't seem to spend much time together."

I smiled. It was nice to know he both cared about the wellbeing of my relationship with Helena, as well as considered Vincent his father. Step-sons could be a real hassle sometimes.

"Titus, she and I have spent almost every minute of the past four years together. That much time in such close proximity can seriously stifle *any* relationship, and we only just started feeling the growing pains a year ago. We're fine now, but trust me, it's not how much time you spend together that matters, but what you do with that time that counts." I paused, shaking my head in disbelief. "I'm turning into Bordeaux…"

"But what is it you two do in your time together?" he asked, oddly squeamish.

For a handsome nineteen year old who didn't speak much and seemed on the sensitive side, he certainly was asking a lot of questions about something I hadn't thought he'd be so clueless about.

"That's none of your business," I replied sarcastically. "Any particular reason for this line of questioning?"

"No," he said too quickly, an obvious indication that he was holding something back.

"You don't have a crush on her do you? I mean, it's perfectly understandable, but…"

"I assure you, Jacob Hunter, that is not the case. She is very beautiful, yes, but I respect your possession of her."

"I don't own her, you know," I pointed out. "Now, she may own me, but that's another story completely. So, what's the deal? Why do you care so much? It's just you and me. We're off the radio. Go ahead and speak your mind."

It was past noon on the day after our encounter with Fadus, and Titus and I were walking through crowds of men and women, on our way to meet with Herod. While we didn't have the direct form of backup we'd had during phase one and two of the mission, the rest of the team was surreptitiously tailing us like they always did.

Helena and Vincent, Bordeaux and Madrina, and Wang and Santino were three pairs amongst hundreds following behind us, appearing like any other Cesarean. We decided to switch up swim pair assignments a month ago, in order to take advantage of our newcomers, but even our current setup was mixed up. Officially, Wang and Santino were now paired together, keeping our best infiltrators and targets for jokes together. Titus and Bordeaux were our heavy support team. Helena and I, inseparable despite Titus' thoughts otherwise, remained as the best sniper team ever concocted. And Vincent and Madrina were our logistics team, one handicapped, the other a noncombatant.

The new pairs gelled perfectly, giving us a solid amount of flexibility, even if we had decided to switch them up just a bit for today.

Titus sighed for the first time since I'd known him, the first indication that he was human after all. "No, Jacob Hunter, there is nothing to talk about."

"It's about a girl, isn't it?"

Titus continued to ignore me.

"Fine. I know a love sick teenager when I see one. Don't ever say I never asked."

He kept on walking, apparently no longer interested in conversation, which was fine by me. The only reason I'd brought him along in the first place was because he was quiet; at least I'd thought he was, but it wouldn't matter for long. We wouldn't have much time for chit chat soon enough, as Herod's residency was quickly coming into view.

Turning a corner, Titus and I saw a majestic building, a palace and a fortress both. It sat on a promontory that jutted out over the Mediterranean and was easily the largest building in the city. Inside the courtyard sat two large statues, one I didn't recognize, but the second was clearly that of my favorite Roman ruler, Augustus. Seeing it brought a pang of anger to me, as I knew this statue would be destroyed and lost at some point in history. As much as I hated the idea of "Rome" these days, knowing so much history and art will be lost still pained me.

The streets here were lined with stalls and kiosks, an interesting commonality among most ancient cities I'd visited over the years. The midday crowd was thick, as was the line of men and women waiting to enter Herod's residence, hoping he would settle disputes between conflicting parties. It wasn't a requirement for the King of the Jews to perform, but we'd learned that Herod apparently enjoyed the task.

In reality, his judicial power meant little in the Roman world. His decrees only covered those concerns that did not interfere with Roman law. Since Rome wanted little to do with the religions of its protectorate constituents, Herod mainly concerned himself with matters of religion and culture.

As for the line of waiting Jews, it extended well outside the doors of the building and into the courtyard. Noticing the crowd, I pulled up short, tossed my hands in the air and shook my head. With this many people in front of us, it could take all day before we saw Herod.

I looked over my shoulder for one of the pairs tailing us and saw Helena and Vincent stopped outside a clothing stall. Helena noticed my attention and quickly looked around in anticipation of some kind of trouble. I indicated with a quick slash of my hand that everything was fine. She nodded and blew me a peck of a kiss. I smiled at the gesture and yanked on Titus' arm, pulling him toward the end of the line.

Thirty minutes later, I was having flashbacks to my childhood standing in line at an amusement park. As a kid, I never really understood what an inefficient use of time it was to spend two hours in a line for only five minutes of payoff. It may have been a fun five minutes, but was it really worth it?

Sure it was. Rollercoasters were a blast.

I still hated lines.

Just as I felt the need to fight off a sudden angry mood swing, I saw a familiar face in the crowd.

Matthias Ben Joseph.

He was strolling through the throng of people, apparently weeding out the more urgent disputes from the lesser ones, prioritizing cases before they went before Herod. He appeared to be placating a pair of old and wrinkly women who had been insistently screaming at each other since Titus and I found our place in the queue, and he was clearly aggravated by the time he managed to catch my eye.

I raised an eyebrow at him and his expression lifted. He said something to the bickering grandmas and made his way to my place in the line.

"*Vani*," he greeted. "Have you come to deal with Herod?"

"We have," I answered. "Is there any chance you can send us to the front of the line?"

The older man looked relieved. "Of course. It will give me an excuse from dealing with these complainers."

I had to smile. Any issue these people had that didn't fall under Roman rule had to be about as insignificant as a single seahorse complaining about a new neighbor moving into the aquarium. I could only imagine the silly squabbling that led most of these people to seek solace in Herod's power. I imagined allegations like someone picking their nose on the Sabbath had to be common in Herod's court. Probably why men like Matthias were tasked with picking out only the ripest cases.

Without another word, Matthias gripped my arm and led me through the mob of people waiting outside. Passing by dozens of arguing Jews, our companion quickly escorted us through a few rooms before delivering us to what looked like Herod's courtroom.

Marble floors, a vaulted ceiling and pillars running along both sides of the room conveyed opulence and power. Mosaics covered the floor and ceilings, and the distance from the door to the only chair in the room was a good forty meters, plenty of time for an offending party to rethink their stance before being heard by the king.

I made sure to take note of any tactical amenities the room offered. The columns supported second level balconies that would give anyone situated in them a clear view of the room below. Also, even though it was late in the afternoon, and the sun was shining brightly outside, there were deep shadows in the corners. Finally, there were only two exits, the large double doors we'd come through, and a small door in the far, back corner.

Twenty five meters in, I was able to make out the man I knew had to be Herod Agrippa. Known as Julius Marcus Agrippa back in Rome, or later as simply Agrippa I, he was the grandson of Herod the Great, and a rather impressive ruler in his own right. I knew quite a bit about the man thanks to my study of the Julio-Claudian family, and had come to respect him as both a person and ruler.

Even though he was seated, I estimated he had to be about six feet tall. He had dark brown hair in neat curls, along with a full beard, left thick but well groomed. He had dark brown eyes that, as we drew closer, I noticed flitted about rapidly, analyzing ever detail he came across. His shallow cheeks and sharp nose gave him a very distinguished look, and for once, it seemed that whoever did the casting for my favorite BBC miniseries, *I, Claudius*, had gotten it right for once.

Thirty meters in, I noticed a line engraved in the floor, and figured it would probably be a good idea to stop. Kings never liked their subjects to come too close as they were often a paranoid bunch. Titus, Matthias, and I performed half bows for him and waited for him to initiate greetings. The few dozen or so retainers and guards gathered around the room's single seated occupant stared vacantly.

King Herod measured us up quickly before letting out an unimpressed sigh, and I didn't blame him since we weren't all dressed up and ready to party right now.

"So you are these *Vani* I have heard so much about," he accused in a rich, deep voice. "Most interesting. From the stories I have heard, I half expected giants, or at least a woman wearing little clothing."

I resisted the urge to smile.

"They are," Matthias answered for us. "This is... Burt," he said awkwardly. "I spoke to him yesterday near the port."

Herod nodded in my direction. "Good. I'd hoped to meet all of you, but I understand your desire to remain secretive. Very wise. Now, what have you come to discuss with me?"

"Sir," I began, taking a small step forward, remaining behind the line. "We have been made aware of a growing threat to your person. The Empress has ordered your assassination, and it's going to happen very soon."

Herod uncrossed his legs and leaned forward, resting his elbows on his knees, and his chin in his hands. "Is that so? How is that you have come by this information?"

"We have contacts within the Empress' Praetorian Guard. We worked with them four years ago and have good friends in high places. The threat is very real."

He leaned back in his seat. "So the *Vani* feel obligated to protect me then, is that it? As I have said, I know all about your exploits in the West, but why should I *trust* you? You owe me nothing."

I made a quick tactical decision and stepped forward, defiantly crossing the boundary between man and king. Herod stiffened at my approach, but no one made any attempt to stop me. Hopefully, they were already nervous about my capabilities and wouldn't interfere later, because I didn't have the time or the patience to deal with kings. There was too much at stake to let the pomp and arrogance of a so-called monarch stand in my way.

"King Herod," I said from beyond the line, "please understand, if we wanted to deceive you, we could have spent this afternoon having a relaxing lunch instead of warning you. Fadus is gathering his assassins as we speak. Whether you want our help or not, I would not sleep in your own bed tonight."

I turned to leave, Titus following obediently, but before we could take another step, Herod stood from his chair and reached an arm out in our direction.

"Wait."

We turned back to face the monarch.

Herod glanced at his feet in a very non-royal manner. "As I have said, I know who you are and what you can do. Please. If you can help, I would not turn you away."

"That is most prudent, my lord," I replied, cringing at the overly formal title. It was hard for someone who had lived his entire life in a free world to acknowledge such a title. "They will come for you tonight. We suggest that you remain here, in your courtroom. We will be better able to protect you here than in your residence."

Herod nodded as he retook his seat.

"Should I not just leave now before they come for me?" He asked.

I shook my head. "Not a good idea. If you leave, they'll just hunt you down. If you hold your ground, the empress may back down."

"What is her purpose in this?" He asked, shaking his head in disbelief. "Is it not enough that she defiles our temple with a statue of her likeness, despite my pleadings to remove it? Not enough that she keeps me here as a mere figurehead with no real power? These people," he continued, waving his hand at the window and the gathering Jews outside, "come here for nothing. I only possess the authority to settle petty squabbles."

"Perhaps that will change once your people see what the empress tries to do tonight," I baited.

His head lifted and I could tell he had taken the bait. "Perhaps. I tell you, Burt, this is not at all how I imagined life would be when I lived in Rome. When I was but a child, the great Caesar Augustus himself assured me Judea would become a sovereign nation within his empire." He frowned and lowered his head, submitting himself to the life he had been dealt.

That *I* had dealt for him.

He continued. "There are days when I miss my friends Caligula and the wise Claudius. Oh, what great emperors they could have been."

I felt my mouth twitch, but I didn't let on that I cared. Even though I did. I cared very much, in fact, and was once again reminded of everything I'd caused.

"I am sorry for what has happened here, King Herod," I consoled after forcing myself to swallow my guilt, at least for the moment.

At my words, his head straightened. "It is no fault of your own, Burt, but of my own making."

I gulped, barely holding it all in, but I could sense Herod's resolve tighten at his misplaced admission.

"Will it be just the two of you?" He asked, obviously fishing for answers himself this time.

The question helped me find my smile. "Perhaps, but you won't see anyone here tonight either way. But rest assured... we will be here."

And with that, I turned on my heels with the military-like precision I thought I'd forgotten years ago, and marched out of the room. I couldn't see Herod's reaction, but I hoped he heeded my warning. Fadus' assassins were really coming for him, only they wouldn't be alone.

"So?" Titus asked, as we made our way into the crowd. "Now, now, now…"

"Shut it," I snapped, snapping my head in his direction.

I hoped to catch some kind of reaction, but his face remained hard. I inspected him closely as we walked, deciding that I had to keep this kid away from Santino. It was clear my child-like friend was a bad influence on the personable teenager. Even I couldn't take two Santinos running around here.

Better play it safe and keep him away from Wang as well.

I sighed, figuring I might as well play along. "Now, we become magicians."

***

"Tangos inbound, north north east. ETA, five mikes. Howcopy?"

"Solid copy, 8-7," I whispered with the click of my radio. "We're in position and ready to receive."

True to his word, Fadus had sent his assassins. Granted, the term "assassin" was used loosely, as his agents for murder were little more than common street thugs. A procurator didn't exactly have the resources or connections to get in touch with highly trained professionals, so he did what most Romans with deep pockets would do. He gathered up fifty or so well-known trouble makers, deviants, and scumbags, paid them an extravagant amount of money, and sent them on their way.

Which was perfect for us. They wouldn't notice a few additions to their ranks.

Helena, Bordeaux, and I were camped out on the high balconies overlooking Herod's courtroom. We'd snuck in through a small window near the back as soon as it had turned dark about an hour ago. There wasn't much room to maneuver on the overhang, so the three of us had spread out as best we could along the length of the courtroom, providing overlapping fields of fire.

Below us sat Herod, his two dozen loyal bodyguards and half as many employees, administrators and servants. They were gathered around a few large tables which had been brought in earlier this evening. They were munching on wine, cheese and fruit, and appeared to be going over legal documents, dockets, cases, and the like. They looked nervous, and they had every right to be. The guards were tense and stiff, and Herod was clearly perspiring.

Frankly, I was still impressed that they were so willing to trust us. I guess the reputation Helena, Santino, and I had built over the past few years was worthy of respect. These people were putting their lives in our hands, and they didn't even know we were there.

"ETA, two mikes," Vincent updated.

He and Madrina were once again waiting outside the AO, working as our intelligence team. Vincent had the UAV up and flying, and was using it to track the incoming bad guys.

As for Titus, Wang and Santino, they were waiting just a few blocks away, along the mob's projected course of entry into Herod's compound. Their mission was to tag along with the assassins, gain entrance into the courtroom, and perform a little play acting.

That put our best swordsmen in play on the ground and our best shooters up top in support, and the three of us in the balcony had switched out or normal weaponry for air guns and tranquilizer darts. Most of what occurred tonight relied on convincing theatrics, and we couldn't risk a few overly curious inspectors discovering bullet wounds.

And we didn't really want to kill anyone we didn't have to.

"ETA, one mike," Vincent reported for the last time. "Good luck."

I sent back a double click. Vincent and Madrina would now fall back from their recon position, and ready our escape plan. We had spent considerable time hashing out the details, and we were completely confident it would work, but it never hurt to be careful. We had the upper hand tonight and all the players in our scheme were already dancing to our tune, but still I stretched my neck and tried to get comfortable. No matter how easy a mission seemed to be, the nervousness and adrenaline never left me.

Thankfully, I didn't have much time to think on it as fifty eight seconds after Vincent's transmission, a horde of malcontents burst into the courtroom with a flurry of noise and shouts. Some seemed drunk, others alert, but they were all tense and ready for a fight, and they didn't make any preamble by ordering Herod to come quietly. They simply charged forward.

Herod's guards advanced in return, ready to meet the interlopers. As for Herod's retinue, many fled through the small door in the back of the room, but some stayed. They armed themselves and made ready to protect their sovereign as well. Finally, near the rear of the advancing assassins, came three other men: Santino, Titus and Wang, who had two, very specific mission instructions: not to kill indiscriminately and ensure Herod's survival.

They were to defend themselves if they were attacked by either side, but they had to leave people alive for when I decided the right moment had come.

Tracking my first target carefully, I fired.

My tranq dart found its target, about three men back in the advancing horde, and he performed exactly as I'd hoped he would. He stumbled and fell to the ground, causing numerous men behind him to trip over his fallen body, and their entire charge faltered. When the two forces met, Herod's guards lost little ground. They were braced and well able to receive the oncoming blow that hit them haphazardly thanks to my intervention. However, once the assassins regained their footing, the momentum shifted, and Herod's guards were systematically pushed back.

Bordeaux, Helena, and I continued to provide fire support, but only at select targets, and Wang and Santino were handling themselves with little problem down below. Both were more skilled with a sword than even most legionnaires, Wang from his martial arts training and Santino from watching too many movies. Titus, however, had learned the trade from his biological father when he was very young and had never seen combat, but as we'd gotten to know him in recent weeks, his prowess with a sword had become obvious, and while there was still the question of his complete greenness in battle, but both Vincent and Helena had vouched for him. Vincent knew him better than all of us, and Helena knew what it was like to be thrust into a situation where your choices were either kill or watch your new friends be killed, but she saw in him what she had felt in herself all those years ago: a willingness to prove himself.

So, we only fired when we feared one of our friends were in danger, which wasn't often. We knew the assassins would wake up sooner or later once the tranq darts wore off, but that was all part of the charade. All we needed to do was to keep the "casualties" to a minimum for the time being.

The battle continued, with Herod's side continuing to lose ground, even though our friends below had inconspicuously switched sides during the confusion and were now fighting against the assassins. I analyzed the battle, and decided now was a good time to do a head count, tallying nine assassins, five guards, and three goofballs.

That would have to do.

"Do it," I said into my microphone.

There was no reply, but there was no doubt everyone received my message.

Almost immediately, Wang and Titus turned on anyone around them, creating utter chaos in the already disorderly battle. Wang skewered a guard through the right bicep, while Titus managed to nearly decapitate one of the assassins that left the man's head dangling by a sliver of skin and muscle. Santino didn't bother with either, focusing his attention solely on Herod.

The King of the Jews hadn't sat idly by while his men defended him, but hefted sword and shield as well. It was a noble gesture, one that almost made me feel bad for what we were about to do, but it wasn't a sentiment that would stop Santino. He stalked around behind Herod as the king dueled with one of the last assassins, while Wang did his job by knocking out Herod's dueling partner with the hilt of his sword and following it up by throwing his shoulder into Herod, just enough so that he was pushed in Santino's direction.

The king stumbled and fell, and immediately saw Santino looming before him, whose face betrayed no hint of what was to come. My friend paused for what I assumed was further dramatic effect, and after performing a quick check to make sure some of the guards were watching, he plunged his sword deep into Herod's chest.

The king didn't scream, a mere wheezing sound emanating from his lungs instead as he slumped to the ground. As Herod fell, I aimed at one of the two remaining guards, and took him down as his attention was focused completely on his king, while Bordeaux dispatched the other.

And with that, the battle was over, only ten minutes after it had started. I looked into the red slicked courtroom as my three friends stood within pools of blood. The three of us in the balcony tossed some rope over the ledge and dropped to the courtroom floor. Everyone, save Wang and me, started the process of policing the bodies, securing any evidence of our involvement.

Wang was already kneeling over Herod's body.

"Is he going to make it?" I asked.

Wang checked his vitals, and nodded. "Santino got him in the shoulder. No internal organs were damaged. His arm will take a while to heal, but he should be fine."

"Good," I replied.

Just prior to Santino's death blow, Helena had shot Herod with a special dart. Instead of containing its typical tranquilizer serum, Wang had filled it with a combination of other serums instead, including some kind of soporific, parasolutrine – I think he'd called it – along with something else called paracin trichloride, and morphine, of course, along with a few others. When I'd voiced my concerns over the amount of crap Wang was planning to dope Herod with, the small medic had simply smiled and commented that he was curious as to how it was all going to turn out as well. But in the end, it had apparently worked, which was why Herod hadn't yelled out in pain after Santino had stabbed him. Morphine works quickly and he probably hadn't felt a thing. The other drugs made for a very convincing death scene once Herod had collapsed.

Many people were going to wake up in a few hours, especially the two guards who saw Herod go down, and when they found that his body had magically disappeared, things in Caesarea should get much more interesting.

Santino sauntered over and held out his hand in my direction. I looked at it and rolled my eyes, but did as I was beckoned and hammered a fist against my palm three times before displaying rock, Santino throwing out paper. He chuckled and smothered my fist with his hand while he clapped me on the back with the other. When he was finished with his little celebration, I moved around Herod's body and placed my hands under his armpits, the much heavier end of the man's body, while Santino took hold of his ankles. On the count of three, we heaved him off the ground and left the building like ghosts in the night.

Santino caught my eyes and lifted an eyebrow.

"So," he started, "now, n…"

"Don't even fucking start!"

Part Three

IX
Besieged

Mission Entry #9
Jacob Hunter
Caesarea, Judea - October, 42 A.D.

Americans have an interesting tradition of meddling in other countries' affairs. Especially when it came to Communism and the Middle East. Oh, boy, does the American government love knocking off democratically elected, or not so democratically elected, heads of state, just to make sure the new ruler was more to their... liking. Not that I had much of a problem with this tradition. It wasn't exactly a novel practice in world civilization, but it obviously wasn't an overly popular one... at least depending on who you ask.

I point this out, because I did the ol' US of A proud a few months back by knocking off a ruling sovereign of my own. Pretty impressive, no?

Well, I thought it was.

Sadly Herod didn't necessarily think so.

Yeah, so I didn't kill him. I haven't gone completely over to the dark side yet. We only faked his death to incite the riot we needed to bring Agrippina here, or at least slow her down in Germany. Remember what I said about pissing off the young Jews of the area to the point where their shit finally hit the proverbial fan? Well, Sociologists, you'll be happy to know that it worked. This place went crazy within a week of Herod's "death."

As for Herod... well... let's just say he'd been slightly miffed. He lost quite a few good men in the botched assassination attempt and was furious we lied to him concerning our intentions for him and the city.

Not to mention the fact that we had to stab him.

He hadn't been cool with that.

He'd ridiculed us, belittled us, yelled at us, and generally tried to make us feel bad for what we did. Especially me. He'd told us we should be ashamed of our given moniker as Vani, *and I'd had to keep reminding myself that in order to make an omelet, a few eggs had to broken.*

We gave him a few days to cool down in isolation with us where we tried to explain what we were trying to accomplish... without all the time travel stuff, of course. In the original timeline, Herod never lived to see the rebellion in 66 A.D., but he'd ruled under a compassionate and tolerant leader in the original Claudius. In this new timeline, however, his reign hadn't been nearly so peachy, and he must have known that it had only been a matter of time. When he learned how quickly events sped up after his death – how his citizens rallied against Roman rule in open rebellion – his tone had steadily shifted to that of acceptance, and soon, he was ready to admit that, perhaps, we'd done the right thing... except for the whole stabbing him thing, of course.

Local Zealots had preached fanatically about how Rome had come in and ordered the assassination of their beloved king, and how their next step was the complete extermination of the Jewish people. The local procurator, Cuspius Fadus, tried to quell the fires, only to have his home stormed by rioters where he was summarily beaten and executed.

Whoops.

That had been enough for Rome. A few weeks later, the local legion garrison had laid siege to the once great city of Caesarea, and had gone about destroying both it and its citizens with systematic efficiency. Once the Romans showed up, King Herod revealed himself to his people, explaining how he'd escaped capture and that his death had all been a plot to further subjugate the people. He'd spoken of how proud and touched he was of his fellow Jews, and urged them to stand up against the Romans. Thus began the local resistance against Rome, led by Herod. We hadn't seen him since, mostly keeping to ourselves, and the only additional information we had was that the rebellion had spread well outside of Caesarea and into the surrounding province... but we haven't received any further intelligence in a while.

Hence why Helena and I were currently sitting atop one of the few surviving towers the city still had, playing our role as sniper support for the besieged citizens and to make sure the rebellion lasted as long as possible, at least in this city.

We came up here every evening, or one of the other remaining high points, and dissuaded at least two dozen legionnaires from invading the camp. That was generally enough to stall any potential large scale invasions for the immediate future.

We were only facing one problem.

We were finally running out of ammo.

Our shortage was forcing us to pick our targets more selectively to conserve what we had left, and we still didn't know if Agrippina was going to show up or not, but I was still confident she would.

The woman loves getting her hands dirty with unruly men.

It was kinda her calling card.

Anyway, Helena's just finished setting up shop for the night, so I might as well end this. There isn't much more to say. I do want to officially apologize to Herod – and to history – for what I did. He may have grudgingly accepted what we did to him, but I still get the feeling he doesn't like me, so I want it on record that I'm sorry. Desperate situations call for desperate solutions, and we need to put things right and get home...

We were willing to do anything at this point.

Anything.

Well... adios amigos.

From beside me, Helena suddenly broke the silence once she was ready for tonight's activities. "Do you think you'll stay in the military when we get home?"

"Hmm?" I replied, blindly trying to place my journal back in my bag.

"The military. Will you stay in if we get home?"

"Hmm." I said, pulling out my binoculars and laying them against my bag, scanning the horizon. "I haven't thought about it to be honest..." I paused, "...check, check, two tangos, twelve o'clock, six hundred meters out... At least, I try not to. Why do you ask?"

"Because I have been thinking about it," she answered, squinting through her scope. "I've been thinking about a lot of things, actually. For a few weeks now."

"Such as..." I prompted distractedly.

"What my life will be like for one. What I'll do with it, another," she paused. "Like what kind of boyfriend you'll be when life is more..." she fired off two rounds, "... normal. Tangos eliminated."

I confirmed her kills and marked them on a kill sheet I'd been keeping since the siege began, tracking numbers and troop movement. I placed the binoculars in front of my eyes again, but thought better of it and turned to look at Helena instead. She was seated a few feet to my left, sitting wither legs folded comfortably on a rock that placed her about a foot or so above my position. She had her arms crossed in front of her chest, holding her rifle in a way that balanced it across her body and in the crook of her elbow, the stock against her shoulder like always. Using her knees as support, the position was extremely comfortable and very efficient for sniper work.

I smiled. "You mean in a place where romantic Friday night outings, like tonight's, won't be filled with killing Romans? Sounds dreadful."

She didn't respond, a frown forming on her lips.

"Come on," I joked, looking back through my binoculars. "That was kinda funny."

Her lips twitched. "Maybe a little," she relented before sighing. "I guess I've just been fantasizing too much. Giving myself false hope as to how our lives could be if we weren't here. Dreaming about things that will probably never happen... as I said, I've had a lot on my mind lately."

"Can't be any more than usual," I said, still scanning the horizon.

She didn't answer, and when I glanced back at her again, I saw that her frown was still in place.

I had to admit, she had been acting strangely of late, even more so than a few months ago. Her level of patience with Santino and me seemed to be at an all-time low. We weren't that much worse than normal, but she was displaying less patience with us than ever. And then there was the physical part. Always waking up early and wandering off on her own during the day, and her pain attacks seemed to occur more frequently these days. Something was bothering her, and her silence on the matter had made me think that she was turning into me.

Except I knew better than to tell her that.

I tried to cheer her up. "Hey, with the two of us, it's got to be pretty fantastic."

"To be honest, I have my doubts," she said, her voice filled with an odd mix of honesty and playfulness. "Don't get me wrong. You're cute, occasionally humorous, and a nice guy when you want to be, but something tells me you're going to be no better than most lazy American men. The ones who want little more from their women except sex and having someone to bring them food."

I winced, trying to hide the expression by turning back to my scope. She wasn't completely wrong. I hated dating. I liked my "me time" and would generally prefer just staying home or hanging out with friends, like back in college when all we'd do is play Beer Pong all night. Of course, I preferred having a woman do those things with me, and after all this time, I knew that any part of my normal life would only be that much more complete with Helena in it.

That said, the old beat up couch I had back home was one of the things I missed the most these days.

"Are you kidding?" I asked excitedly. "We'll do lots of stuff. It'll be great. Like this, just without the Romans, and the killing, and the running, and the…" I trailed off, Helena's point finally hitting home.

What we had together here in Rome was really little more than a happy product of convenience and necessity than an honest relationship. We loved each other, sure, but if we were ever faced with an atmosphere conducive to building an actual relationship, like any twenty-first century couple, would we cut it?

"Okay," I sighed. "Give me the bad news."

Her tone immediately perked up and lightened. "Don't worry. It's not that bad. First, you take me dancing three times a month, out to eat every Thursday night, with something fancy at least once month. We'll also need an activity like hiking or rock climbing, something to get your lazy ass off the couch and keep you in shape. Finally, you must agree to go to a play, ballet, opera, or musical. Four to six times a year."

I was speechless. 'Not that bad?' It was everything but. That was an extremely belligerent set of demands for someone who preferred their couch and Chinese takeout over just about anything. I had to put an end to this before she got too carried away.

I looked back at her. "It's obvious you've taken my personality into account when trying to come up with your *entirely objective* idea of reality, am I right?"

She finally pulled her eye from her scope and offered me a mischievous smile. "I try."

"Funny. Well, here's the compromise. I'll give you dancing once a month, dinner every week is fine, but the fancy stuff needs to be reserved for special occasions only, and I'd rather hike since rock climbing seems too strenuous, but only as long as we get to camp as well."

"Haven't we camped enough over the years?"

"Yeah, but this time with no Santino."

She returned her eye to her scope and grinned. "Deal. But dancing twice a month."

I gritted my teeth and groaned. "What is it with you women and dancing? Is that all you ever did?"

"Of course," she replied. "Especially when I was in America. I was there with three of my Oxford girlfriends after all, and honestly, there's not much else to do in your country for a group of pretty European college girls. Papa arranged for our attendance at many trendy hot spots in New York, L.A., Miami… We were quite popular, actually. Many men…"

"Great, I get the picture," I said hastily. "Spare me the details."

She laughed at me. "What about the theatre, Lieutenant? Don't tell me, the momma's boy that you are, that you didn't attend plays all the time and actually found yourself liking them?"

I growled as she was right again, of course, at least about part of it. I couldn't count how many times my father and I had been tricked into attending plays and musicals, thinking that we were getting dressed up for dinner at a fancy restaurant only.

It had been one of the few things he and I had ever bonded over.

Then again, I had to admit that after the fifth or sixth time, I actually found myself enjoying The Nutcracker, and I did have a soft spot for The Fiddler on the Roof. I'd never actually tell anyone that, of course, but I couldn't help but be fan, even now.

I looked back at her with a frustrated face that was just begging her to challenge what I had to say next. "I'll give you twice a year, but never during football season, especially the playoffs... Check, check. Two tangos, two o'clock, sector 4H."

"What is it with you American men and your stupid American football?" She asked, throwing my question back at me, panning her rife to her right. "Bunch of men hitting each other. It's barbaric... tangos eliminated."

"It's an institution!" I nearly yelled, looking for additional targets. "It's what every *real* man lives for. And since we're on the subject, I have but a stipulation for you then as well."

"Oh, this should be good," she joked.

"It is..." I said malevolently. "It is... So, in regards to football, first off, you will attend ever tailgating party I do. There, you will wear a beer can helmet, colored face paint, and a jersey of my choosing. Additionally, you will wear booty shorts and tie off your jersey like a hot sorority girl. Once properly attired, you will consume excessive amounts of alcohol, hamburgers, hotdogs, chicken, and steak at said tailgating parties, but still maintain your sexiness... that's a very important point, by the way. In addition, you will flirt and cavort with each and every one of my friends, making them excessively jealous of me, which will obviously inflate my ego. Finally, you will love every minute of it, from the shirts vs. skins flag football games, where you will, of course, be a skin, to the end of the night where we'll have to carry Santino home because he's too drunk to do it himself."

I let out a long breath and cracked my neck at the verbal exertion.

Helena stared at me with wide eyes that could have been perplexed, frightened, or both. "You're not implying that Santino's going to be living in our basement... are you?"

"Maybe..."

Helena looked away and sighed. "You've been planning this for a while, haven't you?"

"Since the moment I met you," I replied, completely honest.

"Really?" She asked, her voice suggesting I'd said something cute, and looking back at me. "Even after I almost knocked you out and made it seem like I wanted nothing to do with you?"

"It was love at first sight," I partially joked.

She buried her eye back in her scope, a tiny smile creeping onto her face. "I'll think about the shorts."

"Hey, the only wardrobe appeal you're going to get is if you add thigh high socks."

"I'll keep that in mind," she said, chuckling.

I smiled. We were going to be fine. No matter what challenge we faced, we'd overcome them. We'd gone through enough over the years, and even more over the past twelve months, so there was no way some petty dispute like my drinking directly from the milk carton could break us up...

Although, she'd really better prepare herself for that one.

Of course, neither one of us discussed what life might be like should society be different from how we remembered. I think I could survive an alteration to the timeline like the Yankees being the worst team in Baseball history, but if life as we knew it ended up beyond recognition, it might just be worth staying in Rome. It's why we had to stop Agrippina in Germany, and get her to back down. Placing a good emperor like Vespasian on the throne now would probably do little to make history better for Rome, but it would allow him to fix all the shit Agrippina has broken, and ensure Nero didn't do anything worse. If I had to guess that if we succeeded, even after all the deaths, history wouldn't change too much. There would be differences, I was sure, but the vast majority of the social, political and military decisions would remain unchanged.

At least, thoughts like that helped reassure me that I wasn't somehow responsible for the possible extermination of mankind.

Then again, the world hadn't been all that great when we'd left it either. Helena and I could joke about the ballet and football, and a life filled with little more than relaxation, love, beer, and plenty of sex, but I wasn't so sure such a thing was even possible, at least, not in the long term. I'd almost forgotten what the world had been like before we had left it five years ago, but thinking about it now reminded me just how little really was there for me. For any of us. Nothing but war and the potential for mutually assured annihilation. Perhaps it was best to just stay, but even if I later decided that was the best course of action for us, I wasn't about to let the timeline continue in a state of change.

I knew I'd better drop that line of thinking quickly.

As long as I had Helena, I could make my life happy.

Clearing my mind, I returned my attention to the battlefield and the sneaking Roman horde, when an unexpected voice from behind me nearly scared me right off the roof.

"What's happening kids?"

I turned, my heart racing, to see Santino crouching just outside my peripheral vision, wearing full combat gear, his rifle gripped between his legs.

"What the fuck are you doing here?" I asked with a heavy breath.

I hated being snuck up on. My sister and I had spent our entire childhoods' popping around corners, scaring the shit out of each other, but instead of it hardening my resolve when it came to sudden appearances, it had only made me jumpier.

He tilted his head. "Besides proving the point that we need some kind of super-secret-identification-spy-system-code to let people know when we're coming?"

Helena and I glared at him.

"That's what the damn radios are for!" Helena hissed at him. "Go away!"

He looked between us, oblivious. "Well, I can certainly tell when I'm not wanted," he said, remaining where he was. Normally, when people said something like that, they left, but not Santino, who wouldn't shut up. "So what's happening over here? The rest of the city is pretty quiet tonight."

"About the same," I replied, still a bit startled, retuning my attention once again to the Roman siege entrenchment system. "Only a few targets so far."

"How long have you been there anyway?" Helena asked.

"Long enough to know I like the way Hunter thinks," he replied, flicking his eyebrows at her. "I call shirts."

She groaned and returned her attention to her scope, and I couldn't help but smile.

"So, what exactly are you doing here?" I asked.

"Oh, you know… Wang's stuck playing medic and I got bored, and you know how I am when I get bored…"

"Annoying," Helena mumbled.

"… and, well," Santino continued, "Wang told me to go bother someone else. So who else am I gonna bother but my two most favorite people?"

"Lucky us," I whispered.

He clapped me on the back happily, nearly pitching me over the edge. "Damn right you are. Besides, I figured you might need a chaperone. We all know what happened the last time I left you two alone to watch my back."

"That… only happened a… few times," I reminded him while Helena turned and glared at me because of the admission alone.

"Yeah…" Santino said, stifling a laugh and moving near to where Helena was situated to sit against the rock she was seated on, "…and the last time was only a few weeks ago. You two are practically like bunnies, even after all these years. Impressive. I give no credit to Jacob…."

The first time it had happened had been completely innocent, and a short story, but one he rarely let us forget. About three years ago, Helena and I had been tasked with providing sniper cover while he snuck into a warehouse of some sort to recover stolen goods. For some reason, he had taken an excessively long time, and it had been a full moon… and Helena and I got a little distracted and a little… frisky.

It had been one of our first missions as *Vani*, so early on in our relationship that we were always in the mood, but the next thing we knew, Santino had caught us in the act, looking more pissed than we'd ever seen him before. He'd then angrily explained how he had been forced to extract under pursuit and deal with those chasing him all by himself, and he hadn't even batted an eyelash at us as we'd gotten dressed in front of him, focusing instead on his frustrated rant.

He'd been fine, of course, but it had been a pretty dumb thing to do on our part.

"Anyway," Santino continued, tapping a finger against Helena's boot like a child until she shooed him away, "since the Romans have been pretty quiet this past week, I figured I'd come up here and…"

"Shut it!" I ordered, waving my hand at him.

"Well that's not very…"

"Shut up, Santino," Helena ordered, jerking her rifle left and right across the horizon, "What do you see, Jacob?"

"Ten o'clock, sector 2A. IR strobes."

"I see them," Helena confirmed. "Two of them."

"Think its Gaius and Marcus?" Santino asked, squinting out into the darkness.

"No," I replied flippantly, "I'm sure it's just some freak atmospheric anomaly screwing with our night vision."

Santino smiled. "Nice."

I rolled my eyes and clicked my com. "8-5, 8-1, over"

"8-5 here," Bordeaux replied.

"We've got some bogies out there. IR strobes, meaning you know who. They're in your sector. Take 8-6 and go round them up. Bring them to HQ. Everyone else, rendezvous with us in thirty mikes."

"Wilco, 8-1," he acknowledged, followed by a series of double clicks from everyone else on coms.

"Think they have good news?" Helena asked, packing up her rifle and gear.

"Hopefully," I replied, following suit.

"I just hope it gets us out of the city," Santino said, offering Helena a hand to help her from her perch. "I think Madrina and Helena are the only two ladies left for me to conquer in this dump."

Using his helpfulness to his benefit, he yanked on Helena's arm and spun her like a ballroom dancer into his arms and against his body. He wrapped an arm around her waist and swung her into a dip, puckering his lips and smooching the air in front of her face.

"In your dreams," she said, as he allowed her to stand. She nudged him away from her and slapped him lightly across the face. "And that's for even thinking about it."

"Ow," he said, rubbing his cheek, still smiling. "So close..."

"Come on, Romeo" I said, smiling at their show as I hooked my arm through Helena's, leading her off the roof. "Let's go see what Gaius and Marcus have to say."

***

Caesarea didn't look quite as posh as it had two months ago. Once the legion had showed up to suppress the uprising, they had immediately gone to work laying siege to it. That meant constant bombardments by catapults and *onagers*, which laid waste to the once beautiful seaside city, leaving it to resemble any number of the war-torn and ravaged locales like the ones I'd see on CNN every night back home. The city even had men scurrying about with wraps around their heads, only these men carried swords and shields instead of AK47s and RPGs.

The image was surreal and almost nostalgic, and it was also very dangerous. Within the first week, we had our first casualty: Wang. He'd been on a patrol when a random boulder the size of a Volkswagen Bug had come crashing into the building next to him. The ensuing rubble had killed two of his Jewish companions and had crushed Wang's left leg. He's been laid up ever since, relegating him to maintaining our small field hospital instead of having him out on the lines. As Santino had just complained about, it kept him from getting into the shit more as well often, and this past night hadn't been the first time he'd sought out Helena and I while on sniper duty.

However, while the bombardment had toppled buildings and left large chunks of the city uninhabitable, it had also created extremely defensible positions for us to utilize. Within the rubble, the Jewish rebels had carved out vast networks of connecting chambers and hidden passageways. Tons of concrete and adobe buried on top of itself had left strong positions for us to hold out in during the siege, and also ensured the Romans would have plenty of trouble exterminating the rebels should they decide on a full out assault.

It also made traversing the city annoying, especially in the dark. After rappelling from our sniper hide, my two companions and I climbed, jumped, and carefully made our way to the small bunker we had turned into our headquarters. Three large buildings had collapsed onto a smaller fourth one, the smaller one having remained more or less intact, but with a ton of rubble atop it. The only entrance was a small skylight left open from the impediment.

It took us twenty minutes to reach it, long enough that even Bordeaux must have made it back already with Gaius and Marcus. Santino and I shifted aside the planks of wood covering the entrance and waited for Helena to drop in. Santino followed, and after a quick look around, I joined them. Landing in a crouch, I reached up and gripped a pole connected to the planks and shifted it back to where we'd found it.

Our bunker secure, I did a quick head count.

Everyone was present and accounted for, each wearing their night ops combat fatigues, except for Madrina. While Titus had been given McDougal's set of night ops and Multicam combat fatigues, Madrina had simply been given our late commander's BDU duty clothing, even if they didn't quite fit. McDougal had been Helena's height, just shy of six foot, but Madrina was almost as tall as I was. Combined with a figure that was shapelier than our old commander's, she fit into them snuggly, but it was worth it for their added durability and comfort.

And just as I knew they would be, Gaius and Marcus were also here, already chatting with Wang and Santino, two pairs of Tweetledees and Tweetledums. Their faces were dirty and they wore their blackened *lorica segmentata* armor over their ninja garb.

I ignored them and moved to a small cranny excavated from one of the walls. It had served as my bunk for the past few weeks, ever since the city fell into ruin, and it was the most comfortable place in the room. I plopped myself down on the extra wide cot and took note of our latest home. It was dark, dreary, and drearily pessimistic, although still not the worst accommodation I'd ever been forced to live in. Cramped, dank and with poor ventilation, the eight bodies that hadn't showered in weeks and resided here had left it a reeking shithole.

But it was still home.

Leaning back, I reached into a small shelf I'd created out of the rubble and reached for a jug of wine, some of the last we had. Pulling the stopper out with my teeth, I spat it out against the wall and took a swig. I got comfortable and watched as Helena walked over and seated herself next to me on our bed. I offered her the jug, and she took a long swallow, coughing as she tore the container away from her lips. I smiled, returned it to where I'd found it, and wrapped my arm around her shoulder. She rested her head against my chest contentedly and we simply waited.

No one paid us any attention. Everyone was too tired. Of all the inhabitants of Caesarea, we had been the most active, averaging only a few hours of sleep a night, if that, and we were all doing our best to cope with the stress in one way or another.

Madrina and Bordeaux sat at our small dinner table, one of the few pieces of furniture we'd managed to salvage. They were eating the very last of our MREs, ironically, one of the dreaded meat patty variety. At the far end of the room, Vincent and Titus chatted together quietly.

Their relationship constantly surprised me.

While I'd known Vincent for going on five years now, I'd really only spent just a year with him. We'd grown rather close, I thought, despite his secrecy about the orb and what it could do as well as how he'd impersonated a priest for a time – for a good reason. He'd become more than just a friend, comrade, and fellow scholar of ancient history, but the closest thing to a father I'd ever had. So when I watched him interact with Titus, I tended to forget the fact that they'd known each other far longer than I'd known either of them, and was certainly jealous of their relationship. I hadn't had much of one with my own father, and a part of me had always appreciated the moments when Vincent had filled that role on his behalf. If only Vincent had been around for my childhood. The only positive memory I had of my father and I was the time we'd spent together playing baseball when I was eight. Too bad even that ended badly on the day he'd decided to coach my little league team when I was nine. It had been the beginning of the end for father and son, as his overbearing and authoritative nature had driven a wedge between us that would never mend.

Finally, I turned to Helena, who rested in the nook of my arm, with her head turned to our right, her eyes locked on something in that part of the room. I tracked her gaze but saw nothing of interest. I squinted, trying to discern what had escaped me but came up empty, just a dank corner of the room where we'd piled our remaining cargo containers.

I glanced back down at Helena. If she'd noticed I was paying her any attention at all, she certainly wasn't letting on that she was; odd behavior for the usually hyper-sensitive woman. I reached out gently and gripped her chin, turning her head so that she was looking at me. Her eyes still seemed vacant, but a small smile tugged at her lips.

"Everything all right?" I asked.

She didn't reply immediately, her eyes now darting back and forth rapidly as she examined my face. The smile at her lips grew broader and she leaned up to kiss me.

She pulled away and settled herself back in my arms. "Everything's fine, Jacob. Just fine."

I narrowed my eyes, her behavior suddenly odd. "Something you want to talk about?"

She smiled at me mischievously and closed her eyes. I waited for her to elaborate, but she simply rested her head against my chest and breathed deeply. Knowing her she'd be asleep in seconds.

Puzzled at her odd behavior, I let her rest and waited for everyone to finish what they were doing, no sense in rushing right now. The Romans were quiet and we could use a break – we could always use a break, it seemed. There was no sense going off halfcocked again because we didn't take a moment to catch our collective breaths.

Fifteen minutes later, the four musketeers ended their little chat and gathered up the others. They started maneuvering chairs in my direction so I shook Helena to wake her up, but as expected, she remained stubbornly asleep, mumbling indecipherably and biting my t-shirt in response. Switching tactics, I tilted her head up and laid a kiss on her. She didn't react immediately, but I knew she was awake when she started kissing me back, and she was slow to tear herself away, her lips pursed and her eyes still closed.

"That was nice," she said quietly, biting her lower lip.

"Don't get a chance to do that too often these days, do we?"

Sadly, it was true. Signs of affection were hard to come by – a few minutes ago notwithstanding. We'd only had the few opportunities Santino had mentioned earlier to find moments of intimacy since the siege had begun, and the only time before that had been way back when we were in Byzantium after I had bought her that necklace, which she was wearing even now. There just hadn't been many opportunities with all the training, scouting, and relocating, not to mention Santino's constant presence.

She opened her mouth to speak, but stopped to look out toward the open room.

I tracked her gaze, noticing immediately how everyone else had seated themselves around us and were staring at us. I felt my cheeks burn, but Helena shrugged off the embarrassment with a heartwarming smile. She shifted in my arms so that we had some distance between us, but with my arm still around her. She noticed Santino's look in particular.

"What?" She asked him.

He sniffled mockingly. "You two are just so darn cute."

She laughed. "Get a life."

She punctuated her insult by retrieving an apple from our shelf and hurling it at him, which he managed to snag out of the air easily. He let out an exaggerated sigh as he bit into the piece of fruit, perhaps thinking about how little action he'd gotten in the past few weeks. A besieged city was hardly the place to find a Friday night hookup.

"So," I said. "Gaius. Marcus. What brings you to this neck of the woods?"

They looked at each other.

"We are practically in the desert, Hunter," Marcus pointed out. "What woods are…"

"Never mind." I took a deep breath and thought of home, and all the mindless ne'er-do-wells who at least understood a simple euphemism. I looked back up. "I meant what are you doing here?"

"As we were explaining to Santino and Wang," Gaius said, "things have changed dramatically in Germany."

"We finally have our supply trains established," Marcus continued, "but the Germans are fighting harder than ever, and the empress has been too stubborn to reconsider her strategy."

"Right," Gaius annoyingly confirmed. Sometimes I wondered if these two had been separated at birth. "Making matters worse is this uprising in Judea."

"Any information on how that's going?" I asked. "We don't get much news around here."

Gaius sighed in discontent. "These Jews are running amok all over Judea and into Syria. After the supposed death of their king, the Jewish factions in cities everywhere rose up against Rome.

Most uprisings have already been put down, except for in Caesarea and Jerusalem, with a number of Jews moving towards Masada. Do we have you to thank for their success here?"

"More than you know," I intoned.

"What do you mean?" Gaius asked.

So, I told them how we had instigated the rebellion and set off the chain reaction that had pitted Roman against Jew. He didn't seem surprised.

"I should have known," he said, crossing his arms. "You people have always been very good at causing trouble."

We certainly were that.

"We did it to draw Agrippina away from Germany, find the last orb, and find a way to get her to abdicate. Speaking of which, did she buy you're explanation as to why all your comrades ended up dead?"

The two Romans glanced at each other.

"We believe so," Marcus answered. "We *are* still alive."

"That is true," Gaius picked up, "but when we told her we had been following another lead, therefore avoiding certain death, I immediately felt she didn't believe us."

"Did you tell her about the orb?" I asked.

"We did," Gaius responded. "She was not happy. Especially when we told her we suspected your involvement. No one saw her for two days, but as Marcus said, we are still alive, even though reassigned."

"Reassigned where?" I asked, it finally dawning on me that I had no idea why these two were actually here.

"I'll get to that," he answered, "but there's more about Germany. Despite the Empress' blunderings and lack of strategic acumen, her legions are not amateurs. In fact, while many of our brothers are dead who shouldn't be, far more Germans are being killed than legionnaires, and they have already been pushed north of the Danube River."

I whistled. If that were true, they were carving out more land for the empire than even Trajan did a hundred years from now.

"In fact, there is talk of peace amongst the Germans," Gaius continued. "They're breaking, but it could be another three years before they break completely. There are even non-aggression talks among many Sarmatian tribes, who have been rallying to stall our progress should we subjugate Germany."

"So, where is the problem?" Vincent asked, just as curious as I was about all this. "If the legions are in fact doing so well, why have things changed so much?"

Gaius looked back at me. "Because you will receive what you hoped for. Agrippina is coming. She hopes to quell any future recalcitrant behavior here through diplomatic efforts. She's left Galba in charge of the campaign in Germany."

"Galba?" Bordeaux asked, still untrusting of our old ally. "What about Vespasian?"

"As I told you," Gaius replied, "we were reassigned. Our current role is to protect Vespasian. Agrippina has sent him here to put down the rebellion along with two of the German campaign's legions, including the *XV Primigenia*."

I looked at Vincent. He was shaking his head when he glanced at me, and when our eyes met, we started laughing together.

"What is so funny?" Marcus asked.

"Nothing," I answered, shaking off the last laugh. "Absolutely nothing."

Twenty five years from now, it was none other than Vespasian himself whom the emperor Nero sent to put down this rebellion. It was frustratingly hilarious how the timeline was constantly repositioning itself, screwing with my sense of humor in the process. Were we changing things or not? It was impossible to tell anymore, but if things kept falling into line like this, maybe we had nothing to worry about after all. Maybe the timeline would be just fine – just like that.

"So why are you two here?" Helena asked, always tackling the most important questions.

"Vespasian wishes to speak with you," Gaius answered," but about what, we do not know. All we know is that he is aware of our friendship and has asked us to assure you that you will not be harmed. He also asks that only two of you go."

"Great," Santino said, clapping his hands and rubbing them together. "When do we leave?"

"You're not going," I said offhandedly. I was about to ask Gaius for clarification when Santino interrupted.

"Why not?" He asked, his face obviously upset.

"Because I'm going," Helena answered for me.

Santino looked at me, his eyes pleading for clarification.

"She's right," I said, switching to English. "First of all, she's my swim buddy, and yours is laid up right now..."

"Actually, Hunter," Wang said, rotating his ankle easily, "I'm good to go now. I should be one hundred percent by..."

I shot him a look and he clammed up, taking the hint.

"If anything is going to happen out there," Helena said from the crook of my arm, "whether Vespasian is setting us up or not, it's going to happen to the both of us. I'm not going sit around wondering if he's all right or not."

"Besides," I picked up, "we don't need you obfuscating things."

"No problem there," Santino whined childishly, "because I don't even fucking know what 'obfuscating' means."

"It means to make something more complicated than it already is, Mr. Linguist," Helena chided.

"Easy for you to say, Mr. Oxford," he grumbled, like a moping teenager with his arms crossed against his chest, head down.

Poor guy. He probably just wanted to get out of the city for a few hours. Although, I wasn't sure what kind of tail he was expecting to find in a legion camp.

"When is Vespasian expecting us?" I asked, ignoring his tantrum.

"Tomorrow after midnight," Gaius answered

"Great," I replied, rising to my feet and offering a hand to help Helena up. "We'll be ready."

***

A day later, Helena and I made our way through the dying city with our two Roman friends.

Oddly, we didn't have much trouble. Only a few days ago, the hours between sunset and sunrise had been exceedingly treacherous for both the city's defenders and its attackers. The besieging legion, whoever it was, probably the *II Traiana Fortis* if memory served correct, would use the cover of darkness to probe their way into the city, and its defenders would do everything they could to defend themselves.

Every night was filled with skirmishes throughout the city. They would end by daybreak and be followed by more shelling of the city by Roman artillery throughout the day. Those of us from the future had fared rather well, only needing our swords once or twice, but the method was weighing heavily on the Jewish population. If not for our presence, this siege may have been over weeks ago.

We weren't in Masada. This wasn't a fortress. It was a city. A lush and beautiful one.

At least it had been.

As for the ease of our escape, I knew it must have had something to do with Vespasian. If Gaius and Marcus were to bring us to see him unharmed, the most prudent thing for the man commanding the besieging legions to do was to cease hostilities.

And it was a welcome respite.

After all our years cut off from our home, I'd recently found myself caring less and less about humanity in general. I'd killed without remorse, ending the lives of those who may have lived long years without my intervention, and with each life I took, I simply lost interest. I tried to pretend it wasn't my fault, having witnessed so much death that it was no longer so easy to appreciate the importance of human life. Here in Caesarea, when I'd pass a fallen Jew or legionnaire, I felt nothing, even if it had been by my hand.

I guess all that mattered to me *was* the timeline, not the lives that helped make it what it was, and even then I wondered if I really cared or not anymore.

It's why this break felt so good.

Helena was another story. Starting a few years ago, with every life she took, her emotional struggle to rationalize her guilt became more and more obvious. The woman hadn't been trained to kill on this kind of scale. She'd joined the military for that age old adage of, "meet new people and see the world" bullshit. She'd needed something, anything, to separate herself from the life she had been living, and joining the military had been the best option at the time.

She may have been an Olympic gold winning sharpshooter, but she'd hoped to leave her old life behind, especially that of a trained marksmen. She could have spent her entire military career having never fired a weapon. But what was she going to tell her instructors once they learned of her background? No? Had she not accepted any of the choices forced on her, she could have been drummed out of the military and sent back to her restrictive life and oppressive father.

I sighed as I thought about her. It was amazing how horribly ironic her story was. Here she was joining the military to escape the rule and dominion of her father, only to have the military force her to use her natural abilities in a way she never wanted. It had been a testament to her integrity and fortitude that when she'd been forced to deliver by protecting her teammates' lives, she actually had delivered.

And now she was here.

But it shouldn't matter.

Every death since was my fault, not hers, and the fact that she couldn't accept that made it all the worse, and the first few years had been the worst of all. After many an operation, she would sometimes find some lonely patch of solitude where she could just sit and cry softly to no one but herself, even as far back as our time in the *Primigenia's* winter camp. For the longest time, I'd let her do it alone. I'd thought it was what she needed, but ever since that time she caught me checking up on her and she'd run into my arms, sobbing like I'd never seen before, I'd always tried to be there for her.

Every time I took note of her grief, my heart ached, but the fact that she was now hardened to that pain only made it worse. Now, she acted without remorse when it came to killing in the line of duty. She was still an emotional woman, but after all her time here, she'd become a stone cold killer. That's why whenever I saw her face after she put someone in their grave, I died a little inside.

Just as it did whenever I was reminded of her near death experience. Her pain attacks. Vincent's lost arm. Claudius. Caligula. Agrippina. My life in Ancient Rome. Thousands of lives lost. All my fault. It's why I had to set things straight. I had no idea if Vespasian could fix everything. Not completely. Logic and history said he could, and should Rome come out even a smidge better, along with the rest of history, who would fucking blame me for it? Not me. And my opinion was the only one I needed to appease. All I wanted was some peace, something I wasn't sure I could find anymore.

I almost laughed. I often wondered why my mind tended to wander during the times it should be focused most; the times when my life and the lives of others were at stake. I hadn't a clue why. Maybe it made me sharper. We'd made it this far, after all, which incidentally was the entrance to the legion camp.

A simple wooden door, the gate was our first indicator that this camp was temporary, meant for campaign use only. Its defensive stakes, ditch, palisade, and rampart were there, but it wouldn't hold off an invasion like some of the other forts I'd been in before. However, this particular one was built just like all the rest, and that meant a straight jaunt through the middle of the camp, right for the *praetorium*.

As we passed through the threshold, Helena and I were greeted by unfriendly looks from unfamiliar legionnaires. I'd expected expressions of awe, curiosity and, in Helena's case, lust, but none of the legionnaires displayed such emotions. We were instead met by looks of anger and hatred. Many of these men probably recognized us from the thousands of "Wanted" posters displayed throughout the empire, or were perhaps wondering why these people who'd come from the city they had just been besieging were suddenly and nonchalantly strolling through their camp.

Helena shared a worried look with me, and she tucked in close. She gripped her P90 and brought it close to her chest, while I shouldered *Penelope* as well. While we were mostly sure Vespasian didn't want us dead, if we were going to die, it was going to be together and guns blazing.

But as we quickly approached the center of the camp, fewer and fewer looks came our way. Within minutes, we found ourselves at the entrance of the *praetorium*, and both Gaius and Marcus walked inside while we waited. A few minutes later, important looking military and administrative figures offered us dirty looks as they were hastily escorted from the tent by Marcus while Gaius remained inside.

"You can go inside, now," Marcus informed us once they were gone.

I nodded and took a step forward, but he rested a hand against my chest and stopped me.

"Your weapons, Hunter," he said.

I held his gaze for a few seconds, but he didn't flinch. After another second, I nodded and unclipped my rifle from its 3-point sling draped over my shoulder. I handed it to him, while Helena did the same. I tried to step forward again, but Marcus halted me just as he had before.

"All of them," he said, with a flick of his eyes towards my pistol.

I took a deep breath and retrieved my Sig, slapping it roughly into his waiting hand. "You sure he's not going to kill us?"

"Hunter, if he wanted you dead, you already would be."

"Thanks for that," I grumbled as Helena bravely pulled me behind her into the tent.

The interior of the command tent was just like all the other ones I'd seen. Relatively small, about the size of half a tennis court, and sparingly furnished. A chest, cabinet, desk, bed, and a few extra chairs were the room's only furnishings, but there were a few other oddities. A five foot tall broadsword was prominently displayed on a rack, its dark metal contrasting harshly with the white crispness of the tent's canvas walls, as did a set of double bladed battle axes that hung crisscrossing one another. I wagered they were mementos from the only inhabitant's previous two campaigns in Britain and Gaul.

As for the inhabitant, I was immediately taken aback by his presence – by his looks, his countenance, and years of anticipation. Just under six feet tall, he had dark, almost black hair, a broad nose that completely suited his face and severe eyes that didn't seem capable of missing a thing. He was built like a wrestler, a popular sport these days, even if it was nothing like modern day Greco-Roman wrestling, which was also, in fact, neither Greek nor Roman. He also had an interesting scar on his right cheek, not like Santino's, but a simple line from his temple to chin.

I thought back to all the busts and sculptures of the man I'd seen during my college years. None of those facsimiles resembled this man at all, even one in particular that I normally associated with the man: a representation of him struck in coinage maybe twenty five years from now. Even so, there was something fundamentally familiar about him.

Vespasian.

Finally.

But most surprising was that he also seemed happy, even jovial. He rose to his feet and moved toward us, reaching out with his arm, which I gripped just before the elbow.

"Greetings!" He hailed in an impressively deep voice. "You must be Jacob Hunter. I have heard much about you."

I smiled and tried not to look intimidated by this confusing man.

"All good things I hope," I said awkwardly.

"Perhaps," he said, still smiling, before turning to Helena. "And this must be the lovely Helena… van Strauss? Am I saying that correctly?"

Helena smiled as well, even more embarrassed than I was. "Yes, yes you are."

"Wonderful," he boomed. "It is an honor to meet you as well. The tales of your beauty precede you. Tell me, is it true you can turn men to stone on a whim?"

She looked at me, completely flushed.

"Well," she said like a love sick teenager, tossing her head in my direction, "maybe only this one."

He belted out a rich laugh. "I have heard you two are together. Congratulations! Your marriage must be happy and bountiful."

"It's not like that…" we both started, before cutting ourselves off. I stood as confused as I was embarrassed. This man was nothing like I imagined he would be. He didn't seem like most people, let alone like most Romans.

"Bah! If two people can fall in love and still fight wars with each other and not against one another, then you have something truly special indeed."

An interesting thought. I hoped he was right.

"Now," he said, his joyful attitude draining immediately, "we have much to discuss. Please sit."

"Such a charmer…" Helena whispered in English as we moved to our seats.

"Don't get any ideas, honey," I replied with a smirk.

As Helena and I maneuvered into our chairs, Vespasian took a seat behind his desk, folding his hands in front of him. He rested them on the desk while he waited for us to get comfortable. He took a deep breath, and in an instant, the cheerful man who'd hit on Helena and shook my hand was gone, replaced by a very stern authority figure. My spidey-sense tingled and I knew something was wrong, something that told me our meeting wasn't going to be all shits and giggles after all.

"So," Vespasian began, making eye contact with Helena and I equally, "I have made a very good friend over these past few months. I must admit, I am almost embarrassed to say that before our campaign in Germany, I considered him little more than an arrogant ass, already past his prime. However, as the fates would have it, he and I grew quite close as we worked together, and I found myself considering him a friend."

I gulped. I had a feeling where this was going.

He continued. "As we campaigned this past summer, he amused me with many stories, the particularly interesting ones revolving around events that occurred four years ago. The stories themselves weren't of particular surprise, as I had heard them many times through camp gossip and with my legates over dinner." His eyes drilled through mine as I tried to maintain my composure. He didn't seem convinced that I had any idea what he was talking about. "Oh, you know the ones. The stories about Caligula and a group of people from... well... that part isn't always so clear. However, what made this man's rendition of these tales all the more interesting was that he seemed to know more than most. Do you know of whom I am speaking?"

I cleared my throat and fidgeted in my chair. Helena didn't seem particularly comfortable either. The tone in the room had shifted completely. How easy it had happened was unsettling.

"Galba?" I answered.

"Galba, indeed," he said with a slow nod of his head. "You should know that when he first told me these stories, I did not believe him. How could I? Claudius a traitor? An orb of magical powers? Time traveling soldiers from an era of flying machines that can reach Luna and weapons that can destroy entire cities? Ridiculous! Yet..." He paused, leaning forward to rest his elbows on the table, his chin held up by his hands, "…here you are. Tell me, is it true your weapons can kill from miles away?"

I deferred to Helena.

She shrugged, smiling meekly. "Yes, but it isn't easy."

"It. Isn't. Easy," Vespasian responded, with a slow shake of his head as he straightened his posture. "A very interesting response. Humble. Yet most would say it was impossible."

"Galba's told you more, hasn't he?" I asked.

"Oh yes… far more."

"Did he speak of Agrippina?"

"Ah, the lovely Agrippina," he said, rolling his head as he spoke, "yes, well, we shall get to her soon enough. But first, I have a question for you. As I said, Galba has informed me of where you come from. I understand how you came to be here, at least, as far as anyone could honestly understand it, and wish to sympathize with you. However, your arrival is an accident, and if I truly understand everything, possibly a detrimental one. Now, choose your words very carefully, for your response is most important…"

Before asking, he leaned back in his chair and held the back of his head with his hands. I wasn't sure if the posture was meant to throw us off, intimidate us or give us false hope. Considering the deviousness the man had displayed thus far, I couldn't even begin to guess. Even so, he stared me dead in the eyes, shifted his attention to Helena, and then back to me.

"This is my home. Rome," he said. "Flawed as it is, it's one I care very deeply for. So I must know, what gives you the *right* to interfere with it as you have for the past five years?"

His question was steady, but strain was obviously evident. He didn't sound angry, but there was sternness in the question. I felt Helena's hand reach out and grip my own, giving it a tender squeeze. Vespasian noticed but didn't comment. I looked at her and she gave me a supportive smile.

This was it. *The* question. The one I had struggled with and attempted to justify ever since we'd arrived here. I took a deep breath and tried to collect my thoughts before answering.

Vespasian waited patiently for almost two minutes.

"The right," I started, glancing up from my thoughts. "A very interesting concept, don't you think?" Vespasian didn't respond, but I didn't expect him to. "Well, I've always thought so. I mean, who really has the right to anything? Has God," I paused, "or gods, ever come down and personally proclaimed anything for anyone? Maybe. I've spent my entire life in the belief of a supreme being, and I still do, but when I think of what 'rights' he has given me, my conclusions always draw me to a single thing."

"And what is that?" Vespasian asked.

I paused and looked at Helena.

"To life," I said turning back to him. "My government added extra little things like 'liberty and the pursuit of happiness,' but those are social constructs, created in the hope that people would strive for more with those principals beneath them. But life, well, there is no one out there who can deny me my right to live, and if they threaten it, I will defend it. I have the responsibility for self-preservation and a responsibility to protect those I love."

Helena squeezed my hand again.

"Our arrival here was, as you said, an accident, and yes, a potentially detrimental one." I took a deep breath. "And it was my fault. I have carried this blame on my shoulders for five years, and it gets heavier by the minute. At times I feel like Hercules taking the world off of Atlas' shoulders for a while. The responsibility seems that great. But because it was my fault, it is also my job to put things right." I paused again, taking yet another breath. "Our interference, as you put it, has possibly changed your history, and very possibly the lives of trillions, but, honestly, I couldn't care less."

Vespasian opened his mouth to speak, but I defiantly cut him off with an upraised hand.

"In fact, I only care about one thing, and that's getting me, my friends, and the woman sitting next to me home. They are all I care about. But we have to fix what we've broken first. Only we know what needs to be done, and only we have the means to accomplish it."

My right hand started shaking in frustration upon my knee as I spoke. I looked down at it and clenched it into a fist to quell it, placing it in my lap before continuing.

"Where I come from, we have a saying. 'If it isn't broke, don't fix it,' but sir," I said with half a chuckle, "we broke something... something that could have ramifications thousands of years from now." I paused, shaking my head at the floor before continuing. "It's something we... I... have to fix, and that gives us... gives me... the right to do everything I need to do. If I can't do that we're as good as dead anyway. The only real question is whether you'll help me or not."

Vespasian remained in his chair, his fingers now linked together in support of his chin. He seemed deep in thought. Perhaps he had already made a decision before we arrived and something I had said made him rethink his position. Or perhaps he'd had no prior thoughts on the issue at all, and was weighing his options carefully.

Whichever the case was, Vespasian had always been a thinker, and he had also been a level headed and compassionate man. In fact, one of his greatest characteristics, in my opinion, had always been his adherence to the codes and mannerisms of Augustus Caesar, who had preached careful management, thought before action, hard work, morality, and simply making rational decisions. He'd been an inspiration for Vespasian, and I only hoped it wasn't a sentiment the man before me was still destined to develop later in life.

"You speak well, Hunter," he finally said. "I feel the conviction in your words, as well as this burden you speak of. I have to agree that if I were in your situation, I would want nothing more than to find my way home as well. That is why I have decided to help you."

"You have?" Helena asked skeptically.

"Yes," he replied. "Even before Galba spoke of you, I had heard your stories. Everyone has. *Vani*, correct? I did not know you were these vigilantes at the time, but there isn't a man, woman or child in the Empire who has not heard of you. What you have done for all those people is beyond reproach. You are noble and valorous, having had no reason to help them at all. With your abilities, you could have taken control of Rome itself had you desired, but you did not. You did the right thing. Meeting you both has reinforced what I already suspected: that you are worth helping."

I cleared my throat. "Do you even know what it is we're trying to accomplish?"

"Of course," he said, that jovial attitude faintly returning. "You wish me to remove Agrippina from power."

"Galba told you, I take it?" I asked, almost annoyed at the ugly Roman legate.

"Yes. As I said, we have become good friends. At first his stories were but idle entertainment, but as they went on, I realized just how real they were. As for Agrippina, I took issue with her four years ago when she took over Caligula's throne. Few know this, but I spent time with the Imperial family when I was younger, and had grown quite fond of the man, but his sisters were note quite so endearing. Agrippina had been the worst. Always plotting and scheming, it would not surprise me if she, in fact, was responsible for his death."

I repressed the urge to whistle, knowing full well her actual role in the assassination. It was also interesting to learn that Vespasian had been hanging out with the Julio-Claudian clan in his youth. He was right, I hadn't been aware of his early friendship with Caligula, and as far as I knew, neither did the rest of the academic 21st century world.

I wondered how that had worked.

"Therefore," Vespasian continued, "I have decided to take it upon myself to remove Agrippina from office and find someone more suitable to govern our great empire."

"I believe Jacob told Galba who he thought..." Helena started before Vespasian cut her off.

"Yes, he informed me of your thoughts on the matter."

"We don't think, we know," I enforced.

"Yes, yes," he said, sighing with a shake of his head, "but I am not yet forty years of age, and am far less experienced than most, Galba included. How can I govern all of Rome if I doubt even myself? No, we will find the most appropriate man for the job."

That wasn't part of the plan, but I shouldn't be surprised he would think that way. It was a typical Vespasian answer, but even so, he *was* the only surefire candidate. Others may do a good enough job, but there was no way to ensure that. The safest and most logical thing to do was to follow history.

"Now," Vespasian said, shifting into a more comfortable position in his chair, "tell me more about this blue orb and how it works. Galba was very inconsistent with his details, and I can only assume that was because he had little information."

On his orders, I set out to tell him my ever-expanding and unreliable theory on time travel. I explained the rubber band theory and wormholes, using the worm burrowing through an apple analogy. I then went on to describe the numerous paradoxes we were possibly dealing with, or even possibly proving wrong. I explained what Varus had told me of Remus and the orb's connection with Druids, as well as the Etruscan mantra apparently needed to use it. I finished by indicating that, in reality, I had no concrete facts about how the thing worked, just rough ideas.

"I think I understand," Vespasian said when I was finished. "Your story of fixing what you've changed certainly makes sense now. Any alterations to history today, could change your home completely."

"Exactly," I said.

"But how will you know when this… timeline… is fixed?"

"Well, I have a theory," I offered unsteadily

"You do?" Helena asked curiously.

"In theory, I have a theory," I clarified

"Well, that's helpful," she commented, folding her arms across her chest, a typical Helena reaction whenever I brought up yet another of my theories.

"It requires the orb," I said. "When Claudius was in the midst of torturing me all those years ago, there was a moment when he pressed it against my face. It made contact with my skin but nothing happened. Why not?" I asked both Helena and Vespasian.

Helena worked her lips in thought while Vespasian leaned back in his chair expectantly.

"Okay," I said, "I believe the answer lies in the claim that, according to a fella named Einstein, time is relative."

"What do you mean?" Vespasian asked, ignoring the name drop.

I cringed. Even Helena, the pop culture ignoramus that she was, knew of the science fiction concept of time travel. She, at least, had some very vague and theoretical background knowledge on the concept, but Vespasian had nothing. Nothing in his life could ever have prepared him for the idea of traveling through time. Even Greco-Roman mythology lacked any concise story of time traveling beings, at least as far as I knew of.

"Look," I sighed, "this stuff is very confusing, and I will be the first to admit that I am by no means an expert. Even the most fundamental and scientific knowledge from my timeline is little more than guesswork and theory."

"Just keep it simple, Jacob," Helena advised.

I nodded. "When we first went back in time four years ago, we immediately altered the timeline. Now, think of time as a river and us as a rock being tossed into it. At first, the rock was very small, just a couple of people standing around in a cave, not impacting much of anything. The river still flowed around it easily. Had we never left the cave and gone back home right away we would probably find that very little, if anything, had changed. However, the longer we spent in this point in history, the bigger that rock becomes, so much so that we run the risk of it becoming so big that the water may flow over the embankment, a natural dam builds and the flow of the river slows or diverts, or in a worst case scenario, stops the flow of the river completely. Do you understand what that last part means?"

"I think I do, yes," Vespasian said slowly.

Helena was also nodding, completely enraptured.

"Now, we don't know how big the rock is at this point, it could be huge, it could be small, but my theory as to why nothing happened when I last touched the orb is simply that the rock got big enough to divert the flow of water down another channel, so much so that it deposits the water in a completely different location, meaning that because of what we've done, the timeline is now fixed so that any future encounter with the orb, by anybody, no longer occurs."

"How?" Vespasian asked.

"Well, remember what I said about time being relative? That means that from the perspective of someone from the future, no matter what we do, it has already happened for them. It's done. The reason why I couldn't see anyone on the other side of the orb here in our past is simply because there is no one there in our future. We haven't yet activated the sequence of historical events that will lead to the point where our future selves," I said, pointing to Helena and I, "encounter the orb again. Or anyone else, it seems. Once I look through the orb and see ourselves, I'll know the timeline has reoriented itself to the point where nothing has changed in our present… or at least very little," I finished with a hopeful chuckle before growing serious. "Then again, there is the chance that the rock we've created has already become *so* big, that no matter what we do, I'll never see myself on the other end of the orb. Which could mean a thousand different things."

I let out a slow breath and looked over at Helena. Her chin rested on her hand and she wore a vacant expression on her face, something between complete boredom and being totally lost. After a few seconds, she finally noticed my attention and gave me a supportive smile and nod, like she'd been following along the entire time. Vespasian looked equally as confused, but he let it pass with a shake of his head.

"Are you sure you do not wish to stay in Rome?" He asked. "Once Agrippina is taken care of, I am sure we can find you a position in one our academies."

I looked at Helena with a mock smile on my face.

"A teaching job? In Ancient Rome? Tempting…"

She rotated her face at me with another wide eyed, but completely different expression on her face.

"Never mind," I said quickly, turning back to Vespasian. "Sorry, but I'm a historian, not a pseudo-scientist."

"I see," Vespasian said, "well, I must admit that your explanation is mostly meaningless to me, but it sounds like you understand the problem. Theory or no."

Vespasian stood from his chair, moved over to his bedside stand and poured himself some wine. Goblet in hand, he sat on his bed and took in a deep breath, a moment of weakness I had not yet seen in the man.

"It is time for us to take our leave," he said, "but not without sharing some information you with first." He sighed again. "Even after all we've spoken of, I still can't believe I am about to do this…"

He trailed off, before finally looking at me.

"Agrippina is near. She is staying a few miles outside of Tripolis, just north of Caesarea in Syria. She has brought her Praetorians to aid in the Jewish subjugation and to quell rumbles of insurrection in Parthia, providing us a unique opportunity. The best way for us to remove her is for you to do it. I cannot allow my legions to become involved. Find her and bring her to me, and we will take her back to Rome together in chains. The Senate is fickle, weak. She may have many senators under her influence now, but once I'm through with them, she will be hard pressed to retain their loyalty."

"You want us to capture Agrippina for you?" Helena asked dubiously. "She could have thousands of Praetorians with her. There are eight of us."

"Take your friends Gaius and Marcus," Vespasian offered, waving towards the entrance and our two friends waiting just outside. "That should make it an even fight. She may even have your orb with her."

That got my attention. If we could bring her to justice, remove her from power, and get the orb all at the same time, we might actually be able to get home sooner than expected. Of course, I still had no idea how to work the damn thing, but with Agrippina out of the picture, Varus and I would at least have time to figure it out.

"We'll do it," I said, receiving a shocked look from Helena in return.

"Good," Vespasian remarked. "You may go back to your friends now. I will order Gaius and Marcus to join you soon to inform you when it's best for your group to leave. Speaking of, I must say that I look forward to meeting all of you at a later date, especially the one Galba referred to as, 'the funny one.' He seems quite entertaining."

I smiled. I'm sure Santino will let that go straight to his head.

He always did.

"I'm sure they would like to meet you as well," I replied. "When should we expect to leave?"

"Perhaps two days from now. I'll make sure siege operations are light so you can prepare."

I nodded my head and rose to my feet, following Helena as she rushed unceremoniously towards the entrance. I let her through, but paused briefly, a moment of weakness, or perhaps compassion, hitting me.

"Just one more thing, Vespasian. A favor, really."

"What is it?"

"Once you put down this rebellion, please, go easy on the Jews. It wasn't... completely their fault. Let them have some peace."

Vespasian looked up from a document he was reading to look at me coldly. He held the look for a few seconds before he laughed to himself and punched his desk.

"I knew these Jews were acting bolder than I gave them credit for. They never would have had the balls to rebel on their own. Perhaps in a few years, but not now. Fine. In honor of your deeds as *Vani*, I will make sure the rest of this war is as devoid of bloodshed as I can help. What's done is done, however, that I cannot change."

I nodded. "Just remember when you're settling terms to be gentle. I hate to break it to you, but from where I come from, Jews are still around to pester people, but Roman History is just a course taught in school."

Vespasian lost his smile at that comment, so offering him an innocent smile of my own, I turned and left the *praetorium*. I waved farewell to Gaius and Marcus after retrieving my weapons as Helena finished by giving them quick kisses on the cheeks in parting. Together, my female companion and I marched definitely through the camp and out into the quiet, cold night.

It only took two steps before she had something to say.

"Attack Agrippina when she could have her entire Praetorian contingent with her? Are you fucking crazy?!" She was almost yelling.

"No, I'm not crazy," I answered calmly. "I'm opportunistic, not to mention verging on desperate. If Vespasian sent his army, the potential political ramifications may completely defeat the purpose of what we're trying to accomplish. We, on the other hand, can sneak in and take her without anyone being the wiser, and maybe even grab the orb in the process."

"Jacob, you're getting cocky again. What if she's expecting us? Sets another trap?"

I let out a slow breath. I wasn't getting cocky. Not this time, but how was I going to convince Helena that this plan had nothing to do with the overly obsessive one we acted on months ago?

"When we get back to the city, we'll discuss it with everyone else, and only act on it if it's agreed upon by all," I said. "Besides,

Vespasian is obviously on our side. If he wanted us dead, we would be. Agrippina may be expecting us, but she won't expect all of us. We can do this, Helena. We can get home."

She didn't look nearly so convinced, and she moved her hand down to her stomach, wincing at perhaps another stab of pain. She still seemed very angry and I figured it was about time for another Jacob/Helena speaking hiatus.

"You'd better not be wrong this time," she threatened, with a finality that told me that was going to be it for the near future.

I sighed, condemning myself to the fate of silence that was sure to come, and looked at the road again. "I'm not."

X
Recon

Mission Entry #10
Jacob Hunter
North of Caesarea, Judea - October, 42 A.D.

Pardon the handwriting as I'm writing this on horseback. It wouldn't have been a problem had we purchased those camels I'd wanted, but everyone overruled me on that one. Something about them smelling and having a bad tendency to spit.

I argued that it was llamas that spat, not camels, but no one listened.

Oh, well.

So, guess who we finally met?

Vespasian.

Pretty cool, eh? I love how plans come together in the end. With the way things had been going, I wasn't sure if we'd ever meet him. Apparently, I wasn't very good at plans.

As for Titus Flavius Vespasianus (his Latin name), the man was an enigma. Easily the most confusing Roman I knew, he came off like Santino at times but Vincent at others. He was a tough read and it was hard to know what he was thinking, but that didn't mean he wasn't worth listening to. In fact, he was the reason I was here.

It seems Agrippina's pissed off one man too many. No surprise, there. Vespasian's been done with her for a while now apparently, and has tasked us with capturing her and bringing her to justice.

I had to admit that going after Agrippina felt great. It was time for a little payback, and it felt especially good having Gaius and Marcus with us. I guess it was just great to be working for someone again. Working for ourselves for the past few years had its benefits... kept our own hours, the pay had been good, but it lacked fulfillment. While we weren't on Vespasian's payroll, simply having him send us on a mission was a nice enough change of pace. It felt more purposeful having someone like him making the decisions for once.

Everyone thought the same. Except for Helena. She's never been a proponent of doing anything that put our lives at direct risk, but she's been exceptionally cautious ever since Byzantium. Whatever her reasons, it bothered me. In the past, her bad feelings tended to manifest themselves in real life, but while I've always trusted her judgment, we couldn't stand down now. Home was just a melon sized ball away. If she had a bad feeling, then we'd take it into account and be more careful, but we weren't giving up. Everyone else was on board, and she hadn't been willing to offer anything that could sway the others.

And as always, it's become a point of tension between us. She stopped talking to me about four days ago, just after our conversation with Vespasian. I swear. One day I will figure out what make women tick.

At least that one.

But I digress.

There isn't much else to say right now. No news on the orb, except that Vespasian believes Agrippina may have it on her, but I still don't have a fucking clue how it works.

I'll have to get back to you on that someday.

Great... Santino's radioing me. Some kind of roadblock up ahead. Just another snag to deal with.

I'll try to write one more time before we hit Agrippina. No promises though.

Don't miss me.

I quickly bound my journal and tossed it in my bag. Checking to make sure I looked as inconspicuous as possible, I signaled for everyone to hang back before double timing it to Santino's position. He was on forward recon today, scouting out the area a few hundred meters ahead of us while his swim buddy, Wang, was on rearguard a few hundred meters behind us. It may have split up the swim pair, but it assigned them likeminded tasks to keep the rest of the group stable, at least as stable as this group could get.

Gaius and Marcus had joined us after Vespasian had sent us the go-ahead to leave. They were now 10-9 and 10-10 respectfully, and not only had they been integrated into our chain of command, and given call signs, but they were also given that which they'd always wanted:

The truth.

Now that the cat was out of the bag with Galba and Vespasian, we'd decided it was time to let our best friends in on our little secret, along with Madrina. We told them everything during our first night on the road. It wasn't a surprise that they were initially shocked but quick to accept. In fact, since the truth had been Marcus' guess all along, they'd even joked about it, Gaius grudgingly paying him some money as a result of the bet they'd had.

Madrina, however, had not taken it as well.

She'd known Bordeaux hadn't been a simple Gaulic local, but there was no way she could have guessed where he truly came from. She'd been pretty angry that night. She'd stalked off almost immediately, giving none of us any time to explain. Helena had gone to talk to her, but had come back a few minutes later, having little luck at consoling her. However, Bordeaux, the big snuggly kitten that he was, managed to calm her down rather quickly, and she eventually came around.

Her main concern must have been the orb and what it represented. Once she knew what it was, it had to frighten her that her hulking meat slab of a man might choose to go home, instead of be with her. I had no idea what Bordeaux would do, but I knew he wouldn't just abandon her. He may even choose to stay with her, but it was his decision, and he'd have to deal with it later.

Gaius and Marcus, however, were an entirely different story. They'd practically demanded we take them with us to the future. I had no theoretical problem with them coming, but I had no idea if they even could. I hadn't told them that, but it was just another thing we'd have to figure out later.

In the meantime, we decided now was the best time to get them more acquainted with how we plied our trade. So, we gave them some spare BDUs and boots, our extra com units, and even rifles. Our supply cache had come with my SR-25, Helena's M82 sniper rifle, a few shotguns – just in case we had to face Roman zombies, I suppose – a number of assorted M4-A1 carbines, your standard run of the mill infantry weapons.

Unfortunately, ammo was now at a serious premium. Most of the 5.56mm ammunition used in the G36, M4s, and HK416s, was practically gone thanks to the siege of Caesarea. We only had enough for three full magazines each, barely one hundred rounds. Everyone else fared slightly better. Unfortunately, Helena had given most of her ammo for the DSR1 to Bordeaux, so she wouldn't be doing much more sniper work with it. At least she still had the M82, but she couldn't lug that thing around everywhere.

The shotguns had plenty of ammunition since nobody had ever used the damn things, but we had kept them well maintained. We gave one to Madrina, as it had the easiest learning curve to operate, but we didn't expect her to ever have to use it.

After rationing out the ammo, Santino managed to find an extra box of 5.56 in one of our crates, so we went through the very basics of rifle shooting with Gaius and Marcus. Titus easily out shot them with the G36, but he'd had years of practice under Vincent's tutelage. They did fairly well at medium ranges, each achieving close groupings at about fifty meters or so. Shooting wasn't a hard thing to learn, but it took a certain amount of skill and time to practice. It didn't hurt that they were consummate professionals, soldiers born and bred. They wouldn't give up or stop trying until they were more than competent with whatever weapon they were given.

It was that same legion discipline that I respected more than anything else in this asinine and fucked up time period.

Each of us from the future also offered some skill set to help them fit in. Santino taught them how to move, Helena how to shoot, Bordeaux how to best cope with explosive detonations, Wang some basic medical treatments, Vincent to use the com system, and I instructed them to simply not do anything stupid.

Despite the crash course in modern Spec Ops, the two Romans were in nirvana. They were finally given the chance to prove to the rest of us that they could do everything we could.

I called out to the two of them as I passed by them. "Remember, if this ends up in a firefight, short controlled bursts. Conserve your ammo."

Both men saluted in a more modern fashion than their chest pounding standard, another thing we'd showed them. I hadn't been sure if it was appropriate or not, but given the circumstances, I couldn't have cared less. I returned their salute with an uninterested wave.

I nudged my beautiful Spanish horse in Santino's direction, and we moved out in a trot. It took me five minutes to reach him, but about twenty meters out he was emphatically signaling for me to take cover. Instinct took over and I swiftly swung my left leg over Felix's back and dropped to the ground next to him. In the same movement, I grabbed his reins and gently tugged for him to fall into a sitting position. Horses didn't like lying on the ground, but they did if needed. It just took a little coaxing.

Felix was a good horse though, very obedient, so he fell on his flank as though he did it all the time. I patted his mane, fed him a carrot I'd pulled from my pocket, and told him to stay. I wasn't sure if he'd listen, but I didn't have much of a choice. Leaving him behind, I bear crawled to the small sand dune separating Santino from whatever had his attention.

"What's up?" I asked him, pulling out my binoculars. "A four star resort with comped room service and a pool shaped like a palm tree with lots of hot ladies in bikinis?"

Santino looked at me. "She hasn't talked to you in four days, and already you've got ladies in bikinis on the brain?"

"I just want to see her in a bikini one of these days," I said, peering through the lens. "Not much in the sexy-ware department in the stores around here."

"You're pathetic."

I glanced at him with a mock frown on my face. "I'm so lonely."

Santino chuckled.

"But seriously," I said, returning my attention to my binoculars, "what have we got? Some kind of picket station?"

"That's what I'd call it," he replied, looking through his magnifiers as well. "I've seen about thirty guards manning the post, all acting unprofessional and lazy. Ten archers in the tower, ten guards on duty, with another ten milling about. Stables around back with horses for each of them."

"Hmm," I hummed. "Shouldn't be too much of a problem."

"We *could* just go around," Santino pointed out.

"We could, but I'd rather not have anyone behind us. This post means we have to be pretty close to the AO. I don't want anyone sneaking up on us while we're reconnoitering Agrippina's location."

"You're the boss."

I nearly missed my next breath at the comment, but quickly recovered. "Any thoughts on a tactical approach?"

"I'd say the best way to take care of them is to have them come to us," he suggested.

"Yep," I agreed, squinting through my binoculars.

He glanced at me. "You don't actually have a plan?"

"Well," I said, meeting his look. "One could call it that."

"Call it a plan?"

"Yeah." I shrugged. "Sure. Why not?"

He snickered. "This should be good."

***

Twenty minutes later, Santino and I rode our black horses toward the guard post, our pace innocent and nonthreatening. Before setting out, we'd radioed for the rest of the group to move up to our recon position and wait to receive the bad guys. Once they'd set up the perimeter, the two of us had set out.

"You ready for this?" I asked him.

He turned to me and grinned.

"Try not to laugh too hard," I said.

"Man, this should be *really* good."

Only a few meters out, I gave the post a quick perusal and noted the posture and positions of each guard. Santino had been right. Most looked like they didn't want to be there, and the rest merely let on like they cared. They were so out of it upon our arrival that those out front were visibly surprised by our presence, even though we had been in view for the past ten minutes. A centurion came out to meet us, one of his buddies not far behind.

"Halt," the centurion called. "State your business."

I gave him a warm smile. It was easy to smile. I've always wanted to do this.

"My name is Ben Kenobi," I told the centurion. "This is Luke Skywalker. Let us through. We're on a diplomatic mission to Alderaan."

"You're on a diplomatic mission to…" the centurion looked at his companion curiously, "…Al-der-an?"

"You don't need to see any identification," I continued, waving my hand at him as I looked at Santino. He was staring at me, his mouth hanging open, no grin in sight. Even he couldn't believe I was doing this, and he didn't even seem to care that he was possibly blowing the entire ruse.

"We... don't need to see any identification?" The guard repeated slowly, again looking to his partner for clarification.

Was this actually working?

"These aren't the droids you're looking for?" I asked with an inkling of hope.

"What?!" The guard yelled, indicating to his comrades. "Seize these fools!"

He reached out to grab the reins of my horse, but before he could grasp them, I pulled out my Sig and shot him in the chest.

"Boring conversation, anyway," I said, my smile evaporating. I pulled hard on the reins, orienting Felix back towards our convoy, enticing him to put on some speed. I turned to Santino, conveniently galloping at my side, and offered him a toothy grin. "I've always wanted to do that!"

"Really?? That was your plan?"

"Don't tell Helena."

"Oh, you owe me big time, buddy," he replied, his grin returning. "Big time."

I didn't think he'd say anything to her, but my impending romantic doom wasn't nearly as important as the thing that had just struck my back. I craned my neck to see an arrow sticking out of my shoulder, luckily stopped from impaling me by my body armor. Santino looked over and noticed it as well.

"Move it," he said, pushing his horse even faster for the last hundred meters to our waiting teammates.

Arrows started falling all around us and Roman soldiers mounted horses to give chase. We had a good lead on them, but sniper fire from our comrades was already picking the Roman archers off. By the time we reached the small recon dune, most of the Romans giving chase lay dead behind us. The half dozen remaining Romans noticed their predicament, and turned tail and fled. We couldn't let them alert anyone of our presence, so we picked them off as well, one by one.

From the time I shot the first centurion to when the last Roman fell from his horse, only three minutes had passed. Quick, clean and proficient. Once we were sure no one was getting up, the team moved quickly through the bodies and policed them. Only Helena neglected her duties, rushing over to me instead to examine the arrow stuck in my back.

I didn't feel any pain, and I knew there was no way the primitive arrow could have penetrated the Kevlar that lined the combat fatigues I wore under my robe. Even so, she examined it carefully before diagnosing that it was clear for extraction. With a quick yank, she pulled it free from my MOLLE vest. Stepping around to face me, she broke it in half and threw it at my chest angrily.

I knew what she was thinking.

Another stupid mistake that could have ended much worse than it had. She stood there for a few seconds, just staring at me silently, but then she threw her arms around my shoulders and pulled herself in tight. She hung there for a while before pulling back, holding me by my arms. Her face revealed her concern, but then she shook her head at me and turned away to help the others.

I watched her go.

Women.

***

"I've got two guards in the Northeast cupola," Vincent reported over the radio. "Two more at the base of the tower."

"Copy," I replied, making a mark in my notebook.

"Five more at the gate." That was Wang.

"Uh-huh," I mumbled, scribbling furiously.

"Three on the south wall." Helena this time.

"All right, all right," I commed. "Slow it down. So far we have forty Praetorians scattered throughout the perimeter. Keep going. Slowly."

Their constant updates were disheartening. We'd arrived three hours ago around midnight, and had set up shop about an hour after that. All of us from Madrina to our former legion buddies were scattered around the decent sized seaside resort, counting and cataloging bad guys. We'd expected plenty of guards around the site, but things were quickly getting out of hand. No one had bought into Helena's theory of there being thousands of guards, but we were at least expecting her Sacred Band of three hundred Praetorians. Granted, she'd co-opted many of those men into her new ninja battalions or whatever, and since we'd just got done killing fifty or so of them, I thought maybe we'd get lucky.

"Ten near the docks," Santino radioed.

I marked it.

I personally didn't care how many men were there. Only one person mattered and that was Agrippina. The caves five years ago had housed just as many terrorists, and those men had been equipped with AK47s, not swords and shields. If not for my piss-poor driving skills, we would have been fine. Clearing out a village no bigger than a downtown city block, full of Romans who weren't expecting us shouldn't be a problem, especially if we were well prepared.

There seemed to be a lull in the team's updates.

I glanced up from my notebook, the same one I'd been scribbling nonsense in for the past few months. "Any more tangos?" I asked

"I've got one more coming out of the building," Helena updated. "Maybe back from a bathroom break."

"Anything else?"

Silence.

"Good," I continued. "Hold your positions for thirty mikes and maintain visual contact, then report back to camp."

I received a chaotic series of clicks in return, but it sounded like everyone got the message.

I was already at our camp, maybe five miles from the villa Agrippina had occupied inside the village. Wang had spotted her on a balcony earlier, so we knew exactly where she was staying.

We were near the beach behind a few high dunes in case the Romans came snooping. In preparation for the team's arrival, I moved down to the shoreline and sketched an accurate representation of the town in the damp sand.

North of Tripolis, Syria, modern day Tripoli, Lebanon, the town was negligible in size, but the villa that sat in its center was formidable. The complex sat on a little more than an acre of land, but half of that space consisted of the interestingly designed villa.

Some kind of amalgamation of Roman, Greek, Egyptian, and Mesopotamian architecture, it sported arches, columns, cupolas, minarets, and some designs I was unable to identify. It looked like a piece of junk in my opinion, but I was hardly an architectural expert. At least it had enough entrances and hiding spaces to sneak in a ten man squad from random trajectories.

To my sketch, I added the four walls, towers at the corners and every guard lookout station we had identified. I added the dock, and made sure the size was as close to scale as I could manage.

I took a few steps back and admired my handiwork. It would do. I started adding some more detail to the dock area, probably the most accessible route into the complex, when I noticed the first arrival. I looked up to see Helena making her way toward the camp, unaware that I was on the beach. She looked in our tent to find it empty, so I called out to her before she grew concerned. She waved back and entered the tent for a few minutes, emerging without her gear and wearing shorts and a tank top, her feet bootless.

She walked down to the beach slowly and sat next to my diagram, burying her bare toes in the damp sand. She extended her hand to me. I looked at it for a second but she was insistent, so I let her pull me down to the sand next to her.

I followed her lead and took off my boots.

The sand felt good between my toes, almost like a massage, and I suddenly felt as though I were elsewhere. Alone on the beach with our toes in the sand, the moonlight streaming down from out over the Mediterranean, I almost thought we were on vacation.

"Jacob, can we talk?"

I let my eyes close shut of their own accord, feeling the image slip away with her words. The last time she'd wanted to "talk" was during that first month in Rome when she told me she'd been a green rookie covering our backs in combat. That had been bad enough.

"If it's about the mission, I really don't want to hear it," I told her matter of factly. "We have to do this. With luck…"

"It's not about the mission," she said, cutting me off quietly, her voice devoid of anger or frustration. "Or timelines or Agrippina or anything like that."

Her tone threw me. She'd been our most vocal advocate for taking down Agrippina since this whole mess started. She'd always had more reason to hate her than any of us. Even me. But now she sounded as if she didn't even care at all.

"Then what's this about?"

"It's about... us."

"Us?" I asked, curious. "You finally breaking up with me?"

"What?" She looked stunned that I'd ever say such a thing. "No. Of course not." She shook her head distractedly. "I love you more than..."

"I love you too, Helena," I interrupted. "I don't think I say it enough, but I do. More than anything else."

"I know you do, Jacob." She sighed. "I'm sorry I've been so distant, but I've had a lot on my mind."

"This have anything to do with what we talked about in Galba's tent a few months ago?"

"In a way, yes," she replied, still very distracted, "but also no."

She picked up a handful of sand and I watched as it streamed between her fingers, the wet clumps making tiny mounds as they impacted the beach.

"It's okay, Helena. Just tell me."

She choked a halfhearted laugh. "It's really so simple..."

"Hey, lovebirds," Santino called out from the dune, Wang, Gaius, and Marcus beside him, "leave room for the Holy Spirit down there."

I sighed and batted a hand at him in frustration, but I shifted my attention back to Helena. I was on the edge of my seat over what she was going to tell me. All the tension between us aside, I wanted to know what was bothering her. Had to know. She was staring at the sand and looked sad, rather than annoyed. I simply could not guess what was bothering her.

What could do this to her?

I reached across my body and gripped her cheek with the palm of my hand, rotating her face toward me. I waited until she met my eyes, her bright green ones confirming her sadness.

"Now's not the time for jokes," I said. "I'd really like to know what's going on. Once we're done with the briefing, we're going to sit back down, right here, and we're going to talk about it."

She managed a small half-smile and leaned in to kiss me.

She pulled back and said, "I'll be here."

***

Fifteen minutes later, Helena and I were still waiting on the beach for our remaining teammates to make their way back. We sat there looking at the moonlight, her head on my shoulder, listening to the crashing waves and annoying banter from the peanut gallery back in the camp. I held her hand as we sat, my mind processing everything I could think of.

Everything besides the mission, of course.

But at least my mind wasn't wandering *on* mission, for once. We weren't planning to hit Agrippina until the following night, so I had time to think. But it was still frustrating. I couldn't get Helena out of my head. This was a prime example of why the military frowned on combat operatives engaging in romantic ventures with one another. It was feared that one member of the pairing would becoming over protective of the other, usually the male towards the female, and in an act of desperation or overprotectiveness, do something that could threaten a mission. As chauvinistic as it may seem, it was basic social upbringing 101. Since our cavemen ancestors, it had always been the man's job to protect the women, and the sense of duty subconsciously stuck.

But, it was hardly my fault Helena and I ended up this way. Maybe it was fate. Stupid fate. Or maybe it was simply dumb luck on my part. Either way, it was currently spelling my downfall and leading toward my distraction right now.

If tomorrow was going to be as important and dangerous as we all thought, we had to talk now. Tonight. Not later.

Thankfully, I didn't have much time to focus on it because Vincent, Bordeaux and Madrina finally arrived. Santino, Wang, Titus, Gaius, and Marcus were already on the beach, likewise shoeless, and examining my piece of art. Five minutes later, ten bodies, all lacking footwear, stood around my little drawing of our target location. Santino, of course, felt the need to point out that his five year old equivalent could have done a better job, but after I threw a clump of wet sand in his face, everyone was laughing at him; not with him.

Once everyone settled down, I started the briefing. "All right, everyone, let's keep this short tonight. We'll go over the finer details tomorrow after a good night's sleep." Everyone nodded, pretty tired after our journey from Caesarea, so I continued. "Based on UAV scans and ground based observations, our clearest point of insertion is the docks." I used a small stick to circle the appropriate area of my sand painting. "A small team will amphibiously assault that spot, while the rest of us provide cover and sniper support from the north and south."

I pointed at the shoreline I'd added to my diagram.

"Once inside the perimeter, our scout team will clear the guards within the courtyard while the rest of us make our way to reinforce them. From there, we'll sneak through village and make our way into the villa. Once inside, we have three objectives; one primary and two secondary. Our primary one is to obtain Agrippina. Wang, as always, you're on hostage detail."

I glanced at Wang. He stood with his arms crossed, all business. He nodded in affirmation.

"Good. Our first secondary objective is to find Varus. The last time I encountered him, he was not happy about being employed by Agrippina, but chances are he still is and I'm certain he'd appreciate a rescue effort. Finally, if we find the second orb, we take it."

I sighed. "Keep in mind, the orb is still a secondary objective. Finding it means shit if we can't fix the timeline, and that means turning over Agrippina to Vespasian. Once we have Agrippina, we extract immediately, no matter what. Understood?"

I glanced around the circle, receiving nods and quiet affirmatives all around. Everyone seemed confident, maybe a little nervous, but that was normal. Only Titus and Madrina seemed a little worse for wear, but at least they had close companions to look to for guidance and reassurance prior to the mission.

"Any questions?" I asked finally.

There were none.

"Good. Go get some sleep."

***

I glanced over at Helena as Vincent helped me wash away the diagram. She'd moved closer to the water and sat close enough so that the waves could lap up against her bare legs. I watched her draw circles in the sand, only to observe them disappear with the ebb and flow of the tides. She looked so distracted. So flakey. It was so unlike her. That was my MO.

I patted Vincent on the back, thanking him for his help with the diagram.

He gave me a reassuring smile. "Good luck, Jacob. It looks like she has a lot on her mind."

I nodded and parted company with the elder sage. Taking a deep breath and letting it out slowly to build up my courage, I made my way to Helena at a slower pace than she deserved. I couldn't believe it. I was actually worried.

Upon my arrival, she was so out of it that I caught her completely off guard. She actually flinched at my touch, even though she must have known I was coming. Smiling to cover it up, she took my hand and guided me to sit in front of her. I plopped myself down in the sand, and spread my legs in a V, my feet extending past either side of her waist. She scooted in a bit closer, arched her knees over my legs, and gripped my hands.

"You ready to talk?" I asked.

She smirked. "Not really."

"Just keep it simple. Like what you said with Vespasian."

"The issue is simple by nature," she explained. "Saying the actual words is not. I've been struggling with whether you should even know, considering what we're about to do." She laughed again. "I don't even know how to put it in a way you, of all people, can understand."

"Then start with the most confusing," I suggested. "Blindside me with it."

Her smile lingered. "Okay…well, let's start over then."

"Works for me," I said, shaking my shoulders to ease the tension. "Hit me."

She cleared her throat. "Jacob, there's something I need to tell you."

"What is it, Helena?"

"I… I think I missed a period."

I leaned in and squinted at her in confusion. "In which sentence? I'm already lost."

She rolled her eyes. "Why do I ever listen to you? Of course that would be too confusing. No, Jacob. I think I'm pregnant."

Neither one of us said anything for a long time. I just stared at her as I attempted to process this new information when for no apparent reason, I felt nothing but suspicion.

"And who, may I ask, is the father?" I blurted.

She started to laugh, but then noticed my unflinching expression, causing hers to shift almost immediately. Angrily, she pulled her hands away from mine and slammed them both into my chest, pitching me backward.

"Ow!" I yelped, putting my hands up defensively to protect myself. "What was…"

"You are, you fucking asshole!" She yelled as she rained more blows against my body.

I tried to grapple with her to calm her down, but she stubbornly avoided me. Her punches turned to wild slaps as she frantically tried to bat me away. She was so wild that I wasn't ready for her when she shoved her open palm into my nose with almost as much strength as her original shove. The assault knocked me into the water where a large wave crashed into me, soaking me to the bone, and I could feel blood streaming down my chin as I pushed myself up onto my hands and knees

Helena stared at me angrily, taking a moment to gather her energy before she kicked me in the gut a moment later. It knocked the wind out of me and sent me careening back into the waves. She reared back and kicked me two more times before she threw her hands down and screamed in frustration, doubling over in another uncontrollable pain attack at the same time. But her pain wasn't going to quell her anger, and I watched as she turned on her heels and made her way down the beach.

Idiot! How could you be so stupid?

Pinching my nose, I cleared my head with some sea water and limped my way after her, my hand clutching my abdomen. She was hugging herself as she fled, and was also crying. I ran up behind her and put my hands on her shoulders, but she shrugged me off. I tried again, only to have her turn around and beat against my chest again, this time, however, with considerably less force. After enduring a few more blows, I was finally able to successfully grab her by the wrists and keep her at bay while she continued to cry.

God, I was a fucking idiot.

I pulled her in close, but she continued to struggle, and it was minutes before she finally ceased her assault and cried against my shoulder. I dropped us down to our knees, trying to pacify the situation while waves continued to flow around us.

"I'm so sorry, Helena, I don't know why I said that. Please, I… it was a stupid thing to say. I wasn't thinking. I have so much on my mind, I can't…"

I stopped, realizing there really was no excuse for what I'd said, but her sobs began to slow as I spoke and she eventually pulled back and sat on her heels. She coughed and cleared her throat, rolling her eyes at the sky as she did both.

"And you wondered why I couldn't tell you," she said around a few lingering sobs. "I knew you would react like a child. Say something stupid like that. I just knew it."

"I'm sorry, Helena. It was the only thing that popped into my head. I can't think straight anymore and you surprised me," I paused. "I still can't believe it."

"Well you'd better start, you jerk."

"But how?" I asked, looking at the sand for answers. "It hasn't happened before. We were always so carefu…"

"These things sneak up on people all the time, Jacob." She sniffed. "It must have happened that night during the siege when we were supposed to be covering Santino again." She shook her head. "Or even back in Byzantium, I don't know. Tracking these things has become more and more difficult the longer I've been here. I can't tell for certain how far along I am."

"But you're certain?"

She pounded my shoulder again. "I know this isn't the kind of thing you know anything about, but everything has been mostly normal for a long time and to miss…"

"All right, I get it."

Female biology not only confused me, it practically scared me.

Still.

A baby? A son? A mini-Jacob…

My family had never been large. It had been left small and became strained because of my father. As a result, ever since I could remember, I'd always wanted kids of my own. Fifty, for all I cared. But I always figured it would be in a cushy suburb with a white picket fence, and a guy who still delivered milk to our front door. Not in the first century A.D., surrounded by people who wanted to kill me, not to mention an empress who probably wanted to chew on my guts *while* she killed me. I couldn't imagine raising a kid in Rome. It almost seemed… irresponsible.

"What are you thinking?" Helena asked.

Most of the anger was gone from her voice by now, but traces of her tears were still evident on her lovely face, tears that caught me off guard. She really must have been worked up over this child to actually cry. Her reserved attitude over the past few weeks made sense all of a sudden… over the past year really. Had she wanted this all along? Was I really that blind?

I glanced up at her. "A baby?"

She smiled. "Yes, Jacob. A baby. Yours and mine."

She reached out and placed my hand against her stomach. I didn't feel anything. I suppose I wouldn't this early on, but something told me she was right. My child was there.

"But how can we raise him here?" I asked. "Now? He doesn't deserve to grow up in the ass end of civilization."

"She won't. We'll find a way to get home."

I pulled away from the future mother of my child, stood, and walked back towards the scene of our fight. I rubbed my chin and thought.

"What?" she asked as she slowly caught up to me.

"I… it's… look, I just don't know if we can responsibly raise him here. Not only that, but we also have no idea how a journey through the orb could affect him. Remember how painful it was? And what if we go when you're still pregnant? Who knows what could happen. I just don't see how we can do this."

She stepped around to face me, her eyes narrow.

"You're not suggesting that we…"

"What? Of course not. I just feel…"

"Jacob, stop. There's something else I need to tell you."

"We're not having twins are we?"

She smiled. "You know I can't know that, but there is something else you need to know. The reason I debated telling you for so long, and especially tonight, was because I have no idea what's going to happen to us tomorrow. If I die, I wasn't sure I wanted you knowing you lost your unborn child as well..."

"That's not going to happ..."

"Let me finish," she said, cutting me off with an upraised hand. "It was hard to tell you, yes, but I always knew deep down that you deserved to know. This child is as much yours as it is mine. You had to know. But, I didn't want to you to know because of this exact conversation. I wasn't sure what you would think. That's what worried me most because, well... the fact is simply that I want this baby. More than you can possibly imagine."

She turned her back on me and looked at the ground, her hands massaging her stomach. I stepped up behind her and wrapped my arms around her, gripping her wrists in my hands.

"I've been thinking about this for a long time," she continued. "It was something I've wanted to talk to you about for months, but I didn't think under Galba's bed was the appropriate place to do it, even though it was relevant even then. This child – our child – is something I've wanted ever since I was thirteen years old. A little girl of my own. Someone who I could play with, spoil, love, raise as a lady. Everything. At the time, I suppose what I really wanted was a sister, but later I knew what I wanted was a child. But like all dreams, every day I had to wake up to the truth."

"Your prearranged marriage," I said softly.

She nodded. "I told you I never hated him. But I could never see him as the father of my child either. I knew that, like the marriage, children would inevitably be forced on me as well. It scared me. I didn't know if I would love them or not. Half of each child would be his. Someone I didn't love or even really like. How could I only love half a child?" She turned around. "Then I met you, Jacob. Yours is a child I could love." She squeezed her eyes shut. "We have to do this. This may be our only chance."

I gave it some thought before I pinched her chin with my thumb and index finger, tilted her face up, and waited as I mulled over her words. After a few moments deep in thought, everything pointed to only one conclusion.

"I want this too," I said, before a smile grew on my face. "Looks like you won't be going dancing as often as you'd hoped."

She returned the smile and hugged me tightly. "I can live with that."

Finally. This was the reaction I should have provided ten minutes ago. I held us there for what seemed like hours before the gravity of the situation dawned on me. I separated us and looked down at her.

"I forbid you from going on the mission tomorrow."

"No." She pulled away, surprise in her eyes. "No! You're not going in there without me!"

"Helena, you can't. It's irresponsible."

"Jacob, I'm pregnant, not crippled, and it's too early for it to inhibit me in *any* way."

"Nope. Not happening."

"Yes, Jacob… it is."

There was no hint of backing down in her voice. She wasn't going to take no for an answer.

I met her stare. "You are the most frustratingly stubborn woman I have ever met!"

She smiled. "I know. It's why you love me."

I wanted to yell at her. Bay at the moon. Punch her in the face. Something. My emotions were all over the place. Happiness. Fear. Joy. Anger. Frustration. They were all there. This woman never ceased to amaze and confuse me. It was my turn to get angry.

In mock frustration, I gently pushed her away and kicked sand at her.

"Fine!" I yelled making my way back to the camp, "but you'd better not let *me* die, or your ass is haunted! Haunted!"

Her smile continued to enchant. "Just go back to the tent. I'll meet up with you soon. I want to enjoy the moonlight for a few more minutes." Then her smile turned coy. "At least now we don't have to worry about getting pregnant anymore if you want to have some fun lat…"

"Bah!" I waved my hand at her, and with half of me actually frustrated, the other half joking, I stalked my way back to the camp with my own smile still beaming.

A baby!

I thought getting myself stuck in Rome was crazy enough. Now things were really starting to hit me. I knew nothing about raising a kid. What was I supposed to do when I had to go shoot someone? Let Uncle Wang and Uncle Santino watch him while Helena and I were off on a mission? The kid would be sarcastic jackass in a week!

My head started to swim and I felt like collapsing as adrenaline from both the news and the fight waned.

Somehow finding my way back to the tent, I started working on the zipper, only to have it stubbornly fight me back. Just as I finally yanked the thing open, I heard Santino call out from the small camp fire where he sat with Wang, Gaius, Marcus, and Titus.

"Congratulations, Hunter," he said nonchalantly.

I turned awkwardly. "For what?"

He looked at his companions like I'd just asked the dumbest question of all time. "Helena's pregnancy, of course."

I stared dumbfounded. "What makes you think she's pregnant?"

He cleared his throat. "Well, when a man comes stumbling back from a long talk with a woman where a brawl goes down, it means one of two things. By the way, she really kicked your ass back there." He paused while Wang saluted me with some money he must have won from a bet. "You know... most couples just yell at each other, not throw down like that."

My head started spinning again.

"Anyway," Santino continued, "it means she's either been lying to you this entire time and that she's really some kind of transvestite or... an unexpected pregnancy. But I've seen her naked. She's definitely not a man."

"You've..." I mumbled, before catching on. "You what!?"

"Hey, don't sweat it, buddy," he said grabbing at his chest over his heart. "I'll cherish the image forever."

My swirling emotional storm wanted me to go down there and beat the shit out of him more than anything, but my lack of adrenaline was holding me back.

"I hope they name the kid after me," Wang offered.

"Wang Hunter?" Santino asked, meeting Wang's eye for a few seconds before the two of them burst into laughter. The three Romans were thoroughly confused until Santino translated what the slang word "wang" was as well as what a "hunter" was. The little English lesson barely lasted the time it took for a full translation because now all five of them were laughing hysterically. Even fucking Titus, who rarely showed any emotion, held his side as tears streamed from his eyes. Marcus even fell off his log.

I threw out a few chuckles at my own expense with them.

Trying to ignore the pack of hyenas outside, I pounded my fist against my forehead and escaped into my tent. After drying myself off, I snuggled into my bunk, bringing my blankets up to my nose. I felt like I'd aged three decades.

I still couldn't believe it.

A baby?

A baby.

I couldn't help but smile.

XI
Assault

Mission Entry #11
Jacob Hunter
Tripolis, Syria - October 42, A.D.

Well, folks... it's been fun.

This may very well be my last journal entry because two very different things might happen in the next few hours. Behind door number one, and a much more preferable outcome, is a successful mission consisting of Agrippina's capture and our obtainment of the last orb. Behind door number two, and the more attractive game show girl (that's always how they get you!) is our deaths.

Fun, eh?

Oh, should I mention Helena's pregnant?

Pregnant!

As if I didn't have enough to worry about. Apparently, there really isn't a stork that magically brings children into the world. Well there goes that bubble. Poof. Cue little wisp of smoke. To make matters worse, Helena insists on going on the mission. We couldn't leave her behind since she'd find a way to join us anyway, and even though Madrina is staying behind, she couldn't stop Helena even if she tried, despite her size. And as much as I want to, chaining the mother of my child to a pole doesn't exactly seem like the best option either.

Sigh.

I think I'm going insane. I can only imagine what my blood pressure must be like. Maybe I should ask Wang to give me a checkup...

The human body is not designed for so many fluctuations in emotions.

But anyway, I know I said I wouldn't bring it up anymore, but this is a biggie. I'm going to have a baby for crying out loud.

And isn't this what journals are for? Writing down my thoughts and feeling!?

What's that you say?

You don't want to hear it?

Fine!

Look at me. I'm arguing with myself in a print medium. Normally I just fought with myself in my head, and that was bad enough. This is getting ridiculous.

As for the mission, we're going in slow and meticulous. We don't know what awaits us within Agrippina's little stronghold, but we're used to unknown terrain. We also have a full complement of troops with us, and the additions of Gaius, Marcus and Titus will help our odds just that much more. The two former legionnaires are handier with a sword than any of us, and Titus has been training with rifles for years. He isn't the best shot in the group, but in the CQB environment we'll soon operate in, he'll do just fine.

All right then. There isn't much more to say. Nor is there much time to say anything, if there was anything to say at all.

There's a mouthful.

Well. Wish us luck.

It's been real.

"Are you done with that thing yet, Jacob?" Helena whispered from atop the sand dune.

"Yeah," I replied, tying off the notebook and tossing it in my bag, maybe for the last time. "Any word from Bravo Team?"

"Not yet," she said, scanning the dock area of the complex with her DSR1. "They're late."

"You know how Santino likes to make an entrance," I quipped.

Helena didn't respond, diligently performing her sniper duties, only five rounds left in her rifle. I glanced over at Vincent, who crouched next to me behind the dune. His rifle hung at his right side by a strap around his neck as he practiced reloading magazines one handed. I'd watched him practice the maneuver over the past few months now, and he was good at it. Every attempt he made to secure a fresh magazine into the dangling rifle's magazine had been successful so far. I just hoped he'd be able to do it during the insanity of a combat situation.

"Ready to get back in the saddle, Vincent?" I asked.

He looked up at me when my interruption caused him to miss his reload for the first time. He gave me a disgruntled look.

"I'm not so old that you can put me out to pastures quite yet, Hunter," he reported. "I am not completely worthless." He smiled. "Not yet."

I heard Helena grumble something similar from atop the dune.

So far Santino's little comedy posse only assumed Helena was pregnant. His little joke, as it turned out, had only been just that, and not an insight into her internal workings. After she'd joined me in the tent, we'd decided to keep her situation under wraps for the time being. We didn't need to worry everybody.

So, I ignored her and offered him a smile. "The thought never crossed my mind, sir."

He nodded and went back to work practicing his maneuver. Meanwhile, I hunkered down against the sand and looked up at the stars. They were far brighter than any variety back home and there were so many more. More than I could ever hope to count.

"Get up here, Jacob," Helena ordered, interrupting my stargazing.

I rolled onto my feet and climbed my way to the top of the dune. On my way up, I accidentally knocked sand on Vincent and he glared up at me as he shook himself clean.

"What have we got?" I asked, pulling out my binoculars and focusing them down range.

Once again, she didn't respond. She didn't need to. The view was telling enough.

By the time I focused my optics, two men were already climbing out of the water, their dark figures slowly emerging from the murky depths like in any good Navy SEAL promotional video. I watched four guards fall to the docks before the two figures even climbed onto the wooden planks. Once they hauled themselves up, they cautiously made their way towards the shore – low, slow and silent. A third figure emerged behind them and quietly lowered the dead bodies into the water as the first two men passed by them.

I quickly shifted my attention to the right, and watched as two more guards sitting near the seaside entrance to the courtyard stood from their chairs. They must have noticed something was amiss, but they didn't have much time to think on it before Wang and Santino of Bravo Team gunned them down with their suppressor equipped rifles.

As gravity pulled them to the ground, all three members of Bravo Team were rushing forward to plant themselves firmly against the perimeter wall. My view was obscured in that moment, but I was able to watch as Wang and Santino rounded the corner of the outer wall's entrance and disappear into the complex. I shifted my attention to the other known guard positions within my line of sight. Each contained their occupants, seemingly unaware of what was happening around them, and then they too were removed from the game.

Two minutes later, Santino's voice came over the com. "Alpha Lead, this is Bravo Actual."

"Go ahead," I answered.

"Beachhead secure. Give us five mikes to change out of our wetsuits, and regroup at rally point one."

"Roger, Bravo Actual. Charlie Actual, howcopy?"

"Solid copy," Bordeaux's voice came back. "Rally point one, five mikes."

I sent him a double click and waited with Helena and Vincent for a very long five minutes. When time was up, we rose to our feet and double timed the one hundred meters to the southern end of the beach side perimeter wall. Charlie Team would be coming in from the north. We made the trip in seconds, arriving at the outer wall just before Charlie.

At the head of our three person column, I led Alpha Team forward as we scooted our way along the wall, approaching the entrance Bravo Team had already cleared. I tracked Charlie approaching from the opposite side of the entrance, Bordeaux with his Big Fucking Gun on point.

I reached the corner first.

When Bordeaux arrived, he pulled up short and sent me a nod. I returned the gesture, rounding the corner just as he did, and dropped to a knee while Bordeaux plunged straight through. Helena stood above me offering additional cover.

The immediate area was clear. No sign of Bravo Team.

With a quick flick of his wrist, Bordeaux gestured for both teams to follow him in. I complied, moving into the complex with Helena and Vincent right behind me. We fanned out to the right while Charlie – including Gaius and Marcus – went left.

I took a quick look around. The interior of the courtyard was pleasant but rather unremarkable, decorated with cobblestone pavement, a few hanging gardens scattered about and a fountain with a sizable swimming pool alongside it. It was almost as nice as that four star resort I'd dreamt about a few days ago, sans bikini clad women. There were also a half dozen bodies scattered about, each with neat bullet holes in their chests. Alpha and Charlie quickly went to work concealing them in the shadows.

The job took about three minutes, and there was still no sign of Bravo. Definitely not part of the plan. Helena and I were just about to toss a body into a pile of his friends when we heard a twig snap behind us. Reacting instantly, we dropped the body and spun around, aiming our weapons in the direction of the sound. A single silhouette appeared in the darkness, only to reveal himself as Titus when he stepped into the light. Realizing his blunder, his masked face glanced at the ground in embarrassment.

Two other figures emerged out of the darkness like shades in the night, the more experienced Wang and Santino. One of the masked figures, I assumed Santino, stepped up beside Titus and whacked him in the back of the head in admonishment. The other figure, Wang probably, patted Titus on the shoulder consolingly.

I looked at Helena. She rolled her entire head in an exaggerated gesture of annoyance.

Everyone's masked faces made the whole scene as comical as a Three Stooges routine.

I stood and moved towards Santino while Helena rolled the body amongst his buddies.

"Sit-rep," I demanded once I was within whisper distance.

His masked face glanced around the courtyard. "Perimeter secured. Eight additional tangos down and out. There's only one entrance to the town that we can find and it's been cleared." He paused while he consulted the lens situated in front of his right eye and manipulated the screen attached to his forearm. "UAV confirms all sighted tangos in the courtyard have been eliminated. Tagging new targets inside the town. Transmitting."

I nodded and checked to make sure Alpha and Charlie were done cleaning up the bodies. After confirming that they were, I turned back to Santino before tapping my own forearm screen to call up the information being sent by Santino's UAV. Red blips popped up at set intervals throughout the town, some stationary, others on patrol. It was a standard security detail found in any legion fort. I watched as four red blips walked past two green ones, the ones representing Santino and me. The distance between us had only been a handful of meters, but they were on the other side of the inner courtyard wall, completely oblivious to our presence.

My heart didn't so much as skip a beat.

While it was pounding at a consistently accelerated tempo, the sensation was normal, and I was focused – on mission – a rarity for me these days. A ticker in the upper right hand portion of my eyepiece reported forty six hostiles scattered throughout the village, the same number as last night.

I clicked my com and radioed Madrina, who sat safe and secure in our forward operating base, little more than a mile away. "Base, Alpha Lead. Prepare to receive UAV control from Bravo Actual now."

I nodded to Santino and he returned the gesture with the tap of a finger. In an instant, Santino relinquished control of his UAV over to Madrina. While he could still update intel through his touch screen, Madrina now controlled the flight pattern for the UAV and would be our primary eye in the sky. She was using our spare set of interfacing equipment, something she hadn't a clue how to use mere weeks ago, but could now operate with a certain amount skill. The hardest part had been convincing her she wasn't practicing some form of black magic.

"Okay, Jacob," she said and I winced at her lack of radio discipline. Santino rolled his eyes at the slip up but I pushed it out of my mind. She was doing her job as well as any fish out of water could. I'd had my doubts about allowing her to use anything we'd brought with us from the future, but Bordeaux had vouched for her, and that was good enough for me.

Everything seemed ready to go.

"Flash my eyepiece if you need to update our intel," I ordered her, tapping Santino on the shoulder at the same time. When he turned, I hooked a thumb towards the door. "You're on point." I turned to Bordeaux. "Charlie's rearguard."

The Frenchman held his thumb up and signaled for his people to fall in. Helena and Vincent were already behind me, but by the time I looked back at Santino, Bravo Team was already stacking up behind him as he knelt by the door that would lead us into the town. I quickly moved to catch up, Santino already using a fiber optic cable that he had snaked under the wooden door.

The cable had a small monocular lens attached to the end, with two rings encompassing the device. Santino held it up against his eye, manipulating the rings to twist the cable beneath the door left and right, and to focus it. We used to have a fancy version that connected to our computers and projected images directly to our eyepieces, but I broke it two years ago. Stepped on it. Santino had not been happy.

Apparently satisfied, he pulled it back and tucked it into a pouch on his rig. He sent a nod to Titus, who slowly gripped the simple ring door handle and carefully opened the door inward. Wang stood just to the side, sticking his UMP into the opening. With a quick nod, Santino and Titus moved in, Wang following, with Alpha and Charlie behind them.

Laid out before us was a simple walled city, no more than a village by modern standards, and like any good Roman city, it was easy to navigate. Built along a simple grid pattern much like any legion fort, the city possessed five main roads that ran along its length. Its center road was twice the width of any two of the others, and ended at the steps that led to the largest building in the town, Agrippina's villa. Bisecting these roads were maybe twenty shorter ones that ran parallel to each other.

Along these roads were a series of smaller buildings. During our recon, we hadn't noticed movement from any structure other than Agrippina and her Praetorians, so we weren't sure what they were meant for. Whether the town had been abandoned prior to their arrival or if they had evacuated the city at the same time, we couldn't determine. Either way, dozens of buildings were left scattered throughout that could contain any number of hidden problems.

I led Alpha Team to the very first of these buildings, Charlie stacking up behind us while Santino directed his team to a building opposite the road we'd emerged onto. I kept one eye on my eyepiece to keep track of the patrol's progress as I peeked around the corner to get my first real look at the villa.

It was huge, almost half as wide as the town itself, its bulk cutting off the inner two roads that flanked the main road. Our UAV scans had shown that it sat in the back half of the city from our position, and dominated everything around it. Maybe six or seven stories high, its peak offered a three hundred and sixty degree view of its surrounding area. The view must have been spectacular, with the Mediterranean Sea to the east and nothing but scrub desert as far as the eye could see in every other direction.

I nodded to no one but myself as I completed this analysis in a thought. I pulled my head back, but something caught my eye and I had to force myself from doing a double take. It seemed that many of the villa's surrounding buildings were incomplete, or in various stages of construction. Some were finished, but the majority consisted of little more than a roof and its support structure. While, nothing seemed out of place by the scene, something about it tickled me in a bad way. Maybe this was a new town under renovation, but something felt off about its varying stage of completion.

Before I could think on it more, I felt Helena's hand squeeze my shoulder, indicating everyone was ready to move out. I reached back and tapped her leg, confirming I understood her gesture. With another glance at my eyepiece to confirm the patrols were out of sight, I rounded the corner and set off into the town.

I pushed forward, my rifle held out in front of me in a ready position, my eyes partially focused through my scope. Walking us forward at a quickened pace, my team and I swept the roads for previously unknown assailants, stopping at every intersection we encountered. Our objective was to avoid contact before entering the villa by not drawing attention to ourselves. There were too many Praetorians patrolling the exterior grounds to ensure we remained undetected if we started dropping bodies.

It was child's play. Back in 2021, even the most primitive of guerilla forces could be equipped with signal jammers that could block our communications or low level disruptors that sent out the briefest of EMP pulses that could short out everything from our UAV to our red dot sights. Needless to say, infiltrating this town was even easier than sneaking into the Roman provincial compound back in Caesarea.

But that didn't mean I thought our infiltration would be effortless. We were about two thirds of the way to the villa when my eyepiece indicated one of the patrols was about to turn a corner and put them into direct line of sight with our line of movement. I raised a fist to signal a halt and shook two pointed fingers towards the wall to my right. Like most of the buildings, it was still in an early stage of construction. Built of clay, adobe or some such material, the building had multiple large windows cut into place. I leaned to my right and rolled myself over the lip of the sill and into the empty shell of a home. I crouched and leaned against the inner wall, keeping an eye on my eyepiece and waited for the four red dots coming up behind us to pass by.

Their progress was slow, calculated, and when they moved near enough for me to hear them, I heard nothing but the shuffling of their feet and the subtle clinking of metal on metal, be it armor, sword or both. No words were exchanged, nor was there any sign that they were doing anything but their jobs. It was almost disconcerting the level of discipline they were putting on display tonight. They were dedicated beyond reproach, stalwart warriors without equal. Either these guys were the last of Agrippina's original Sacred Band, recruited from the best and most loyal Praetorians, or her new band of miscreants were more formidable than we thought – an idea that gave me further pause for thought. Roman legions trained and equipped in the art of modern warfare would be something worth considering. A few thousand of them wouldn't sway the course of a world war, no, but they'd be an interesting variable thrown into the mix.

Something worth considering for the book I'll have to write some day.

Out of the corner of my eye, I noticed Helena and Vincent rise to their feet. A quick glance at my eyepiece confirmed the patrol had passed by us and were moving towards the villa. I rose to my feet and climbed over the ledge more carefully this time. Santino and his team emerged from a similar house across the road and stacked up, my team and Charlie doing the same. Without a word, I started moving again, following a safe distance behind the roaming patrol.

I could see them ahead of us as we approached the villa, their capes billowing in the light wind behind them, their feet marching in silent union. We paced them like patient panthers stalking prey, and I watched as the large villa loomed into view. It seemed far bigger than the aerial recon first indicated; the equivalent of a six, maybe seven story building, wide and long. It was an intimidating structure.

After another minute or so, the patrol peeled off in front of the villa and moved to the opposite side of the town. I paused at the last intersection until they were well out of sight, checked my eyepiece, and picked up the pace towards the villa's outer wall. It's most obvious entrance was up the exterior main staircase that pointed in the direction we had just come from, but it was too exposed. Maybe thirty meters long, the staircase rose almost a third of the way up the building and was well lit by torches that lined the steps.

A far more suitable entry point was on the side of the villa, a door Santino had identified when a small numbers of heat signatures entered and exited from that point at consistent intervals during our recon. The next use of the door wasn't scheduled for another hour, plenty of time for us to access it.

Bravo Team was already at the door by the time the rest of us caught up a few minutes later. Santino had his snake eye cam under the door again and was scanning for potential threats. By the time Alpha stacked up behind me, he was already pulling it back under the door. He stood and coiled it up before placing it in a pouch on his MOLLE vest. He stepped to the opposite side of the door and nodded. I responded by placing a hand on the handle, yanking it open, allowing Santino and his team to stream in.

I led my team through at a more reserved rate, allowing Bravo Team to handle any immediate take downs, but when I stepped through the door there wasn't a soul in sight. Instead, I was greeted by a long, narrow hallway that ended about thirty feet down where it branched off at a four way intersection, illuminated by a number of torches.

And this was when the entire mission rested squarely on Santino's shoulders. If the rest of the village was any indication, the interior was liable to be level after level of random corridors and empty rooms, but I was confident Santino could find his way. When the hallway that led from the door deposited us into a large receiving room, little more than a gigantic hallway, I felt better about our situation. We'd been in dozens of administration buildings over the years and they were all laid out very similarly. Santino would know exactly where to go.

Like any castle or palace throughout the centuries, the large staircase outside delivered people here. The Great Room was immense, with the square footage of maybe three basketball courts placed end to end. Opposite the main entrance was another staircase that led up to the second level. Surrounding the room were a number of doors that led to offices, kitchens, maybe servant quarters and dotting the room's flanks were a number of columns supporting the entire structure.

Santino's team fanned out into the room, taking up defensive positions behind the columns. I led Alpha to the staircase where I took a knee just at the foot of the structure, making sure I knelt hidden in the shadows. Bordeaux swept Charlie to the left towards the main entrance, taking up position behind the columns there. We hunkered down and waited, suspecting a patrol would soon reveal itself.

A minute later, my night vision dimmed, the result of a bright light creeping up from somewhere.

"Alpha Lead, Charlie Actual," Bordeaux's voice said over the radio. "Tangos inbound from staircase. Headcount: twenty."

I replied with a double click, turning to Alpha Team and flicking my fingers towards the rear of the staircase, where an opening would allow my team to cross beneath to the opposite side of the stairs. Helena and Vincent nodded, and Vincent led the three of us under the stairs to the opposite side. The two of them took up position beside the steps, but I stepped off to the right to hide behind the nearest column.

It was at about that time when the patrol descended to the bottom of the stairs, their progress indicating they were heading towards the main entrance. I flicked on my infrared laser sight, watching as another eight beams of light joined my own, and centered it on the nearest Praetorian's back.

When I confirmed the others had found targets of their own, I pulled the trigger, the quick burst of lead finding its mark just below the neck. Helena and Vincent dispatched their targets in a similar fashion, the three men crumpling to the floor in a pile. I immediately shifted my aim towards a second Praetorian, and put a single round efficiently in his head. By the time the bullet was making its way towards my second target, Bravo and Charlie had opened fire on the lead Praetorians. Before I could blink, in a hail of coughs and the faintest flashes of lights, there was a large pile of corpses lying in the middle of the room.

"Wait one," I radioed, and with the flick of my wrist, ordered Alpha to follow.

I walked to the scene slowly, silently crossing one foot over the other, falling on the outer sole of my feet to ensure complete silence, keeping my rifle trained on the pile as I crept forward. Within the bloodbath, I found one Praetorian still among the living. He was gurgling blood from a neck wound that had missed his artery, but had nicked his windpipe. He reached a hand out toward me, but before I gave it another thought, I put a round through his forehead.

My eyes lingered on his lifeless face for a few seconds, fascinated by the fact that I felt nothing. Five years ago, I would have understood putting someone out of their misery, but it would have eaten me up inside.

Now, I didn't feel anything at all.

Then it struck me that this man may have well been a father himself. A husband. A brother. Certainly a son. He may have had a lovely family he was only trying to provide for. Or he was one of the ruthless scum bags Gaius told us Agrippina had been recruiting for her Praetorians.

Still, I felt nothing.

I was the one with a baby on the way

I did, however, feel a hand on my arm. A familiar gesture that confirmed it was Helena's well before I turned to face her, and any lack of feeling was gone, replaced by happiness that I'd gotten him before he'd gotten her.

I looked down the hall and saw Bravo Team approach with Charlie behind them. Wang was already checking doors, looking for an unlocked one. He wasn't having much luck, so he borrowed Santino's fiber optic device, and looked for rooms that were at least empty. He found one on the second try and pulled out a small bone saw from his medic bag. With it, he sawed through the plank of wood on the inside of the door that kept it barred shut, through a small gap between the door and the wall. It didn't take long, and with a quick jiggle, he finagled the door open. He let the rest of us haul bodies into the room while he cleaned and sterilized the saw before replacing it in his bag.

I hated to think about it, but Wang may need to use that saw again, and not for cutting through planks of wood.

Once the bodies were secure, we took a moment to mop up the floor with towels and sheets we had stowed in Titus' pack, dumping them in with the dead Praetorians as well. Once the door was secure, Santino took us out once again, heading in the direction of the stairwell.

We climbed to the second floor, little more than a balcony that overlooked the atrium below. Santino ignored it and continued straight up toward the third floor, its staircase even longer and higher than the last. By the time we reached the third floor I estimated we'd traveled nearly half the length of the building. Our UAV flying silent overwatch outside confirmed my suspicion as it projected our position within the building directly onto my eyepiece.

At the top of the stairs, we encountered a long hallway that ran perpendicular to our path. No other options presented themselves so Santino simply chose to go left, and the rest of us followed. Halfway down the featureless corridor, we came to another intersecting hallway that ran both ways along the length of the villa this time. Santino halted, checked his corners and reached up to activate his radio.

"Charlie, post up here. Alpha, follow," he ordered. Bordeaux double clicked his com, and by the time I turned the corner and was following Santino down the corridor, Charlie was already dug in and covering our backs.

As we crept along the hallway, I felt an odd sensation beneath my feet. There was no need to stop and investigate because the sensation only came when I was moving. It felt as though the floor was not level, and was in fact sloped, giving me the impression that we were not only moving deeper into the villa but moving higher into it as well. It was one thing our UAV couldn't confirm as we continued our journey.

Another minute later, we were faced with yet another T-junction intersection, this one heading back towards the center of the building or continuing straight back to its end. I felt a sudden twinge of frustration at the uninspired design choice of the building. Not only that, but I was starting to feel thoroughly creeped out. I couldn't be sure, but it felt as if the corridors were not only gradually elevating, but also narrowing as well.

I couldn't help but feel like we were being corralled somehow.

The building was just like one of those carnival funhouses with all the mirrors and windows, except opaque and blank, and it felt the same and was just as freaky.

I sighed when Santino ordered Alpha to hold out at the junction while he and his team scouted forward. I assumed if we ran into yet another T-junction, he'd order Charlie up and we'd continue to leapfrog.

Helena and I moved to cover down the long hallway, while Vincent watched Bravo's backs. We sat there for a few minutes, waiting in eerie silence.

"It's quiet," Helena whispered to me.

"I was just thinking that."

"There aren't any rooms. Just hallways."

I nodded. "I've noticed."

"It's creeping me out," she elaborated.

I didn't smile. "Me too."

She started to speak again, but was cut off when Santino voice came over the radio.

"We've got a bogie. A doorway with a large room behind it. Minimal visibility. Suggest Alpha and Charlie regroup."

I sent a quick double click and heard Bordeaux's follow just after mine.

I patted Helena on the shoulder, letting her know I was moving out, and made my way down the hall at a trot. I quickly found myself at the door Santino described. It was very plain, almost dull in its simplicity, but the doorframe was far different. Ornate, decorative, and possibly colorful – although I couldn't really tell through my NVGs – it could easily allow four Bordeauxs to walk through shoulder to shoulder.

I squinted at the frame, noting some kind of serpent-like dragon stretched along the length of the doorframe, from base to ceiling to base again. Small wings protruded from it body along the portion that ran horizontally along the ceiling, while at the foot of the door on the left side I could see a head with a forked tongue extending from its mouth and at the base on the right was a tail that more closely resembled that of a rattlesnake.

Very interesting. The design was clearly Asian in origin, and had no reason for being in ancient Syria. There were many fantastic creatures in the mythologies of the Mediterranean area, but none as straight forward as a simple dragon. There were creatures like Cerberus, the three headed dog, or a chimera, an animal with a lion's head, a goat's body, and a serpent's tail, and creatures like griffons and the Pegasus, of course, but no dragons.

Fascinating.

"What's with the décor, professor?" Santino asked.

"I have no idea," I answered truthfully. "There's something off about this entire building. Besides the exterior and first level, there's nothing about it that resembles a Roman structure. Maybe whichever Roman ordered its construction hired someone from Asia to do the decorating and they decided to leave their own architectural and mythological mark here."

"That seems like a bit of a stretch," Helena mentioned, catching up behind me.

"Any better ideas?" I asked her.

She thought for a second. "No."

"What about the tail?" Vincent asked. "Correct me if I'm wrong, but rattlesnakes are indigenous to the Americas, yes?"

"Last time I checked," Santino said unhappily.

I shrugged. "It's not that complex of a design. I assume it must symbolize something else. Any of you an expert on ancient Asian cultures?"

No one said anything.

"Wang?" I asked, turning to the small man of Chinese descent, who stood beside Santino.

"I'm from Cardiff," he replied matter of factly.

There was a chorus of nervous chuckles from the group and I smiled beneath my mask. I let it go for a few seconds before motioning for Bravo Team to breach the door. As they had done twice already, Santino's team silently opened the door and streamed into the room in a manner that would make any SWAT team proud. By the time Charlie pulled up the rear, both Alpha and Bravo had fanned out through the large room, covering all the angles.

The room seemed clear, but was so expansive that our NVGs had trouble penetrating the darkness. To remedy the situation, Wang withdrew a number of yellow chemlights from his pack, snapped them, and tossed them throughout the room. Santino did the same, and I followed suit. Awash in an almost day-colored glow, I twisted my NVGs up so that they sat on my head, and viewed the room with my regular vision, but saw little of note.

At least there weren't any people in the room, people we'd probably have to kill. There was, however, a shit ton of evidence that indicated Agrippina was nearby. Gold, silver, jewels, statues and all sorts of trinkets lay scattered about. Further evidence of her presence was some of her obscene Venus/Agrippina art Santino and I had admired on her pleasure barge.

Santino noticed as well and looked at me. "Can I..."

"No."

He flung his head forward in a pout, but continued his sweep of the room.

There were four levels to the room, each about four feet above the last, with a small stairwell running through the center, all the way to the top. Charlie stayed near the door, while Alpha and Bravo slowly made our way up the stairs, clearing each level as we ascended. Each level had piles of treasure that reminded me of *Aladdin*, specifically the scene when the genie conjured up all that loot to impress the title character in the cave.

I always liked that part.

Great musical sequence.

As it happened, I was the first person to reach the top. The highest level not only had the highest density of treasure, but also had the most real estate to walk on. Among the goodies scattered about, at the very back of the room, stood three columns that came up to my chest. The center column had a gold box atop it, the one on the left had what looked like a burlap sack, while the one on the right was shrouded by a piece of fine cloth.

The display seemed too distinct to simply ignore as simply more treasure, so I continued.

I approached the middle column carefully, a sudden reminder of what happened in an Indiana Jones movie during an oddly similar moment creeping into my mind. It did occur to me that the whole scenario seemed a bit off, but having trophies on display didn't exactly go against the grain. Vespasian had had spoils of war displayed in his *praetorium*, and if Agrippina was planning to stay, there was no reason she wouldn't do the same.

Even so, I reoriented myself towards the column with the burlap sack atop it. Gripping a corner tightly, I yanked it away.

Beneath it lay a spherical object, radiating a dim blue light.

I grunted, my sudden exposure to what I immediately knew as the orb hitting me like a wall of bricks. I didn't feel pain or pleasure, compulsion or apathy, only surprise. To see it so innocuously placed and easily accessible was staggering. I half-expected to have to mow through a hundred Praetorians just to reach it.

But then I felt the compulsion set in, an addiction I'd contracted long ago that forced me to reach out with my gloved hand and pick it up. As it had on Agrippina's pleasure barge, time seemed to slow as my hand moved steadily toward the orb, and my mind could barely even comprehend the fact that my friends were, for some reason, failing to intervene.

I tried to think about something else, anything else to focus my attention away from the orb. I thought about my future life away from Rome and with Helena in it. When that didn't work I tried to think of Helena in that skimpy imaginary bikini I'd hoped to see her in back at the outpost a few days ago and all the countless times we'd made love, but even thoughts such as those were unable to take a firm hold in my mind.

My subconscious spirit was broken, left adrift on a mission of its own, one I couldn't hope to fight against. Every precaution I'd planned to take was suddenly left at the door to this villa when I'd stupidly pulled away a piece of cloth that should have stayed where it was. Days and weeks seemed to drift by; time wasted as my mind and body continued their losing battle against what the orb was trying to make them do.

After what seemed like a lifetime, my bare hand finally touched the orb.

And nothing happened.

In a bout of clarity, my body no longer fought against my mind and I held the orb out in front of my chest and gazed into it like a crazed fortune teller. After months, years really, worrying what would happen should I come into contact with the orb again, my confusion and surprise only grew as I now felt nothing. I waited for something to happen. Anything. But nothing did. I tossed it between my hands for a few seconds, juggling it back and forth.

I was so confused that I couldn't even formulate a question to ask myself when, for once, questions were worth asking. Instead I felt my mind start to wander, and a sense of calm flowed over me. I felt almost peaceful as I daydreamed with my eyes closed before I finally caught myself. I forced myself to focus on the situation. With one last look, seeing nothing within, I secured it back in its burlap cloth with one last shrug.

I turned to see Helena and Santino finally join me at the top.

"What was that light, Jacob?" Helena asked.

"Hmm? Oh, I guess it must have been this," I said, holding up the orb. "It wasn't very bright though. Good eyes."

She exchanged an odd glance with Santino, but shook her head and reached out to take it from me. As she placed it in her bag, Santino pushed past me and moved towards the gold box.

"Don't..." I warned him.

"What? I was just looking at it."

"Sure you were," I said, returning my attention back to Helena.

She gave me a thumbs-up after securing the orb. I clicked my com.

"All teams report to the top level."

Really, I only needed Bordeaux up here, but it was best to consolidate all of us on high ground where we could more easily defend ourselves.

"Uh... Jacob?" Santino asked from behind me. "You'd better take a look at this."

"What is it?" I asked, figuring he'd probably broken the golden box.

Surprisingly, he was at the column with the fine cloth, peeking beneath it at what lay beneath. He brought his head up and tore the cloth away from the column.

It revealed another blue sphere.

"Am I missing something?" He asked before looking back down at it.

I wasn't sure. It certainly looked to be the same size and color, but how could it be another one of the orbs? Unless my math really was that bad, there should only be one left after we destroyed one of the two. Where did this third one come from? Where was the sense of compulsion and draw like the other one?

"You think Agrippina got it to work?" Santino asked. "Made a second one just like we did?"

"Maybe," I replied, unsure. "Bag it and tag it. Might as well bring it along."

"Wilco, boss," he said, securing the orb.

I left him alone and went to find Bordeaux, who was pulling something big from his bag.

"How big is that bomb?"

He looked up at me. "Big enough."

"Big enough to bring down the entire building?"

He smiled. "Just remember that it would be best to not be here when it goes off. I'm setting it for forty five minutes."

I looked at my watch. 0230. We'd only been in the building for about twenty minutes. Plenty of time. I watched as he buried the bomb beneath a pile of treasure, but turned when I heard Titus' voice from atop the treasure room ask, "What's this?"

I finished my turn just in time to see him open the gold box Santino had been eyeing earlier.

"Don't touch tha..." I started, but never had the chance to finish.

As Titus opened the small box, a small spark ignited within. When the spark touched the contents of the box, a simple bowl containing a white, glittering powder, a flash of light as bright as a flashbang went off and engulfed the room. All I could see was white, and even my ear protectors had trouble dampening out the sound it had created.

I groped at the world around me, seeing nothing, the only thing my confused mind allowing me to sense being the abysmal white emptiness that engulfed me. Disoriented and blind, I wasn't able to avoid tripping and falling onto a pile of gold. I tried to push myself up, but before my hands could find purchase on anything stable, I felt a horribly sharp pain in my head, and instead of white, all I saw was black.

***

I've been knocked unconscious quite a few times in my life. A few more than the average person I would think. Normally, when these lovely episodes of rest and relaxation were provided to me, hallucinations always seemed to manifest themselves. They tended to revolve around loved ones or personal relationships, old nightmares or new fears, and were generally ambiguous as to their tone and meaning.

But not today.

Today I saw nothing, and as I came around, I wondered if the lack of a hallucination meant something ominous was lurking. All I felt was a horrible throbbing inside the back of my skull, as if a tiny construction worker had burrowed his way into my head and placed his jackhammer against my brain, and was having his way with me.

When I regained consciousness, I did so tentatively, my eyes doing all they could to regain focus. But as it always was at this point of recovery, all my vision could discern was a dull, amorphous haze clouding everything I looked at. I blinked a few times and shook my head to clear it, cringing as the motion doubled the number of jackhammers on duty.

Despite the pain, I knew I had to come to my senses quickly, and did everything I could to fight through it. As my senses returned, I found myself lying on my side with my hands tied behind my back. All my MOLLE combat gear had been stripped away, including my thigh holster and my eyepiece system, and I realized that my shirt and boots had been removed as well. I lay there bare-chested, unable to move my head, at least not without pain, but I found that I could at least move my eyes.

Titling my eyes downwards, I saw the legs of one of my team members. Based on the size and clothing, it could have been Wang, Santino, Titus, or Vincent. I had no idea which. Tracking my gaze upward, I saw another body, this one lithe and shapely, also having been stripped naked from the waist up. It had to be Helena. I could see her hands were bound behind her as well, but blood dripped from her fingertips.

Adrenaline coursed through my body, fear for Helena and my unborn child manifesting itself. It drove me as I struggled against my restraints, but before I could make much progress, I found myself being manhandled by two thugs. I struggled against them, but was too weak to put up much of a fight and they maneuvered me into a kneeling position, my hands still bound behind my back. It made my head swim again and I struggled to stay conscious. With a jerk of my head, the pain ever persistent, I grunted and breathed heavily before everything started to clear.

I looked up, hoping to better understand the situation, and it didn't take long to come to an assessment.

We were pretty much fucked.

The room we were in was large, easily twice the size of the treasure vault, but was only a single level room. It was rectangular in design, had no windows, one door that I could see, and only a single chair. There were no decorations in the room, merely torches hanging from the ceiling and attached to the room's half dozen support columns. Lighting was negligible. The room was dark and there were deep shadows in the corners.

Arrayed around the solitary chair stood dozens of armor-encased soldiers, Praetorians if I had to guess. Most had his right hand on his *gladius* and none appeared friendly, familiar or sympathetic. They stood at attention in a semicircle around us and the chair, ready for anything. There were also a dozen or so Praetorian ninjas scattered about in a much more disorganized fashion. These men still wore their facemasks. Some were leaning against pillars, others crouching in the shadows, but each was just as ready as his soldier counterparts.

Those who were not standing at attention were manhandling our weapons and gear. I immediately identified *Penelope* by the numerous gadgets and tools attached to her. A pair of Praetorians was fondling her roughly and I felt my rage continue to grow.

Finally, seated upon the simple chair was none other than Agrippina. Clothed, for once, she wore a simple dress, cut in a fashion more akin to modern day gowns. As was normal for her, it was low cut and had a long slit along the left leg. She looked elegant and evil, like some kind of cross between Aurora and Maleficent from *Sleeping Beauty*, and I had to give her credit. She had a shtick and she kept with it.

She was seated with her right leg crossed over her left, her hands resting in her lap. Her light blond hair was tied up in an efficient bun with a few loose strands dangling on either side of her face. As opposed to the last time I'd seen her, when she had been completely naked and exposed, this woman could almost pass for regal and respectable monarchy.

I continued to kneel, unable to quantify the rage that boiled within me. Only Agrippina could bring out hatred like this and I knew learning to fly would be easier than calming myself at this point. But I had to try. Anger had led me down a dark path last time. The only thing I could rely on was my old self, the one that could stay calm in a time of crisis, no matter how forgotten that man was.

"Agrippina," I said hoarsely. "How's the ass?"

She smiled unexpectedly – a mischievously alluring one – stood and slowly strolled to where I knelt and I almost expected her to fling herself sexually at me, but she merely leaned down and tilted my chin up with the tip of a fingernail, forcing me to gaze into her eyes.

"It is quite perfect," she said quietly, "but you of all people should already know that, Jacob Hunter."

I gritted my teeth and tore my head away from her hand. As was the case with my anger, only she could make me eat my own words like that. She continued to smile and walked to my left, glancing down at Helena as she passed by. Thankfully, she didn't touch her, but simply made her way back to her chair and sat down.

"Why do you continue to bother me, Jacob?" She asked. "I offered you access to the orbs once, but you denied me. Are you here to steal them from me now?" She scoffed and tilted her head up so that she could peer over her nose down at me. "Is it that you have seen me naked and now wish for more? Is that why you brought your Amazon this time?"

I bit my tongue and forced myself not to rise to her bait.

"We just want to go home, Agrippina," I said, my voice starting to clear. Before I continued, I noticed movement to my right, and saw the rest of my team begin to regain consciousness as well. Santino was first to his knees, also the person who had been right next to me. I turned back to Agrippina. "The orbs are dangerous. You have no idea how harmful they can be."

"I know all about their potential, Jacob," she said, nodding to one of her guards.

In response, he briefly exited the room before reappearing, dragging a body behind him. He dragged it out in front of Agrippina's seated form and dumped it there disrespectfully. I looked at it, seeing that the body was absent a head. I looked at it in confusion for a few seconds before glancing up at Agrippina. She gazed at me coolly, her eyes widening in realization a few seconds later. She held up a finger.

"How silly of me. You need the head, of course."

She turned to reach for something behind her. In one quick motion, she reoriented herself and tossed whatever she was holding in one deft movement. As it flew through the air, I identified it as a human head. It hit the ground a few feet in front of me with a horrible squishing noise and rolled its way to rest between my knees. It landed face down, and all I could see was a mop of dark hair.

Agrippina rolled her eyes and motioned with a hand to the same guard who had brought in the body. He marched over and rotated the head so that a set of all too familiar grey stared back at me.

Varus'.

I snapped my head away, averting my eyes from the man I had come to call a friend. A man I knew to be some long lost ancestor of mine. A family man who would never again hold his wife or help raise his son.

Without wanting to, I moved my attention back to his face. Even if his features had been horribly mutilated, I would have been able to identify him by his eyes alone. They were a cold almost-blue, and were set exactly like mine. But his face wasn't harmed. His features were as unsullied by violence as they had always been. Even his normal expression of contemplative thought was still there, preserved eternally on his severed head.

I closed my eyes and turned away.

The guard retrieved Varus' head and brought it back to Agrippina. She accepted it, and by the time I reopened my eyes, had it in her lap and was stroking poor Varus' hair like a Bond villain would his cat. I clenched my teeth in anger once again and stared daggers at her. She was unphased by my attempt at intimidation and continued petting my friend's head.

"This fool," she said, "managed to operate the orb." She haughtily lifted her chin again and continued. "But he did not share in my excitement. While I may know what it does, I have been unable to personally operate it, or find anyone else who can. I may have lost my temper." She raised her shoulders just slightly. "I am the first to admit my mistake, but sometimes our emotions get the best of us, do they not, Jacob?"

I kept my mouth shut.

Everyone had managed to get themselves up into a kneeling position by now, all strung out in a line, kneeling shoulder to shoulder. I looked the other way but saw that Helena remained inert. Noticing my attention, Agrippina tossed Varus' head over her shoulder and moved to crouch beside Helena. She reached down and stroked her hair momentarily until she grew bored and pulled on Helena's shoulders, mounting her on her knees. I was now able to see that the source of her blood was a small cut on the side of her temple, probably from a blow taken when she was knocked unconscious. It had to be why she was still out. No one else seemed to be bleeding.

Once Agrippina managed to balance her upright, she caressed Helena's naked body with a hand, humming in satisfaction as she poked one of Helena's breast – but not in a sensual way, more like as a curious pre-teen boy seeing one for the first time – but a heartbeat later, she reeled back with a hand and slapped Helena across the face, snapping her out of her daze. She cried out in pain from both the slap and quick transition to consciousness, coughing and choking, her eyes unable to lock onto anything. Her head lolled lazily until Agrippina grabbed her by the hair.

She turned to me. "I've wanted to do that for a very long time. I must admit that I've suffered from sudden bouts of jealousy on occasion."

Helena mumbled under her breath indecipherably. Agrippina noticed, and brought her head closer, pretending to try and hear what she was saying.

"What's that, dear? Oh, does it hurt. I'm sorry." And with that, she brought her head in closer, and kissed the side of Helena's cheek, right where she'd slapped her. I couldn't watch.

She turned back to look at me once again. "I've always wanted to do that, as well." She sighed. "If only there was time for more. The three of us could have had something truly special, Jacob."

My stomach churned at the thought.

She smiled at me and kissed Helena on the forehead before standing up and moving down the line of captured and beaten warriors, looking at each in turn. She stopped at the very end, in front of Gaius and Marcus.

"Traitors," she hissed. "Your deaths will be first."

They sneered at her but she ignored them and snapped her fingers, summoning a handful of her guards. "Take them outside and crucify them."

Gaius and Marcus struggled against their Praetorian handlers, trying anything to break away, but there was nothing they could do. With three Praetorians on each of them, they might as well have been David against Goliath without a sling. They were hauled through the room's single door and never brought back. Everyone else struggled against their restraints, all except Helena, who was doing everything she could to stay on her knees.

Agrippina ignored Gaius and Marcus' removal and walked back in my direction. She turned her head and saw Titus.

"You, I have not met," she said, gripping his chin with her fingers. "Lovely, though. And young. I think I will keep you."

She continued, leaving each of my friends with a comment as she passed by.

"Brute," she said to Bordeaux.

"Cripple," as she passed Vincent

"Oriental," to poor Wang.

"Ah, you." Her final comment was to Santino. She almost sounded happy to see him, but it wasn't hard to read between the lines. "Stamina you may have, but as I told you before, your performance was hardly worth remembering."

Santino just smiled at her.

I blinked as his smile reminded me of something, but what was it exactly? Oh, that's right: that he was an asshole. But he was my kind of asshole. It's who he was. And it was a good thing, at least in this moment, because it also reminded me who I was as well. It reminded me that I was always prepared for anything, and that I always had a knife behind my belt.

I would have smacked myself if I wasn't tied up, but I didn't let myself grow too excited just yet. We were still in it deep.

Agrippina moved back to her chair to consult with one of her Praetorians, and I used the time to check on Helena. She was still mostly out of it, her head bobbing from side to side as it hung near her chest. Occasionally she'd snap it up like she was waking abruptly from a nap, but it would just as quickly drop again. I hissed at her, trying to get her attention, but she remained incoherent.

I decided to ignore her as I tried to budge my knife from its hiding place at my back. It was tricky. My hands were tightly bound and the knife was in there good. It was going to take me a few minutes of finagling to get it out without anyone noticing.

I decided to multitask by trying to physically get Helena's attention with a kick of my foot. I probably hit her harder than I should have, but I had to make sure she was all right. Luckily, she reacted, and her eyes finally popped open. She craned her head to look at me and I could tell her vision wasn't quite there yet. Her eyes were normally so piercing that she always seemed to be looking right through me, but instead, her eyes were swollen and tracking all over the place.

I snuck a quick peek at Agrippina, noting her Praetorian commander had left again, and that she was impatiently tapping her foot for his return.

I looked back at Helena. She was blinking rapidly and she seemed to look at me with much greater focus now. When I thought she was coherent enough to communicate, I mouthed, *are you okay*? She jerked her head in an abbreviated affirmation and I breathed a silent sigh of relief. I was about to ask about the baby, even though I knew she couldn't possibly know anything, when Santino interrupted me.

"Tell me you have a plan, Hunter," he whispered.

"Me?" I replied quietly, turning to him. "It's your turn."

He shook his head, mumbling something about lazy leaders and inept commanders.

"Where's your knife?" He asked.

"I'm working on it."

He opened his mouth again but Agrippina interrupted, strutting back towards us.

"Now, Jacob, are you prepared to help me?"

"I told you. I don't know how the thing works," I insisted.

She hummed a disbelieving noise, and pulled the orb from behind her back.

"Tell, me," she said. "Do you see anything within?"

Just to please her and buy us some more time, I looked, not expecting to find anything, but to my surprise, I did see something within. Something I'd never seen before, but couldn't quite make out, so I played dumb.

"There's nothing there, Agrippina. There never is."

"That is too bad." She snapped her fingers. "Perhaps some incentive will be required."

A Praetorian answered her call, bringing with him what appeared to be Wang's 9mm Beretta. She held it in her hand, inspecting it briefly, before pressing it against my forehead.

"Now?"

I smirked. "You don't even know how to use that."

"I don't?" She asked, shifting her aim towards Helena. "And now?"

I opened my mouth to speak, but I didn't say anything. She was bluffing, but even if she wasn't, I had to hold out as long as possible. I was gambling with the two most important people I had in my life, but I had to stall. The power of the orbs could not be allowed to fall into her hands.

She noticed my stubbornness and lowered her aim.

"Hmm... that won't do," she said. "Besides, I want you to watch her suffer. Perhaps one of your friends."

She walked out before Bordeaux, Wang, Vincent, and Santino, pointing the gun at each, humming as she switched from target to target in a Roman version of eeny, meeny, miny, moe. She passed back and forth, over and over between them before finally settling on Bordeaux.

She smiled. "You."

She pulled the trigger. The suppressor equipped pistol's bang was barely loud enough to reverberate off the walls or hurt my still dazed brain, but the memory of Bordeaux's skull shattering open would resonate in my mind for the rest of my life. I watched as the large Frenchman took the round defiantly, but fatally. The bullet entered through his left eye socket, and exploded out the back of his head, covering the wall behind him in blood and grey brain matter. My friend's body didn't move much at first, his large mass holding him firmly against the force of the small, fast moving object. But soon, gravity took its toll, and he slumped to the floor – lifeless.

I stared at his body in shock, unable to comprehend that such a violent death could come to a friend as close as he was.

Was.

Was...

Everyone else struggled against their restraints again, and I found myself mindlessly joining them, momentarily forgetting about my knife. I wanted nothing more than to rip Agrippina's heart from her chest and shove it down her throat. Only Helena, still in a daze, managed to avoid the image of Bordeaux's death.

"You fucking bitch!" Santino screamed, his insult standing out amongst all the rest, spittle flying from his mouth. I'd never seen him so angry.

She turned angrily to face him, pointing the gun at his head.

"Perhaps you shall be next?"

Santino defiantly turned toward me, switching to English.

"Don't tell her anything, Hunter! Wait for the b..."

But Agrippina pistol whipped him before he could finish.

Wait for the b...?

Wait for the what?

What had he been talking about?

The bitch? The batman? The bomb? The bomb!

Perhaps Bordeaux would have the last laugh after all.

But, what time was it? I couldn't see my watch or anyone else's. How long had we been out? I had to stall.

"You can continue to watch friends die all night, Jacob," Agrippina said, as I watched her slowly squeeze the trigger. "But remember, your Amazon's death won't be anywhere near as quick or easy."

I opened my mouth to speak, but my response was suddenly drowned out by an insistent *beep beep beep* noise, emanating from somewhere in the room. I glanced around. My ropes were almost cut but I had yet to determine what was making that noise. It seemed to be coming from Bordeaux. Agrippina looked at my friend's body as well, hoping to discover the source of the annoyance. I realized what it was a half second later.

Agrippina turned to look at me, anger in her eyes. I met her stare, and offered her a cold smile. A smile completely devoid of happiness, joy, or relief. The only emotion it conveyed was vengeance.

Through clenched teeth, I whispered, "boom."

And then room was engulfed in flame.

The explosion originated from some place above us and seemingly on the other end of the building, but that didn't save us from the deafening blast or the concussive wave that sent those on their feet flying across the room and those of us kneeling to skid across to the floor. I watched as Agrippina bounced off one of her Praetorians and careened across my line of sight, landing somewhere near Helena.

Luckily, the bomb hadn't been close enough to inflict traumatic nerve damage on any of us, so we'd survive. Had we been too close, we could have died from any number of factors. The fire from the explosion could have melted the skin from our bodies, the blast wave may have disintegrated our brain matter, or the pressure build up could have liquefied our bones and left us as little more than a puddles of goo on the floor.

Even so, my ears were ringing and I knew I wouldn't be hearing anything for several minutes, but I was conscious and I finally had the opportunity to use my knife to finish cutting through my ropes. Santino was also up, patiently waiting for me to palm the knife off to him, which I did immediately.

I didn't wait. I got to my feet and searched for *Penelope*.

Off to my left, I could see Helena was slow to rise, sluggish at first, but she'd also been furthest from the explosion. I watched as the limber woman managed to squeeze her feet through her bound hands so that her tied wrists were now in front of her. She stumbled away from me and I had to assume she was searching for Agrippina.

I couldn't worry about her now. Praetorians were getting to their feet all around me. I needed a weapon. My weapon. It was time to end this. Vespasian could live with it if we killed

Agrippina. We weren't leaving without her, but the state in which she came with us was up to her.

I thought about Bordeaux. He wouldn't have a choice in how he was coming home. Gaius and Marcus might also have little choice. I had no idea where they were. It was possible they were already dead.

My mind focused when I finally found *Penelope*, still in the hands of the bastard Praetorian that had been fondling her earlier. He was only a few feet away, but the after-effects of the explosion made it feel as if I was wading through Jell-o to get to him, and it seemed to take hours for me to gain any ground.

I pushed through it.

He saw me coming and attempted to draw his *gladius*, but I was on him before he could even fully take it in his hand. With a quick punch to his wrist, his grip loosened and the sword dropped back in its sheath. The move came at the same instant as I stomped on his foot, following that up by kneeing him in the balls. He doubled over in pain, still holding my rifle, so I snatched his head with my hands and smashed my knee into his nose. My kneecap felt like it had burst apart, but he was probably dead. I pushed him over and he released *Penelope* into the air as he fell.

I snatched her out of the air, turned, and fed a round into the chamber. Checking to make sure she was ready with a quick, practiced motion and look, I determined that it was time to go hunting. It was dark after most of the torches had been snuffed out by the explosion, but the room was now dimly illuminated by the night sky, visible through the collapsing roof. Rubble was strewn everywhere in big slabs, chunks, and toppled pillars. The level above us was visible in some places, and I notice at least one enemy Praetorian buried alive, only his head exposed.

I activated the night vision on my rifle's ACOG scope.

Peering through it, I noted two Praetorians making their way toward Helena. Once again, even through the dim green glow of my night vision, I saw ravenous intent on their faces, just like the Praetorian four years ago that had almost killed her.

The rest of the guys were up now as well, searching for weapons of their own. Wang was already getting in touch with his inner martial artist, having taken out two Praetorians with quick karate kicks to the head. He'd been close with Bordeaux as well, former swim buddies, and his anger was obvious. Vincent was up as well, but he wasn't fighting.

He was grieving.

A large chunk of the ceiling had fallen during the explosion right on Titus. I could only see the upper half of the young Roman's body, everything from his belly button down having been crushed by the concrete. Vincent held Titus' visible upper body in his arm, and cried for his adopted son.

Watching the old man cry caused me to hesitate, and I nearly missed what happened next.

Santino never saw Vincent in his time of grief, or if he had, he focused on the Praetorians going after Helena instead. He bravely body checked one of them into the other, leapt on him, and beat him to death with his fists. His action snapped me from my own sadness at the loss of Titus and the pain Vincent was feeling, and I shot the second Praetorians in the back as he got to his feet with a three round burst, just before he could exact some measure of revenge on Santino.

Helena had noticed what Santino had done as well, and helping him to his feet after he was finished with his target. She reached up and touched his cheek in thanks for the save, an intimate gesture only friends as close as they could share without it seeming awkward. He threw her a goofy smile, gripped her hand momentarily, and rushed off to find someone else to kill. Helena, meanwhile, spotted Agrippina and went directly for her.

A slight motion to my immediate left pulled my attention away, and I spotted one of the ninjas trying to flank me. He rushed at me with his small scimitar blade, but instead of waiting for him to skewer me, I ran out to meet him. Spinning at the last second as we closed the gap, I managed to guess which way he was going to lunge and avoided his blade. He stumbled past me and I put a three round burst into his back.

Six down, another thirty or so to go.

I unloaded the remaining rounds in my magazine on whatever targets I could find.

Nearing empty, I watched Wang take a sword to his thigh, forcing him to fight on basically one leg. A group of five Praetorians tried to overwhelm him, but I evened up the sides considerably by putting four of them down before they even reached him. The last was no match for even a handicapped Wang.

The only thing keeping the enemy at bay was my gun fire, and as I fired off another round into the last of the ninjas, I knew there could still be as many as ten Praetorians still lurking about.

I looked around frantically for Helena and found her wrestling with Agrippina a few dozen meters away. Both women had more bruises than they'd had just after the explosion, but Helena clearly had the upper hand. Her hands may have been bound, but she was a warrior now, honed and seasoned after half a decade forced to kill or be killed.

Agrippina may have known how to fight, but she wasn't a match for my woman.

I fired my last round at a Praetorian approaching the two of them, shattering the left side of his skull, but Helena's luck was about to change despite my intervention. Agrippina had found the orb lying on the ground beside them, and took hold of it like a blunt weapon. Helena was on top of her, pounding into Agrippina's chest with her bound hands, when Agrippina managed to swing the sphere upwards, smashing it into the side of Helena's head. The impact sent Helena rolling off her foe, but it had only been a glancing blow. Agrippina jumped on top of her, hoping to get the upper hand, but a very nimble Helena placed a foot against Agrippina's midsection and kicked her away. Helena quickly took advantage and repositioned herself back on top of Agrippina.

Helena had the orb in her hands now, having torn it from Agrippina's grasp as she had lain stunned on the ground, and I watched as Helena smashed it into Agrippina's beautiful and terror stricken face over and over and over again, not wasting any time on tricks, fancy moves, or ultimatums that offered a chance for survival.

The first thing that was destroyed was Agrippina's nose.

It had caved in after the second impact of the orb, and even though I was busy beating a Praetorian across the face with *Penelope*, I saw Helena's face grow even more enraged as tears and spit and sweat flung all around her as she relentlessly pummeled the empress, years of searing, pent up rage and frustration driving her to continue. She slammed the orb again and again into Agrippina's face, turning eye sockets into an indistinguishable crater while another blow shattered her teeth into oblivion. With yet another blow, the orb was now buried halfway through Agrippina's head, past her none existent face, crunching and crushing bits of her skull into powder.

She'd been dead after only the third strike.

Helena's rage was dwindling, but not before one last heave of the orb, this one slamming into the floor, having gone completely through Agrippina's skull. The mother of my unborn child reared back from Agrippina's lifeless corpse, leaving the orb where it was, and her arms fell to the floor beside her. She sat back upon Agrippina's stomach, as blood covered her from head to toe, arched her back, and screamed, releasing everything she had in her. She slumped forward again, placing her hands on either side of Agrippina's corpse to hold herself up, and slowly composed herself as she turned, finding me seconds later.

Her eyes were vacant, distant, and blood streamed down her near perfect face, and while I knew she understood what she'd just done – that she'd finally exacted the revenge she'd wanted for years – I only hoped she wouldn't let it eat away at her.

As for myself, I let out a huge breath of relief at the sight of Helena sitting victorious over Agrippina, and I couldn't help me feel like the battle around me was dying down, but I couldn't be sure.

My night vision scope had broken off earlier, and the darkness was so deep that I had no idea who was still alive and who was dead, but I made my way to Helena, determining it was time to extract ourselves as quickly as possible. She sat there, waiting for me, perhaps too drained to move, when her eyes opened wide in surprise.

She saw, before I did, a previously hidden Praetorian emerge from the shadows and take a swing at her with his *gladius*. His attack hit her square in the chest, pitching her backward into a slab of rubble, but the blow had been with side of his sword, not the edge, so instead of slicing her chest clean open, it only knocked the wind out of her. It was enough to disorient her however, and allowed the Praetorian the chance to place his foot against her neck and push her over the rubble. She slid down a slab of concrete, and I lost sight of her as she tumbled into the darkness.

I bellowed in fear and anger at the sight of what had just happened, alerting her attacker to my presence, and my fear for her evaporated when he stepped around and leapt at me, his sword held at the ready. He thrust for my abdomen, but I sidestepped left – not nearly fast enough. The sword grazed my ribcage and I felt pain race through my entire right flank. I stumbled as I turned, clutching at the wound, but I couldn't let it slow me down, because this mother fucker was going to die. I found a broken *gladius* on the ground, its blade snapped in half, and picked it up. I reached out with my free hand and motioned for him to bring it.

He did.

He came at me hard and fast, putting me on the defensive almost immediately. Block. Block. Stab. Block. Riposte. I did everything I could to stay alive. As long as there was still a chance Helena had survived, I would too. But my broken sword was no match for his intact one, and he was clearly the better swordsman. His face was mature and hardened, and it was clear he wasn't some young rook fresh out of boot camp. He knew how to fight and he was fighting for his survival just as I was.

He stuck to his training as we dueled, stabbing with the point, rarely slashing with the blade. He made another jab at me, which I managed to block down and to the right, causing him to stumble from the force of my parry. His sword found itself lodged between fallen slabs of concrete, temporarily jamming it, so I took advantage by stepping down on the blade, disarming him in an instant.

But the bastard wasn't going to give up that easily.

While I had his sword pinned, he threw an open palmed smack into my flank, right where he had slashed me earlier. A fucking sissy-boy slap, but it hurt like hell, and I grunted in pain and stumbled backward, giving him enough time to retrieve his sword. He came back at me with a downward slash, easily defendable with my upraised sword, but the force of the strike was so great that I wasn't able to keep him from pushing my arm down, allowing his blade to slice into my shoulder. His blade cut deep into the muscle, maybe an inch or two, and he yanked it out, pulling out bits of flesh and muscle as well.

My right arm immediately went numb.

I switched my sword to my off hand and he smiled, knowing I was done for. He took only a moment to pause for a quick breath before rushing headlong at me. My mind raced for a response to his attack, but found none, so I did the last thing he, me, or anyone would expect.

I dropped my sword.

His expression of confusion was exactly what I was hoping for. In his hurry to kill me, he hadn't noticed a piece of concrete directly in front of him that was precariously balancing on another. I'd noticed it earlier before I had temporarily disarmed him, and had somehow managed to avoid it.

The Praetorian fell into it, and he went down hard, something snapping in his leg. I didn't bother reaching for my sword. It was too inaccessible. Instead, I grabbed one of the few torches still ablaze from a fallen pillar nearby and leapt at my foe. I brought the torch down in a stabbing motion, impaling him through his mouth.

The flames barely even sputtered as his face melted away.

But he somehow managed the last laugh.

Whether it had been a planned attack, a gut reaction, or merely an uncontrollable spasm, he managed to bring his *gladius* up and stab me in the stomach with it. It didn't go too deep, but I could almost feel it tear up my insides. It got me a few inches above my bellybutton, and a few to the right. It could have hit my liver, maybe my stomach, I didn't know.

I figured I was dead anyway.

My only thought was to find Helena.

I left the Praetorian to sizzle behind me and found the pile of rubble she'd fallen down, stepping over but barely noticing Agrippina's lifeless body. I crawled in after her and found her at the bottom, lying on her side, her left arm splayed out beneath her head so that it could rest atop Helena's outstretched bicep. I edged next to her and reached out for her cheek with a bloody, shaky hand. She wasn't moving, and it wasn't until I bumped into something hard and sharp, that I discovered she'd been impaled through the upper chest with a piece of metal shrapnel.

But she was still breathing, which gave me hope. She was still alive, and where there was life, there was survival, especially after she'd successfully returned from beyond the grave before.

Hope for myself, however, was quickly becoming scarce.

Her eyes were still open and moving, but foamy blood frothed at her mouth, and her chest wound sputtered noisily. My own wounds were not faring much better.

My eyes moistened.

"Not again, Helena," I said through tears. "I can't... I..." but I wasn't sure if she could hear me anymore.

She couldn't move. Not even to lift a hand like she had the last time. All she could do was take one last breath and go still. My hand continued to tremble with increasing severity. I touched her stomach, hoping for something. Anything. But I felt nothing. Nothing to indicate that life remained in either of the two people that shared this wonderful body and soul I loved so much.

I started to cough. Blood came out this time. My vision started to narrow and the edges got hazy. I fell to my side, right alongside Helena.

This story couldn't end now.

Wang could still show up.

He had to show up.

He always showed up.

But, before he did, I felt my own last tendrils of life slip away as copious amounts of blood from all three of my wounds pooled around me and my foggy eyesight continued to close in.

It was only a matter of time.

I closed my eyes, reached out, and groped for Helena's hand, hoping to hold it one more time as we made our final journey together. Finding her right arm hanging behind her back, I slowly slide my hand down her bare arm, slower and slower, death's twisted joke gaining the upper hand with each passing second. I could feel her skin beginning to cool, but when I finally reached her wrist and found her fingers, just before I felt no more, my hand felt something large, hard, and round.

The haze and fog I saw through my eyes flared in one last, bizarre glimmer of resistance, and I waited, alone, for my final journey to commence, knowing such a flash could only mean one thing. I could see the light coming, bright as I always thought it would be, but oddly colored blue instead of...

XII
Foresight

Tripolis, Syria
October 42 A.D.

Death was such a sudden thing.

And I knew I had to be dead, because it was the only explanation for how I felt:

Fantastic.

Like new, in fact. Reborn, maybe. Not even a hallucination to speak of. That part was refreshing. No fatigue, no soreness, no numbness, aches... pain, just... nothing. No complaints. That seemed like a good definition of heaven. A place where there was simply nothing to complain about. That sounded poetic.

I think I'm going to like it here. If only I could see something. Everything was still black.

And then I wondered where St. Peter was and why I couldn't see his pearly gates.

St. Peter?

Hello? Anybody home?

Anybody...?

What the fu... I caught myself sheepishly. It probably wasn't a good idea to swear just before you meet St. Peter. He, quite literally, held the keys to the kingdom, and I doubted The Big Guy was much of a potty mouth either.

I had to admit, this wasn't exactly what I figured my final transition to the glorious afterlife would be like. I always thought there'd be little cherub like angels, clouds, loved ones to welcome me, or at least some topless women. But I didn't see any of that. All I saw were the backs of my eyelids, and I felt very surprised at just how coherently I was able to form intelligible thoughts and process this new information.

Wasn't I dead just a second ago?

Maybe ol' J.C. was testing me.

I risked a peek by opening my eyelids just slightly...

And almost vomited at what I saw.

No angels. No clouds. No gates. Not even any breasts.

Just...

Santino.

Of all the guides to the afterworld, I get Santino? I mean, Dante got fucking Virgil as a guide! Where was my ancient Roman poet? I'd take Virgil too; he seemed like a Roman I could actually stand to be around right now.

There weren't many of them left…

"You all right, Jacob," the Ghost of Christmas Santino said to me. "You look like you've seen a ghost."

"I *am* seeing a ghost," I pointed out, surprised when the finger I jabbed at his chest touched something solid. I recoiled my hand like I'd just touched a hot stove, gripping it protectively against my chest with my other hand. I opened my eyes fully and gave him a suspicious look. "Because if *you're* my guide to heaven, you must be dead too."

He chuckled and glanced behind me. "Jacob, what the fuck are you babbling about?"

Suddenly, I wasn't so sure. My eyesight had been pretty blurry when I'd first opened them, but now I could see that while the room was lit in an amber glow, it was still dark, not exactly the brightly lit area I assumed was heaven.

"Oh, my God." I dropped my voice to a whisper and leaned in closer to Santino. "Am I in Hell?"

Santino's eyes narrowed, and he put his hands on his hips. "You're about to be if you don't tell me why you've gone insane on me all of a sudden. You off your meds?"

Another voice from behind me spoke up. "What's wrong, Santino?"

It was an angelic voice.

A feminine voice.

Helena's voice.

I turned to see her standing there. Alive, healthy, and as beautiful as ever. I blinked. Nope. Still there, and no wings. Making my way to her in two long strides, I wrapped my arms around her and kissed her as hard as I could. If God was in fact sending me to Hell, I was going to drag her with me. I didn't care what she thought.

Helena's ghost shoved me away, but she didn't look mad.

"Jacob," she whispered bashfully, "what are you doing? We're on a mission."

A what? Is that what they called it here in… purgatory?

Was that where we were?

Helena's ghost pointed to her right.

I looked at what she was pointing toward, hoping it wasn't Satan. The room looked oddly familiar. It was large, with numerous tiered levels that descended from where I stood. I also saw people and enough treasure to fill Ft. Knox. Vincent were there. As was Wang. Gaius and Marcus as well. Titus. Bordeaux!

I was in the goddamned treasure room.

The same damn room I'd stood in fifty minutes ago!

But how was that possible?

I looked at my hands.

I was holding the orb.

I looked toward the heavens, or at least just the ceiling, my eyes furrowed in confusion… thinking.

Déjà vu?

Had I gone back in time?

I had to have.

Wait, wait, wait…

If I'd gone back in time, where was the second orb? And why hadn't the transition hurt like hell? And if the orb transported all matter within a room with it, where was all the rubble, dead Praetorians, and a horribly disfigured and definitely dead Agrippina? In fact, since I was transitioning back to a point in time where I already existed, shouldn't there be a copy of me and of all my friends too?

I looked at Helena and poked her cheek, definitely feeling resistance. She looked at me angrily and poked me back. I felt that too. Just in case, I gave her a little shove. She stumbled back a step. In response, she slugged me in the shoulder.

It hurt.

I met her eyes. "You're alive?"

"Last time I checked, Jacob," she said, looking at me like I belonged in the loony bin.

I smiled and leaned her back as I kissed her again, pulling away quickly and tossing the orb in her direction. She made a grab for it but bobbled it a few times before finally catching it awkwardly. She called after me, but I ignored her as I made my way to Bordeaux, who was setting the bomb he'd already set once upon a time.

I nearly tackled him as I ran to where he was burying it beneath the treasure. "Wait, you big, beautiful beast of a Frenchman, you!"

He gave me a funny look. "I'm flattered, Hunter, but I'm married."

I shook my head, still amazed at what was happening. I would have kissed him too if I'd had the time.

"Set it for thirty five minutes," I ordered.

"I was going to set it for…"

"Just do it. Trust me."

He shrugged, but didn't seem happy about it. "You're the boss."

He reset the timer and placed it beneath the treasure.

Everything made sense. Everything! I knew how the orb worked. I knew what it was intended to do. How it could take us home. And I knew what was about to happen. And how I could fix it.

I turned to see Titus once again analyzing the box, his hand poised to open it.

"What's thi…"

I struggled to find my voice as I grinned like an idiot. "Wait, stop, don't do tha…" I repeated for no one's benefit but my own.

And then came the white burst. My eyes immediately went blank, but unlike last time, I laughed, groping about stupidly, playing it all up this time. Then I waited for the sound of clinking armor running into the room. And there it was. Now, time for the…

***

I've been knocked unconscious quite a few times in my life. More than the average…

I squeezed my eyes tightly, the muscles in my face recoiling from the pain.

Really? Even my post black out monologues were the same? I suppose I shouldn't be surprised since the pain sure felt the same. Despite knowing what to expect, I still felt like shit as I slowly regained consciousness, and used the time while my body recovered to hash out the last of the details about the orb. I couldn't believe how simple it was. Varus had been right. Our use of the orb had been much too complicated. Far too random. Using it properly was in fact almost elegant, if not genius.

I still couldn't explain the kind of trance I'd gone into when I'd first touched the orb, but now I understood the flash of blue light Helena had noticed. Somehow, somewhat, she must have clearly seen the orb activating itself. How I activated it was something I still didn't know, but I suspected I knew someone who did. I only hoped he left a trail for us to follow when we got out of this.

But that could wait. For now, the elegant part.

When Agrippina forced me to inspect the orb earlier, I *had* seen something beneath the swirling white clouds that always seemed to indicate the orb was... active, for lack of a better term. I hadn't understood it at the time, because I thought I had only seen a reflection of myself, but I had seen a reflection because it had in fact been me. It had been me at the point in time and space when I had first touched the orb in the treasure room.

An hour later, when I came into contact with it as Helena had held it in her cold hand, the orb finally had the chance to operate in the way it had always been meant to.

Instead of haphazardly transporting everything in a room and replicating itself, it took its sole user on a ride back to its starting point. My rubber band theory actually made perfect sense. The ball was never supposed to be used by two different people. It was meant as a transportation device for one person to travel back to a prearranged point on the timeline, taking only the users' consciousness with it, not the body. All the pain and wounds I'd received during the previous timeline were gone, leaving only the memories.

And hence, its true elegance.

Conventional time machines from the movies transported the entire entity of its user. Mind, body, spirit. All of it.

That never made much sense to me. A time traveler would still be susceptible to the effects of time. If I'd taken my DeLorean off joyriding through the timeline for twenty five years in total, when I finally decided to return to my original point on the timeline, I would be twenty five years older. The body still ages at the same rate. I couldn't come back twenty five years later from the starting point, or else there'd be a twenty five year gap where I simply didn't exist.

Unless I wanted to go the whole "fake death" route.

But the orb only transported the consciousness of a person.

Their memories. Their experiences. Their essence.

This thing would have been great to have back in college. Set this puppy a day before a test, go in to take it the next day, learn all the questions, sit through the damn thing, return to my dorm room, and proceed to warp myself back to the day before, all the knowledge of the test's contents still in my head. And no physical aging to go along with it. I don't even want to think about how well I could have done with the ladies. It wouldn't even have been a challenge.

Simply elegant.

But how did I activate it to begin with?

I grunted. All that thinking made my head hurt even more, but still I managed to regain consciousness before the others. And just like last time, when I opened my eyes, I confirmed that everything seemed the same and everyone was in their places, ready for the final scene.

Again.

Lights, camera, action.

"Agrippina," I said hoarsely, looking up. "How's the ass? Oh, that's right. It is quite perfect and I of all people should know that. By the way, your face looks a lot better than the last time I saw it."

I almost shuddered at the memory of the faceless Agrippina, but thoughts of watching Helena die for a second time hardened me.

No, it would be the third time this time around.

Agrippina looked at me from her chair. She offered me a blink in recognition that she'd heard me but not much else. She directed a cool look in my direction, displaying her ever impressive poker face, but she shifted her toga over her bare legs at the same time, revealing even more skin.

Interesting.

I wasn't much of a poker player myself; never was. I'd never been very good at counting cards, nor did I have a very good poker face, but I was good at reading people. Detecting subtle nuances that said someone was hiding something, or even outright lying, came pretty easy for me. I figured it must have come from trust issues with my father and past relationships, friends who I constantly schemed with or against as a kid, watching too much TV, or maybe even from my work with the CIA.

Whatever the origin of my talent, when Agrippina shifted her toga, a nuance, I definitely detected. For such a seasoned poker player, as she surely must be, she'd just revealed her tell. In fact, it was a pretty obvious one. It was a testament to her obvious sex appeal that I, or anyone else for that matter, never picked up on it.

But her face was another matter. It remained impressively stoic as she rose from her chair, whispering something in her closest Praetorian's ear. When he left the room, she strutted over to where I knelt and lifted my chin, just as before, recovering from her slip perfectly.

"Why do you continue to bother me, Jacob?" She asked. "Is it that you have seen me naked and you now wish for more? Is that why you brought your Amazon this time?"

I smiled. "Now that you mention it, yes, that's exactly what I'm here for. How nice of you to offer." I glanced at Helena but leaned my head in closer, dropping my voice to a whisper. "It's good that you've already stripped her half naked, but we should probably wait for her to regain consciousness first. Doing it while she's just lying there seems a bit weird. Don't you think?"

Agrippina's face twitched and I had a hard time suppressing the urge to mimic Santino's goofy ass grin.

Score one for Hunter.

And in that moment Agrippina didn't seem so threatening. She was just like me. We only appeared more confident than we really were because we hid our fears behind defense mechanisms. I believe the clinical term for it was Narcissistic Personality Disorder. I remember because my sister tried to diagnose me with it when I was sixteen years old. It's basically a disorder in which people have an inflated sense of their own self-importance. Generally, they used some kind of grand show to hide how fragile and low their self-esteem really was.

But unless you knew that a person suffered from the disorder, it made him very hard to read. It was obvious when some people were happy or sad, but that wasn't the case for people like Agrippina and me. I hid behind my sarcastic wit and the idea that I could outthink just about anyone, and Agrippina covered herself with her sexual audacity. We disguised what we were truly feeling with a phony façade of self-confidence and bravado.

At least I had before recently. I seemed much more open now, and it was ironic that I had Agrippina to thank for that. In that moment, everything I felt concerning what had passed between the two of us was gone, and I felt a renewed, legitimate sense of confidence.

"You know, Agrippina," I said, with a shake of my head, even though it still hurt. "I think I finally understand you."

"You do?" She asked sternly, taking a step back and crossing her arms across her chest, the maneuver pushing up her breasts and exposing them even more. I would have laughed if I didn't need to stall, and wondered if she even knew what she was doing.

"Yeah, I think I do." Now that she'd pulled back, I went to work freeing my knife behind me belt. "You use your looks and promiscuousness to get what you want, never taking no for an answer. You bat your eyes, pucker your lips, and shake your ass, expecting everyone to drool all over you and do whatever you want them to do. We have a name for people like you where I come from. They're called cheerleaders. But, just like most of those pompom-waving charlatans, deep down, you wish you were something else. Something more. A person people actually like, not someone they fear and loath. Deep down, you're just a child, clawing for a way out."

Agrippina's eyes narrowed at my little speech, and I almost thought I saw something shift in her expression, but if it did, the evil inside her quickly suppressed it. She frowned at me before turning back to her chair, speaking as she walked.

"I think I understand you as well, Jacob Hunter," she said as she sat back down, shifting her toga again. I smiled at her as she continued. "Men like you enjoy giving long speeches, letting your words and eloquence engage in battle for you. You are a very intelligent man, adept at reading people and determining what makes them who they are. You like to talk and you use this advantage to overcome your other... shortcomings," she said with a small grin as she flicked her eyes downwards, but in the next second she grew very serious. "But this also makes you very dangerous, and not in the ways you may think."

I narrowed my eyes, wondering where she was going with this.

"Your mind is an infection," she continued. "It is a disease that threatens to reduce your conscious thought to a bubbling mess of sheer confusion. You lead yourself down dismal paths that you convince yourself are worth traveling, taking others with you, making the poorest of decisions as your paranoia overcomes you, crippling your ability to discern between what's truly right and what's truly wrong. But you are very stubborn and will forever fight against this certain eventuality. One that will ruin us all."

My smile drained from my face along with the color in my cheeks. Agrippina's face grew sterner, and she let her arms drop to her sides. In that moment, not a millimeter of cleavage or a sliver of skin along her thighs was showing, and my mind whirled at what that meant. And then I caught myself.

"You don't know anything about me," I said coldly, that old sliver of self-doubt slowly clawing its way back into my psyche.

"You're wrong," she said, leaning forward. "I know everything about you. That's why I have to kill you, Jacob; to keep you from destroying what so many have worked so hard to accomplish. Your presence is an offense to my society and my empire. I have to do what's right for both."

The elation I'd felt earlier was quickly evaporating, once again replaced by what seemed like my constant companions for years now: rage and fear.

"What do you know about what's right and wrong?" I asked, trying to go back on the offensive. "You're nothing but a power hungry fraud who will do anything to ensure your schemes and manipulations succeed."

"You know me so well, is that what you think?" She asked from her position above me. She let the question linger before leaning down and placing a hand on my shoulder. "But where does this knowledge come from, I wonder? By my count, you and I have spent very little time together. Were you so quick to judge my brother? Or my uncle?"

Of course I had been. I'd judged them against what I'd already known about them, but... that hadn't turned out very well. They were different when they'd died. They weren't the men I had read about in history books. I'd always assumed it was the orb's influence, but that wasn't necessarily the case. Claudius had been healthy and without ailment well before I arrived in Rome, a historical inaccuracy not easily lost on me.

Did that mean I was misreading Agrippina? Perhaps I was missing something beyond her aggressive foreign policies, blatant mismanagement of client-state governments, irreprehensible lust to murder potential claimants to the imperial throne, or even in her zealous witch hunt for my friends and me.

In all honesty, I didn't want to think about it anymore. I just wanted to get out of here with our lives this time, and preferably with the orbs.

I looked up at her. "Why don't you just kill me then?"

She pulled back. "I am not without a cruel streak. Most would agree to that, but I tried to help you before, and while you rebuked me once, I will continue to be magnanimous with you, as I need you now more than ever."

Because you killed Varus, you bitch – but I didn't say it.

"Why?" I asked. "So that you can have yet another powerful weapon to use against anyone who would dare stand against you?

She brought a hand to her cheek and her eyes were furrowed in dumbfounded disbelief, an expression that couldn't believe I could even *think* to utter such words. "You cannot possibly think that I feel any less suspicious of you having it!"

She punctuated her statement by twirling around and moving back toward her chair. I barely even noticed how revealing the movement had been. My head was too busy once again, my brain on the brink of exhaustion. I tried to get a handle on it by reminding myself I could think about it later, but it was difficult.

Was Agrippina simply trying to do what she thought was right? Did she see me as a threat?

Was I the threat?

I shook my head at the thought and glanced quickly to my right. Santino and the boys were already on their knees, all shirtless just the same as last time, so I peeked left. Helena, shirtless this time too, was coming around as well, not quite as quickly as last time, but perhaps more peacefully. My conversation with Agrippina had saved her from the painful beating she'd received last time and I suddenly felt the need to ask myself why Agrippina had been so conversational this time, far more reasonable than violent. Had my trip through time altered her sensibilities as well?

That didn't make sense.

Did it?

I turned back to Santino as I finally remembered what would soon happen, keeping my voice very low.

"Tell Titus to move as far from Vincent as possible."

Santino looked at me questioningly.

"Pass it on," I insisted like a third grader.

He narrowed his eyes but turned to do as I asked.

"Jacob?"

The sound of my name came from Agrippina, and I turned my head to face her. Her Praetorian had returned and I saw Varus' headless body crumpled at her feet. She didn't seem aware of its existence at the moment, and since her demeanor wasn't nearly so cruel this time around, I suspected she wouldn't even reference it.

"I must know something, Jacob," she said from her chair, her legs crossed as they always were. "If I offered to give you and your friends – even your Amazon – everything you ever wanted and needed, promising to protect you and keep you from harm, would you help me?"

"I..." for the briefest of moments, I thought about it, but it was never an option. "I can't do that. There are things about the orb that you'll never understand."

"And you won't tell me?"

I shook my head. "I know what you're capable of. I've seen the kind of cruelty you can inflict with your own hands. I've watched it here myself."

I winced at the slip, but didn't think she'd understand what I'd meant.

But she must have because she stood again, this time with purpose. "You have been here before, haven't you? You used the orb!"

I almost laughed in her face. "Wouldn't you like to know?"

The control she'd displayed for the past ten minutes was gone, but instead of coming at me in a furious rage, she simply smiled, but then the insistent *beep, beep, beep* of Bordeaux's watch sounded all around us and just like last time, confusion set in immediately.

Agrippina looked at her Praetorians.

"What is that noise?!" She yelled.

They looked just as confused as she was, glancing about the room in search of the nuisance. It was at that point when I started to chuckle and she turned back to glare at me, her eyes wide and angry. My chuckles grew into a rolling laughter.

"Boom."

A half second later, I was flying through the air again before slamming against the back wall. The impact knocked the air out of my lungs, but I was ready for it. I kept my head against my chest and braced for it by slowly exhaling as I flew. It took me a full minute less than last time to get to my feet. I saved another twenty seconds knowing exactly where to look for *Penelope* and another fifteen because the Praetorian I'd fought the first time was still completely out of it. I shot him in the head with one bullet and quickly scanned for targets.

I had thirty rounds left and I was going to make sure I killed every last one of these fuckers before any more of my friends died.

Again…

I scanned left first, remembering Gaius and Marcus were here this time, each rising to their feet. Two more bodies for the fight. Titus still hadn't come away unscathed, but at least the concrete hadn't killed him, landing lower on his leg instead. He couldn't move, but it freed up Vincent to fight from the beginning. Wang was already a blur of motion and Santino was on his feet and had his ropes torn open as well. He moved to help Helena again while Helena went in search of Agrippina, just as she had last time.

I couldn't forget Bordeaux. Fate my ass. That big lug was up as well, alive and fuming. After the explosion, he'd ripped open his bonds through a sheer exertion of muscle alone.

After confirming everyone was alive, I started dropping Praetorians. Some were still struggling to their feet. These were easy kills. Others were up and moving to engage either myself or someone else. These were only slightly more troublesome. Thirty rounds, twenty five kills. Remorseless.

Not bad.

I looked around for Helena. Hers was the only fight I knew for sure had a bad ending.

I found her deadlocked with Agrippina once again, only this time there was no spherical object to be used as a weapon. The two women rolled each other over and over and over again, whoever ended on top momentarily gaining the upper hand. I wasn't wasting any time to watch this time. They were on the other side of the room, so I was already on the move.

Helena finally managed to pin Agrippina to the ground, positioning herself more on her foe's legs than her stomach this time, allowing Helena to keep more control over her desperate adversary. Agrippina tried to punch up at her, but Helena impressively caught her arm with her left hand and managed to snatch Agrippina's other hand as well. With a quick motion, Helena jerked Agrippina into a sitting position and head-butted her.

I was ten steps away when I saw the Praetorian who had almost sliced Helena in half the first time, looming in the rubble. I noticed this time that he had been buried beneath fallen concrete and wood during most of the fight, and was only just now able to extract himself. Agrippina's head rested against the ground, stunned by Helena's blow, and Helena looked like she was ready to choke her to death.

The Praetorian moved closer.

I moved as well.

Maybe fate simply had it out for Helena. The woman *had* impressively escaped death on multiple occasions, after all. Perhaps Death was getting angry at her constantly snubbing him out of a pay check. It didn't take a leap of logic to assume that Death could be a pretty ornery guy.

But Fate, or Death, or even God for that matter, could all go to hell right now.

Helena made her own fate, and so did I.

The Praetorian had his sword in hand now, cocked for use, and he looked excited for the chance to plunge it through Helena's back this time instead of slashing at her. He still had a few more steps to go, but I only had one.

I dove at Helena, tackling her harder than the toughest of linebackers, praying I didn't do any damage to my child. But I had to break her grapple with Agrippina, and the only way to do that was to really nail her.

Unfortunately, even with all my momentum behind my leap, Helena's hands stayed firmly clamped around Agrippina's wrists. It slowed us just enough so that when the Praetorian finally came through on his stab, he didn't just meet air like I'd originally hoped. Instead, his *gladius* tore right through my left flank, just below my armpit, opposite the side he'd sliced open the last time.

I yelled in pain, and Helena finally released Agrippina's wrists after she heard my cry of pain. When we hit the ground, we rolled together, Agrippina still lying where we left her. Once we came to a stop, Helena and I were separated, but all I cared about was the gaping wound in my side. I risked a glance at it.

I immediately wished I hadn't.

I wasn't sure if it looked worse than it felt, or not. I wasn't even sure I wanted to know. The laceration was at least six inches long, from my *seratus* muscles around to my shoulder blade. The thing had to have been splayed open an inch deep and I swore I could see my ribs.

Helena noticed it too and scampered to my side. She sat behind me and tried to hold me in an upright position in her arms. I felt her bare breasts push up against my back and a flood of warmth from her active body surged through my own. The comforting feeling helped stave off the shock that was sure to come, I was sure, but Helena didn't have anything to treat my wound with, so she simply slapped her hand there and held on tight.

Just like all the other times, her first aid treatment hurt more than the actual wounding, and I yelled in pain for a second time.

My attacker ignored us, knowing Helena and I weren't going anywhere. He moved over and helped Agrippina up, and I knew she was going to order him to kill us. I locked eyes with her for just a brief second as she swayed weakly and saw something I'd never seen there before.

Fear, perhaps?

She flicked her eyes at Helena, who glared back at her silently, refusing to leave me to die, even to kill Agrippina. The empress took a second to evaluate all her options before finally settling on that of the fleeing variety. Without another look, she and her Praetorian savior found an opening in the wall and got the hell out of here

Helena shifted her hand on my wound and I groaned.

"Just hang on, Jacob," she said. "Wang will be here in a second."

"I'll be fine, Helena. It's just a scratch."

She looked at it again, shifting her hand to do so.

Another yell.

She hissed, one that was clearly an *oops*. "If it's just a scratch, quit crying you big baby."

I smiled around the pain. She wouldn't joke if she truly thought it was serious.

More at ease than I'd been thirty seconds ago, I looked out over the fallen rubble, collapsed columns, and dead Praetorians, trying to glimpse an outline of my friends through the still settling dust from the explosion. I couldn't hear the obvious sounds of a battle going on, but I did hear plenty of people moving around.

I blinked twice, and by the third, I could see two figures moving in our direction through the debris. I tensed at first, wincing at the pain from my wound, and heard Helena breath in sharply as well, readying herself for anything.

I was reaching for *Penelope,* even though she was empty, when Wang and Santino came barreling through the cloud of dust and debris, heading right for us. Both men rushed to our position, each still shirtless and sweating heavily. Wang moved to my left side, already pulling off his medical bag, which he must have found after the battle.

He hastily batted Helena's hand aside and inspected the wound. He used his thumb and forefinger to gently part it before shaking his head after I yelled again.

"Always have to be the hero, don't you, Hunter?" He asked, pulling a syringe out of his bag.

"Of course he does," Helena replied, resting her chin on my shoulder.

I winced. "Give it to me straight, doc. Am I going to make it?"

Wang flicked the syringe, but spared a moment to glance at me. "Don't be a drama queen, mate. It's just a flesh wound."

I sighed in relief and patted Helena's arm, which she still had wrapped around my stomach.

I shifted my attention to Santino as Wang jabbed me with the needle.

I winced but kept my attention on my friend. "Sit-rep."

Santino coughed up some dust as he turned to survey the room. The blown dirt and debris continued to swirl around him, caking his perspiring body in a thick coating. He looked more like a ghost than ever.

"We're pretty fucked up," he reported. "Titus is immobile. His left leg is pinned beneath a giant slab of ceiling. Gaius and Marcus are helping Vincent get him out."

He hesitated for a moment as he glanced at a blown out portion of the wall. I traced his look but could discern nothing of note, except that we had been moved down to the first floor of the villa.

"What?" I asked.

"Bordeaux is MIA. The first thing he did after the last Praetorian went down was to radio Madrina. When she didn't answer, he checked the UAV feed." He paused again with a shake of his head. "The GPS beacon we gave her indicated she's just outside and not moving. She must have come to investigate during our little nap earlier. Bordeaux ran that way." He raised a hand to indicate the blown out wall.

Another loose end, but he'd be back after he found her. "What about everyone else?"

"Everyone else has cuts, scrapes, scratches, and a few knife wounds, but you're the worst." He paused once again. "Of course."

I smiled. It did always seem like I managed to get myself hurt more often than naught.

"What about Agrippina?"

"She's gone. Scurried her tight little ass out of here like a cockroach. I *was* able to find this though," he said, holding up what I knew must have been the orb wrapped in a black cloth.

"At least this mission wasn't a total wash," Wang said sarcastically as he stitched me up. "But we should look for Varus. If he was here, he may have survived the explosion and be in need of medical attention."

My chin dropped against my chest at the thought of poor Varus. I knew what the others did not; that he was already dead, probably buried somewhere here in the rubble. We owed it to him to find his body.

"What about the other orb?" I asked

"Unknown," Santino said, before swiftly pulling back the orb as if something important finally dawned on him. "By the way, how did you know to reset the timer on Bordeaux's bomb?"

I coughed. "Let's just get everyone situated before we get into that."

He nodded and I looked at Wang. He was completely focused on his procedure and was already finishing up the stitches on my side. I barely even noticed.

"Move him forward, Helena," he ordered.

She did as she was told, pushing me away from her so that Wang could wrap my chest up with a few rolls of gauze. After a few wraps around my shoulder, he dug into Santino's bag and pulled out a spare black T-shirt a size too small to add extra pressure. Once he and Helena managed to get it on me, they both helped me up, and Wang handed me a sling and Helena and Santino shirts of their own.

Santino took his immediately, but Helena looked at it stupidly before looking down at her naked upper body, perhaps realizing for the first time how exposed she was, and she sheepishly moved to cover herself with her arms. She readily accepted the shirt Wang held out in front of him, who looked amused at her awkwardness.

I ignored them both, my head swimming as I tried to steady my head and focus. I must have lost more blood than I'd thought.

But it looked like I'd live.

It looked like we'ed all live.

Thank God.

He could come back from Hell now.

Once Helena secured her shirt over her torso, she took the sling from me and pulled it over my head and maneuvered my arm into it. She then gripped me by my other arm and helped move me closer to the rest of the group. She led me to a slab of rock and sat me down. I winced as I sat, but I was glad to be off my feet. She brushed my cheek with a hand and leaned in to kiss me, a single happy tear sliding down her cheek. She wiped it away and moved to help Titus.

It was then that a shirtless Bordeaux came rushing into the room, an unconscious or dead, Madrina in his arms. He threw a disgusted look at me as he passed by, calling for Wang as he set his wife down gingerly on a large, flat piece of concrete. He knelt by her, uselessly mopping her hair from her face instead of helping Titus. Wang went to see what he could do for her while everyone else continued to extract Titus from the rubble.

I watched the endeavor.

Gaius and Marcus already had a piece of an iron pole working as a fulcrum beneath the slab while Vincent tried to clear obstructions with his only hand. But every time they tried to move it, Titus cried out in pain. Luckily once Santino joined in, they were able to lift the slab just high enough for Helena to pull him out. Gaius and Marcus politely pushed her aside, lifted the boy, and carried him next to me.

Wang noticed Titus' removal, said a quick word to Bordeaux, and moved to look at the young Roman's leg. Bordeaux angrily followed Wang's departure until he remembered my presence. I made eye contact with him and gave him a supportive nod, but his response was the last thing I expected. His eyes blazed intensely, all the fury over his wife's injury now directed solely at me. He sprang to his feet and moved in my direction, his hands balled into fists.

If I didn't know any better, I would have thought he meant me physical harm.

I'd never seen such anger in the man before, especially not directed at me. He was normally so gentle despite his size that we always joked he was just a big kitten. But now, it was like watching Bill Bixby transform into Lou Ferrigno on one of the greatest TV shows ever created.

His large body bounded to where I sat in less than a second as I watched in wide-eyed terror. He reached out and grabbed the collar of my shirt, his right hand rearing back behind his head, ready to strike.

"You!" He roared, attracting the attention of the others. "First you tell me to reset the timer!? Then to trust you!? Look what happened to my wife!"

I squeezed my eyes and looked away, bracing myself for the punch I knew would probably take my head from my shoulders. Luckily it never landed. Helena leapt onto his arm before he could take a swing at me, but all she could do was hold on like a child dangling on a playground monkey bars set. Even still, he almost managed to throw it all the same. Santino also tried to get between me and my attacker, but Bordeaux seemed intent on killing me. He shrugged Helena off like she was a rag doll and pushed Santino to the ground. It took the combined efforts of Marcus, Gaius, Santino, *and* Helena to stop him from crushing me.

Once they pushed him far enough away, Vincent stepped in to glare at him.

"What the hell are you doing, Lieutenant?!" He yelled.

It wasn't the voice of a friend or father figure, but of our old commanding officer. Captain Vincent was demanding why one of his men had just tried to strike a fellow officer.

That calmed Bordeaux down.

But only a little.

"He told me to trust him," he yelled. "Said thirty five minutes would be enough time. I would have set it for an hour. This may never have happened!" He finished his point by jabbing a finger at his unconscious wife.

Wang turned his head to face the raging Frenchman, setting Titus' leg as he did so.

"She's just unconscious, Jeanne. Her vitals are good. She'll be fine."

Bordeaux was now taking tremendous deep breaths, his veins pulsing like a blowfish. He stared at me, but I tried to hold his gaze coolly. He was suffering from a post combat adrenaline rush. Nothing gets the blood flowing like fighting for your life, but if he wasn't careful, he could work himself into a coma if he didn't get his heart rate under control. It wasn't a foreign concept to soldiers, sometimes leading to Post Traumatic Stress Disorder.

Vincent put his only remaining hand on Bordeaux shoulder. A very trusting gesture considering his disability.

"Calm down," he said. "Everything's fine. All of us are still alive. That's the only thing that matters."

Bordeaux shifted his attention away from me and down at him. Vincent held his stare like a rock and after a few moments, Bordeaux finally calmed his breathing and settled down. He moved back to Madrina, sat beside her, and held her hand. No one else moved for a few seconds after that, everyone still in shock and awe at not only the battle, but Bordeaux's explosion.

Helena was the first to recover. She moved to sit next to me, wrapping her left arm around my back, holding me well below my wound. She rested her head against my shoulder and placed her other hand against my chest. She immediately pulled it back and moved her head to look at me.

"Your heart's racing."

I turned to look at her. Very slowly. My face must have been completely white.

"I don't think I've ever been so scared in my entire life," I said

She felt the seriousness in my voice and moved her head back to my shoulder. She started rubbing my chest around my heart, as if that would help. I didn't know if it would slow my pulsing blood pressure, but it felt good all the same.

Vincent still stood where he had talked Bordeaux down. He waited there for another second before dropping his head and turning to face me.

"How *did* you know to reset the timer?" He asked without hesitation, his only hand on his hip.

He didn't look angry but to deny him an answer was completely out of the question.

I panned the room, noticing everyone except Wang had their attention on me. Bordeaux especially. Even Titus, who moaned every now and then from the pain, was groggily glancing in my direction.

I sighed, shrugging. "Agrippina was right. I've been here before. This is the second time I watched this fight go down. I figured out how to use the orb in the previous timeline and did so…" I trailed off, expecting someone to cut me off, but everyone only waited patiently. I continued. "The first time, things didn't turn out so good. You two," I said pointing at the former Roman Praetorians, "were taken out back and crucified immediately. And you," I pointed at Bordeaux, "well, Agrippina killed you before the bomb even went off. She shot you in the head with Wang's pistol."

The large Frenchmen held my look for another heartbeat. He tore his eyes away soon after and closed them. Everything must have been falling into place for him.

"And that slab didn't just break your leg last time," I told Titus directly. "It killed you."

The young Roman blinked, still half out of it.

"As for you," I said, shrugging Helena off my shoulders to look at her. "I had to watch you die in…" I looked into Helena's eyes, unable to finish the thought, and her face said it all. She was just as ill as I was at the thought of the both of us going through that again, and I wondered if she was angry at me too for getting us into yet another life or death situation. At my own words, I felt my heart sink into my stomach as my adrenaline left my system and the horrific memories returned.

"What about me?" Santino asked.

I snorted in amusement, thankful that Santino would always be there to pull me from the brink, just as Helena could. "Honestly, I don't know. You were probably fine. I'm pretty sure you can't even die, just so you'll always be around to annoy the world."

Santino crossed his arms and beamed with pride. He looked among our friends hoping someone would give him the benefit of making eye contact with him, but no one did. Each was too preoccupied with his thoughts.

"I even thought *I* died," I continued, my shoulders suddenly very heavy. "I was hit in three different places and was losing a lot of blood. I didn't even know I activated the orb when I did. That's why I thought I was dead back in the treasure vault."

"What did you do to make the orb work?" Vincent asked.

"I'm really not sure," I explained.

But before I had the opportunity to explain, if I even could, another large slab of concrete fell from the roof and landed between Santino and Vincent, and the building began to shake.

Violently.

More slabs of the building and other debris started to fall all around us. Bordeaux moved to cover Madrina, while Wang protected Titus.

Santino managed to look up in time to see a column from one of the floors above him break apart and head straight for him through a hole in the ceiling. He dove out of the way, dropping the orb when he hit the ground. I watched as it shed its cloth and rolled away from him, and I tracked it as it started moving to my left before shifting directions sharply, making its way directly toward me. I tried to justify it by convincing myself that it had met an impediment in its path that knocked it toward me, but I hadn't seen anything.

It rolled as if possessed, seemingly of its own volition.

I looked down at it while I remained nonchalantly seated on my concrete slab, Helena trying to protect us both. But the only thing I could focus on was the orb, the collapsing building not even on the backburner. It rolled up against my boot, bounced off, and hit it again, settling against my toe. The compulsion was there again, but it seemed controllable, like craving a food that I knew I could resist, albeit with some trouble.

Clouds swirled within, just as they always seemed to when it had something to say, but something was different this time. The clouds settled, revealing something I'd never see within the orb before, but something familiar.

I looked closer.

Revealed within was a room with a white ceiling and floor that almost seemed to glow. Two walls on the sides were also white, but the third wall was nothing but glass. The fourth was out of view. Behind the glass wall stood men in white lab coats, complete with pocket protectors and black rimmed glasses.

How odd.

But within the room was by far the oddest part of the scene. Dark forms stood patiently, while others sat on rectangular boxes. Men from the looks of it.

My hand moved on its own, reaching ever so slowly for the orb. I didn't even try to fight it. Something about this one felt right. My bare fingers spread across the smooth surface, now as soft as a stress ball, but it did nothing. As I brought it closer to my face, I saw one of the figures holding the orb as well in a gloved hand. The figure spun the other, bare hand in a circle, a motion that suggested someone should do something.

All I could think about at the moment was how much I wanted to go home but hadn't a clue as to what I should do, and not surprisingly, nothing happened. I remained in the blown out building with Helena still wrapped around me. When the building finally stopped shaking seconds later, she slowly lifted her head. She saw I was holding the orb in my open hand and she looked between it and me.

"Jacob, what are you do…"

With her words came a flash of bright blue light and the hiss of a thick cloud of mist winking into existence. I felt an electric discharge, like a static bubble building up all around me followed by the wash of cool air against my face and a gentle blast of pressure as it burst.

Thankfully, the building remained still, unless of course we weren't in the building anymore.

The orb dimmed and went inert, still glowing its dull blue, but seemingly inactive.

Helena snatched it from my fingers and threw it back to Santino.

Nothing had happened. I hadn't thought so. The figure within hadn't been me.

Then I saw movement. Something clawing its way out of the mist. Figures. Dark ones. Six of them.

In that moment, I knew exactly how the Roman augers must have felt five years ago. The ones who'd intended to find nothing but treasure but instead found us.

As the mist cleared, the figures looked more and more familiar.

They were dressed in black clothing, simple BDUs from the look of it. They wore harness type rigs over their chests, somewhat akin to the ALICE webbing worn by grunts in the 20th century. They also carried weapons.

Rifles.

Most appeared to be M16s, even if certain details seemed… different.

I was speechless. Helena rose off my shoulder at a snail's pace. Her mouth was open and she was staring at them as well. The rest of our team was arrayed around them in a circle. Those who had found their weapons trained them on these new visitors, even me, despite the fact *Penelope* was empty. All we needed was for Romans to show up before the standoff turned into a Mexican style one, but the lead figure in the group finally stepped forward, raising his rifle over his head.

Then he spoke.

In English.

"Stand down!" He bellowed – to everyone it seemed.

His men lowered their rifles, except for two, who already had their rifles slung and were tending to another figure resting on his back. The one who held the orb.

Another fucking orb.

Those of us with weapons lowered them as well. The lead figure took a step forward in my direction. He was wearing a type of balaclava, revealing only his eyes. His entire appearance surprised me less than what I saw in those eyes:

Recognition and relief.

He took another step and reached up to pull off his mask, and my eyes grew as large as his own. The guy looked like a model, or an actor, or any number of those kinds of people who were too good looking for their own good. He had blond hair fashioned in a longer style crew cut, bright blue eyes, a chiseled jaw line, and shallow cheeks. The guy's look screamed, "d-bag," and I knew it was true.

He smiled a toothy grin and opened his arms wide in a friendly gesture.

"What's wrong, Jacob?" He asked. "You look like you've seen a ghost."

I stared at him.

"You know this clown?" Santino asked, still peering over his gun sights.

I did know this clown. I knew him very well, in fact.

I rose to my feet painfully, motioning for Helena to stay back, and took two steps closer to the blond haired phantom. I knew he had to be a phantom because he was right. I *was* seeing a ghost. He was dead, after all. At least, he was assumed so. Two months before I'd activated the orb, this man had been sent on a mission, one he had not come back from. No one had seen him since, but his locator beacon had placed him deep in the North Korean mountains where it had continued to pulse for months, unmoving.

Since I knew he had to be dead. Therefore a phantom. Therefore not real. Therefore a ghost. I had absolutely no problem with what I was about to do.

Taking one last step forward, I reared back with my right arm and socked him in the face with a very solid, Helena-worthy, right hook. He went down hard and his troops raised their rifles again, but he motioned for them to stand down almost instantly. I stepped forward to loom over him and pointed down at his face, ignoring the blazing pain in my side.

"That's for Artie, you backstabbing piece of shit!"

That felt good. Very good. Great, even. I've wanted to do that for over five years. Even after everything that had happened to me in between. Too bad he was just a figment of my imagination and the real man I'd wanted to relieve my frustration on was stuck back in the 21st century, if he was even still alive.

The man sat up and spat out a glop of blood. He wiped his mouth and stared up at me.

"I deserved that, Hunter," he admitted, "I really did. But I've made my peace with her."

"Fuck that!" I shouted, our interchange seeming more and more unreal with every word.

"You can ask her yourself," he said, pointing behind him towards the figure holding the orb.

I shifted my attention. The figure was smaller than the rest, but not overly so, but now I noticed more curves. The man was in fact a woman.

Once she pulled off her mask, my suspicion was confirmed. The blue eyed bastard had been right.

It was Artie.

I took a step forward, my heart beating faster than it had during Bordeaux's charge and I was unable to believe what my eyes were seeing. The shock of identifying the first man was completely drowned out by my excitement at seeing this particular woman. She wasn't supposed to be dead, and seeing her told me these people were, in fact, real.

"Artie?" I called out tentatively, trying not to get my hopes up.

I took a wobbly step toward her, oblivious to my friends' stunned and confused reactions over the interchange occurring before them.

The woman looked up at me. "Hi, Jacob."

I smiled down at her. She smiled back.

She shot to her feet like a jackrabbit and ran the few steps to me in a blink. She threw her arms around my shoulders and I didn't even care that it hurt like hell. I wrapped my non-bound arm around her back tightly, and she hung there while I rocked her.

Helena stepped forward, coughing politely into her fist.

I pulled away and looked into her jealous face. Besides Agrippina, she'd never seen anyone offer me anywhere near as much affection before. And I wouldn't even call what Agrippina offered me as affection. I laughed at the whole thing.

"Sorry, Helena. This is Artie. She's..."

"Good evening, *mademoiselle*," Santino interrupted, brushing past me to take Artie's hand so that he could kiss it gently. "Jonathon Archibald Santino the Third, at your service. Pleased to make your acquaintance."

Helena looked at me. *Archibald?* She mouthed.

I shrugged. I thought he'd headed his lone mission entry with that.

"Ah," Artie said, her voice high and smooth, not quite at the annoying pitch. I smirked at how she drew out the sigh in knowing recognition. "So, *you're* Santino..."

He smiled dashingly, but I shoved him to the side and out of the way.

"Artie, that's Santino," I said, waving my hand dismissively at him. "And this is Helena," I said, indicating Helena. "Helena, this is Artie, but her full name is Diana Hunter."

Helena snapped her head to look at the young woman.

"Diana?" She whispered.

Diana "Artie" Hunter.

Engineer. Astronaut. Genius.

My little sister.

Diana was tall, although not quite as tall as Helena, and was athletic enough to cut it for the space program, weighing exactly one hundred and forty one pounds last time I'd heard. It was a vital statistic I knew only all too well, as she and my mother had argued relentlessly over who was taller and in better shape. The two had been as competitive as Wang and Santino, only far more loving. They'd practically been like sisters for the few years between when Diana had entered adulthood and mom had died. It was unfortunate it hadn't lasted longer.

She had brown hair, darker than mine, and kept it about shoulder length. Brown eyes and a cute round face gave her features more like Dad's, but she was just as lovely as Mom. That said, she was my sister after all, and while to me she had proportionately pleasant features, I wasn't an objective source of criticism. She'd been good looking enough to date the D-bag I'd punched out a few minutes ago though, so that must have counted for something.

Her nickname also came from our mother. An avid reader of anything she could get her hands on, my mom had read everything from romance to history, mysteries to biographies, and the classics, but her passion had always rested in mythology. Later in my life, I'd always found it odd how much she'd enjoyed the subject, considering her staunch Catholicism, but it didn't matter which society the stories came from because she loved them all.

As for Diana's nickname, it came straight from Greco-Roman mythology. Diana was the Roman derivation for the Greek goddess, Artemis, Apollo's sister and goddess of the hunt. Mom used to love telling infant Diana all of Artemis' stories, about how independent and strong she'd been, and about how she never took crap from men and always blazed her own path. After a while, my baby sister started saying the name Artemis in that cute little gibberish way kids that age do, and after a while, mom just started calling her "Artie," and the name stuck.

Santino was as confused as ever.

"Diana? Hunter?" He asked as he turned to look at me, his hands on his hips. "You never told me you were married!"

I rolled my eyes while Helena answered for me. "She's his sister, you dimwit."

Santino looked between Artie and me, back and forth, disbelief still evident. He pointed a finger at her and scanned her from head to toe. "This... this is your sister?"

I ignored him, my mind and my heart racing uncontrollably. Diana and I had always been very close. Up until college almost inseparable. Seeing her now made me feel something I hadn't legitimately felt in a long while.

Hope.

And then reality kicked in.

"Just what the hell are you doing here, Diana?" I asked.

"We got your message, Jacob. Your journal." She paused, and reached out to grab my shoulders. She looked up at me with her big, dark, doe eyes. "I'm here because they needed someone with Remus' bloodline, and since I have a higher security clearance than you do, the President called me in."

Jesus, her short sentence was a lot to take in. Here was someone, other than myself, speaking as though she knew exactly what the hell she was talking about. I wasn't used to that. It was exciting on another level as well. I guess my journal wasn't a complete waste of time after all.

"Is that true?" I asked the blond haired leader of the group.

His name was Lieutenant Paul Archer, US Navy. SEALs. Built like a linebacker, he'd been in the same BUD/S class as me and we'd continued our training together at SEAL Qualification Training and had bonded from the moment we'd gotten to know each other. Some of the enlisted men in the class had thought we had interestingly similar names, despite the fact they were completely different, and in the rigorous world of SEAL training, participants needed anything they could find to latch onto, and the two of us had figured since everyone else thought we already shared a bond, we might as well make one.

It hadn't been hard. He'd been a good friend. He and I were the only two officers in our BUD/S graduating class, and we'd both admitted later that without our friendship, it was possible neither one of us would have made it.

It was at our graduation ceremony where he had met Diana.

Despite being literally planets apart most of the time, their friendship grew into a romance that lasted nearly two years, to the point where he'd considered popping the question. All of which had changed when I'd visited him during the very random instance when the both of us had leave on the same weekend. I'd gone to his California home, sneaking in a window as any good SEAL would since we only used doors when we were kicking them in.

Inside, I'd found him with some floozy.

I remember grabbing him by the neck as he went at it, throwing him out of the bed and against the wall. The girl had grabbed a sheet and high tailed it out of the room before I could toss her out as well. I hadn't beat the shit out of him like I should have, but I did tell him that our friendship was over, and that I wouldn't go so easy on him if we ever met again. I'd also told him that if he wasn't upfront about it with Artie, he was a dead man.

The next day he'd called her and told her the news.

She had been devastated. She'd been poised to take the next trip to the US-EU Joint Operation Moon Base later that day. She went, but it had not been easy on her. I remember talking to her via a satellite uplink video conference, watching as her tears floated all around her as they pulled away from her face to free fall in the low gravity. She'd gotten over it, but it hadn't been easy. That had been three months before I'd transferred to the Pope's Praetorians. Archer had disappeared in Korea two months before that seminal moment as well.

I don't remember Diana shedding a single tear.

Archer got to his feet and nodded.

"Give me a sit-rep then," I ordered. "From the beginning."

Archer took a look around, clearly not happy about being undermined in front of his men. I looked around as well. My people were gathering closer around where Artie, Helena, Santino, and I stood while Archer's men closed in as well. I looked at their faces, but they were all still covered by their facemasks.

"Three days after you and your team went dark," Archer started, "the President ordered a search and rescue operation to find you. He called us in."

"The President?" I asked with a sigh.

"Of course," Archer answered, before shaking his head. "Oh, right. The timeline is fucked up. You guys were working for the Pope."

"What do you mean by, 'fucked up'?" Vincent asked. I'd never heard him swear like that before.

The cuss word also brought up another interesting question. How were Diana and Archer even standing here? Let alone speaking English? The guy was talking about being sent by the President, not the Pope. That single change alone was significant enough to suggest the timeline was in some form of disarray.

If that was the case, how also are they exactly as I remembered them?

"We can get to that later," Archer said politely. "As it stood, you were two days past your deadline. We were sent to your last known location off the Ottoman Coast in Syria."

Ottoman Coast?

"We found the caves along with plenty of dead bodies. None of them members of the North Atlantic Federation Forces."

North Atlantic Federation... What?

"Most of it had been blown to hell and we immediately feared the worst, but we found something that gave us hope. We detected a locator beacon transmitting so weakly that we almost didn't pick it up. We found it a few miles east of the cave, next to a lake."

I narrowed my eyes, suddenly very curious.

"We had to dig about forty feet down. What we found surprised the hell out of us, and we hadn't even opened it. A standard issue, ballistic grade cargo container, but of a design unfamiliar to us. It also looked as old as the world itself. What we found inside confused all of us even more..."

As he spoke, consciousness started to elude me and my head grew foggy. I felt myself passing out. I really must have lost more blood than I thought and it was starting to hit me."

"Jacob!" Both Helena and Diana called out simultaneously as they reached out to steady me. Both women looked at each other, still technically having not been introduced to one another. Santino's stupid interruption hadn't even given them the chance to shake hands. Even so, they both helped me shuffle back over to my slab of concrete. Wang stepped over and gave me some water and an MRE cracker.

"Thanks, Wang," I said with a nod, turning back to Archer. "Sorry about that."

"Don't worry about it," he said.

I was surprised at the lack of animosity between us. Maybe he really had made his peace with Artie. Maybe what had happened hadn't even been the same?

Helena moved to sit to my right, making sure I wouldn't fall.

Archer looked around the ruined building, as if noticing its dire state of repair for the first time.

"Shouldn't we get out of here, Hunter?" He asked. "This place doesn't seem stable."

I hesitated. If the building hadn't moved after the force of the orb's activation, it would stand long enough to find Varus. "We can go after we find someone. Have your men look for..." I paused again, looking at Helena. "Have your men look for a head and a body. The body should be wearing a toga. He was with us."

Helena looked at me curiously.

"Varus..." I whispered.

She gasped and looked at the floor. Everyone else who'd known the man dropped their heads as well. None of them had been as close with him as I had been, but they'd all respected him just as much. Varus had been a good man. We had to get his body back to Rome so that his wife and small child could pay their respects.

Archer flicked his hand to verify my request and his men spread out through the rubble strewn room. I watched as they broke glow sticks to brighten the area, their green glows only making the situation more morbid. It made me think of Varus' family, especially his son. The thought ate at me. His son would have to grow up fatherless.

Because of me.

"I'll help them," Santino offered respectfully.

I nodded in thanks and watched him go. I noticed Artie watch him go as well. Trying to forget about Varus, I eyed her in that big brother kind of way. She shrugged at me and returned my big brother look with a little sister scowl. I sighed. So it was going to be like that then.

Only Wang and Bordeaux hung back from the search. Madrina was still out, and even though I assumed Bordeaux had put all the pieces together, it was best not to anger him. That left Archer, Artie and Helena with me. Definitely not the most ideal double date, but at least I only disliked one of them.

"So what was in the container, Archer?" I asked.

"Well, we couldn't open it in the field. It had been sealed with something kind of sealant epoxy and we were worried about damaging its contents. We had to carry it back to the States for analysis. It took the techs four hours to pop it open. Inside were three objects, and it hadn't been pretty."

I was on the edge of my seat. I really was. Ever since I started writing the journal earlier this year, the only thing I wanted to know was how all this ended.

"First was a blue sphere. This one," he said holding up the one Artie had used to get them here.

How many did that make now? Three? Four? The math was officially too much now.

"Second, was a very interesting notebook. It was brittle and falling to pieces, but I bet you know what the very interesting part was."

"Let me guess," I said with a half-smile. "That it was written in English, blue ink, and in poorly worded grammar and syntax."

"Exactly," he replied. "I have to admit, it was a pretty interesting read. At least it was after an antiquities preservation team from the natural history museum in New York managed to transcribe it. I'm sorry, but the notebook is pretty much trashed."

"Nuts."

Archer smirked. "The third object was the most interesting, not to mention disturbing. It was the source of the locator beacon. A human body." He paused, glancing at his feet hesitantly. "After close examination, it was determined to be identical to your body type and size, with a crack in the left tibia, carbon dated as two thousand years old."

I looked at Artie, who leaned against the wall near us, her arms crossed.

"I confirmed it, big brother. The leg had a break right where you cracked it when you fell out of the tree house when we were kids. I didn't believe it at first. Your body... your skeleton... just lying there. I couldn't believe it." She shuddered and shifted her arms to hug herself. "It was creepy."

I smiled nervously, but not at the thought of my own body having withered to little more than a skeleton, still in existence at a point where my sister could view it. I didn't let existential things like that bother me. At least I tried not to.

I smiled because Diana had always been so blunt, so childishly naïve in the delivery of her thoughts that I found her to be a walking enigma. She was eighteen months younger than me, but by the time I graduated from Dartmouth, she was already walking away from MIT with a Masters in Aerospace Engineering. She was a child prodigy, but even with that big old brain stuffed in her head, she was as silly as Santino… and that thought caused me to pause in my tracks.

I shook my head. I'd have to watch those two. Just another thing to worry about.

Helena held up a hand like a student in a classroom.

"Excuse me, but are you telling us that when you found a two thousand year old body in a historically impractical container, along with a notebook spewing forth all sorts of nonsense," she looked at me, "no offense, Jacob…"

I shrugged. "None taken."

"…that you actually believed our team traveled back through time?"

"You must be Major Strauss," Archer said with a halfhearted salute. "Senator Strauss will be very happy to learn that you're unharmed."

Helena and I exchanged glances, our eyes wide and surprised.

Major Strauss? Senator Strauss?

Oh, boy.

As for Archer, his look lingered on "Major Strauss" a second longer than I would have liked. Considering his past, I immediately grew suspicious.

"Just as an aside, Hunter," he said, covering his look rather well, "the President wasn't too happy about certain parts of your journal…" his voice trailed off, and he settled with just pointing between Helena and I.

"Excuse me?" I asked.

He looked at me sharply. "Don't play dumb with me. You two are supposed to be officers. We have rules about these things for a reason. The President feels…"

"Listen buddy," I interrupted angrily, "you get stuck in ancient Rome for four and a half years and we'll see if you do something stupid…"

Helena offered me a sour look.

"…Oh, you know what I mean," I said with a dismissive wave before turning back to Archer. "You can go tell this so-called *president*," I said throwing up air quotes, "that he can take my journal and shove it up his a..."

"That's enough, Jacob," Artie interrupted. "He understands where you're coming from; he just wished you would have been more professional in your journal."

"It's not an AAR," I told her, even though memory reminded me that it was. "It's just a stupid journal. I didn't even think anyone would actually find it. It was just something to keep me focused."

Helena almost laughed at that comment.

"Whatever," Archer piped up, annoyance obviously evident in his voice, "but to answer the major's question, no, that wasn't our first thought. Remember, it took us a few weeks before we could translate the journal. The fact that we picked up a transmitter signal was odd, yes, but hardly confirmed anything. The tech was so far beyond us that we thought it was Persian. It wasn't until we called in Diana after we had the first part of the journal translated that we confirmed it was Hunter. A final DNA and dental record test confirmed it. Like Diana said, Jacob... it was creepy. Even for me."

I nodded absentmindedly. I couldn't imagine what that must have been like. The sheer absence of any kind of normality to the situation had to have been mind-blowing. I tried to picture Archer, a tough guy SEAL through and through, trying to sit and listen to a bunch of eggheads attempting to explain what was going on. Despite being a jack ass, Archer had always been a patient thinker, exactly what the military looked for in their 21st century officers. It had made him a good platoon leader, if not a good person, but I knew that if I had been in his shoes, even with all the TV I had seen over the years, I'm not sure how I would have dealt with it.

Helena always joked that when we'd first been sent back, I'd handled it so well because it was almost like I welcomed it, or even planned it. She'd been fairly right, as always, but I countered by explaining how I'd always been good at adapting to new situations, which was true, and that I'd always hated movies where people could never actually figure it out that zombies were in fact attacking, or aliens were invading, or monsters were maiming, when it was clearly happening right in front of them.

Did people not watch movies in the movies?

That never made sense to me. It was partially why I was so impressed that Archer and whoever else was involved managed to come to the logical, if not obvious, conclusion as quickly as they had. These kinds of things don't happen every day.

"Just out of curiosity," I started, "just how much time has gone by between when we disappeared and now?"

Archer and Artie exchanged glances.

"A month," Artie answered sadly.

"A month, eh?" I asked calmly, but then grew angry. "A fucking month!? We've been stuck in Rome for five years! Five years!"

"How could you possibly blame us for that, Jacob?" She asked.

"Do you know what we've gone through?! What I've gone through?! Do you know how many times I've had to watch things happen that have been slowly pecking away at my sanity? My soul?!" I yelled, poking my head and chest in frustration, my anger burning inside me. "Years!"

"Hunter, you're the expert here," Archer said, holding a hand out to calm me down. "All we know is what you described in your journal, some of which was lost, I'm sorry to say. And you didn't really do a great job describing time travel theory in there, anyway. Like you've said, you have had five years to think about this. Your sister and the other scientists back home have only had a few weeks."

Artie looked at Archer, finally some of that original resentment I knew she felt toward him surfacing. If it had only been a few weeks like Artie said, theyir breakup was still technically rather fresh. Peace or no, I couldn't imagine she was enjoying working with him.

"I'm an engineer, Archer, not a scientist. I do math. I don't spend my time developing theoretical concepts about wonky time travel theses." She turned her attention back to me. "We don't have much, Jacob, but I know how you think. To me, your journal read more like a movie script than a doctoral thesis. You always did watch too much TV. By the way, I'm sorry to say, your movie isn't going to happen. The whole thing is classified."

I looked at Helena again. "Figures."

"You had a lot of pseudo-science in there," Artie continued, "and don't get me started on your claims of 'magic.' You can't even imagine the laughs that got from the scientific think tank assigned to figure out your story."

"That hardly seems fair," I snapped in annoyance. "Those dorks are probably just compensating for all that time playing their little games about fairies and dragons. Losers..."

"Jacob, don't pretend like you never played those as a kid..."

"As a kid!" I quickly defended, glancing at, but not quite making eye contact with Helena. "I grew out of that like forever ago."

Artie glanced at Helena.

"He's the worst bluffer on the planet. It's always so easy to tell when he's lying. He hates the word, 'like,' but uses it constantly when he knows he's wrong."

I saw Helena looking at me out of the corner of my eye, but I didn't dare turn to look.

This is a nightmare. Sister and girlfriend in the same room together? God help me.

"No offense," Archer interrupted, "but I can do without this little family reunion. I need to check on my men."

"Wait, Archer, quick question," I called before he could leave. Of all the questions I could think of, oddly, there was only on my mind. "Where's that Balisong knife I gave you a few years ago?"

He cocked his head to the side quizzically. "What's a Balisong knife?"

I gulped. "Also known as a butterfly knife..."

"Oh, right," he said, pulling out a very familiar looking object from his pocket, flipping it open. "You mean a Xenophon knife."

My head dropped to my chest before I snapped it back up, turning it towards Helena. "That fucking kid."

"I told you," she said, patting my hand.

Archer pointed at me, his face in a state of shock. "Wait a second... Xenophon Knives have one of the most mysterious origins out there. More so than Stonehenge or even the Bermuda Triangle. Legends go that it was designed by a child from Greece. They said it was impossible because it was made in a way and with materials that couldn't be replicated for another two thousand years. The National History Museum in London still has the original one on display. No one understands it…" he paused. "Don't tell me it was you!"

I shrugged. "Maybe…"

He grasped the side of his head with his hands and laughed. "I can't believe it! I've discovered one of the world's most unexplainable mysteries, and of all explanations, it was you who caused it! Why doesn't that surprise me?"

Still laughing to himself, and without any further ado, Archer threw his hands in the air, turned on his heels, and left.

Both Artie and I watched him go.

"There's a history there with you three, isn't there?" Helena asked.

Artie turned to face her, lowering her arms as she moved to stand in front of me. "You have no idea." She stared at me for a few seconds, her eyes typically unreadable, before she punched me in the arm on my good side.

"Ow!" I barked. "What the hell was that for?"

She started punching me again, each of her next words accompanied by the jab of her fist.

"That's. For. Scaring. Me. Half. To. Death!" She finished with an excessively hard slug.

"Stop it," I whined. "I'm wounded."

"Don't give me, 'wounded.' Mom never wanted you to join the service in the first place, and now I know why! Look at where we are! I mean… you hate dad, why'd you even sign up?"

"Seemed like the right thing to do at the time," I reasoned with a shrug.

She punched me again. "That's not an answer."

Helena leaned forward and smiled. "I like her."

I groaned. It was bad enough Helena and Madrina were friends.

This was a hundred times worse.

Artie turned to face her, looking at her as if legitimately noticing her for the very first time. After basically checking Helena out, scanning her from head to toe, Artie smiled and moved in to give her a very sisterly hug. Any stranger would think they'd known each other for years.

Artie could be like that. She'd always been the kind of person, even as an eight years old, who had no problem walking up to a complete stranger and saying "hi." I never understood it, but at least as she got older, especially after the episode with Archer, she had matured when it came to putting herself out there like that.

"So, you must be Helena," Artie said, still holding her tightly.

I looked at Helena. Her face was as nervous and awkward as I've ever seen it. She wasn't used to this kind of personal affection from anybody but me either. Even a friend as close as Santino had rarely ever offered her a hug, but then again, hugs weren't really his cup of tea as well. She patted Artie on the shoulder embarrassedly and looked at me uncomfortably.

Artie pulled back and held Helena out at arm's length, analyzing her.

"I must say, Jacob," she said, glancing at me. "Good job. She's way prettier than I thought she would be."

Helena blushed and looked away. She looked no better than she had a few months ago prior to the operation where we'd rescued that young Roman girl, Julia.

Artie noticed her bashfulness.

"Oh, I didn't mean it like that," she reassured. "I'm just surprised to find someone who even just likes Jacob, let alone a hottie like you who apparently loves him. Did you know that he never, not once, brought a girl home to meet mom and dad?"

Helena looked at me, astonished. "Really?"

"Oh, and you did?"

"My situation was a bit different."

"I said you weren't allowed to use that excuse anymore."

"Since when do I listen to you?"

Artie smiled at the interchange. "It's hard to imagine you've known each other for so long, when for me, Jacob's only been gone a month, but... it's not that hard now."

"Tell me about it," I joked. "You should have seen her ten months ago when she was ready to dump me."

"Me?!" Helena yelled. "You were the one who wouldn't talk to me *six* months ago."

We glared at each other, but they were loving glares.

"And you're pregnant!" Artie exclaimed loudly, performing the Ms. America fanning motion. "Congratulations! I'm going to be an aunt!"

"Shut up!" I said as loud as I could but still under my breath, while Helena shushed her as well. "Nobody knows yet."

"You haven't told anybody?" Artie asked.

"I just found out two days ago," I said with a shrug.

She ignored me and turned towards Helena. "So, tell me, what are you…"

I shook my head and tried to focus on anything else besides the two women and their baby talk.

I was saved by Archer returning with one of his men who held some kind of bag in his hand. The man was bald, with blue eyes and reddish hued beard. He also carried an M14 rifle, with a large scope on it. The M14 was a rifle rich in history and had still been used even in my original timeline, but its glory days had been far in the past. I had to assume this guy was a sniper, but along with their outdated uniforms and rigs, his use of an M14 only enforced my fears that the timeline had definitely been altered

And not for the better.

"Hunter, this is Gunnery Sergeant Alex Cuyler. Sniper."

"Gunny," I greeted with a nod, receiving a salute in return.

"Lieutenant," he said.

I blinked. Oh, right. I was a lieutenant. I almost forgot.

"We found multiple heads among the rubble," he reported. "Each is pretty messed up, but your teammates think this is your friend. It's… so mangled they couldn't be sure. They said you'd be the best person to identify him."

I sighed and glanced at Helena. Artie cut off their conversation and gave us some space. Helena picked up my hand.

"I'm ready."

Cuyler took a breath and unfolded the piece of cloth carefully. Peeling away the last of the blood soaked layers, he revealed a mangled and bruised face. The lower half of the jaw had been torn away, and the rest of the face was so cut up that even though I saw Varus' telling grey eyes, it was still hard to identify.

I looked away and motioned for him to close it up.

"Did you find the body?" I asked.

"We believe so. It was the only one not wearing any kind of armor."

"Thanks, Gunny," I said softly.

"We also found this hidden behind a sash he wore around his waist," Sergeant Cuyler said as he held out a piece of rolled up papyrus that had been flattened. "We don't know what it says."

I accepted it, turning it over in my hand until I saw writing over the seal. Scrawled there in neat little letters was my name, spelled as *Iakob*.

"It's my name," I pointed out. "It's in Latin." I sighed. "Did you find anything else?"

"No, sir."

I nodded morbidly and he saluted and left to tend to the body.

"Were you two close?" Archer asked.

I wasn't sure how to reply to that. We really hadn't been overly close. We'd been friends, sure, but hardly BFFs. I batted the piece of papyrus into my empty hand a few times, wondering if I should open it.

I needed answers to all the things I'd experienced tonight. Answers to how exactly the orb worked and how I'd used it only an hour ago. Answers to Agrippina and how she seemed to know so much. I wanted those answers now more than ever, and while Varus' note may have the ones I sought, we had more pressing matters to deal with. I passed it to Helena, who tucked it away in a pouch.

I'd read it later.

"Yeah," I replied. "We were."

Archer pursed his lips and glanced at Artie. She wasn't paying him any attention.

I tried to push Varus from my mind. I didn't have time to grieve. Now that we'd found him, we should get out of here. I started to rise when a loud shout from Santino nearly dropped me back to my seat.

"Jacob! Get over here! You really need to see this. Bring your pal, the clown."

I mumbled under my breath and allowed Helena to help me to my feet. Archer and Artie followed behind us.

"Santino," I said as I approached him, "I swear to God, if you ever say I really need to see something ever again, I'm not going to be responsible for what I let Helena do to you."

Wang, Vincent, the Romans, the new time travelers, and Santino stood near a bombed out corner of the building, open to the rest of the world. They were all looking through the hole, past the knocked over perimeter wall, toward the north. Those who had optical devices had them trained outside, while Santino turned to face me, anything but a happy expression on his face.

"Now's not the time, Hunter," he said. "Although, I do feel obligated to mention that Hunter and Archer are eerily similar names."

I looked at my former friend, and watched him roll his eyes, mumbling under his breath.

"So, what's the problem?" I asked, turning back to Santino.

"The problem?" Santino repeated angrily. "Just look out the fucking window."

I held my gaze on him for a few seconds before slowly shifting my look in the general direction of his outstretched arm. What I saw stopped me in my tracks.

Laid out before us were men. Soldiers. Legionnaires. Praetorians. Thousands of them. Their torches indicating they were far off but perhaps approaching our location.

Aw, shit.

My mind started processing the information as quickly as it could, which wasn't anywhere near efficient enough. Even with Archer's reinforcements and additional supplies, we wouldn't be able to put up a suitable defense. Those of us who'd been in Rome more than thirty minutes were weary after the close call we'd had with Agrippina and it was amazing how much traveling through the orb weakened a person. Archer's men weren't showing signs of fatigue yet, but having been there, I knew it was only a matter of time.

I turned to look at Archer. "Just how many chapters were in my journal, anyway?"

He met my eyes. "Twelve. Why?"

"Because I've already written eleven... and I'm suddenly feeling the urge to write another."

Archer motioned for his men to fall in. "Get ready to move out!" He shouted. "Get the crates and the body bag, but be prepared to stop and offer cover fire. We're heading south."

I swore under my breath. I didn't need to offer any orders to my people. They were too used to this kind of situation. The two sets of Tweetledees and Tweetledums moved to help the new arrivals with the cargo containers. Each were a little smaller than our original containers, but something told me they wouldn't even stop a spear, let alone grenades. Finally, Vincent helped Titus on his crushed leg, while Bordeaux picked up Madrina, who was still out cold.

Meanwhile, Helena and Artie stuck close to me as we gathered up whatever gear we could find. Luckily, our camp was south of this shithole of a building, so we'd be able to recover the rest of our gear, whatever little we had left, and avoid the approaching enemy.

I tentatively strapped *Penelope* around my shoulder, while I tossed my bag to Helena. I couldn't hang on to the heavy rucksack with my arm in a sling, or with the pain in my side. She helpfully accepted it, along with her own, checking her last P90 magazine for ammo. I could see through the clear plastic magazine that she only had a dozen or so rounds left.

I found my MOLLE rig and slipped it on, keeping it unattached on my bad side. I clipped my pistol holster to my thigh and felt like a complete man once again. I pulled out my Sig, checked that it was loaded, and felt exponentially better knowing I at least had my sidearm.

I caught Archer's men already blazing a path through the blown out corner of the room, immediately turning south to avoid the approaching horde. Our best bet was to get back to Vespasian, even though we were coming back empty handed. I rushed to catch up to Archer on the way out.

"I need to know something, Archer. Something that doesn't make much sense on your end."

"And what's that, Hunter?" He asked pretentiously.

I almost stumbled at his tone. It suggested dismissal on my part, almost as if I were in his way, or that we were on a need to know basis, and I didn't need to know.

I let it pass. "What exactly are you doing here?"

He looked at me as we ran, his expression all of a sudden very angry. "We're here because your journal's final entry had a lot to say, Hunter. The President was very interested. We're here because somewhere along the way, something goes seriously wrong."

"So?" I replied. "You were in your own timeline before you left, and you seem exactly as I remember. It can't be that bad."

"That's the problem, Hunter. It is that bad. We're here because you fucked up beyond measure, and you need to fix it." He threw me a cocky grin. "And we're here to help."

To be Continued

A Note from the Author

Throughout the past four years of my life, as I've labored to both write and publish the book you have just read and the one that preceded it, I never considered myself a writer. How could I? Writers are something special. The Great Ones. The Wayne Gretskys of their craft. Guys like Steinbeck and Salinger, or my personal favorites like Herbert and Heinlein. Ladies too. Wonderful writers like Woolf and Austin. Hell, J.K. Rowling.

And yeah, maybe even guys like Crichton.

Just not this Crichton.

Writers make it look effortless, and it shows in their product. Writers may struggle to get where they are, but once they've reached the mountaintop, they rarely disappoint those mere mortals beneath them. Sure, many of them have an army of alpha readers, agents, editors and publishers, all of whom have the simple job of ensuring the product is as good as it can be, but it doesn't matter. Even without all that, Writers are amazing and do what few can even dream of doing.

But I've dreamt of it for years, and the end result is what has been laid out on these pages before you, and other pages you may have already read or are soon to read. It's not much. Just my humble attempt at doing what the greats do so effortlessly: entertain others with original stories.

And despite it all, I'm proud of my efforts. I know you must have slopped through some distracting grammatical errors, dumbly placed commas..., , inane character quirks, and questioningly dumb decision making capabilities, but the story is what it is. Nobody's perfect, like Helena likes to say, least of all the author, me, who is in fact only human. Perhaps if my wife had more time to read my work or if my friends would actually turn in *edited* drafts of the stuff I give them or if I'd taken more writing courses instead of history classes back in college, this story may have been something more.

But despite all that, I'm completely happy with my work. Proud of it. Ecstatic to share it with the world in fact. Because every story I write is like a new baby entering my life. No matter how it turns out, I'll always love it and will always be there to support it. No matter what quirks it accumulates over the years and trials it has to endure, I'll always be there. And with some luck, I'll have made some good friends along the way who share in my love for it, willing to support it as much as I do.

That's all I can really ask for, and I hope you'll be there as the ride continues.

Coming Soon

**Keep Reading for a look at the third book in the ongoing
Praetorian Series: *A Hunter and His Legion*, due out in the fall
of 2013:**

Not quite as far in the future as last time…

"Quick to the point, I see," Vespasian remarked. "Why don't
you introduce your friends first?"

I started with Artie and Archer. I made no mention of the fact
that they had just arrived, or that Artie was my sister. Vespasian
gave her a curious look as he made his way to grasp her hand,
maybe noticing she wasn't the military type, maybe thinking she
was attractive, I didn't know. He already knew Gaius and Marcus,
who simply saluted smartly as he passed by. He kissed Helena's
hand, just as he did last time we'd met, my frustration at the
gesture the same then as it was now.

"Can I marry him yet?" Helena whispered to me in English.

I ignored her and finished by introducing Santino, who looked
as uninterested as usual, but Vespasian perked up at the name.

"Ah," he remarked, "so you are the 'funny one' then."

Santino turned to me and smiled, "I've always liked that
Galba."

I rolled my eyes. Of all of us, Santino was the only one our
old Roman comrade, Galba, had liked.

None of us had any idea why.

"I have something for you actually," Vespasian remarked
causally, making his way towards his chest.

Only taking a few seconds to rummage through his gear, he
brought out a long, thin object wrapped in a heavy cloth. He
brought it to Santino, who looked at it stupidly before accepting
the gift, only to continue looking at it stupidly. Noticing his
hesitancy, Vespasian beckoned for him to open it. As opposed to a
kid on Christmas morning, Santino gingerly gripped the cloth and
peeled it away slowly, carefully.

I leaned in for a better look but all I could see was something metallic and sharp. Santino squinted at it curiously, as though trying to piece together the puzzle of what the object could be before revealing it completely. The process was agonizingly slow, and I couldn't even care less what it was. Either Santino was acting particularly stupid, which wasn't hard to imagine, or whatever he was holding was familiar to him.

Finally, unable to contain his curiosity any longer, Santino ripped open the cloth to reveal a long fixed blade knife. But not just any knife. *His* knife. The one he had lost all those years ago the day we tried to recover Agrippina's baby, Nero. He'd thrown it at the then villain of this story, Claudius, but it had been intercepted by one of the Caesar's Praetorians.

It was an incident that had oddly bothered him ever since.

I'd never understood his attachment to the thing until only a year ago after Helena had bought him a replacement blade, a twelve inch curved blade, reminiscent of an Arabian scimitar. I had caught him one day daftly balancing the knife by the blade on the tip of his fingernail. A clever party trick, to be sure, but it was also something he did when something was bothering him. I'd about had enough of his annoying sorrow over his lost knife, so I'd confronted him on it. For someone who treated women like disposable paper cups, his attachment to the thing was disconcerting, and my curiosity had been driving me insane.

His story had been surprisingly heartfelt.

I never knew much about his family, something he'd always been reluctant to talk about, but I knew he had a younger half-brother still in high school, but other than that, his family story was a void. As it turned out, Santino had been very close with his father, a bond formed living on the mean streets of one of New York's seedier areas. His father had been a welder, a salt of the earth blue collar man who worked hard just to put food on his family's table every night.

As a hobby, his father collected knives. Everything from kitchen tools, to ornate decorative ones, to military grade ware. His collection was immense, but he never squandered his money at the expense of his family. It was his only hobby.

But the hobby ended when Santino was thirteen and had discovered his father dead in his bedroom, paramedics later diagnosing it as a heart attack. The very next day, a package came in the mail addressed to Santino's father. Young Santino had opened it to discover the same knife he had carried with him ever since. It was the last in his father's collection, and the only one Santino had decided to keep. His mother had sold the rest in preparation for their move away from New York after she had remarried and gave birth to his half-brother.

I glanced at Santino, who stood dumbstruck by what he saw balancing in his palm. I've seen him speechless before, embarrassed to the point of sulking, sad, happy, but never what I was seeing right now. He looked as though his life was complete or that he had somehow reclaimed a piece of his lost soul.

"How?" He stuttered. "Where?"

Vespasian smiled. "It was sent to me during my time in Germany. It had a note on it saying to deliver it to, 'the funny one.' At the time, I had no idea what that meant as Galba had yet to inform me of you people."

"Who sent it?" Santino asked

"The note was simply signed: Varus."

Now Santino looked almost heartbroken. He dropped his hands to his lap, and his jaw hung open slightly. Every second Santino had spent around Varus, he had spent it pestering, annoying and bullying him. But now he's learned that the man who had once probably hated him had in fact risked his life to send him his knife back, a man who was now dead, a man Santino had pestered even upon their last meeting.

I wondered if the reality of Varus' death had truly hit him until just now.

Slowly, he looked back up at Vespasian.

"Thank you." He said, about as speechless as it came for him.

"You're welcome," Vespasian said. "We've sharpened it for you."

In response, Santino tossed the knife in the air and caught it on the palm of his hand, balancing it upright by the handle. He flipped it again and caught it before spinning it around his finger like a Wild West cowboy would do his gun, managing to sheath it in his belt in one fluid process.

Winking at Vespasian, he said, "thanks."

Vespasian nodded, amused, and turned back to me.

"So, now that formalities have been taken care of, let us get down to business."

"I hope you mean the business of crucifying this man," Herod remarked from the corner.

Vespasian turned. "Herod, I am sorry about your shoulder, but please, leave it be. There are bigger forces at work here beyond Judea."

"Is that so?" Herod asked. "Please enlighten me."

"Sorry," I interrupted, "but you don't need to know."

"Do not speak to me, traitor."

I rolled my eyes and bluntly said, "We need to go to Alexandria."

"Then go," Vespasian said. "You do not need my help to get there. If you leave now you could be there in a matter of days."

"Well..." I said, dragging it out like children would do with their parents. "Alexandria isn't our final destination, and where we're going may require a little help.

"What kind of help."

"The military kind."

Vespasian waited patiently for me to continue.

"I need a few cohorts of legionnaires, an equal amount of auxilia, enough equipment for three times that size of a force, and enough naval vessels to transport it all from here to..." I hesitated, wondering if maybe I'd overplayed my hand, "to Britain."

Vespasian scoffed. "Is that all?" He asked nonchalantly.

"What?!" Herod's face was growing redder by the minute and his disposition was quickly degrading. "You are not honestly considering helping these people."

"I'm not considering anything," Vespasian snapped. "Yet."

At this point, I wasn't sure what the enigmatic Roman was thinking. It was completely possible that he had already somehow deduced that I would come to him with these exact same demands or he could just be as clueless as Herod.

"So, is that all?" Vespasian asked again. "I wonder if I should consider such a request insulting, especially since you have returned without Agrippina as we'd agreed." He waved a hand. "Besides, this city, and this man here especially," he said indicating Herod, "are in quite a state of disarray, and we should not forget how fractured this once great empire has become, oddly enough, all thanks to you and your actions."

I glanced at Artie and Archer, wondering if their *Prophesy of Doom's* origin was about to be explained right now.

"What's happened?" I asked.

Vespasian casually made his way to his desk before answering my question. Herod moved to stand behind the Roman, his good arm folded across his chest, clutching his injured one. I was still amazed how familial these two were. Up until a few weeks ago, I had no idea Herod and Vespasian had ever even met.

"It seems you are the catalyst for a great many things, Jacob Hunter," Vespasian said matter of factly. "I know little of Rome's history from where you come from, but from what little I have learned from Galba, I have surmised that it went on for quite a time after the reign of Caligula. Is this correct?"

"Yes, quite a while longer. Five hundred years more. Fifteen hundred more some would argue," I finished making the tired argument that Rome's true existence lasted until the end of the Byzantine Empire in 1453, a fact that sadly only a select few college students ever learned.

"Well then," he said, "it seems we have quite the problem then."

"Can you please get to the point," Helena asked, never one for historical digressions.

Vespasian smiled even though I suspected he had nothing to smile about.

"The vast empire of Rome has fractured," he said. "Rebellions have flared up everywhere. The Germanic peace in the North has come to an end and Sarmatia has made veiled threats to attack our legions there, justifying it as self-defense. Gauls are growing restless in the West, the Parthians are ready to advance into Anatolia, and the senate of Rome is completely divided on what to do. They're as frightened as Vestal Virgins on a windy day."

He paused for a moment to survey us, but none of us moved. I couldn't speak for my companions, but my mind was alternating between shock and vindication. I always knew we'd screw up so bad that something this big would happen, but I'd assumed it would manifest itself years from not, perhaps even well after we were well and buried. But the magnitude and suddenness of what Vespasian had described was shocking.

"Oh," Vespasian said with a smile, "I believe I forgot to mention that Britain has rebelled against the legion I left there last year as well."

My mouth opened in preparation for words to emerge, but nothing came out. Vespasian noticed my hesitation.

"So..." Vespasian said slowly as he lurched to his feet. "I have a proposition for you, Jacob Hunter. I give you everything you ask for and more, and in return... you reconquer Britain for me."

Now I was truly stunned.

"Me?"

"Not you alone, of course," Vespasian comforted as he leaned against his desk his arms crossed in front of him. "I have already sent a courier to Galba to make haste to Britain and wait for your arrival. He is the most experienced military commander I have, and will serve you well. German forces are weak. Tired. They still have much fight in them, but will be little more than an annoyance and Sarmatia will take some time to mobilize . We have bigger problems elsewhere."

"So what do you want me to do?" I asked nervously.

"As I said, Britain has launched hostilities against Roman forces. We left only a single legion when Agrippina ordered us to the German front, even though I argued we would need at least another year to quell the country side and leave no less than three legions to maintain control."

"So how many are you sending with Galba?"

I tried to do the math in my head of how many legions were currently with Galba, Vespasian, here, located in Britain, and in the rest of the empire, but there were so many units in play at the moment I couldn't keep track of them all.

"Zero."

"None, huh?" I quipped. "What do you want me to do, win Britain over with my looks and charms alone?" I paused. "Well, that might actually work."

Helena elbowed me in my rib cage, luckily on my unwounded side, and Vespasian smiled.

"That will not be necessary. I will send the *XV Primigenia* with you as well. I believe you are familiar them?"

"Yes, we've worked with them before."

"Good, then you should be familiar with the officers at least. Furthermore, you will have its compliment of auxilia, the legion and its auxilia already present in Britain, and of course you will have Galba as well."

"Oh good," Santino mumbled under his breath.

"But you're not even giving me what you consider a *peace keeping* force," I countered.

"I have full faith in your abilities, Jacob Hunter. You can do things that ten legions cannot. You will need that kind of precision if you wish to succeed."

I held Vespasian's eye for a second before I turned to my companions. Artie and Archer wore blank expressions, unable to understand the words exchanged between us let alone the context of the conversation. Helena looked worried and distractedly rubbed her belly, and Santino, like always, wore a completely unhelpful expression, choosing to keep his opinion to himself until he could complain about whatever decision I made later.

"What about Agrippina?" I asked, folding my arms in a mirror position of Vespasian's.

"There is not much we can do about her now. She has brought her entire Praetorian force here to contain the Parthian threat until I can lead my legions against it. I believe she'll return to Germany then, but she has not made any intentions available to me in weeks.

"As I said, brush fires have ignited all over the empire, and we are spread very thin. Luckily," he said, clapping Herod on the shoulder, "Herod has agreed to appeal for his forces to stand down and upon his successful completion of that task, I shall be leaving within the month."

"I would not have agreed to such terms had I known you would be working with him," Herod growled.

"Herod, for the love of the gods, will you shut up," Vespasian snapped, turning to glare at his friend. "If you knew the full extent of his reasoning, you would not be so quick to condemn. This man did what he thought was right to do. At the time, I may have done the same. None of this, not even your arm, was personal. Trust me."

"Wasn't personal?!" Herod yelled. "Thousands of Jews are dead. Our peace with Rome in shambles. And people on both sides are still clambering for blood. How can you say this was not personal?"

I didn't want to frown, or show any kind of emotion, but I couldn't help but do so. Despite Vespasian's rationale, Herod was right. The killing of all those Jews and the deaths of all the Romans who came to fight them were nobody's fault but my own.

I sighed inwardly before saying anything. I tried to think of the fact that I may have actually saved thousands of Jewish lives. Not killed them. For all I knew, the rebellion today may circumvent the rebellion that would have occurred in 44 A.D., where even more Jews died in a much longer war.

That justification would do for now.

"Herod," I spoke softly, "please believe me when I say that there is more at stake here than you can possibly imagine. We used you, yes, but it was very necessary. Take solace in the fact that should Vespasian wrest control from Agrippina, things will change for you and your people. Forever and for the better."

Herod stared at me with icy eyes. I knew he would never trust me again, and that if I ever saw him again I'd better watch my back. I just hoped he wouldn't get in the way now because there was too much at stake.

He kept his gaze on mine, only a second longer before turning to Vespasian.

"I am done here," he said before storming out of the tent.

On his way out, he made sure to bump against me with his good shoulder, hitting me of course against my own bad side, muttering under his breath as he made his retreat.

"Nice to see you too, buddy," Santino called out to his retreating backside. When Herod failed to respond, Santino turned back to me and clicked his tongue. "Don't people say goodbye anymore?"

I smirked and turned back to Vespasian.

"He will be all right," he said. "He has a fiery temper but a sound mind. We shall soon have peace in the region and I will be allowed to move on to more important matters."

I couldn't help but let out a small sigh of relief.

"Good."

"Now, on to said more important matters," Vespasian said while moving to stand directly in front of me. "How do you feel about becoming a general of the legions, Legate Jacob Hunter?"

I blinked in shock. "Me?"

If you're interested in Edward Crichton's Sci-Fi epic *Starfarer: Rendezvous with Destiny*, released in the spring of 2013, keep reading for a sneak peek at the first few chapters.

INCOMING TRANSMISSION . . .

TO: John Paul Sterling, Admiral, Allied Space Navy (ASN)
FROM: Alexander Mosley, First High Admiral, Allied Space Navy (ASN)
ORIGINAL REPORT: Richard Alderman, Colonel, Office of Strategic Space Intelligence (OSSI) - Original Report Attached
SECURITY LEVEL: **CLASSIFIED**

XXXXX - XXXXXXXXXX - XXXXX

SUBJECT: Anomalous ISLAND Activity - Action Required
SENT: 11.13.2595 (11:20:11)
AUTHENTICATION CODE: **Echo Echo Bravo Zero Zero Seven Echo**

Admiral John Paul Sterling,

This could be big, J.P., so I'll dispense with the usual pleasantries. Word has been sent to OSSI that our Chinese friends have encountered an anomaly along ISLAND Transit Route AlphaCOL-BetaCOL. The spooks haven't been able to get anything specific out of the Chinese yet, but it has The Star Destiny Corporation, at least, very concerned.

They're going to lose contact with the ISLAND Liner *Sierra Madre* on the aforementioned course very soon, and while OSSI isn't saying much, we could be talking about another rumored contact with alien technology aboard an ISLAND. That or they may have simply experienced their first mishap with WeT Tech.

Consider this your unofficial readiness report. Prepare the Third Fleet for immediate redeployment back to Earth and launch the *Alcestis* as soon as possible. I don't think I need to remind you to keep your wits about you, John Paul. There's more at play here than even I'm aware of, and I can't offer you much more advice than that. This won't be some silly sim we mucked about with back at the Academy. Something big is about to happen and something about it stinks.

Regards,

First High Admiral Alexander Mosley, ASN
Admiralty Board, Chair
Washington Aerospace Naval Headquarters, Luna

P.S. Should we get through whatever this thing is, I'll get you a case of that ancient Jamison swill you love so much.

<<<<< SEE ATTACHED FILE FOR ORIGINAL REPORT >>>>>

SECTION 1
The ISLAND

High Earth Orbit /
ISLAND Liner *Sierra Madre* – Red Zone /
Power Conduction Shaft – Delta /

11.06.2595
07:35:08 Zulu

That which defines mankind is nothing more than what he leaves behind. In no other way will he be remembered when his presence in this universe becomes little more than dust to aid in the formation of new celestial bodies, and the onset of space travel centuries ago only added to this legacy. Later, the ability to travel to other planets cemented it. If every human in existence simply vanished from reality, the ISLAND Liner *Sierra Madre* would remain, drifting through the depths of space for time immemorial.

And whoever finds it will think it little more than a hulking piece of junk.

Senior Chief of Electronics Dhaval Jaheed knew that was unfair assessment of a large portion of the ISLAND, but in the presence of so many undocumented, unbundled, ungrounded, and unfamiliar wires, connectors, cables, circuits, and other forms of electronic mayhem before him gave him pause to curse the wretched ship. It was a safety inspector's worst nightmare, and the Red Zone was already an extremely dangerous, almost mystical, place, quarantined from entrance by all ISLAND passengers and staff.

Senior Chiefs never sent technicians into the area, mostly because they never needed to, but the occasion had arisen today, much to the dread of every technician under Dhaval's supervision. His rank of ISLAND Senior Chief of Electronics gave him seniority over every electrician or technician aboard the *Sierra Madre*, and made him the only person he was willing to send into such a hazardous portion of the ship. The rest of them were all back in the Green Zone, the outer layer of the ship that surrounded the Red Zone like an egg encasing its yolk.

Despite knowing it was in his best interest to focus on his work, it was difficult for Dhaval not to wonder exactly what kind of genius would let something as important as an ISLAND Liner fall into such disarray. ISLANDs were the sole means of transportation to Earth's colonies, and the only way to keep humanity's presence amongst the stars connected. The mess he was in now was a disgrace to mechanics, technicians, electricians, and engineers alike, but he supposed that's what happened after hundreds of years of neglect.

"Find the breaker yet, Chief?" Asked an unwelcome voice that infiltrated every recess of his mind. It came so suddenly that

Dhaval stumbled from his perch overlooking the exact breaker box he had in fact been searching for. He shot his hand out to seize the nearest stabilizing handle, only to have it break away from the shaft in his grip. His life was spared by a safety cable that secured his belt to a ladder rung – which amazingly held firm. Dhaval dangled there for a few moments, his forehead glistening with sweat as he stared down the conduction shaft, noticing the green safety lights fixed to the wall descend only about ten meters before becoming overwhelmed in darkness. The shaft descended for hundreds of kilometers, all the way to the Core, but few knew what was down there.

Dhaval touched a red button on his exo-suit, and a small object shot out from a mechanism on his back. The magnetic wafer attached itself to the metal wall and reeled him back into a standing position upon his perch. Once upright, he deactivated the magnetic anchor and took a deep breath as it recoiled.

"Chief?" Came the disjointed voice in his head again, somewhat more worried.

Dhaval gritted his teeth in frustration and keyed his com. "This is Senior Chief Jaheed. I've found the conduit. Initiating repairs now."

"Copy that, Chief. Be careful down there. Some of that equipment could be a hundred years old."

Dhaval paused for the briefest of seconds in frustration before returning to his work.

As far as he knew, he was the first person to visit this realm of the ISLAND since the last round of ship wide upgrades and renovations that had expanded the *Sierra Madre's* overall size and mass to its current level. There may have been the riff raff and Unwanteds who had inherited the bowls of the ship over the past few centuries, but even they were smart enough to stay out of the conduction shafts and rarely breached the Red Zone.

The only reason he was even down here was because the ISLAND's Senior Systems Officer had identified a small power drain that originated in the very spot Dhaval now occupied, one that threatened the ship's next WeT Jump. Such a problem hadn't arisen in the thirty-five years since Dhaval had been conscripted to work aboard the *Sierra Madre*, but it wasn't Dhaval's position to question how such a problem had arisen. His job was simply to fix the broken conduit and bring the conduction shaft back to peak efficiency. All he cared about was that the one hundred year old power box he was currently manhandling seemed repairable. He pulled a data cable from his chest rig and jacked it into a port that seemed like it would accommodate the plug. Numbers and figures poured across the Lens in front of his left eye, most of which was meaningless gibberish even for someone as experienced as Dhaval, but he comprehended enough to tell him it was at least fixable.

Just as Dhaval thought he had enough information to begin, he heard a loud metallic bang above him that reverberated through the shaft. It was repeated a number of times before ending just as suddenly as it began. It sounded like someone carelessly knocking over machinery as they moved through the area.

"Hello?" Dhaval called into the darkness, knowing he was supposed to be alone. He hadn't been sure what he'd heard, but it sounded distinctly like moving people. "Hello?" He repeated. "Is anyone there?"

Only silence answered him.

Dhaval shrugged and eyed the darkness above him one last time before returning to his work.

You're getting paranoid in your old age, Dhaval.

He shifted in his seat and got comfortable on his perch, locking his exo-suit into a comfortable sitting position for a long repair job. The *Sierra Madre* wasn't due to depart on its two year voyage for another nine hours, and Dhaval had no idea how long this was going to take. The last thing he wanted to do was report a failure to Ship Master Na and risk delaying the ISLAND's departure time. This was the young woman's first voyage as ship master of an ISLAND Liner, and rumor had it that she was as ruthless as she was new to the position. Upsetting her would not bode well for even a veteran like Dhaval Jaheed, for no matter how good he was, he was still an Indian aboard an ISLAND – little more than a slave on a farm.

Earth /
Havana, Cuba /

ISLAND Departure Spaceport /

11.06.2595
08:00:00 Zulu

In a time of great prosperity, the most obvious course of action is towards progress.

Growth.

Modernization.

To build towards the future and create a utopia of high tech splendor.

It's what happened in the days following the end of Earth's population crisis and later economic boom that came with the advent of interstellar trade and colonization. Cities across the globe became shining, glimmering metropolises of glass and light, more beautiful than ever, but not Havana, Cuba. Its spaceport was the sole means of transportation to the High Earth Orbit ISLAND Docking Facility in the western hemisphere, and a prosperous city because of it, but it appeared little more than a dirty small town on the cusp of social annihilation.

At least that's how it seemed like to Carl Lawson as he sat in a local cantina, waiting for the departure time for his shuttle to arrive. The seedy bar was something out of a Western vid, an entertainment genre made famous once again after centuries in obscurity. It was a setting that belonged in a museum, like the one Lawson had in fact seen at the Cleveland Museum of Ancient American History when he was eight years old. The only difference being the lack of holographic personifications of living, breathing humans performing any number of mundane, yet clichéd tasks like bartending, piano and card playing, wenching, and the like. This bar was authentic, with real live people enjoying the relaxed, stress free setting which Havana still exuded. On any other day, Lawson probably could have died content as he sat amongst fellow travelers in seek of a cold *cerveza*, but life was never completely stress free, especially not with his folks visiting to see him off.

"This isn't what you want to do," his father, John Lawson, said from across the table. "ISLANDs only come back to Earth every three years."

"About two actually," Carl Lawson replied, not understanding his parents sudden desire to dissuade him from leaving. He ignored his father and turned towards the bartender. *"Señor, otra cerveza, por favor."* The bartender nodded and tossed him a can of beer and Lawson couldn't help but smile.

Where has this place been all my life?

"But you won't know anybody," his mother, Eileen, chimed in with her ever chipper voice. "All your friends and family are on Earth, not to mention your friends in the military."

Outwardly, his mother was the sweet and caring type you'd find in any homestead across the galaxy, but Carl had known the truth behind it since he was a toddler. Underneath that façade of motherly kindness was the attitude of a woman who simply didn't give a shit, and only kept up her disguise to fit in with societal pressures. The fact that she still treated him like a child, instead of the forty-five year old man that he was, said something about her. She was the kind of person who would shop for yet another needless product to sooth her own fickle desires on her Lens' Inter-Lens Service, while maintaining only the barest semblance of attention during what someone else would consider a very personal conversation.

"Mom," Carl said with a sigh. "Why do you think I'm even doing this? The only actual friend I have left is coming with me, so why stay."

The statement wasn't a question, and he didn't expect his mother to answer anyway. Not because she knew it hadn't been a question, but because he knew she didn't actually care.

John Lawson ignored his wife and pressed on. "You realize, son, that if you leave, you'll be doing little more than admitting your own guilt and running away in shame?"

Carl turned away from his mother, who no longer seemed interested, fixating her attention instead on the young Cuban bartender whose biceps were at risk of bursting through the sleeves of his tropical style shirt. He fixed his father with a stern gaze and lowered his voice.

"Is that why you're here? To convince me to stay on a world that would rather see me hung by the gallows because the firing squad would be too quick? There's nothing left for me here. At least if I go, I can visit in a few years when things have quieted down. In time… who knows? Maybe I'll be able to return one day."

"No one is saying you should go on the Lens and draw attention to yourself, son, but if you stay and lead a quiet life, at least you can say you kept your honor intact and stood your ground."

"Whose honor exactly am I protecting? Yours or mine? Better be careful, dad. You don't want to be taken off the list of all those holiday parties you're always invited to."

"Don't take that tone with me. I'm past caring about whether what happened was your fault or not, but our reputation has already been blemished by all this as it is, and the only thing you can do to repair it is to stare your accusers in the face and refuse to admit defeat."

"I already did that. Don't you remember when they stripped me of my rank and all my accomplishments and held me up as an example to save face with the Chinese? No, I did my part thank you much. I think I'm well and done with all that bullshit."

John Lawson folded his arms and glared at his son, watching as Carl swallowed that last of his beer.

"Don't do this, Carl. Don't expect a home to come back to if you do."

Carl smirked at his father and picked up his travel bag before getting to his feet and throwing some anachronistic monetary coins down on the table. Physical money may have been extinct on Earth for centuries now, but for those traveling to the outer colonies, it was a necessity, not to mention for those few who knew to stop at this lovely hole-in-the-wall before departure. "Don't worry, father. I haven't been coming back to one since the day you tried to save your *own* face in all this at no one's expense but my own."

With nothing left to say to his father, he reached out and grabbed his mother's arm before passing by her. He leaned down and gave her a kiss on the cheek, knowing he'll miss her despite all her faults. "Say goodbye to Lilly for me, mom."

Eileen flicked her eyes away from her beefcake pretty for just a second. "Oh, your sister will miss you terribly. Won't that help you cha…"

"Goodbye, mom."

"Oh, well, goodbye, dear." She turned back to her lustful desire and said nothing else.

Lawson looked back at his parents, now both ignoring him for completely different reasons. He couldn't believe it had come to this. His own parents had turned their backs on him in a time when he needed them the most. When the entire world was against him, he should have been able to turn to them and expect comfort and reassurance, but no such sentiment existed, and he was on his own.

Carl Lawson versus the universe.

He turned and headed towards the door, stopping only briefly to take in the surreal atmosphere of one of the most unique places he'd ever visited. With a nod of approval he walked out into the dusty streets and turned north towards the only sign of progress and hope as far as the eye could see: the spaceport.

And his future.

High Earth Orbit /
ISLAND Liner *Sierra Madre* – Green Zone /
Command Deck – Bridge /

11.06.2595
08:35:16 Zulu

"Ship's status?"

"All indicators save one show green, ma'am."

"What's the situation in Power Conduction Shaft – Delta? Are we on still on schedule?"

"Senior Chief of Electronics Jaheed is on it, ma'am. His controller indicates he should have the problem locked down well before our time of departure."

"Good," Ship Master Mei-Xing Na replied behind a cool smile, pleased at her new crew's performance.

She abhorred incompetency – a cancer that had to be rooted out of as soon as it was discovered – and would not have been pleased with lackluster personnel. Whether her perfectionism was a byproduct of her Chinese ancestry or her own tenacity for perfection was anyone's guess, but she knew that her own personal level of expectation came from hard work and a selfless dedication to the fruition of her life's goals, and today would mark her first steps towards fulfilling her destiny. Today, she would take her first voyage as the ship master of an ISLAND Liner, and she wasn't about to let incompetency blemish such a step.

"Ship Master," another voice called out from her right. "Docking Control has indicated the first wave of shuttles are on approach. We should expect our first class passengers to arrive within the hour."

Mei-Xing nodded, but a sneer crossed her face at the continued use of the Common language amongst her crew. It was an excessively antiquated speech, an ugly speech, burdened and littered with the drivels of the old English language.

It may have been the language of international trade, commerce, and cooperation centuries ago, but the galaxy is so much bigger now! She thought. *With Chinese as the dominant language on more planets than any other, isn't it time for us to speak our own language, with our own people, on our own ships?*

She frowned. There was little hope to be found in such thoughts. The Americans were still too heavily involved in galactic affairs for Common to just go away, even if all they'd been reduced to was a security guard for planet Earth. There was also the problem that while all ISLANDs were crewed by Chinese, they were still staffed by their subservient Indians, creating yet another language barrier. Mei-Xing sighed to herself. Common was taught to every new born baby alongside their own native languages. There was no changing that now.

No matter how disgusting it felt on Mei-Xing's tongue.

"Ship Master?" The voice spoke again.

"Very good, Mister Chen," She said, glancing at the chronograph in the upper right hand corner of the oval Lens situated in front of her left eye.

08:36:02.

Only about a minute late. She supposed that was within even her standard of punctuality, especially considering how complex the last twenty four hours before an ISLAND launch was.

She blinked and sent a slight mental nudge towards her Lens, and a visual feed of the docking bay sprang into view. She saw the deck crew scurrying about with guidance lights in their hands, red carpets sprawled along the deck to help facilitate the boarding of travelers, and concierges, ready at the beck and call of any passenger to set foot aboard the *Sierra Madre*.

Good, good.

With another mental nudge, the Lens feed shifted back to her To-Do-List, which she kept as her default setting. She checked off the numbered event concerning the arrival of passengers and looked at the next thing on the list. She already knew what it was, but the internal comfort of continuously checking her lists gave her piece of mind. Item number five for the day was to rest until 14:00:00 when the next item on her list came about. It was barely nine o'clock in the morning, but she'd already been on the bridge for nine hours performing the ISLAND's pre-flight check lists with her bridge crew. Feeling weariness creeping in, she stood and surveyed the bridge.

The bridge was built like the quarter of a sphere removed from the remainder, with the ship master's at the very center, raised above all other stations by a semicircular platform about a meter above the deck. Arrayed around her from left to right, along the curved interior of the viewport that encased the bridge were her officers' duty stations. Everything from navigation to communication to ship's systems and a half dozen other flight sensitive tasks. Beyond these stations, wrapping around the entirety of the curved section of the bridge, was the transparent viewport that connected the bridge to the emptiness of space. It wrapped above and behind and around Mei-Xing as she stood at the foot of her dais, and all she could see was space. It was something she had enjoyed immensely since her first moment on the bridge of her new command only one week ago.

Immaculate, the bridge was lit with bright lights and streamlined interfaces. It had red carpeting on the floor and wood paneling along the bulkheads, luxury items that simply screamed: civilian. It was nothing like the cold steel and colorless white Mei-Xing had seen aboard the Allied Space Navy's ships of war she had toured during her training.

Interestingly, she had to admit that she approved of the sterility of those ships more.

Finally, directly behind the ship master's chair was the lift, which she promptly started for.

"XO," she said as she stepped off her dais. A small man with a well-greased comb over straightened from his position overlooking the shoulder of the ship's Communication Officer.

"Ma'am?" He asked.

"The bridge is yours."

"Aye, ma'am," he replied with a slight nod. Mei-Xing did not return it but made sure her look lingered just enough to be obviously suggestive. Her executive officer didn't dare make mistakes while she was away, and her subtle look served as a reminder that he'd better not. It wasn't that she was unsure of his abilities, in fact, she couldn't ask for a more competent first officer, but that she never dropped her persona, not even for him.

She didn't want her crew to fear her, but she demanded their respect all the same.

She turned and entered the lift, but instead of indicating her intended destination with a simple thought through her Lens, a door whooshed open in front of her, opposite the one she'd just came through. Stepping through, she entered the atrium of her personal quarters, a space about the size of a small living room despite its sole purpose as a place to receive guests and store her footwear.

Once through the lift doors, which silently closed behind her, she immediately slouched her shoulders and rolled her neck. She wasn't a machine, despite what others may think, and she needed to relax as much as the next person. She slipped off her bulky duty boots and placed them in a small compartment that quickly retreated back into the bulkhead after she'd placed them within, and opened the large, ornate door to enter her new home.

Those who knew anything about space travel, especially those like the Chinese or Americans who dominated the practice, understood that space was always at a premium aboard a spacefaring vessel. The Americans would especially understand this, as their use for space travel revolved almost solely around combat, where every cubic inch of a spaceship was used to fit ammunition, life support, provisions, berths, or any number of mission critical essentials. The Chinese understood this as well, and abided by such a concept with most of their ship designs.

But not for ISLAND Liners.

Inter-System Luxury Aerospace Destination Liners had no need to worry about space constrictions. Each ISLAND was almost five hundred years old, beginning their lives as simple transport shuttles that ferried supplies from Earth to China's first colony on Mars in the late 21st century. But as time progressed, repairs and refits had been necessary, giving designers the unique opportunity to build on top of the existing infrastructure, creating larger and larger ships. Four hundred years later, those original ships had grown to immense sizes, each slightly different from the next. Each ISLAND was literally the size of Europe's largest countries, hundreds of kilometers long, and half as wide and tall. Shaped like an angular, blocky cone, the engine block was the wide base and the bridge its tip. They were space worthy countries capable of supporting millions of passengers.

Designed for comfort and leisure, Mei-Xing, as ship master, was entitled to the most extravagant suite on the ship. Two stories with five rooms, three baths, a solar to view the stars, a central atrium, dining room, and equipped with an emergency escape capsule, it was easily the most opulent accommodation available. Decorated in mainly Chinese motifs, Mei-Xing could almost pretend she was back on Earth in her ancestral home that had provided her with so much.

She looked at the vaulted ceilings, tassels, hangings, bronze sculptures, and gold inlaid furniture and sighed. Here was a place worthy of her accomplishments. It was a place where she could relax and enjoy the fruits of her labors. She glanced at the central fountain that flowed gracefully into its basin and touched the water. It rippled at her gesture and she smiled, continuing her way towards her room and up the port side staircase, having already chosen that she would only descend down the starboard side one.

It took her nearly thirty seconds to climb the stairs to the landing separating her quarters from the rest of her suite. Reaching out to grasp the intricate handle before her, she twisted and opened the wide double doors and entered her immaculately furnished room that gleamed in pristine opulence. She started the process of undressing herself as she strode across the room, removing each piece of her uniform carefully, meticulously folding each article of clothing and placing them on her dresser and throwing her undergarments down her hidden laundry chute.

Before stepping into bed, Mei-Xing moved towards her full body mirror she'd brought with her from her childhood home. It was an ovoid with gold designs twirling around the edges, coming together at the top to form two small cherubs blowing small horns at the other. It had been a gift from her grandmother for her eighth birthday and she had always treasured it.

What she really loved about the mirror, however, was how it presented her body. Of course, Mei-Xing knew it reflected her no differently than any other mirror, but something about the gold designs and cherubs framed her in a more perfect way.

She was tall for a Chinese woman, standing at 1.75 meters, with a strong body most women would be hard pressed to replicate. Her face was just as hard as her body, with small but full red lips and dark eyes that could look as intensely serious as they could sultry. Her skin was smooth and soft, but it was the angle of her cheeks that provided her with the prized sternness she was so proud of.

Assured that her face was clear of any blemishes she may need to take care of, lowered her hand and examined her breasts. They were firm and well sized and Mei-Xing hummed in satisfaction. She then turned to the side to inspect her backside, likewise content at its shape and firmness, but then she frowned. Upon closer inspection, her abdominal muscles seemed less defined than normal, showing almost an imperceptible amount of paunch over her otherwise taut stomach.

We'll have to do something about that, won't we, Mei-Xing?

The last week hadn't left her much time for physical exercise, and she could now see the results of her sedentary lifestyle. It did not make her happy, but she knew once her ISLAND was successfully under way, she'd have time to work on it again. With one last look at her behind, she nodded at her reflection and quietly padded her way towards her bed. Slipping in beneath her silk sheets, she nudged her Lens to deactivate the lights in the room and set her alarm to wake her in four hours.

She needed to be well rested. ISLAND departures were still a big deal for the citizens of each planet it visited, and even though the ship wouldn't be back for two years, and in that time any mistakes her crew may make well and forgotten; *she* would not forget them. She would take them to the grave – should such a day ever in fact arrive for Ship Master Mei-Xing Na.

ABOUT THE AUTHOR

Edward Crichton, a native Clevelander, lives in Chicago, Illinois with his wife, where he spends his time coming to grips with his newfound sports allegiances. A long time enthusiast of Science Fiction, Fantasy, History and everything in between, he spends his time reading, writing, and overusing his Xbox.

Until recently, Crichton had often hoped for a cat, but his wife decided to let him have a baby boy instead. Due in November of 2013, he and his wife could not be more excited.

His Sci-Fi epic *Starfarer: Rendezvous with Destiny*, was released in April of 2013, and the latest book in his *Praetorian* Series: *A Hunter and His Legion*, was released in September of 2013. Crichton hopes to spend a few months bonding with his wife and newborn child before getting back into writing, but he still hopes to release his next book by the summer of 2014.

Edward's website and blog can be found at
EdCrichtonBooks

You can also Like/Comment on his Facebook page here
Edward Crichton

And you can follow him on Twitter
@EdCrichton

Or Email him at
EdCrichton85@gmail.com